THIS STRANGE ENGINE

PHILIP LIGON

Jumpmaster Press
Birmingham, Alabama

Cover Artwork: Steve Beaulieu
Library Cataloging Data
Names: Ligon, Philip , (Philip Ligon) 1972 -
Title: *This Strange Engine* by Philip Ligon
5.5 in. × 8.5 in. (13.97 cm × 21.59 cm)
Description: Jumpmaster Press digital eBook edition | Jumpmaster Press
print edition | Alabama: Jumpmaster Press, 2018-2022. P.O Box 1774
Alabaster, AL 35007

Summary: Alexander Asherton, Ash to his friends, has reached the low point
of his life. A once promising future with the Church of England has given
way to a clandestine organization which tracks and collects items of a
magical nature. They provide the elixirs that keep Ash alive, and in exchange
he uses the power the elixirs grant to 'acquire' what they desire.

If he succeeds, he lives. If he fails, he dies.

ISBN-13: 978-1-958448-97-7 (eBook) | 978-1-949184-84-6 (print) |

1. Steampunk 2. Fantasy 3. Airships 4. Automatons 5. Historical fantasy 6.
Gaslamp 7. Alternative history 8. Robots

Printed in the United States of America

THIS STRANGE ENGINE

PHILIP LIGON

To Heather,
The adventure
begins!

[signature]

Aug '25

*To my wife and children for
their unending patience and support.*

*And to my mom for her encouragement and for
helping to instill a love of all things books.*

CHAPTER 1

Two gables at the crest of a gentleman's town home provided a needed refuge from an airship circling over the town of Campden, where the marvels of modern science and technology met the strange machinations of magic. Two lamps shining from the gondola on the airship illuminated the streets as they searched for me and the statue nestled in my pouch. The secure warehouse where the valuable was stored proved to be...well, not so secure for one with my power. Yet a lack of securities on their part did not indicate a lack of dangers.

My employers were anonymous individuals I called, at least to myself, The Misters. The term was bit foolish considering they frightened the gargoyles out of me, but it was a small way to defy them and their deadly assignments.

Case in point was my current mission in which they insisted I go after the statue on this night. To further complicate matters, they insisted I complete the assignment within the span of darkness. Such terms led to poor planning and increased the opportunity to make a mistake. And to compound the problems, I hadn't plucked a magical trinket from under the nose of a commoner, or even a lesser lord. No, I snatched it from Duke Schaever himself, the man who controlled the town and its flow of magic and wealth.

If The Misters were capable of humor, I'm sure they found much in sending me out under such duress.

Speaking of sending out, that is what the Duke had done with the airship and its company of Guardsmen, pulling it away from its assignment to catch refugees from the magical realm. Fortunately, the craft appeared to be of the smaller size, about three-hundred feet from nose to tail. Such a size restricted the number of Guardsmen it could carry, but meant it was faster and more maneuverable.

Curse the contraption and its lights.

For the moment, the hum of its engines, one on each side of its wire frame, grew fainter. Its lights moved across the next road as it displayed a fish-like tail, and gave me a moment to take a deep breath, to calm the pounding of my heart.

What's the next move, Ash? How will you escape such a chase?

To best carry out their desire, The Misters granted the power to leap far higher and farther than normal. The magic elixir that mixed with my blood and gave me such an ability worked better than I hoped. It not only kept me two steps ahead of my pursuers, but also from certain death if they caught me. The Duke had a reputation for dealing with thieves in a prompt and final manner, especially if magical items were involved.

The possibility of torture and death urged me to abandon my refuge with a jump. As I sailed through the air, the wind tore at my face. It whistled in my ears as it took my breath away. The sensation was so close to flying...so very close.

I landed on a roof on the opposite side of the street and rolled, ending the sensation, the freedom, all too soon. The slates gave way and sent me all the way to the edge. I flailed and caught myself with all fourteen fingers...well, ten fingers and four thumbs to be exact. Not all of them were useful or cooperated like they should have.

These powers always had a side-effect. Too often they caused a hindrance, such as when one of the extra thumbs snagged the corner of the glass case that once protected the statue in my pouch, and sent it tumbling to the floor. The sound of it shattering alerted the Guardsmen. Yet such was the price of having a power. So long as I lived it was one I'd pay without regret.

As I dangled above the street, an old man with wispy white hair and bushy gray eyebrows appeared from a dormer window. "Who's up there?" When he spotted me, he added, "What's this? What do you think you're doing?"

My feet scraped the stone next to his window as I tried to scramble back to the top. But an extra thumb wedged between two slates.

The man spoke with a knowing tone. "I thought that airship chased another band of those orcs who've been terrorizing decent people, but it followed you across half this town. I had this ready in case trouble came to these parts." He brandished a double-barreled rifle with the velocity enhancer above the chamber. The air intakes glowed red, showing their ready state.

"Wait," I said as I continued to gain better footing. "Hold your weapon."

"Why should I, thief?" The barrels of the man's gun stared at me like a pair of black eyes. The hammer gave a distinct click.

His accusation made me pause as it struck something deep within, like when another child calls you a name in the park. "Who says I'm a thief?"

"I do. Who else would run about on the top of decent people's homes? And be dressed from head to foot in black?" He shifted the gun. "And I'll bet you're helping those creatures."

He had a valid point about being a thief, one that settled uneasy in my belly. Once, I never would've considered stealing. Once, I never—

There's no time for such thoughts, Ash. The past is best left alone.

Desperation made me push away, breaking the thumb. Pain shot through my hand and arm as I flew across the road. I slammed into the side of a bakery, well above the ground. Chips of mortar fell from the surrounding stones.

One crack followed another in quick succession, and time seemed to slow in the face of death. Bullets pinged as they hit the stone next to my left ear. My heart beat once. Twice. An ache arose in the back of my skull where I had hit the wall. My weight pressed against the stone, stopped, and shifted downwards. Nausea arose in the pit of my belly, the sort that speaks of a bad ending. In this instance, I dropped two stories onto the bluish-gray cobblestone.

The impact jarred every bone in my body, and I heard, more than felt, my right arm crack. I rolled and regained my feet though my arm hung limp. What should have been a searing pain running through my shoulder and neck, and into my head was little more than a throbbing, due to the damaged nerves from the burns I received on the darkest day of my life. The scars on my right side ran from my face to my legs.

The man with the rifle yelled, "Thief! Stop! Thief! Guardsmen!" His voice encouraged me to continue running before anyone answered his call.

The airship's lights danced in a crossing pattern over the buildings and homes just ahead.

I jumped with all the power my elixired-up legs could manage and landed on the roof of a three-story inn. After cresting the gentle slope of red shingles, I leapt onto a boarding house with a flat roof. I splashed through standing puddles and prepared to leap again as I reached the edge overlooking an alley.

A squeal gave me pause.

Below, a lady struggled with two men who looked worse than the thief the old man accused me of being. They had the lady pinned to the ground. One emptied the contents of her purse while the other emptied those of her bodice and said with a thick Scottish accent, "Quit struggling, or I'll slit that bosom. A shame that'd be, lassie, since our fun has just begun."

The woman whimpered and struggled all the harder as the second man stuffed a rag into her mouth. "Where're you going dressed so? An engagement at this hour? And when the moon isn't near to full? A pretty thing like you should be more careful."

The airship still circled and searched. It faced my direction now, and if it discovered my whereabouts, I might not out-jump the Guardsmen who'd descend from it.

But I could not - would not - allow such an atrocity as these two men appeared determined to commit. A thief I was, but even thieves had honor. The canon within, the little voice of righteousness remaining from my old life, refused to be ignored. It said, "The hand of providence has given you this power at this moment. You are obliged to assist."

The voice encouraged the bravado the elixirs always gave me. Was there anything I couldn't do?

Better sense made me whisper, "You're a lunatic, Ash," as I backed away from the ledge. A short sprint and jump took me to a building across the way, which I pushed off with one leg, struck another, pushed off it, and landed on top of the first man. As we rolled across the cobblestone, I struck a blow to his face.

The Scot advanced with a knife in hand. "What've we here? A black knight come to rescue his fair maiden?"

Unlike after the fall, my right arm sent a pulsing, sharp pain through my shoulder as I stood. It hurt such that I took short breaths to keep the men in focus.

This is stupid, Ash. And foolish.

But necessary.

I moved between the lady who lay on the ground, frozen with fright, and the scoundrels.

The men charged as a pair, both with knives at the ready.

I met their challenge with my own knife gripped tight in my left hand. The lady screamed as I threw myself to the right. My broken arm took the brunt of the impact and the tip of a knife. The sensation jolted me. I gasped. My knife slipped. I fumbled to hold it. Somehow I stepped behind the attackers.

The Scot spun to face me while the other moved for the lady, who remained on the ground, shivering.

I needed to protect her, shield her, so she could escape. Yet my arm hurt worse, and the street tilted to the right. The Scot knocked my outstretched knife to the side. He lunged, and I jumped ten feet high from a standing position.

The men must've been just as impressed as I, for they both stared.

But not long enough.

The Scot dodged when I kicked at his face.

The other man pulled the lady up and gripped her tight as he held his knife to her throat. "One more move and I'll bloody her up." For emphasis, he pressed the blade hard enough to draw a dark line across her pale skin. The act made her cry out and the pitiful sound filled me with equal parts anger, helplessness, and determination.

You won't hurt her again.

The Scotsman wrenched my weapon away. "Look at this one, will you? That hair's white as a ghost's. Does that mean you're a magic freak? Are you so bloody out of your mind that you have no sense?" He laughed as he waved his knife around to frighten me. "Can you feel it if I do this?"

When he tried to slash across my chest, I caught his hand. A twist of his arm made him hold the knife against his own throat. "Magic freak?" I asked with no little annoyance. "Is that the best you can do?" True, I was a magic freak, but who were they to judge?

He bumped my broken arm, which made me suck in a quick breath as the street tilted right again.

Foolish, Ash. Foolish, foolish, and more foolish.

He pulled away. "Oh, I'll do better, freak. Much, much better. When I'm finished with you, I'll have you beg—"

Lights blazed down like Heaven itself opened. A voice from the airship boomed, "You three! Stop!"

This wasn't what I wanted to happen. Yet what did I expect? A quick rescue? A kiss of gratitude from the lady? An easy escape from the ones hunting me?

I couldn't help but to smile and laugh, for part of me expected such a go of it. Whether or not the influence of the elixir controlled that part could be debated.

The two men looked at me with mouths open in surprise. Did they see confidence? Invincibility?

Madness?

A Guardsman struck the ground behind them with a distinct crack of stone. I expected to see the man broken and bleeding. Instead, he landed in a hunched position, with his left palm and right knee down. He stood with neither grimace nor flinch as if he had merely tripped.

That was a sure sign of an elixir at work. It was also a sign the coming confrontation wouldn't go well, the thought of which made my hands sweaty as it subdued my overflowing optimism.

The Guardsman wore the fine, crimson-colored overcoat that reached to his knees. A patch on his left chest displayed the white badger of Duke Schaever's crest. His collar hugged his neck, not unlike the proper constables in London. But, this being Campden, instead of carrying the clubs and pistols of their peers in other parts of the empire, he carried a sword along with his pistol. He was big, seven-feet tall with shoulders as broad as a blacksmith's.

The Scot engaged our common foe while his friend scooped up the contents of the lady's purse.

With their attention averted, I hurried to assist the lady. She still shivered as she hugged herself. Her discarded coat I wrapped about her delicate shoulders and said, "You should leave. Go home. Go to those who love you."

Tears dropped from her cheeks. She whispered, "Thank you." And when she looked up, her eyes grew large.

So did mine.

"Alexander?" Rebecca asked. "What...what are you doing here?"

The daughter of Bishop Donnavan, my old mentor and friend. She was a part of my best-forgotten past, a time far removed from my current situation.

I swallowed the lump in my throat before saying, "I could ask the same of you."

As if embarrassed, she pulled her coat tighter around her slashed bodice. She had blossomed into an attractive and mature woman.

When I took her hand, its softness combined with its smallness to give rise to...what? Something I should've felt years ago? An opportunity I should've seized instead of being a fool and chasing after Aimee's skirts? A longing that remained unfilled for many seasons?

No! Her touch encouraged a feeling best forgotten. I wouldn't allow it. It didn't belong in this world, in my life. Caring. Tenderness. They led to love and heartbreak and betrayal.

I wouldn't suffer them again.

A shot sounded from behind. The smaller man fell, clutching his belly.

The Guardsman remained still as if he savored the moment of death. The still-smoking pistol in his hand only added to his air of enjoyment. He turned on the Scot, who now backed away. The Guardsman closed the gap far quicker than an ordinary man.

The Scot growled and threw his knife as he dodged left. While the blade caught the Guardsman in the belly, it did nothing to slow him. He grabbed the Scotsman and threw him across the alley like he tossed a small child.

The Scot struck the wall with a sickening crunch. A dark streak smeared the wall as he slid to the ground.

Two deaths within seconds. I had seen my share of lifeless bodies during my service to the Church, so I was not a stranger to the unnatural state. Yet none bothered me so much as those who died from violence. The faces of those victims, their memories, were the reason I vowed never to kill.

Never.

The Guardsman pulled the knife from his belly, then threw it aside like it was a mere nuisance. Not a drop of blood marred his clothing.

What sort of elixir flowed in his veins? What gave him such strength combined with such invincibility? How had he received two powers and survived?

He turned to us, and Rebecca shivered again as she pressed against me as if I could protect her. I held her tight in spite of myself. Having her so close felt...comforting, even in the face of danger. I whispered, "You're safe now, and that man will help you. But I had best call this an evening."

She shook her head. "He's strange. There's something wrong with him. Stay with me, please. I know you, Alexander. I trust you."

Her words struck a blow worse than my fall from the building.

You don't know me, Rebecca. Not anymore. You cannot trust me.

Though she was wrong about me, she was correct about the Guardsman. The way he moved was not smooth and graceful, but erratic, almost mechanical. Was that the side-effect of his elixir?

"Release the lady," the voice said from overhead. "Back away from her."

What? And face the magic Guardsman? A lunatic I am, but not one such as that.

I whispered, "Tell your father I appreciate all he did for me." Before Rebecca could reply, I ran.

The Guardsman followed. His heavy footsteps echoed in the alley, yet he covered a dozen yards with the quickness of a cheetah. He reached for me, but I knocked his arm away. My left hand ached like I slapped a rock.

"Wait," Rebecca called from behind. "He helped me. He saved me."

The Guardsman spun me around by the shoulder. He aimed his pistol at the bridge of my nose.

I held my good arm up. So Alexander Asherton would die in the streets of Campden. Would anyone mourn my passing? Rebecca, perhaps? Would anyone else care? Or would I be another victim of the town's magical ways, another magic addict who met an untimely end, a note in the morning paper next to the advertisement for airship travel? Was my end to be so meaningless? So empty?

I longed for death once, but now that I faced the possibility, I wanted to live. Crazy that I didn't appreciate life until it was about to be taken back.

Rebecca hurried towards us. She reached out as she said, "You have the wrong man. He saved me."

No, sweet lady, he has the right man. He has his thief.

The Guardsman paused as I looked him in the eyes. What I saw weren't eyes at all. They were colorless glass balls.

"What..." I had to look away. Yet I couldn't stop staring. "What..."

Rebecca grabbed the Guardsman's arm. "Run, Alexander!"

The Guardsman lifted her high by the coat. She cried out as she tried to keep her modesty. When he turned and gently placed her on the ground, I had the assurance I needed to know she was safe.

I jumped away, leaving her behind with the rest of my past, and pushed from building to building until reaching the top of a three-story one. The airship hovered closer, and ladders dropped to the roof. Having no desire to see what other monstrosities would descend, I continued to run. The infernal lights followed.

From rooftop-to-rooftop I raced across a world of dormer windows and gables and chimneys that made the landscape an ever-changing and challenging complex of routes. Across courtyards behind some of the inns, over the carriage houses and blacksmith quarters behind others, across well-tended gardens offering quiet respites from the business of the day, I jumped.

Still the airship pursued. Its engines hummed all the louder as it sped forward. The strange Guardsman followed, too. He jumped the same space I moved across, but he landed with thuds that sent tiles and bricks to the ground. He showed a single determination to keep pace with me, refusing to let me slip away no matter how I tried.

After scampering across the wooden shingles of a building housing a bakery on the ground floor, I stopped. My breath caught in my throat despite my pounding heart and aching body.

What a strange night, to have reawakened a reminder of the past, then to bring me hereabouts to the one place I experienced peace and contentment during those days. The irony and absurdity almost made me laugh.

It sat across the street, taunting and beckoning, and demanding the utmost of respect. Its great, unfinished spires rose above the city in a reminder of the fact we owed all to the God of Saint James Cathedral. The sanctuary was the size of five buildings. It had row upon row of red velvet-covered pews. Its windows sparkled with inset diamonds. On the north end sat a dais that invited all who sought saving grace. Behind the dais were doors leading to the preparation rooms. There, Bishop Donnavan and his deans and canons all donned their robes. There, they talked and fasted, prayed, and took part in the morning and evening prayers and lessons. There, they rejoiced at the saving of a soul, and wept over the sins of mankind.

They were men I once called friends and colleagues. They were good men, respectable and dedicated. How had I ever been their equal? Surely that Alexander Asherton never existed.

"Send down upon our Bishops, and Curates, and all Congregations committed to their charge, the healthful Spirit of thy grace; and that they—" I stopped the canon's voice from quoting The Book of Common Prayer, lest it remember too much and draw me further into the past.

"I apologize for the trespass," I said to no one as I leapt to the left-most spire, the one half-coated with gold. I grabbed the bottommost gargoyle with my good arm and swung behind it. I stood on its back, between its wings. It was the white one that seemed to laugh at the mortal world, one I looked upon many times from below.

The night had grown quiet and still. For the moment the hunters had lost their fox, and afforded a rare opportunity to look over the entire town, to smell the enticing aromas rising from Paul's Bakery. There, one could find the best cinnamon bread this side of the Malvern Hills. In the days of my former employment under Bishop Donnavan, I'd give excuses to walk to the shop just to buy a piece as a mid-morning treat.

Speaking of the good Bishop, had Rebecca reached her home? Was she safe again, perhaps escorted by a different Guardsman with marble eyes?

A chill rippled through me at the thought.

What if we had fallen in love as her father once hoped? Would I have been a parson in a quiet village, raising a family now? Would I have been on my way to more prominent positions in the Church? What if I hadn't met Aimee at the same time?

I caught myself gazing towards the estates on the outer edge of town. There, I once lived. There, Aimee lived still. Did she sleep a sound sleep? Did she sleep free of guilt and shame for her betrayal? The image of her as she stood just outside the import shop, Smith's Oriental Treasures, would forever haunt me. That day, my former wife wore the black dress that ran from neck to ankles. Large, silver buttons ran in a line down the right side, from shoulder to waist, accenting her curves. Smaller, matching buttons adorned her elbow length gloves.

I followed to ask, one last time, that she reconsider the divorce. As I stepped across the road I saw the purple smoke pouring from the grate in front of the shop. As I raced forward, I yelled.

That day she left my spirit in shards in the same way the bomb left my body in tatters. Like Job, everything in my life fell down about me in the subsequent days. But my response wasn't very Job-like. The following months found me seeking refuge from the pain, the emotional more so than the physical. My willingness to pay any price for relief cost far more than I ever imagined. It cost me everything and brought me to this moment, to another mission for The Misters, and to a future of more dangers.

Was I bitter? Yes...no...sometimes...only when I dwelled on what was. After all, what could I change now?

Nothing and everything.

The hum of the airship grew louder behind, breaking me out of the memories, out of the thoughts. The ship's nose, like the end of a pike, seemed to reach for me.

Below, the Guardsman paused as he - it - watched. The light glinted in his marble eyes. He didn't jump as I had. Rather, he dropped twenty feet to the street. A normal man would've been injured by such a fall. But as quick as the Guardsman landed, he dashed for the cathedral's entrance.

The airship, meanwhile, turned its side to me, and displayed the lines of wire across its frame. It attempted to flank me.

I jumped higher, swung around four more gargoyles, and reached the scaffolding surrounding the bell tower. Two young canons lived in rooms just below where the final bells would be placed. Plans called for a set of gears and pulleys to take responsibility for ringing the hour and the service times. Until that day, though, the canons were charged with the physical task of ringing the smaller, temporary bells. I tried to land as quietly as possible so as not to disturb their slumber and alert them to my intrusion.

Not that my caution mattered, as one of the men asked, "What's this?" He wore the cream-colored wool robes that kept him warm. I didn't recognize him, which was both a blessing and a surprise considering the way the night had progressed.

"Bear this sinner no mind," I said as I motioned for him to go about his business, and ran to the other side. "Pray, rather, grant a blessing to a poor man?"

He did his position proud, for he recovered enough of his wits to say, "Of course. But why not take the opportunity to confess your sins, sir?"

Why, indeed.

Because I didn't deserve forgiveness? Because one doesn't spend his life fighting against the horrors of magic addiction, only to become entangled in those very things? No, I was beyond confession.

When I jumped, he cried out in fear as if he thought I'd plummet to the ground. Instead of realizing his concern, I grabbed onto the scaffolding around the northern spire, swung around it once, and jumped again. I landed hard on another roof. My broken arm sent new shots of pain through my shoulder and neck.

Maybe thieving wasn't worth the effort. Or the pain. Maybe...

The airship illuminated the spires of the cathedral with its searchlights, casting a majestic glow over the structure.

I hurried across two more streets. Was I lucky or blessed to have eluded both it and the Guardsman? I believed the former while the canon still within me said the latter.

Either way, what mattered was living to see another day.

You're a lucky man, Ash.

I almost laughed at the thought, at the relief that ran from my feet to my head.

Yes, I was lucky to see the light breaking over the horizon.

Daylight?

In answer to my question, Saint James' bells rang through the morning air. They gave the long tolls indicating the time for the Morning Prayer.

What would be the text for Brother Donnavan's Morning Lesson? This being the seventh day of June would mean a reading from Job chapters eight and nine. I cared not to delve into such a providential message. Other matters concerned me, specifically The Misters' coming wrath at my lack of punctuality. Yet I secured the statue. Would such an accomplishment not be worth something more than threats and chastisement? Or death?

A glance left and right showed empty streets. I dropped down and hurried across the way, then into an alley between two of the most respectable-looking businesses. One was a merchant's cooperative, an exchange that took up as much space as a warehouse. Both the practical and the luxurious filled its walls. The merchants employed a company of Guardsmen to patrol the perimeter after proper business hours to discourage the curious on-looker or potential thief.

In the alley opposite the Exchange stood a regal building fronted by marble columns, reminiscent of ancient Greek architecture. Gold trim stamped with a Latin phrase – *et justitia praevalebit* – *and justice will prevail* – repeated on each side of the building. Six windows lined the two upper floors, while the first floor contained ten niches on the front, each with a small statue. The ground floor had doors, on the alley side of which there were three. It was the furthest to the left to which I hurried, then knocked twice.

The door swung open. The attending doorman kept to the shadows behind it. He liked to believe he remained a mystery, but after the Gerrerd business, when I had enhanced sight and the ability to see at night, I spied him out. He was a cyclops, named as such because he resembled the creatures from Greek mythology. His people were known for their size and simple minds. This one, like all others I had met on this side of the Gateway, wore a protective shield of glass over his face, held in place by a metal helmet that reached across his cheeks in the Roman fashion. The shield was a necessity to keep the creature's enemies from exploiting his greatest weakness: poking his one eye.

Why I enjoyed aggravating the creature, I couldn't say. Perhaps because he tried to be so secretive, or because I had to make light of anything before I faced the darkness of The Misters. Since the cyclops was the last creature I would see, he provided an opportunistic victim.

I tipped an imaginary hat and spoke with a delightful sarcasm. "Evening Lord Mayor."

"I'm not your Lord Mayor," the creature grunted, "and they're waiting on you. You're late. Again."

"Thank you, Lord Mayor. I wouldn't want to disappoint them by being punctual, would I?" My words rolled off my tongue too fast, revealing my nervousness. "It's such a reputation I must maintain. And believe me, it takes no small amount of effort to do so."

Though it did take a great deal of effort to remain in The Misters' good grace.

He grunted again as he closed the door.

I walked down the dark hallway where not a lamp was lit. The omen was not lost on me or my slowing steps.

"Your arm is broken," the cyclops said from the doorway.

"Yes, it is, Lord Mayor." It hurt, too. The pain had moved over the top of my head and settled between my eyes.

I stopped before the door at the opposite end. The elation of finishing the assignment gave way to dread, for these interrogations never went well. I straightened my shirt, stood a little taller, and took a deep breath. Before I knocked, the door swung open, releasing a wall of heat and blinding light.

As I entered, the first to speak was the one I christened Mister Important for his always haughty, all-knowing, self-righteous tone. "You are late."

"I did my best," I said and resisted the urge to shift the blame to their restrictions on my time. Awaiting pronouncement of their justice felt like a two-ton weight rested on my shoulders.

The one I called Mister Mercy, for his always kind and feminine tone, asked, "You have it in your possession, hmmm?"

Both remained behind a light that threw a penetrating brightness over the sparsely furnished room. They maintained their anonymity, always keeping out of sight. It was part of their grand game, and though I cared little for it, I had to indulge them. For now.

I held the pouch up.

"Yes, place it on the table," Mister Important said. "Open it so we can verify its authenticity. It had best not be a counterfeit."

Mister Mercy said, "We do not deal well with counterfeits. We had the last courier ripped apart at the limbs for trying to deceive us. His death was most...gratifying. Hmmm, but I can still see the stain of his blood on the floor about you. And on the walls, too." He delivered the threat while still sounding kind, like a grandfather espousing wisdom to his grandson.

They wanted me to look at the spots, but I refused to give them the satisfaction. Instead, I placed the bag on a small, rickety table. A lawyer's office should've had the means to afford finer furniture, but perhaps they enjoyed inspecting the empire's most valued treasures on such a decrepit piece of wood. It was another part of their game.

"The item is genuine," I said as I opened the bag and revealed a small statue that had to be the ugliest piece of art ever created. It made *The Ugly Duchess* look like the *Mona Lisa* in comparison. From one angle its brownish-green clay form could be accused of appearing like a distorted pregnant woman, and from another angle it looked like it could have been a troll with an enlarge stomach. The difficulty was deciding which, for the head was missing. It held its arms up like it wanted to wave, except its hands were claws. A dark red jewel embedded in the middle of the stomach soaked in the lamplight, and seemed possessed of its own will, if that were possible, like a judging eye staring out at the world and condemning it, condemning me, for all crimes. A ring of small jewels around each wrist, everyone of them black, added to its strangeness.

Did a mandate exist in the magic community that said the most powerful objects had to be the most grotesque and disgusting? If so, this was dangerous.

Mister Important gasped while Mister Mercy said with a lustful tone, "This is the object we wanted. We are well pleased, Mister Asherton. Well pleased."

His words brought some measure of relief, for they meant I'd live, remain in their employ, and see another day, another elixir, and maybe another power. What else could I expect? I deserved nothing more.

Mister Important said with an equally possessive tone, "Yes, and it appears our information regarding it was correct. Someone has removed the head. Had we not obtained this in time, The Gatherers would have stolen it and attempted to rejoin the pieces."

"The statue contains but a small fragment of its true potential so long as it remains incomplete. We cannot allow them to keep the most important piece. No, that cannot be allowed."

The Gatherers were a small group of thieves whose purpose in life was to gather magical objects from all corners of the town. Much like my employers, who called themselves The Company, they claimed they saved the world by maintaining control over everything capable of destroying it.

Both groups ignored the fact there were plenty of mechanical creations capable of doing that very thing. They also forgot English law required all magical items not possessed by a creature from the other side of the Gateway, the portal connecting this world to the magical realm, to be turned over to the Gateway Secretary for cataloging and examination.

A quiet stretched throughout the room as the disgusting statue mocked me. It felt as if it wanted to reach out and grab me, that it would pull me into the stone on its stomach and digest me in its bowels.

It drew my eyes like I discovered the beauty of an unclothed woman for the first time. Its form shimmered, and appeared to rock forward and backwards. Tears filled my eyes and blurred my vision, and yet the statue remained as clear as ever. Cold emanated from it, of the type that made bones ache.

My hand trembled as I reached out. I hesitated mere inches from its surface and, strange enough, heat radiated from it.

Black magic. Whoever created such a monstrosity had been in league with demons.

Whether or not The Misters wanted me to, I covered the piece of hell with the pouch. I proved its authenticity. That should've been sufficient.

Still, I couldn't help but wonder what I collected. Had I saved it from being put to less than honest use? Had I willingly given it over to the wrong hands? Part of me wanted to ignore the answer while the canon's voice said, "You know what havoc you wreak. You understand the consequences."

Mister Important said, "Yes, it seems this is a powerful statue. I can imagine the power it will grant once we have possession of the head."

"Ummm, hmmm," added Mister Mercy, "and that is where you will help us, Mister Asherton."

I bowed in humility and said the opposite of what I thought. "I was glad to be of service again, good masters. As usual, I will await my next assignment." I paused. "I would advise, though, that you allow Duke Schaever's anger to run its course. After this night, he will increase patrols and watch everyone's movements even closer."

Mister Important laughed his deep, bellowing laugh. It echoed through the room. "Then you will have to be more careful, for we have your next assignment prepared."

You didn't...did you?

I asked, "Perhaps there is another who has not been in the field as recently who would be more appropriate." Pain shot through my shoulder as I held up my broken arm. "As—" A sharp ache broke my words off, and I cleared my throat. "As you can see, I have injuries and require treatment. Also, the Guardsmen know my face too well."

What I didn't say was I needed the opportunity to recover from the events of the night. I needed to deal with the feelings Rebecca had aroused. I needed to forget the Guardsman with the marble eyes. To do either required a visit to Branagh's Tavern. The ale, as much as I could hold before passing out, beckoned.

Mister Mercy said, "The price you pay for being negligent with your powers. You enjoy them too much."

A rather large smile broke across my face despite my attempt to remain stoic. "The powers have their moments, I must confess. You should try the—"

"You will receive healing," Mister Important said with irritation. "We will inform Pienne that he is to restore your arm."

I held up my good hand to display the extra appendages. "But the latest potion runs through me still. I cannot take another combination of elixirs until the previous one has left." Why did they need me to remind them?

"Yes," Mister Mercy said, "but there are ways to hasten the process, though none are pleasant. Still, what does a slave concern his masters? Do you not desire more of the magic? Hmmm? And what new power shall you possess this time? Hmmm? Does that not gnaw at your belly, the possibility of something new and extraordinary?"

Yes, it did. Though I tried not to, I shivered in expectation of another round of magic injections. The feeling it gave – the sense of living beyond one's mortal shell – was as inviting as a grand feast of mutton and ale to a starving man. Curse The Misters for a millennium for introducing me to the ecstasy and pain of the procedure.

Mister Important spoke with a tone of amusement. "Yes, our brave slave desires our power. And we shall continue to grant his desires. Yes, we shall continue in our business arrangement, although he arrived late this time." He took a quick snort of satisfaction. "Yes, and you might even find a special enjoyment with your next assignment."

"Perhaps he will," Mister Mercy said. "Hmmm, perhaps he will. It is more complicated than usual. It will require more consideration, more delicate maneuvering, and less charging through obstacles like a bull."

The way he spoke set off the voice in my head, which said to run. Their game grew tiresome. My arm throbbed, my head hurt, and I needed rest. Yes, even more than wanting to feel the magic in my blood or drinking Branagh's Ale to excess, I needed rest.

He continued, oblivious to my physical ailments. "It might require killing this time. In fact, I am sure it will. Call it an assassination if you like."

The words shot cold through my back, which settled at the base of my skull. I glared into the light and the brightness made my eyes water. "I don't kill. That line I refuse to cross. You know that."

I had a sense that Mister Mercy was a smiling cat as he said, "Though we have never asked you to do so, you should have realized the extremes to which we can, and will, call you to service."

"I won't kill. I'm not an assassin. Thief? Yes. Murderer? No."

I would not send a body to Saint James for a funeral. I would not subject his loved ones to such senseless loss.

Mister Important said, "Then you will have the third potion administered immediately. However, the choice is yours. Agree to this assignment and live. Refuse and die."

To kill and live was no choice. It was a mandate to end Ash as I knew him. Many sins I committed, but of physical murder I remained innocent.

The canon within me howled in anger and despair. Like Joseph, I should have fled and removed myself from the situation.

Yet no one could flee The Misters. No one escaped their justice. Those who tried always died horrible, violent deaths. Always. I might not be a murderer, but I was a coward. I was a thief. A quitter. A failure. Why else would I let myself fall into the trappings of my addiction?

So did it matter if I became a murderer, too?

Well, yes.

But...

Unease moved from my belly and into my throat, like I swallowed a pint of lamp oil. I wanted to soak in a bath for days, and cleanse myself of The Misters, of my life.

Mister Mercy asked, "What is your decision, hmmm?" His tone was too eager, too full of self-satisfaction.

"I'll do it," I whispered so low I almost couldn't hear my own words. Did I want to hear them?

"Was that an affirmative? Speak louder."

I swallowed the lump in my throat, then growled, "Just tell me who I have to kill."

Both men laughed. It was Mister Important who delivered the fatal words. "You will kill Aimee, your former wife."

CHAPTER 2

"Who?" I asked as I rubbed my left ear. An extra thumb jammed into it. "I thought you said Aimee."

Mister Important continued with his gleeful tone. "Yes, our sources tell us she was chosen to transport the Head of Forneil to her employers. Such is its importance that if she fails, she dies. Therefore, she will not lose track of it unless she has either delivered it or met an untimely end while safeguarding it. What she will not do is give it over to the first gentleman to ask. Need I say more?" He sniffed as if already dismissing her. "A nice assignment, yes? You know your former wife's habits and friends, her strengths and weaknesses. What better assignment for you?"

He should have asked, "What worse assignment?" They just introduced new rules to their cruel game...unless they wanted to elicit a reaction from me, one worthy of death.

I asked, "You're sure she possesses the Head? This is the same Aimee to whom we are referring?"

Though my insides roiled with anger, I tried to maintain a calm demeanor. Silently I yelled, "The banker's assistant who has to account for every shilling and pence that comes through her ledgers? The same lady who wears dresses of a most exacting standard, who believes that a worthwhile evening is spent at an opera?

The same lady who dared to call my life a bore? Who wanted no part of it? Who rejected me? Who threw my love back in my face? Who said I neglected her for two years and convinced the magistrate to agree?

I took a calming breath, then said aloud, "Are you sure you have the correct person? She's too involved in her sums and figures to concern herself with magic."

Mister Mercy said, "Hmmm, and yet she is a member of The Gatherers. She has been for many, many years. At least ten we know of."

Another chill ran through my arms and into my back. "No. She's not—"

"Yes," Mister Important said, "she is an active agent for them. And a fine actress she is, our dear Aimee."

Not our dear Aimee. My dear Aimee.

No, Ash...don't be a fool. She isn't yours anymore – if she ever belonged to you at all.

Mister Important continued, "She was sixteen when she tried her first elixir and started down the path of developing the rather despicable habit of purchasing magic elixirs, the ones that let you forget all troubles. Did you not know that?"

That wasn't correct. He was wrong. "She told me she tried them once, but they confused her thoughts too much. She couldn't stand to lose her ability to think clearly."

Mister Mercy laughed. "She was an addict by the age of twenty, hmmm. She was one of those unlucky few who suffer the worst effects of the elixirs, the slow starvation and lethargy. By the time she was twenty-one, she reached her end."

He was lying. He had to be! "No. She never—"

"The Gatherers saved her, much like we saved you. They introduced her to society and granted her a piece of land you were once owner of. They also exploited her talents and beauty by placing her in a position where she could maintain an accounting of most of the money and wealth flowing through our dear city. Large withdrawals or deposits mean either blackmail or something valuable has exchanged hands. She could tip her masters and let them learn the nature of the transaction. If you are ignorant of these facts, then what else do you not know about your former wife?"

The accusation hung in the following silence. I wanted to yell, to tell them they were wrong. I knew Aimee like no one else. Did they know she slept on her right side? Or that she had such nightmares she often awoke twisted in sweat-soaked linens?

No.

Did they know a ray of sunlight through a slit in the curtains made her smile?

Again, no.

Did they know she yelled and screamed when she was angry, especially if I dared to buy a bouquet for her without her approval, because I spent coins not authorized by her accounting?

Sadly, no.

Aimee. My dear, beautiful Aimee.

But if they were right...

"Go," Mister Mercy said with a tone expecting no further argument. "You have your assignment. The Head of Forneil will be brought to us in no more than two weeks."

I said through clenched teeth, "You're wrong about her."

Mister Important replied with no little anger. "Do not question us, slave. It is a credit to your target that she hid her secrets from the one most intimate with her. Do not underestimate her abilities. Do not underestimate her motives and desires."

Mister Mercy said, "Hmmm, perhaps he already did."

The bastards. They tried so hard to get a stronger emotional reaction from me. They wouldn't have the satisfaction.

I turned to leave.

Mister Mercy continued, "Yes, and one more item to know about your former lover. She has a magical power, to the point of a fetish. She seems to derive the most pleasure from using it."

"Aimee has no magical abilities," I said, not wanting to hear more lies. "I would have known if she did. One cannot hide that." *Not for three years.*

"Hmmm, and yet it seems she can create magical explosions. I am sure you are intimately familiar with their effects."

The lamps went dark as I turned back to them. The audience ended, and on their terms, not mine.

Never mine.

My right side ached with ghost pains as I left the room. The hallway felt colder.

She wouldn't have done that. She couldn't. We shared a love as deep as possible. Even at our lowest point, she would never have created the explosion and tried to kill me.

But what if The Misters were right?

No, they weren't. She never would have tried to kill me. She was not capable of such cruelty.

I counted the steps: one, two, three, four...

But she could be so cold, too. And change from warm to cold in a second, and back again just as quick. It was her greatest fault.

Where was I? Step seven or eight?

I returned to the door.

Twenty steps, Ash. Now count. Don't think about her. Not even when your arm throbs and your heart aches, or you want to drown all the memories in ale.

One, two, three...twenty. I entered the room. The overwhelming smell of sulfur, oil, rosemary, and vinegar burned my nose. It made me sneeze.

A short, round man with a French accent wobbled over. "A blessing upon you." His eyes were deep-set between his protruding forehead and the blubber of his cheeks. His small lips somehow made a rather high-pitched voice for a man. Bushy brown hair covered his head and hung low in the back. It also covered his ears.

He held up a handkerchief embroidered with lace. "The Masters sent word that Alexander was coming." He laughed a wheezing, somewhat nasally, but quiet laugh. "Pienne has prepared a special concoction for him this time. A special one indeed. Took him most of this week just to prepare it, though he was surprised he would have a use for it this soon." He looked me up and down. "A rough go of it, eh?" He grabbed my broken arm, which made me wince. "Tsk. Tsk. Those extra appendages caused Alexander some trouble. Oh, well, nothing Pienne cannot fix in short order."

He pulled me along by the wounded arm, but not to the side of the room with the most interesting gadgets. There, a metal globe bobbed up and down as it spun between two black plates without string or wire to hold it in place. Behind it arose the click and whir sounds of a pump moving a clear liquid through a series of glasses shaped like bells. Steam floated from each.

Instead, he led me to the other side of the room where he sat me in the wooden, straight-backed chair with the leather padded seat and arms, the one surrounded by the tubes and the beakers and the foaming and smoking elixirs of all different colors. Needles of various sizes and lengths waited in a row, like the keys of an organ awaiting a master's touch. Not that he ever used the short, thin ones.

No, his elixirs always required the thicker, five-inch needles that left a bruise for a week.

The needles I despised, but what they delivered was worth the pain.

He whistled as he pulled at various tubes and stared at each far longer than necessary, like he forgot their specific purpose. His half-shrug gave little reassurance as he pulled three tubes out and attached his needles. "A good healing Pienne will give Alexander before he is de-magiced." He laughed his quiet, irritating laugh. "Alexander might need another healing after that, too." The strange man paused to look at me. "He might as well relax. He will be Pienne's subject for a while."

As I tried not to stare at the needles I said, "You enjoy this."

His brow rose, but his eyes remained obscured. "This is Pienne's job. This is his specialty. He could not be happier."

To keep my mind off the needles, I asked, "So how many of us are there? How many of us do you get to experiment on?"

He held the needles up as he released his magic elixirs. "Now Alexander knows Pienne cannot tell. And he cannot say that Alexander is his favorite subject."

"That's supposed to comfort me?" I sucked in a quick breath as he inserted the first needle into my left arm. It gave more than the slight pinch, and I tried not to squirm. "What are you trying to do, finish killing me?"

He held me down with his surprisingly strong arm. "Not quite. Not quite. Though Pienne heard that is Alexander's next assignment." He leaned close and whispered, "Here is his chance to try something new. Pienne put together a pigment-changing color. Ever wonder what it is like to resemble a troll? They have a pleasant green tint, does Alexander not agree?"

"No! Why would I want to look like a troll?"

"Shhhh!" He glanced around, then sighed and let the needle fall. He picked up a different tube and started the flow through it. "This is Alexander's last chance. Imagine how popular he would be with the ladies. Pienne bets they would flock to a man with a handsome green tint."

I hissed, "Then try it on yourself and test your theory."

He nodded and laughed. "But Pienne is banned from experimenting on himself. The Masters...Alexander understands they do not want to lose a man of Pienne's knowledge and expertise." He inserted the second needle into my right arm, which hurt worse than the first. Sweat broke out on my forehead as the room appeared to grow small. The click-whir sound grew louder.

I growled. "This had better work."

He smiled as the elixirs flowed into my arms and into my blood. "But of course it will work. And Alexander will feel better than ever."

The warmth filled my arms and moved into my shoulders. My mouth watered as the sensation reached my neck and then my face and then my brain.

The moment of freedom was upon me, the time when all troubles, when all those past moments, melt into nothing. I could forget the events of the night: Rebecca Donnavan, the Guardsman, The Misters, and Aimee. It numbed me and sent me into a welcomed state of emptiness where I could drift. Alone. Away from all troubles. Away from the world, from life.

Pienne waved as my eyes drooped. "Have a pleasant dream."

A sharp pain shot through my left forearm. I gasped, and tried to strike at the source, but bands held my arms to the chair.

Pienne removed the needles as he asked, "How is Pienne's favorite patient feeling?"

What? Other than the fact that my mouth feels like a wad of wool has been stuffed into it?

At least my head felt clear and my right arm no longer hurt. Yet my left leg twitched. It ignored any desire on the part of my head to tell it to stop and twitched all the more. The bands kept me from holding the stubborn appendage down. "Pienne, what have you done?"

He peered over his cheeks. "That? Oh, it will improve with time. Just a slight effect of the magic." I might've fallen out of the chair had he not kept me strapped down. "How is the arm feeling? All better?"

For that he earned a glare. "Yes, good enough to strangle you."

He nodded as he returned to the tubes and his needles. "As the Masters are insisting Alexander hunt your former wife as soon as possible, they also insist that Pienne should remove the previous magic from his veins." He put one hand on his chest as he continued to inspect the tubes. "He, of course, insisted Alexander would do well to wait, for this much magic in this short a span can have...intriguing effects."

The leg stopped long enough to let me enjoy a calm moment. "I'm surprised at you, Pienne. I thought you always found the effects interesting. What better opportunity to study one of your test subjects?"

When he connected one of the long needles to a tube and released a pink liquid, I squirmed at the thought of being poked again. He tapped the end to release the air. "Quite true. If Alexander survives this, Pienne will be more than glad to make his observations and his studies. If Alexander dies, though, Pienne might feel some guilt for a few days, which would interrupt his work. And Alexander understands Pienne does not like to have his work interrupted." He took my right arm.

"Your concern is touching," I muttered, then sucked in a quick breath to ready myself.

He paused as the cursed needle rested against my forearm. "Pienne is sorry about this, but the Masters insisted."

He inserted the needle into the vein. Instead of the typical warmth, a searing pain like fire moved into my shoulder and into my skull. It shot through my body. I tried to knock Pienne away, but the squatty man's straps held fast.

As I fought the restraints, the fire touched my brain. A nauseous wave erupted from the depths of my belly. I retched just before I passed out.

She took form before me. Aimee. That beautiful woman with her golden hair and her slight frame, with a smile that made her face glow and made all the sharpness disappear. She had perfected her stride, with swaying hips that spoke of a business-like manner, but suggested so much more. Aimee, with green eyes and an attire that was all dress, yet somehow resembled a man's business suit. Her dresses were always unbuttoned one too low for most modest tastes, but accentuated her small, elfish-like bosom. The dress she wore was her favorite: a light-blue topaz with white flowers twisting around her belly, highlighting her curves. She wore the calculating machine on her wrist. It was a six-inch square by two-inch thick black box with numbers just big enough for her fingers. Tubes ran from it to a similar box, albeit without the numbers, on her back. Together, they kept track of instant sums as required for the books or a transaction. She always wore it when she worked.

Oh, how she walked with pride and with a confidant air as she crossed the great hall of the Bank. Her heels clicked on the marble floor and there was not a gentleman in the room who didn't stop to steal a glance or to out-right stare as I did. If there was a picture of an angel taken human form, it was Aimee.

It was always Aimee.

She caught my eye as I watched with mouth open, like a fool. She nodded in respect to my station, for in those days I wore the black shirt and white collar of the canons. A more favorable opening couldn't have presented itself. I moved to intercept her, clearing my throat and trying to make a muddled mind think of an appropriate question.

She made no move to stop, so I walked beside her. "I'm new here," which was a lie and made all the worse for my station. "Where might I make a deposit on behalf of a friend?"

As she continued, she motioned to the left. Her voice carried the assurance of authority. "One of the clerks will help you, sir."

"You work here?" I asked, and in an instant realized how foolish I sounded, especially when I needed quick wits.

She raised a brow. "Because I am a woman, do you assume I would not, sir?"

This required a delicate response. "No...no...it's just I have never seen someone of such beauty working in a place such as this." Too bold? Maybe. But she seemed the type who respected boldness. "If I might say."

At that, she stopped. A smile flickered across her stern yet endearing face, softening it and speaking of something wonderful hidden behind the facade. My heart beat faster. "You are an—"

"Canon, yes. At Saint James."

"Are you people allowed to address ladies in such a fashion? And insinuate the most beautiful should work on the streets?"

What? No, I didn't mean it that way.

My face felt flushed. "No, of course not." I cleared my throat. "Because we dedicate our lives to a higher calling doesn't mean we deny ourselves some of life's joys." My face turned redder still. "And, no, you shouldn't be working the streets. You look just—" I cleared my throat again to stop babbling. "What I mean to say is love is a gift from the Lord. It's not something we separate from ourselves."

"One look at me and you believe you are in love?" She raised a brow and the sternness returned to her features. "Interesting." She began walking again. "Just when you hinted at proving yourself worthy of attention, I find you no better than a typical man."

For a moment, my feet remained planted on the marble. Yet who was I to let such a moment pass without seizing the opportunity to make amends for my boyish babbling? I hurried to her side again.

"Do they teach you bishops how to bother people while they attend to their business? Good afternoon, sir." For emphasis, she punched several numbers on her machine. The box on her back whirred, and four tubes released puffs of air.

"It's still morning by my recollection, and no, persistence isn't taught. It has always been a fault of mine, I fear. That's why I will quit following you only after you agree to allow me to escort you to dinner." Yes, a touch of boldness, and a dash of brashness. Would she respect such a move?

She continued to walk and picked up the pace such that I was hard-pressed to match her. We approached a wall of doors, all with names engraved on gold plates, and she charged towards the middle one. Just before reaching it, she turned. "What makes you think I don't already have someone courting me? Can you not see the eyes of the men following as I go? Have you not noticed the jealousy that you, a man of the Church, have created just by daring to walk and talk with me? Or do you wish to increase your business at your cathedral by enticing others to sin?"

She wanted an angry reaction that would provide an excuse to dismiss me as another religious zealot. A poor attempt at gamesmanship, and I refused to give her what she desired. Instead, I laughed.

She looked me up and down as if she just noticed me. "Doubly insulting, too? What type of bishop are you anyway?"

"A canon who refuses to take no for an answer." One who hoped to hear a yes in the next moment.

My hopes burned away when she reached for the door. However, she sniffed and said, "If you dare to learn the depths of your supposed love, then meet me here tomorrow night after the Bank's public hours. I will allow you to take me to a quiet dinner." Before I could think to ask her name, she entered the room beyond.

After further inquiries, a clerk told me her name and added, "She's all business, that one. Works alongside the banking guild members and is one of their closest confidants, outside of their own circle."

Indeed, and who was I to take her to dinner? Who was I to fall in love with her?

To marry her? To adore her? To try to make her happy?

Or to be betrayed by her? Scorned and cast aside? And, if The Misters spoke true, burned and broken by her?

Another sharp pain in my arm woke me. This time, my head pounded to the point where a crack appeared across my vision. The room spun, and I threw up what little was in my belly. My mouth tasted like bad brown pudding.

"How are..." A voice faded in and out, like my head was submerged in a tank of water. "...can Alexander..."

The room tilted as it spun faster.

My insides burned with agony and I heaved air. I doubled-over and moaned. "What...have you done?"

"...so sorry...blame...Masters..." Pienne's voice came and went like waves against the shore. "...will...have Alexander...ready..."

I tried to punch him, but his straps still held me fast. And besides, my arm felt like cream.

"This time...enjoy it...might make...worth...pain," Pienne added.

Something sharp stuck in my left arm.

What am I, a human pincushion?

The elixir shot through my veins, creating an agony that tested the extent of my nerves. I struggled against the bands. I wanted out. I wanted...

A soothing warmth washed over the pain. It didn't dispel the latter so much as it made the burning worse.

Should I give into the ecstasy or the pain? It made for an utterly confused feeling that followed me into passing out again.

"There now, all better?" The bulbous face smiled at me through a fog.

My mouth had passed beyond dry and my tongue tried to stick to the roof of my mouth. "Water...please."

"Of course, of course. Did Alexander think Pienne would forget such an important ingredient?" He placed a mug to my lips and poured the cold water. I gagged, but held a little in my mouth. I swished it around before spitting it on the floor.

The squatty man shook his head. "Pienne dislikes it when Alexander does that. Make a mess of the place and the Masters, they don't like messes."

"You deserve worse for what you just put me through. I couldn't enjoy whatever this new power is." I leaned forward to be menacing, but his straps continued to hold me in place. "What is it this time? You didn't have the decency to warn me." A wiggle of my fingers reassured me of the presence of all ten...well, eight fingers and two thumbs to be specific. My hands had lost their extra width, too. And my leg no longer twitched.

Perhaps I should've been thankful for such small blessings. But why did Pienne's laugh make me uneasy?

The squatty man said, "Oh, this one Alexander will like. Besides, Pienne didn't know if Alexander would survive so he didn't want him to be disappointed if he died."

With quite a bit of excitement I asked, "You mean I get to fly?"

His smile turned to a frown. "No. No flying."

Why expect anything else, Ash? Why should you be able to experience the freedom, the sensation? To soar with the airships without need of engines and wings, to fly among the clouds...that's what you want.

More to myself than to Pienne I said, "That's the only reason I agreed to work for them. They promised I would get to fly."

Pienne removed the left strap. "That's not the way Pienne heard it and Alexander should appreciate how difficult the flying elixirs are. The Masters use them sparingly. After the last thief tried to fly to the sun...well, it's an unpredictable power. The magic creates an unstable mind." He covered his mouth as he shook his head. "Pienne has said too much already." He removed the right strap. "How is Alexander feeling? All better? Invincible, maybe?"

I stretched my arms as I stood. My right arm worked as it should. The cuts had disappeared. "Well, yes, I do feel the best I have in at least two hours." I squinted at him. "Which is the time this has taken?"

He waved me away as he laughed. "Four days. Four days! Took longer to remove the last bit of magic than Pienne would have liked."

Four days lost when they gave me two weeks? I should've been angry and let Pienne know of my displeasure. Yet I felt too alive, like every part of my being worked in perfection. My skin felt as if it radiated energy and will. Smells were more refined and focused. The lab looked brighter and even the furthest corner appeared sharper.

The magic high, the glorious sensation of two worlds combining in one body. Such a moment deserved to be savored like a fine ale.

I asked with a cheery delight, "Longer than you or the Masters would have liked?"

He shrugged. "There is a difference?" He pointed to the red bottle with the black tube running from its base. "And need Pienne remind Alexander of the agreement?" His face scrunched up in one of his deep laughs and his chin almost touched his forehead. "But of course he does. The Masters require it. Their idea of a joke, Pienne believes. Though it's anything but that. It takes a combination of two elixirs to grant a power. Only the strongest can survive the process of having the magic instilled within his blood. But no one can survive the third elixir, which will be administered if Alexander tries to leave, if he betrays the secrets of the Masters, if he—"

"Reveals any information to The Gatherers, if I fall into the hands of the local authorities." I nodded. "Yes, Pienne, I understand."

The third elixir was the ultimate weapon The Misters wielded, or threatened to wield. Just how much it frightened me, I would never admit. Witnessing the effect it had on one of The Misters' servants just after I joined gave me nightmares for a week. The man's blood boiled. Sores and burns appeared on his skin as he screamed. When the sores busted, blood bubbled from them. In the end, the man became a pile of mushy bones covered with a thick, red pudding-like substance. It's not a sight I would wish on anyone, even on Aimee.

When I tried to walk, my left foot felt wrong like it weighed ten times its normal weight.

I sat and pulled off my boot. What I saw earned a groan.

My foot had turned a dull gray color, like lead. "What's this about, Pienne?"

He touched my foot, but I felt nothing. He whistled a long whistle. "Well, Pienne never expected that one. He thought Alexander might turn silver all over. And wouldn't that have been something?"

He deserved a swift kick for his remark, but I had no hope of moving my foot quick enough. "What did you do, Pienne? Tell me."

He looked up, but remained bent over my foot. "Alexander is invincible. Or nearly enough, anyway." He jabbed my arm with a needle and it bent. "Did Alexander feel that?"

"Well, no—"

He punched me in the chest. "And that?"

"Well, no—"

Before I could move out of the way, he broke one of his empty jars over my head. "Or that?"

I wiped the side of my face with one hand while reaching for his throat with the other. He always moved quicker than his toady body appeared capable, so I missed. With no little dread, I inspected my hand. What should've been a bloody mess was nothing.

Pienne clapped his hands. "Since Alexander is going after someone who loves to create such grand explosions, the Masters thought it best he withstand such destruction. Therefore, he has been granted the power of invincibility. He is, shall Pienne say, thick-skinned. Or a lead body, which is why Alexander's foot seems to have attracted all the particular effect."

The first step, while not impossible, proved difficult. "How am I supposed to chase anyone?"

He shrugged. "Maybe Alexander shouldn't. But knowing him, Pienne would be thankful he could survive another blast."

"I know Aimee," I said as I spun on my heavy foot to face the toady man. Why did these fools keep insisting she had a power? "All of you are wrong about her."

She would never have caused that explosion. She could never have done such a thing. Not for the love we once shared.

In fact, it was her I was trying to save. Again.

Pienne forced a drink in my hand as he hurried me to the door. "Best be getting started. The Masters do not appreciate delays." He pushed me into the dark corridor.

With everything that had happened since arriving at The Misters', I had almost forgotten my encounter with the Guardsman, though I doubt I could forget the sight of the knife in his belly, or the way he moved, or the way he struck the ground, or his strange eyes.

Before Pienne closed the door, I asked, "Are there elixirs to keep a man from bleeding when wounded?"

He paused. "Not that Pienne knows of. The magic would be even more unstable than that required for flying. To attempt such an elixir would risk blowing oneself up, Pienne thinks." He shut and bolted his door.

I drank as I hobbled towards the outline of the door leading into the town. My left foot almost dragged the ground.

So what was that Guardsman? A cyclops? No...he had two eyes...or something eye-like. And the way he moved was reminiscent of a set of gears that required a little grease. Strange. Very strange.

What did the good Duke scheme?

When the door swung open, I almost forgot to leave the same way I entered...with a touch of sarcasm. It wouldn't do to let the cyclops believe I was no longer fond of him. So I tipped my imaginary hat. "Always a pleasure, Lord Mayor."

The cyclops grunted. "For you, but not for me."

The day appeared to be late afternoon, for the shadows stretched long towards the east. What waited was a moment I wouldn't enjoy. However, it could provide a measure of satisfaction when I proved The Misters wrong.

I spoke aloud, needing to hear the assurance of my own voice, "She would never have created that explosion."

Why, then, did the silence of the street seem to mock me?

CHAPTER 3

The Bank would only be open for another hour, so I should have been in a state of some haste. Yet Pienne's shenanigans put a gnawing hunger in my belly. The three shillings in my pocket was just enough to buy a full meal at The Royale, a tavern with a lamb shank worthy of the Queen's table. There, a well-dressed man of business was treated with as much importance and respect as a farmer from the market, though the two sat in different rooms. The ambiance was always enjoyable. Besides, Aimee would be working late. She always did.

By half-dragging, half-lifting my foot, I made my way down the street. My belly rumbled louder in anticipation of the juicy shank, with its hint of pepper and garlic that tickled the tongue. Yes, such would be the perfect reward for completing another mission. The best part was the fact The Misters could do nary a thing to stop me.

I turned the corner onto Queen's Street, where the Merchant's Exchange loomed. A grand set of stairs and a landing ran the front of the building. Recessed upper floors, reminiscent of the great pyramids, created balconies offering exceptional views of the town. Mounted to the roof was a rotating metal globe ten feet in diameter. Lights from the base blazed on its surface, showing those parts of the world whence their latest acquisitions had arrived: Hong

Kong, America, the Amazon, and various parts of Africa. The lights changed from blue to red to green as the globe turned. In a city of magic, the mechanical globe mocked that which provided the money to buy the merchants' imports.

Men ran in and out of the doors as they tried to finish a deal before closing. Within one, a short fellow with his white shirttails escaping his trousers, yelled at another who rushed into the street. The object of his wrath flinched once, but never slowed.

In the distance stood The Royale's outline, with the two bay windows on the first floor and a porch with flowers sheltering the entrance. Did the smell of the kitchen reach me already? It must have, for my mouth watered.

"Alms for the poor?" a high-pitched voice asked from ten yards away. It belonged to a boy of seven or eight who wore a stained shirt that might've once been accused of being white. His trousers reached no lower than his ankles. Holes in the knees exposed the front of his thighs. The tops of his ears stuck out from his tangled blonde hair. They were not quite pointed and not quite round, indicating a half-elf, half-human boy shunned by proper English society.

Recent years had seen fewer of the children running amok, but there were still more than enough. Orphanages once bustled with the business of raising the half-blood children as out-of-wedlock scandals threatened families of all social classes. Those with means paid a hefty sum to rid their family of such disgrace.

I felt a kinship with the orphans as magic also led to my displacement from society.

This lad was in the direct path of the fellow fleeing and, for such a misfortune, received a backhand that spun him down. His tin cup clattered across the cobblestone, allowing a pence to escape. The boy squeaked like a mouse as he scrambled for the coin. Another man laughed as he kicked the cup into the traffic.

Somehow, the cup avoided one set of wheels.

The boy looked at the oncoming horses, wagons, carriages, and the occasional mechanical contraption steaming like an enraged bull. He started to dart in, but hesitated.

I wanted to yell to him to stop, but my words caught in the dryness of my throat.

A horse kicked his cup further away.

That decided him and he darted into their midst. He circumvented a farmer's wagon, now empty of its produce. A carriage driver yelled as the boy almost stepped in front of him.

The little voice within said, "Go to his aid, Ash. This is as good a time as any to test your new power and put it to a good work."

Damsels in distress and children in danger...how could I refuse either?

"You there!" a man called as I hobbled across his path. He rode a metal wagon with a pointed nose on the front of a four-foot cylinder. Six pipes stuck out each side and released puffs of white smoke. It pulled six wooden crates stacked on a cart. He made it a point to pass close enough to kick me. His pointed boot felt like nothing more than a light tap against my shoulder.

The boy continued his dance of desperation as he moved closer to his cup.

A white carriage passed, and I tipped my imaginary hat to the occupants hidden behind drawn curtains. The ornately engraved flowers along the side indicated a lord or lady of some distinction within.

The boy and I reached the cup at the same time. He snatched it up and looked at me with a mixed expression – triumph for having rescued his lone possession, and fear I was about to snatch it from him. A woman screamed as a man yelled, "Out of the way!" I grabbed the lad and cradled him in my arms as a team of six horses bore down. Unable to move out of harm's way fast enough, I did what any sensible gentleman would do. I fell to the ground and covered the boy with my body.

"Blooming fool," the driver said as the horses passed overhead. Four hooves glanced off my arms, proving the truth of his words. However, the pain that should have shot through me felt like nothing more than a scrape. Once the wheels rumbled clear, I stood with the boy.

The rest of the traffic had stopped, along with at least fifty folks along the sides. I tried to ignore them as I dusted the boy off. "Your life isn't worth a cup, little one." I rubbed his matted hair as he stared at me with eyes wide and mouth open. "Be more cautious next time, eh?" When the boy continued to stare, I encouraged him with a small push towards the side, and dropped a coin into his cup. My belly growled in protest, but the voice sighed in contentment.

The boy moved to safety, and as I reached the opposite side, the crowd slowly resumed their business. More than one passerby shook his or her head. Someone muttered, "Luckiest thing I ever saw."

Lucky to him, maybe. Unlucky to me, who was down one shilling and could no longer afford the lamb. The smaller amount meant a meal at an inn within the shadows of old Saint James' Church known as The Eight Bells. There I ate a meal of boiled potato soup, bread, and drank a mug of beer to wash it down.

The fare was such a contrast compared to the first I ate with Aimee. Certain details of the long-ago evening remained as vivid as the moment they happened, such as when the appointed time arrived for the clerks to turn the late-comers away with cries of "Come back tomorrow!"

They directed one at me, and I informed the chief clerk of my business.

He smiled. "You're a better man than I. We'll see how long she keeps you waiting."

Indeed, she kept me waiting for almost two hours. Once during that time she broke away from her business long enough to inform me she would be working late. If I still desired to escort her to dinner then I would be pleased to wait until she finished.

To reinforce her claims, a deep-throated voice bellowed from behind the wall of doors, "Aimee! We need those accounts now!"

That was the only time I saw her flinch. Somehow it made me adore her more, and re-emphasized a human living within the angelic beauty.

In hindsight, the evening was a test of wills as much as anything. It established a boundary, letting me know she did what she did and no one, not even an interest for her affections, would interfere.

Eventually, she finished her work. As we walked out of the Bank, she pulled the pins out of her hair. What fell from her head was long, blonde hair. She ran her fingers through it, loosening it from its bonds. When she stood straight again, the hair bounced down her shoulders in waves.

Oh, she looked so beautiful that it pained me to gaze upon her. Yet I could not help but to stare...mesmerized...entranced.

She said, "I know a small café in the Parisian style. They have tables on the sidewalk, and as the evening has cooled nicely, I should think I'd like to eat there."

"Lead—" My voice cracked, betraying the longing and desire threatening my better senses, and I had to clear it. "Lead the way."

She took me to the place, two streets over, and said nothing the entire way. If she tried to bother me with silence, then she underestimated my resolve. I called solitude and quiet contemplation my friends. The hostess who seated us smirked as if to say I was above my rightful social class. We sat at a table for two, with a wax candle burning between us. The meal was simple. The conversation, the specifics of which I had long forgotten, was short and just as simple. Yet the time went quicker than I would have liked.

Still, when we parted, and I paid most of the coins I possessed, she said, "I suppose you'd like to continue this courtship by escorting me to another dinner?"

"Of course. We barely had the chance to enjoy this one."

She titled her head the slightest bit. "Then you may escort me a week from tonight. But with the stipulation that you refrain from visiting me at the Bank. Understood? My employers weren't happy with the distraction you caused this evening."

The fact that she wanted to see me again made me so happy, I would've agreed to anything at that point. If I needed to wait for a month, I would have, especially when she said, "You make me smile, bishop. Few men can, but you appear to be one of them. I want to know to what extent you can continue to rise to such a challenge."

Better than most. Better than any other.

At least for a time.

I raised my current mug of beer in toast to her and all the street-side café meals we shared. We enjoyed good times together. We shared laughs and dreams and stories of our childhood, all those wonderful, almost insignificant details divulged by lovers. For a time she was happy, or so I believed.

Another round was tempting, for the bitter taste of disappointment settled my mouth. Yet it was time to go. Had Pienne not given me a gimpy leg I would've remained a little longer before continuing to the Bank.

On the streets, the first patrol of Guardsmen who passed I greeted with a nod. They made it a point to ignore me, which had to be a sign of good things to come.

My destination waited closer to the heart of the city. I had read of boomtowns in the American west and long imagined Campden to be of a similar fashion since the coming of the Gateway, albeit with English sensibilities. While the Americans were known for their saloons, we had the long tradition of inns and taverns and alehouses. Where they worshipped in wooden churches, we gave praise in our glorious cathedrals. They had banks, but we did, too. Yet ours were much grander and more proper, paying the pound and shilling and pence and all transactions associated with them the respect they deserved.

The Bank of Campden was no exception. Its marble columns rose an impressive five stories on three sides. The front façade was also made of marble, but while the columns were white, the front was black. There were no windows. The lone door allowed entrance and exit though the door was so large it could've been mistaken as a moat bridge for a small castle or manor home. Its oaken planks had been oiled black, and gold rings hung from it as if it waited for a giant to knock and inquire of his holdings.

In admiring the building, I had thought nothing of the steps until I reached the base. Twelve of them waited between me and the door.

With a sigh, I stepped up with my right foot then pulled my left behind it. The first wasn't too troublesome to navigate, but my thigh burned by the sixth step. So I used my hands to help it out, and we got along tolerably well though a bit weary by the time we reached the level with the door. Still, I hobbled to it and pulled it open.

"In Spera Non Esse Claudit" – *"The Trust That Never Closes"* - read their motto engraved along the frame. Though the business of deposits and withdrawals

maintained proper hours, the business of loans and trading and of summaries of accounts continued throughout the night, signifying the establishment's importance.

And so I entered the hallowed halls of the Bank. My lone step echoed through a room as wide as the building. It opened three stories high with five chandeliers of gold and crystal reflecting the light of a hundred candles though most were extinguished for the night. They awaited the two gentlemen responsible for replacing candles, cleaning the holders of the melted wax, and shining the gems. I passed many hours on many nights watching the men climb up and down their rickety ladders.

Aimee once mentioned a junior associate proposed replacing the chandeliers with modern lighting based on various levels rotating through a system that automated the replacement and lighting of the candles. Her superiors declined even though it would've saved them the cost of the two gentlemen who tended the current lights. They said the old style established certain credence to the establishment. It reminded those who entrusted their money with the Bank that it was as safe as it had been for the previous generations.

I agreed with them if for no other reason than it meant I could marvel at the inefficiencies of the old methods.

On the floor, black marble contrasted with desks made of white marble and chairs of black cherry stained as dark as the marble. Its coldness and business-like austere always reminded me of the Verintain Family Mausoleum, where the Ring of Seven Powers once resided.

A sudden chill made me rub my arms. I almost looked over my shoulder for ghouls as I dragged my foot across the floor. My destination was the first floor where Aimee would still be working, studying her ledgers and her numbers and tapping the keys of her calculation machine, just like she was on the day I proposed.

Our courtship lasted three months though I gave up any hope of not being in love with her after the first. Her beauty grew each day. Her appearance changed, too, becoming more genuine. She kept her hair down more often and wore more jewelry, favoring the low-drooping necklaces that accented the curves of her bosom.

Many of my fellow canons, and even Bishop Donnavan, asked what I saw in her beyond appearance. All I could say was, "She becomes a different person when she leaves the Bank. Once she grows comfortable with you, she becomes passionate and full of life. She reminds me of the rose of Sharon in the Song of Solomon."

Yes, I fell in love with that flower as much as I fell in love with the cold, business-like beauty who existed during the other ten or twelve hours of the day.

She said she loved me after I took the knife for her. And I, the fool that I was, believed her. Some beautiful women never realize the power they hold over a man's emotions. A pretty smile touches deeper than a compliment, a tear deeper than a kiss.

You are not making this easy, Ash. Remember who you are dealing with. Never forget how she spurned you.

At the bottom of the steps, I took a deep breath before proceeding to climb one step, one foot lift, at-a-time. No one else came or went.

At least I could catch Aimee if she left while I made my tortured way up since she never took another way. Her shoes had worn grooves in the steps, a testament to the number of times she flew up and down them each day. Even the clerks joked that everyone taking this flight risked their lives, for one never knew when she would knock him down.

I pulled myself over the top step and leaned against the wall to rest. My arms and leg ached even more. Yet I still had a good thirty yards to reach the door at the opposite end, the white one contrasting against all the other black doors on the floor.

It was at this very place I stood the night of the attempted burglary. She worked later than usual and no one else remained for me to visit, so I wandered the building, trying to uncover some of its mysteries. After spending time on the ground floor, I reached the top of the steps, and saw the shadowy form moving down the way. He blended well with the black marble and made no sound as he moved. Only when Aimee's door opened did I see the dagger in the thief's hand silhouetted against the white. As she turned to close her door, the thief raced forward.

My legs already propelled me forward, and as I ran I yelled, "Aimee!"

The thief turned. I lost track of his blade until it protruded from my thigh. Yet the wound neither slowed me nor discouraged me, driven as I was by love and determination. As Aimee sought the safety of her office, I wrapped my arms around the man at her door. Somehow, he dislodged himself and, before I grabbed him, disappeared in the dusky light.

Then, I assumed he slipped away.

Now?

What if he had been a magic user? What if The Misters sent him? Or the attack was not a random act, but a targeted killing?

That night was the first time Aimee allowed me inside her office. She sat me in her chair, placed my foot on her desk, and tended the wound. She cried, too, one of three times I witnessed her doing so. The best way I knew to make her stop was by kissing her. When I did, she fell into my lap, and took full advantage of the moment's passion. When she pulled away she whispered, "I love you, Alexander Asherton." The words surged through my heart, sending me into a euphoria matched only by magic elixirs.

So what would she say when she saw me now? The last time we were in each other's presence was the day we met in the lawyer's office to make the divorce official. She refused to look at me as she signed the document. Her arm made a quick movement to push it across the table as if my presence made her ill and she wanted to be rid of me. "Sign it, Alexander. And I will not listen to another of your sermons on why this is wrong."

After doing as requested, I followed her to make a final plea. She hurried from me and... Well, what if The Misters were right?

They weren't. This was a matter to put behind me, prove them wrong, and move onto my next assignment.

The names that were once so familiar passed as I dragged my foot across the floor. The first was Jerome, a tall man from Birmingham whose dark complexion complemented the marble.

Next was Sean, an old widower who offered free advice on how to make a woman happy. He advised me of the power held in a bouquet.

Redding's name had been replaced, and the Bank was no worse for his loss. Of them all, I confided in him the most. I called him a good and loyal friend. He visited our home many times, sharing dinner or playing whist. Yet like everyone else, he turned his back on me after the divorce. Like everyone else Aimee and I used to call friends, he shunned me.

As much as I had learned to loathe her, I loathed Redding and the other names even more. They, who sat in marbled offices and pronounced judgment on who should or should not receive a loan for that lovely little cottage or that quaint town house. They, who always seemed so amused when I waited on her. They, who told every secret, every whispered rumor they heard.

There were no secrets at the Bank. That lesson I learned the hard way. It was one of the biggest reasons I never placed a foot in the building again.

I despised the Bank and those it harbored.

Did The Misters know of the disgrace and humiliation they heaped upon me at that moment? Did they laugh with each other even then?

At her door, I reached out to trace the name inscribed in gold. I caught myself prior to touching it. The heat from my hand fogged it over.

How many times had I told myself it wouldn't be like this? How many times did I wish this venerable building would collapse?

Maybe that was why The Misters never granted me the power of explosions.

Put the moment behind you, Ash. Prove The Misters wrong. Prove Pienne wrong.

Remember this is business.

They didn't know Aimee like I did. She wasn't a magic user. She had never been an addict.

Still, my hand trembled as I reached for the latch.

It was senseless to announce myself. It was pointless to make it last longer than necessary. She would be at her desk, scribbling in her ledger. Once she realized who it was, and gave her vocal displeasure at my sight, she would pay me little mind.

So I opened the door and found the office empty. Well, empty of her.

Both relief and disappointment washed through me.

The furniture remained as it always did. The candle on her desk had burned halfway down. Her mechanical quill rested on its white porcelain holder. The tube running from its top to an ink tin was black, showing recent use. Her ledger remained open, and next to it waited the calculation machine.

Where was she?

Like those old times, I would have to wait for her. How appropriate.

I sat down. Or sank down as she always liked to have her visitors sitting lower than herself.

She would not have the satisfaction, so I stood.

The contents of her desk were sparse. No pictures. No flowers. No small decorative glass balls so popular with the ladies those days.

Curiosity compelled me to step over to look at her latest business. A loan, perhaps? An accounting of the day's transactions?

But words were scribbled in the midst of the numbers. "That which you seek is no longer here. Too bad that you will not be here much longer, either."

I wasn't?

How did she know? How did she—

Smoke rose from beneath her chair, from between my feet. It was a single strand of thin, purple smoke.

I had seen that one other time.

"Damn."

The Misters were right.

And I was about to test Pienne's new power.

That was my last thought before the explosion struck.

CHAPTER 4

"Over here!" someone said from above. "Call the fire brigade!"

Smoke filled the air and made my eyes water. A coughing fit took hold. My skin stung all over, like a hundred enraged bees had struck at once.

"Someone's here," another voice said. "And alive. God be praised!"

Was I truly alive? Or did I see the proverbial light at the end of the tunnel shining through the myriad of cracks between the marble rubble above? Perhaps, but those who reported such an experience never talked about pain. Rather, they always spoke of a profound peace and overwhelming comfort. At that moment, all I felt besides the aching, was betrayal and rage.

How could Aimee have tried to kill me? Did she view our marriage as a lie? What did she really mean when she said she loved me? Was that a lie, too?

How had I been such a love blind fool?

Mounds of rock pinned my arms. The top of a desk sat squarely on my chest.

I hated black marble. I hated white marble.

I hated marble.

"Are you there?" the first man called as water rained down. Drops struck my face and I swallowed what I could to relieve the thirst brought on by the dust.

"Down here," I said, half-hoarse. "I could use a bit of help."

Help. Something Aimee would need when I found her. She had much to explain.

The rubble squeezed down, pushing the breath from my chest as someone passed through the light. Oddly enough, in spite of the pressure, there was no pain.

Bless Pienne and his mad elixirs.

So how did Aimee know to expect me? How did she know I would go to her office? The same way she knew I would follow her from the lawyer's office after signing the divorce documents?

In answer, the scars on my right side ached all the more.

Was she truly so cold? What about the time we walked through the King's Gardens? She told me she had never been happier. She said she never imagined someone caring for her like I did. Her orphan's heart had found a home with mine. So after all of that, and other tender, intimate moments, she wanted me dead? What did I mean to her after the divorce? Nothing except a bad moment in her life? What had I done to deserve such an act? Was it something I didn't do?

"But I survived, didn't I?" I whispered. I lived through the first blast and I lived through this one. "What do you think of that, little canon?"

The voice said nothing.

"We'll get you out of there," the man said as he pulled off several broken pieces of furniture. "The physician will be waiting to tend to you, sir." He called for more hands. "You are a lucky chap to be alive. Blessed, I'd say."

Perhaps.

More likely though, I am cursed.

Yes, I owed Aimee much more than I ever dreamt. Oh, how I used to wonder at how blessed I was with her love and affections. How I used to offer up praise for sending such a lovely creature into my life. And look at what path that sent me hurtling down. Burned and broken by her explosion, I turned to the only thing promising relief from the constant pain: magic. And, oh, what lovely little potions I purchased. How they numbed the aches and the breaking of my heart and the throbbing of my soul. They provided an escape from the realities, the coldness and indifference, of my broken existence.

And, oh, how those magics fed upon my body. And how I wanted more and more and more, even as my hair turned white, a permanent reminder to society of my indulgences and weaknesses and of my impending death.

Once I reached that point, I needed the magic to continue living. Ironic, was it not? To live, I needed that which killed me.

Pienne called it an unfortunate good circumstance. He claimed it meant ones such as myself moved closer to the creatures on the other side of the Gateway. We became more than we were, bridging the gap between science and magic.

I said we became much less.

Water sprayed the rubble and more light filled the tiny cave.

Four pairs of hands lifted me. It took a bit of wiggling before the table gave way. When the hands pulled all the harder, the Bank's effort to claim me failed and the marble slid to the right.

"Careful, gentlemen," the first man said, "he is likely to be seriously injured, and we might cause more harm than good. Where's the physician?"

They placed me on the top of the rubble.

"Where are you injured?" the man asked.

Smoky air burned my lungs as I took a deep breath. It felt far better than it should have. I sat up and squeezed the man's shoulder. "Thank you, sir, but I appear to be fine. Praise the Lord!"

Even in the gaslight, the man's face appeared ashen. He looked between the hole and me. "But...but..."

"Just strolling down the street when the blast struck. Imagine if I had been inside." I chuckled. "Probably would've died." As I dusted myself off, I saw the true extent of the damage.

My skin had a definite red tint, like a wall of heat had struck or like I enjoyed a long day in the sun. Almost all of the hair on my front was either burned away or singed. My clothes had completely disappeared. In my nakedness was exposed the scars along my right arm, thigh, and ribs. Not that the crowd noticed those details. To a one, all they could do was stare at the walking miracle before them.

This could be played one of two ways: either act overwhelmed by such a great occurance, or brush it aside with something resembling indifference. The latter seemed wiser and less likely to attract more undue attention.

I patted the man's shoulder, then pushed through the others. They moved like marble was attached to their legs. My lead foot allowed me to only go so fast, but at least the smoke provided some cover for my compromised state of attire.

With my head held high, I hobbled from the scene. I moved past the fire brigade, who worked their water wagon. The contraption reminded me of an elephant, but with wheels for legs. The giant tank ended with a sharp nose on the front that attached to a trunk-like hose. Two men at the rear pumped the water using a handle that resembled a tail. The man controlling the hose let the pressure build before releasing his spray.

Other members of the fire brigade formed a line up one pile of debris, then down another. Their black buckets moved in perfect unison, and contrasted against their red uniforms and white hats.

Not unlike when the old tannery burned last year, dozens upon dozens of citizens turned out to help combat the deadly fire. Its spread would make more lives miserable, all because of Aimee.

One enterprising chap worked a crank on the front of a machine comprised of cracker barrels stacked six high and three across. Metal tubes ran from each, like the spout on a keg, and met at a hose just above the man's head. As he turned the crank, an engine in the back sputtered. Drops of water fell from a hose in response. I tamped my curiosity and didn't wait to see if he could get it to work or see what, exactly, it would do.

Only when I cleared the immediate area did I pause to survey the scene.

The Bank had been dealt a potentially mortal wound. A hole had been ripped into the side, one stretching from the ground floor to the top floor. It ran almost as wide as the building itself. Beams and joists were exposed, and many smoldered. Much of the priceless marble had been reduced to dust and what remained on that side of the building had cracked in at least a dozen different ways.

Did Aimee fear me so much she willingly destroyed her very life? Perhaps, though it was more likely she hated me that much.

I wasn't sure what to think of such possibilities. Sadness, disappointment, relief, and my own anger fought for control, such was the influence the lady still held over me.

Above, the familiar hum of an airship's engines urged me to keep moving. The oblong, balloon-like ship was colored the same red as the fire brigade. The pilot, in a glass gondola attached to the belly of the ship, leaned out his window as he surveyed the scene. He yelled something that was lost in the noise of flames and people. A moment later, the metal tanks at the rear of the ship opened. They released a cloud of water which struck with a loud whoosh. It stirred up a cloud of dust and ash, followed immediately by smoke and the sound of sizzles.

The dust tried to overtake me, but I hobbled out of its path. The prevailing wind chilled my bare skin, making me rub my arms as I made my way home.

Clothing would be the first order of business, followed by straightening out the thoughts swirling in my head.

What will you do next, Ash?

Open more old wounds, of course. Revisit moments and relationships best forgotten.

Did The Misters enjoy their private joke on my behalf? Surely someone laughed at my predicament.

I know I didn't.

Sleep consumed me the rest of the night and through most of the next day, departing only when Saint James' bells struck five in the evening. In spite of the aches and the soreness, I forced myself up and to the wash basin. Into the water went the last of the marble dust. Only then did I dress in my finest clothes, the ones suitable for an evening in society: black coat, black trousers and a white shirt with a red vest.

Such finery was appropriate for any of the much-anticipated events leading to Duke Schaever's marriage, and I would rather be on my way to one of them, rather than where I had to go.

When I entered the streets, I didn't blend in at all with the area's occupants, for this was where the magic addicts, prostitutes, urchins, thieves, and all other sorts of the socially downtrodden and financially challenged made their homes. Here, the buildings remained in a constant state of decay. Boards had given up most of their paint or stain years ago, leaving the wood exposed and, having been beaten by the sun and rain, had turned gray. Hence, the name of this section: the Gray Area.

Once, I dedicated my life to helping these very people, for I understood their predicament all too well. Once, I tried to offer them hope in the midst of their despair, for I once escaped similar circumstances and the consequences of addiction.

Now?

They were my neighbors, for I called the Gray Area home. It served as a reminder of my rise and my fall, of my transgressions and my weaknesses, of my childhood and my loss. Not to say the people living there were bad. On the contrary, most were good people willing to help if the need were great. They kept alive a small hope within me, a small belief that grace did abound in the world, even when such hope was challenged by situations such as I currently found myself.

So Aimee knew I pursued her. Did she believe me now dead?

That depended on who The Gatherers assigned to watch the explosion. Did they watch me rise from the rubble? Did word spread of the miracle, of the man who survived without a scratch? If I were fortunate, such news would be lost in the chaos of the moment.

I tugged my vest to straighten a wrinkle, an impossible task given that it was wool, in anticipation of the next move. We played a chess game now, with all the intricacies and nuances associated with it. Only I never played the game well. My tendency to favor direct confrontation always lost to subtlety and subterfuge.

Walking down the street mostly involved dragging my lead foot along. My goal was the other side of the city, past Saint James', past the Bank, past The Misters, past the green parks and the Duke's home, towards the outer district, to the area I once called home. There, estates had been granted to those deemed worthy of land or who could afford to purchase one or who had inherited it prior to the coming of the Schaevers. Many had gardens and pastures, and well-tended yards. Most of the homes were made of brick or stone and always had fresh paint on the trim. Stone fences marked the perimeter of each holding. To round out the importance of the area, cobblestone lined the streets, and workers cleaned after the horses, mostly at night and beneath the gas lamps.

There lived Aimee still, in the home which her lawyer successfully petitioned the good Duke to legally return to her as part of the divorce. But I wouldn't start there. If she suspected I survived, that would be the last place she'd stay. No, I would go straight to her best friend, Bonni Greenhew, someone she had known since they lived in the orphanage together. Both had risen through society despite their humble beginnings. Aimee confided in no one else like she did with Bonni.

Truthfully, I never did like the Greenhews. Bonni's husband was a banker, too, though he worked for the rival, the Royal Trust. He always greeted me with a smile and a handshake, saying something like, "Hello, Ash. Always a pleasure to see you."

While I would answer something like, "A pleasure to see you, too, Frank," he would say under his breath, "I'm sure it's a pleasure you twit. Now I'll have to wash your filth from my hands." He did that so often I think he forgot he talked just loud enough for me to hear.

I had seen neither of them since before the divorce and truth be told, I never wanted to see them again. If a giant hole opened in the earth and swallowed them, or a flying machine or airship crashed and burned on top of them, it would have performed a great service not only for me, but for mankind in general.

A woman whistled as she leaned against a lamp pole. No one had yet come through to light it, so the shadows obscured her. That was a pity, for Lauree was one of the prettier street workers. She had all the features of a classic beauty, with her straight, raven-colored hair and a heart-shaped face with full lips. "Where're you going all dressed up?"

I waved as I avoided an odorous pile in the gutter. Horse or pig or human, it mattered not. They all smelled.

She stepped away from the pole, and caught me as I crossed over to King's Road. A smile appeared on her face as she brushed my lapels. Knowing it was for me made my heart skip a beat. "You look too distinguished to be here alone. You're not in a hurry, either. Where are you going, magic boy?"

"Places far and wide," I said, which was my usual answer when she asked her usual question.

She slipped her arm through mine. "Then take me with you."

"Baby, I'll take you around the world."

Her head rested on my shoulder. It felt good to have her this close...too good. "But you're spoken for. And Her Majesty put a price on your head."

"All the reasons why we should depart now."

A playful laugh eased the tension in her eyes. "Only you remember those lines so well, Ash. No one else seems to care much about the plays. And Ro—" She cleared her throat. "Well, they're not approved of by some."

We weren't so different in that respect. Masters owned us, commanded us, profited by us.

I gave her hand a reassuring squeeze.

Lauree. The once-upon-a-time actress. I had the pleasure of watching her perform several times in moments far removed from what we now knew. When she made her first appearance as Bianca in 'The Taming of the Shrew' her performance attracted much attention and praise. Critics declared she was a notable, young actress, one destined for fame.

With a light-hearted tone meant to lift us from the dour cloud that had settled over us I asked, "So what's new, beautiful? What's the word on the streets?"

"Did you hear about the miracle at the Bank?" When I shook my head, which spun with dread of what I was about to hear, she continued with enthusiasm, "Some gentleman got caught in an explosion and walked away naked and with not a scratch on him. Some folks get all the luck don't they?"

"Yes," I said with a sudden lump in my throat.

Had she noticed my red-tinted skin?

"What's with the limp?" she asked as she stared at my leg.

"Bruised foot," I answered with a light-hearted tone that I hoped didn't sound forced.

She raised her brow as she gripped my arm tighter. "How did that happen?"

"Long story." I tried to say that in a way that meant I had no desire to discuss it.

She acquiesced by remaining quiet as we passed the boarded-up school with broken window panes on the second floor, and the weed-eaten lot where the old tannery stood before it burned last year at the hand of a suspected arsonist who was never caught. The fire threatened to spread quickly and only because the locals turned out to help the fire brigade was it subdued in time. I didn't care to consider the amount of suffering of those who owned so little losing everything to such an uncaring act.

I looked at Lauree as we passed a row of old, gray homes. If our lives had been different and our paths had crossed years earlier, we could've been Campden's finest couple. It was a shame she had fallen almost as far as I. We could have enjoyed a fine marriage.

When we reached the outskirts of the area, she kissed my cheek. "Thanks for nothin'."

A tip of my imaginary hat was followed by, "A gentleman knows nothin' better than most."

That was the last line from 'Another Day', Lauree's final performance. She made it her best, but the play as a whole was horrific. The other actors were amateurs and the set design fell apart during the premiere, which did nothing to impress the London critics. Once they derided it, the public ignored it. Rather than blame the writer or director, the producers blamed her and blacklisted her, thus bringing an abrupt end to her promising career.

After hailing a cab, I watched her walk away in the dusk with shoulders hunched and steps slow.

The canon within wanted to run to her and hold her tight. It wanted to give her the hope of which I once preached. She needed it, for she faced a long, dark night.

So did I, and it would not do to drag myself across the town, and appear half exhausted from the walk. No, where I went demanded the utmost dignity and respect, even if it meant putting on a moment of airs, of making a performance that would do Lauree proud.

As I stepped into the cab with my good foot, and pulled my other in, the entire contraption tilted dangerously to the side. The driver peered around. "What's this, governor? Heavy packages can be placed in the back."

When he started to rise, I motioned and said, "Oh, I seem to have added the pounds of late." I cleared my throat. "It appears I lost track of just how many." I gave a jovial laugh as I closed the door. Maybe he wouldn't note my slender frame.

Fortunately, no one else sat in the cab, though the driver did pick up and drop off three other passengers along the way. When we turned the corner from the Duke's grounds, I stared at a walled land existing in a time all its own. His home loomed in the distance with its ancient-looking keep and towers rising above majestic oaks in mockery of its true age. They served as a reminder that Campden existed as it did only because of his grandfather's genius and his grandmother's uncanny ability to wield her family's new-found influence.

We passed the Hollese house, a grand structure rising three floors. The family was rumored to be distant cousins to the royals and to reinforce such a belief, had built a home reminiscent of England's finest, complete with a moat as well as two round turrets, and a foyer resembling a gatehouse. They hosted two parties every year, one at the start of spring and the other at the end of summer, and they issued invitations to everyone for three miles around.

Aimee always enjoyed those affairs. Me? I would rather have spent my time in more meaningful pursuits besides drinking and gossiping.

The Jernigans' house passed, with its ivy-covered wall. They proudly maintained a reputation for having a wandering eye. They had rarely acknowledged me, being the canon that I was.

Then there was the Goodmeade estate, where a yard full of flowers in bloom drew visitors from all over the empire. The Queen, passing through for a visit with the good Duke two years ago, took the time to visit the famous yard. Mrs. Goodmeade was a widow with no children, save for the flowers. She worked among them even at that hour, and her mouth moved as she spoke loving and tender words to them.

Next was the Killens', with their eight children. Then there was the Noblair's, a couple who adopted three girls from local orphanages.

Others followed, but my eyes locked on the Greenhew's estate, where a carriage waited at the end of the sidewalk. The Schaever's white badger glowed on the doors and illuminated each side. A footman waited at the side while the driver sat, ready to leave at a moment's notice.

"A popular destination this evening," the driver of my cab said as he stopped.

What business did the Greenhews have with the Duke? They always aspired to higher social circles, but I never knew them to be acquaintances with Campden's leading family.

Maybe the Duke's betrothed visited? If so, could I catch a glimpse of her beauty, which was rumored to be unequalled?

The driver helped me down and when my left foot hit the ground, it made a sound like a lead weight striking. I wanted to check the bottom of my heel to see if it had a dent. Instead, I handed the surprised driver his coins, and began my trek past the other carriage. Neither the footman nor the driver acknowledged me.

The Greenhew home was actually one of the more modest estates in the area. It rose two floors and was made of a red brick obscured by ivy and moss. Their carriage house was in the rear, well out of view. Their yard was comprised of large weeping willows and shrubs cut at a uniform waist-height. Small paths led in all directions, paths down which Aimee and I walked arm-in-arm on many cool nights. Once, we lost ourselves in the maze on a late spring evening. Aimee dared me to catch her and teased me by stripping out of her clothes, starting with her shoes and then her dress and then—

Don't think about the moments, Ash. Take a deep breath and let it out slowly. Those days are gone, and it would've been better if they never happened.

Beyond the house were several pastures where they kept a flock of sheep. A barn and groundskeeper's house rounded out their property.

The front door opened, releasing a flood of light. A man said, "I expect a full report at the Ball. You have the invitation." His voice carried an expectation of obedience. "Find out where the delay is. I'll broker no excuses."

Seeing the carriage surprised me, but that paled in comparison to the disbelief I felt when I saw to whom the voice belonged.

Duke Schaever.

His ever-present cane clicked on the stone of the walkway as he limped towards me. He wore a fine suit with an outline of the badger in gold on each lapel. He wore a top hat and beneath the brim were gray curls extending to the base of his neck. A refined face with deep-set eyes sat amidst a well-groomed beard the same color as the curls of his hair.

No one knew the true reason he limped. Some said a magic curse followed him, some claimed an elf injured him when he refused to keep his part of a deal, while others said he had been caught in an explosion. The last reason made me feel kin to his condition, and was the one I chose to believe.

I stepped off the path and bowed as he passed, even as I looked to see if his fiancé followed. Would he be so quick to give a tip of his hat if he knew I was the one who stole the Statue of Forneil from under his nose? Would he be so quick to return to his carriage and hurry into the night?

Despite my having stolen from him, I respected his position and his authority. In many ways, he helped Campden and promoted the town's unique qualities. Even with his recently announced engagement, he was turning the days leading to the marriage into an affair for the entire town. The paper spoke of the official introduction of his bride-to-be at the Duke's Ball, which would be followed by series of exciting social gatherings over the next several months which included a special premiere at Chen's Dragon Theatre, and a week-long carnivale on the grounds of his home.

Each event would be spectacular, for he always made magic the centerpiece.

I tipped my imaginary hat to his departure, then resumed my journey along the path. When I reached the entrance, I paused.

This wouldn't go well, aside from the fact I was about to make a scandalous breach of etiquette, for I seemed to have forgotten to send a calling card. But then, that would have destroyed any hope of surprise.

Not that the card would've been acknowledged.

A knock summoned the doorman, a dour man whose top hat almost covered his eyes so that you never knew which way he looked. He was older than anyone I knew. He had gray hair, and loose skin that hung down at his cheeks like a hound's. For the first time, I saw surprise flicker across his face, though his voice was as nonchalant as ever. "Mister Asherton, I don't believe you have an appointment. I will inform the master that you called. Good day!"

I bowed and kept my demeanor charitable in spite of the irritation of having to be at the place. More old memories awakened, and I wished they'd go back to sleep. "As observant and knowledgeable as always, Kevin. I gave no prior announcement of my arrival, but I was hoping I might have a word with Bonni and Frank."

"You just missed them, sir. If they wish to see you, they will send a card." He closed the door.

My left foot in the doorway kept it from shutting. "I know they always take their supper at home on Thursday nights, Kevin. They make no exception to the rule. And I just passed their distinguished guest, so I know they are home."

He tried to close the door again and said, "You're not welcome here, sir."

"Is she here?" *Aimee?*

He neither flinched nor hesitated as he continued to try to push the door closed. Was I correct? Did she wait inside?

I tried to remain charitable despite the urge to burst through. "I must talk to her. The matter is most urgent. Don't make this any nastier than it must be."

"You're not welcome here." He tried to push my foot out of the way by using his own.

I'd remain pleasant and charitable no matter how difficult. "I'll give you one more chance. Let me in peacefully or I will force my way."

He continued to try to pry my foot out as he tried to close the door in a most insistent manner.

A solid push moved him back one step, and allowed the chance to get my chest between the door and the frame. Then it was an easy matter to squeeze in, even as he drew a sword.

The man was determined. Foolishly so. Yet he wasn't going to stop me from seeing Aimee.

He waved the sword even faster, grasping it in both hands. "Make no mistake, I will hurt you unless you turn around and leave immediately."

I held my arms out. "I come unarmed, and you threaten me? Let me speak to the masters of the house and then I'll be on my way." I waved his sword away. "You have my word this won't take but a moment."

And oh, what a moment it would be.

Kevin raised his voice. "Leave now, sir! I'll not warn you again."

"What's that?" Frank called from the dining room, which sat on the right side, just off the foyer and the library. He sounded frustrated. "Is something the matter? Has the Duke returned?"

"Nothing, sir," Kevin said. "Just a most persistent...salesman."

Salesman?

Frank barked, "Send him on his way and tell him not to come back unless he wants the Guardsmen called on him."

"It's Asherton," I called, keeping my tone light. "And I'd like a word with you."

My voice echoed twice through the hallways. Everything went quiet. Even the clocks seemed to take a moment longer to tick off the next second.

Kevin advanced to push me out the door. I knocked his blade aside, and limped past the old man. "Sorry to interrupt, but—"

Bonni appeared from nowhere and slapped my left cheek, which made her pause as she stared at her hand. She whimpered as she held her wrist. Both fingers and palm blazed red. "You have no right to be here."

Frank stood beside her. "You had best leave if you know what's good." Under his breath, he said, "Bastard. Bringing your filth into this honorable home."

I smiled the biggest smile I could manage, for such a face would aggravate them all the more, then bowed. Still, the canon's voice urged me to remain charitable no matter the circumstances. "As I was explaining to Kevin, I only wanted a word with you good folks."

Bonni motioned to the doorman. "We've already wasted enough time on you. You have a lot of nerve coming here after—" She pointed to the door. "Get out!"

Not with Aimee hiding in the house. "I'm looking for her." They needed no name to know to whom I referred. "I need to speak with her. Where is she?"

Frank sneered. "Far from here." He tried to push me, but my left foot kept me firmly grounded. "Kevin, you have our permission."

The doorman didn't hesitate and I made no attempt to dodge his strike. His blade struck my back, at the kidney level, and bounced off.

All three stood, stunned, and the house grew quiet again.

Who were these people? Really? Did they want me dead that much?

Bonni's mouth hung open in disbelief. "What...what..." She looked at her husband. "Keep him here while I find out what this means."

I grabbed her shoulder. "Wait. You must tell me where she is. Which room?"

The lady spun and held her hand out, palm and fingers straight like she wanted me to stop. Only, the air rippled from a circle at the center of her palm. It shot out and knocked me back like a barrel struck me. A small table broke my fall as it busted into a dozen pieces.

A lamp fell, shattered, and spilled its oil. Several papers landed in my lap.

One had the imprint of the Duke's stamp, the one with the badger. The writing spoke of the Duke's Ball. I grabbed the invitation and tucked it away as I stood.

Bonni advanced. "That would've killed most people. Who are you?" When she held out her hand again, I lowered my shoulder and planted my left foot behind. In light of two attempts to kill me, any desire to remain charitable disappeared, and they had only themselves to blame for the consequences.

Her shockwave struck, sliding me an inch backwards, but nothing more. Before she recovered from her own surprise, I grabbed her arm and twisted her around. "A magic user, eh? Kept this secret from me all these years? Just like Aimee kept her little explosive secret?" I pulled her close as Frank and Kevin tried to flank me. "How many laughs did you share at my expense, knowing how ignorant I remained of the truth?"

She planted her foot on mine, trying to drive her heel into the bone, but all she did was howl in pain. "Who—what—are you?"

I motioned to Frank. "One step closer and I will kill your precious wife. Don't think I won't enjoy it." Such a threat made the man stop even though I wouldn't carry through on it. I couldn't kill her, no matter how much I might want to. "All I wanted was to ask you where Aimee is hiding. You didn't have to make all this trouble on my behalf." Bonni smelled like lemon pudding with a hint of vanilla, which meant she wore Aimee's favorite scent by what's-his-name, the perfumer with the store across from the Bank. Her hair tickled my nose the way Aimee's once did.

Don't return to those memories, Ash.

Frank spoke with rage and fear. "Release my wife, Asherton. I don't know who or what you're involved with, but you had best let her go." Under his breath, he said, "You're a dead man."

As she held her head higher Bonni said, "Kevin, do what you must."

"But I will not injure you, madam," the doorman said. "I'll be—"

I choked her and pulled her close enough for our cheeks to touch. As she tried to push away, I whispered, "You know where she is. Tell me!"

She quit struggling, and said nothing.

Kevin appeared with an old-fashioned double-barreled musket. He pointed it at my back.

I rolled my eyes. "Are you sure you know how to play with such a dangerous weapon? Put it down before you hurt someone."

Frank advanced, and I squeezed Bonni's neck tighter. Her face turned red as she gagged.

He held his hand out, too, with palm and fingers straight, but parallel to the ground. Flames shot from his fingertips. They glanced off my shoulder and set my coat ablaze. The fire warmed my skin.

You're a magic user, too? They surround me?

I released Bonni so I could pat the flames out.

Frank smiled. "Afraid of a little fire? Let's see what you do when I hit you full-on." He pointed with both hands and a ball of flame raced forward, howling and roaring.

I ducked beneath the heat. When he pushed another ball behind the first, I grabbed hold of Kevin. The man struggled, but I drew him in front of the flames.

The ball struck, setting the doorman alight. Heat washed over me as flames tickled my shoulders and sides. As Kevin screamed, I reached around him and aimed his musket at Frank's heart.

The canon's voice yelled for me to stop.

I can't kill Frank, either. It isn't right.

My hand shook as I pulled the trigger. One round struck his right thigh. He cried out and stumbled even as he released another ball of flame, one that sailed high and set the ceiling ablaze.

Bonni pushed her air and tried to smother the flames, which ate their ancient tapestries like they were parchment. The door and the front wall burned within the span of moments.

I pushed Kevin to her as my skin warmed more, and she tended to the man's flames as I put out my own with quick pats. My vest, now scorched and tattered, hung open. Where my lead-like skin absorbed the heat, I glowed like an ember. Yet the scars on my arm remained white in contrast to the red, making them resemble a doctor's playfield of exploration.

Frank held his leg as he stood. "You're a dead man, Asherton. The Gatherers have marked you. You'll not escape our grasp. You will not know peace until we settle with you."

That was the reward I received for practicing restraint by not killing him?

Bonni said, "Stop!" She held one hand out while still trying to smother the spreading fire with her other.

I all but growled as I said, "This is a matter between Aimee and me. It seems I owe her something for trying to kill me." The subsequent smugness displayed on Bonni's face reassured me of my debt.

Never had those two kept secrets from each other.

Bonni peered down her nose. "Do you believe you're smart enough to stand against her, to exact some sort of revenge? You will never find her. No, she's too cunning for the likes of you." She quit trying to smother the flames and held both of her hands towards me. "Just like you never knew her secrets, you will never know where she is. We of The Gatherers are far above you lesser people, you dredges of the earth. I don't know why she married you."

"Don't go there, Bonni." *Don't say it.*

She sneered. "She never really loved you. Claimed you were boring, but was indebted to you and so she pretended you were her world. How did you repay her? By trying to make her less than she was, by holding her back when she could be free like a butterfly in the spring air." A strand of loose hair fell in front of her eyes. "She said you would never do anything except devote your life to your precious religion. She mocked that, too."

The words hurt worse than they should have. They struck deeper than anything she could summon to hit me. The confidence in her voice and the satisfaction of her smile said she knew it.

"She hated you." She threw her hands forward, side-by-side, yelling as she did so.

The air rippled like a wall. I lowered my shoulder again, but it did little good. The impact knocked me away like she swatted a pesky fly.

I struck the front wall, now completely engulfed in flames. The wood and bricks crumpled and gave way, and I tumbled over the porch and into the yard. A row of hedges stopped me.

Aches filled my body, not on my skin, other than feeling like a kettle over a fire, but deep within, like I suffered internal bruising. My shoulder and arm throbbed at the bones and my muscles felt sore. Yet I refused to lie there in anticipation of another display of the Greenhews talents.

The flames spread through their home. The front was completely engulfed. Fire licked at the roof. The ivy curled and bits broke off to drift high into the air, trailing small tendrils of flame and smoke. Bonni continued to strike at the fire. Small holes appeared where her force of air smothered. But almost as soon as she made progress, the fire attacked the opening with a renewed vigor.

Once I might've felt some pity for their situation, though never real concern. A pang of guilt did arise at the thought of Kevin's burns. True, he tried to kill me, but he was acting the part of the obedient dog.

The fire brigade pulled its wagon over the grass. Two men sat on the top of the water tank and spun a handle on each side. The handles, in turn, opened and closed a pair of metal sheers that looked sharp enough to slice a man in half. They easily carved a path through the shrubs. If they missed any stalk, their yellow-colored wagon with the red-stained tank tore through it.

A dozen men jumped off the wagon's sides and back. The first one asked, "Are you injured, sir?"

"No, but there's an old man within who is." I waved him along as I turned my back to the scene.

Was Aimee in the house? Perhaps not since she didn't appear to help battle the flames. If she was not hiding at the Greenhews, and she was not at the Bank, then I couldn't say for certain where she stayed.

I took the invitation out of my pocket.

One thing I did know was she would be at the Duke's Ball. It was the biggest, most exclusive party of the year. With the new found invitation, I would be there, too.

CHAPTER 5

The Greenhews left a rotten fish kind of taste in my mouth, as they always had. They also made me feel like I needed yet another good bath. While the last would have to wait, only one place could sufficiently take care of the first: Branagh's Tavern.

Within Campden, one could find respectable establishments serving a good mug of ale with an expensive meal. Aimee and I frequented many of those places, located mainly in the newer sections of town, close to the Bank. The Brown Pup was a particular favorite.

There were the places where the locals frequented, where the food was good, the drink plentiful, and cheaper. These were mostly in the old section, along High Street. The Red Lion, the Lygon Arms, and the Noel Arms were but a few of the popular and more traditional establishments. Those were the places I knew the best in my previous life, places where I dragged many men and women out before they made complete fools of themselves. That had been one of my chief jobs as a canon, though it meant assuming deacon type responsibilities. Still, it proved to be most satisfying, if not the most aggravating, especially when the potential fool emptied the contents of his belly all over me.

Finally, there were places where no respectable person would find himself. Those less-than-distinguished establishments existed on the outskirts of every decent area of the city. They made alehouses appear worthy of the Queen's patronage. They nestled themselves in the shadows or at the ends of alleys. Within were all types of creatures, from those dealing in magic to those needing a magical departure from the pains of this world. There were women who would do anything for a price, and men who threw away their last pence for an elixir, even though they might have a wife and children waiting at home. I learned where to find most of those establishments during the days of my recovery, as they catered to my ever-growing need.

Then there was Branagh's Tavern. It was located at the Gateway, the very machine, if it could be referred to as that, responsible for Campden's transformation from a quiet town to the world's center for magic. So dark and foreboding and exotic a clientele did Branagh's serve that it couldn't be found on the main level of the city. No, it belonged on the same level as the sewers and the tunnels beneath the homes and businesses. To reach it, I had to pass through an abandoned warehouse on the north side, a building where vagrants and gypsies staked a claim, and where the poorest of the downtrodden lived with little else besides the shirts on their backs.

I also passed by a group of ever-present Guardsmen whose duty it was to examine every departing human for magical items. There wasn't an honest gentleman in the group, for bribes and favors were always preferred to actually finding anything.

At Branagh's one could talk to humans, or trolls; though their language sounded more like grunts and groans and they tended to be poor conversationalists; or dwarves, with their stocky frames and gruff demeanors; or goblins, which were always quick to laugh and equally as quick to be offended. There were gnomes, little hairy folks who often traveled in packs. When you saw one of them, you best have a hand on your wallet or over your pockets. Their ability to steal things from under your nose was enviable.

Then there were the reptilians, a race of walking lizards. They were not as commonly seen as some of the other races, but it was not unusual to see them sitting and drinking, often as close to the fires as they could manage. They preferred to talk in hisses and slurs, but I passed more than one evening conversing with them. Their unique perspective on life was that flesh was weak while leather-like skin and scales were far superior. They tended to look upon humans as bothersome, but necessary, pests.

There were still other races sometimes spotted at a table or the bar, but were much rarer. Elves, skinny-looking human-like beings with over-sized ears that rose to a point and often-times had blonde hair, sometimes visited the establishment. They almost always appeared as soiled as a farmer fresh from the field, but gentlemen with money valued their too extensive magical abilities. Then there were the orcs, half the size of humans and with faces strangely distorted so they had a severe underbite, bulging eyes, and swollen cheeks beneath an overly large forehead. If an orc and elf ever spotted each other, there was usually trouble, for the two races were mortal enemies.

If stories were true, a centuries-old war raging in the magical world centered on the orcs and elves. Every day, the Gateway spat out refugees seeking safety. Some remained in the tavern for days or weeks to escape the trouble and to find rest, some hoped to work and make a new life for themselves, and others tried to hide from whatever dangers pursued them. Recent months saw more than usual, and many caused trouble in the town. The Duke responded to calls for help by keeping his airships over the town at all times.

Aside from all that unpleasant business, the rarest of the rare creatures were giants and dragons. Fully matured, neither could pass through the Gateway. For the giants, younger, braver and more curious ones would occasionally venture into Branagh's. When they did, it was quite a spectacle, especially for the gnomes, who were said to be both creatures' favorite delicacies. Those little ones scurried for every dark corner while others surrounded the newcomer.

The dragons had been branded a nuisance by the Gateway Secretary and were forbidden past Branagh's front door. They were hardly more than mindless beasts, though they could be trained to do a variety of tasks, as farmers discovered when they experimented with them thirty years prior. The creatures proved their worth when they plowed fields quicker than any pair of oxen. Farms expanded and crop production reached levels unseen and unimagined, at least until the dragons decided to eat all they helped sow. They wrought so much devastation that the country suffered from widespread starvation that winter. Thousands upon thousands either died or emigrated to America.

"Evening, Ash," Hansan said in a friendly manner. He was the doorman for Branagh's and stood guard at the outer entrance, in the basement of the warehouse. He wore a black shirt and black trousers and appeared as much a part of the shadows as the darkness did. Being a cyclops, his chest was as broad as a table and his arms as thick as barrels of ale. His was the only race that could take more than one magic power at-a-time. As such, they were valued by all, but few could afford their prices. The Company and The Gatherers used them only for the most difficult missions, those beyond the abilities of one or two lackeys. Unfortunate for them, though, combining elixirs could be a tricky business that resulted in death as often as success. Not even Pienne felt comfortable combining his magics into one creature.

By treaty, the Gateway Secretary paid for Branagh's security, but a group called The Elders who resided on the other side took care of the necessary details, which always involved extraordinarily powered cyclopes.

Hansan continued, "It's a rough crowd tonight. I've already had to break up two fights, and there are more refugees than usual." He held the door open, and blinked his single eye. "Word on the street is that you're tracking trouble. Best watch your back." He blinked again. "Mind your front, too."

My belly twisted with uncertainty. What if I couldn't get the drink I so desperately needed? I asked rather cautiously, "What kind of trouble?"

His eye narrowed. "The kind that gets you killed. Don't know anything else."

He refused to admit to anything else. He went to great lengths to remain as neutral as he could when something important happened inside.

I didn't bother to hide my disappointment as I said, "Thanks for the warning."

As I limped past, he said, "New effect, eh? What is it this time? Gimpy leg syndrome?"

"Lead foot."

He snorted in amusement. "Ah. Well, enjoy and make sure I don't have to drag you out of here. Understand?"

I waved to him. "When have you ever had reason to do so?"

"Just last week," he said with a tone that was anything but light and playful. "Make sure it doesn't happen again, else I'll have to keep you out of here for good." He closed the door.

Last week happened to be an incident with a reptilian who decided he wanted my table. Could I be blamed for showing him the limit of my patience? The dagger at the base of his tail was meant as a warning. I had no intention of using it.

Next was a flight of steps lighted by two low-burning lanterns, which did little more than reassure the darkness that its domain remained safe. At the base of the stairs was another door.

Jansan, a twin of Hansan in every way, opened the door. "Evening, Mister Ash. Tough crowd tonight, but I think you'll be glad to know Sheela is here. I'd venture to guess she's a bit worried about you, too. Word is you walked away from an explosion."

"Thank you," I said as I entered the smoky air and the stale ale smell and the music of a violin making a vain attempt to screech above the noise of the crowd.

So much for keeping my new power a secret.

Branagh's main room had a ceiling about ten feet high. The length of the room stretched fifty feet and ended at the Gateway itself, a marvel of scientific engineering that, ironically, ushered in the Age of Magic. Duke Schaever's grandfather, a noted scientist for his work with electricity, set out to locate a place where natural magnetic forces converged. He theorized that if he tapped such a source, he could generate an endless supply of power. So he arrived in Chipping Campden just after the start of 1800 and began digging in the precise location he claimed was the confluence of such forces. When he reached his calculated spot, he built a cage of copper tubes twelve feet high, six feet wide and four feet deep. At each corner he mounted six-inch thick spools of wire, each one of which ended in square points made of gold. To make the most of the power source, he claimed he needed a secondary one to begin the process. And so, he connected his cage to a steam engine almost the size of a locomotive.

A crowd of roughly fifty men and women gathered to watch him pull the lever for the first time. Some were fellow scientists who followed his work and assisted him in refining his calculations. Others were curious locals who wanted to see what the odd man who brought such a disruption to the area, and who dug such a big hole in their town, was going to do. But many were skeptics who made no effort to hide their opinions both of the man's theory and of his methods.

Legend said that when the electricity from the engine struck the cage, the copper glowed and the coils hummed like a thousand bees. Lightning flew from the coils and met in the middle with such a clap of thunder that it knocked the crowd backwards. And in that instant, the Gateway appeared with such an inward force that it pulled its creator and his chief assistant into its growing circle.

Neither had been heard from since.

But what they left behind was a ten foot high circle that, did indeed, pulse with an energy all its own. Faded reds and blues swirled in constant motion throughout its whiteness, never repeating the same pattern twice.

More amazing than the strange and mesmerizing pulse, though, was what happened when something stepped through. The milk-like membrane stretched and contorted into the creature's shape as if it fought to keep the realms separate. Yet it fought a losing battle, which it gave up with a light pop. It then returned to its normal state in an instant, and left the new arrival in a dazed and confused state. Branagh's Ale, which was a true malt, was supposed to be the best elixir for helping the creatures regain their senses.

It is said the first creature to cross from the other side was a gnome and its appearance set the stunned crowd into such a panic that the cage was nearly torn apart. Fortunately, more sensible men moved to protect the new discovery, and from that day on, Campden was never the same.

To add to its strangeness, the comings and goings through the Gateway were almost exclusively by those of the magical realm. Of the hundreds of humans who had tried, only two had returned. The first lived for three days and was said to have been insane as soon as the Gateway released him. The second appeared as an old man of eighty or ninety, though his actual age was twenty. Guardsmen gathered him up and no one had seen him since. Many speculated that he died from his aged condition not long afterwards.

Of the magical realm itself, few details were known. In spite of the war and the suffering, almost all of the creatures refused to speak of their home. The ones who did talk all told such fanciful tales that they had been deemed unreliable in light of the fact that it took a large amount of Branagh's Ale to loosen their tongues.

I dragged my foot across a hardwood floor as nice as any to be found in the better homes. Ale and blood had stained it through sixty some-odd years of use. Two bars, one to the left and one to the right, served all. Between them were hundreds of tables and chairs, which were almost always filled no matter the time of day or night.

Branagh's prided itself on being the city's only twenty-four hour alehouse. While the others closed, being respectable and reputable places of business under government license, Branagh's continued to serve. Being underground as it was, time never mattered. Night was as good as day and vice versa.

As I entered the room, first one set of eyes looked at me. Then another and another and another and another. Turning heads rippled through the room in a wave, and the conversations quieted. Some of the looks directed at me were admiring. Some were curious. Others were questioning.

But most were of an out-right unfriendly sort. Crossed brows, twitching ears, flickering tongues of the forked variety, and many hands on weapons indicated the precariousness of the situation.

Only the assurance of my power kept me from leaving...well, that added to my desire for an ale. Together, they gave me enough bravado-inspired confidence to half-smile as I headed for my usual table. I needed to play this the same as the moments after the Bank explosion. If I let them know how my heart raced, they might sense weakness in their prey and descend like a pack of hounds.

The tip of an arrow glinted in the light to the right.

"Ash!" a woman squealed as she threw herself into my arms. The smell of winter nights and apple cider provided a refreshing sense of comfort.

She wrapped her arms about my neck and whispered, "Keep me between you and the room." Then she said, loud enough for everyone to hear, "How is my favorite thief this night? What have you brought me this time? Jewels? Another necklace?"

I made sure I remained between her and the arrow. Whatever was going on, she had no need to be in unnecessary danger. I produced the invitation and said, "How about the biggest social gathering in town?" She snatched it out of my hand and whistled as I continued on.

The crowd returned to their business, though more than one eye watched my every slow step.

The arrow followed.

At the table, two others waited. First was Reckard, a fellow Company thief. He also bore the white hair, marking him as a magic user, as well as the unfortunate problem with his lack of weight, which manifested itself in his hollow cheeks and thin arms. He could move fast, though, sometimes faster than he realized. It wasn't uncommon for magic users to manifest their own abilities, but it was rare for such a person to live more than a few months. Reckard was that rarity.

Second was Leesal, Sheela's best friend. She had brown hair cut short enough to expose the bottom of her neck. And, like Sheela, she served tables at Branagh's.

Reckard pushed a chair towards me with his foot. "Join us, old chap. Tell us about The Mister's latest quest." He cocked an eyebrow. "Gimpy foot, eh? What did Pienne do this time?"

No sooner had I settled than Sheela squeezed between the table and me and onto my lap, which earned a scowl from Reckard. She held the invitation against the light. "This is a good counterfeit. Who made it for you?"

I couldn't help but to smile. "That's the original article." I waved to a different barmaid for a drink. "Lifted it off the table of a respectable family." One I hoped to never see again.

Both Reckard and Leesal placed their elbows on the table and leaned forward with expectation. The former said, "Sounds like we get to hear a story. Don't keep us in suspense, old chap. Tell us of this good turn of fortune. Tell me you snatched two of those." He held a hand up as he glanced left and right. "But first, tell us what you're so involved in that most of this tavern wants you dead. And tell us why your finest clothes are scorched."

A fine tale, indeed. Hatred, betrayal, attempted murder, and love. Where to begin?

I kept my voice even as I said, "Concerning the ill-will this evening, I can make no conclusion." Drool threatened to slip out of the corner of my mouth as I peered into the just arrived mug. "Any chance this is poisoned?"

Sheela slapped my shoulder and glanced twice at her hand. She gave my shoulder a push with her finger. "What's the news, Ash? What's this power?"

As I recounted the events of the last week, between drinks of ale, they grew quieter and more somber. Reckard studied his own mug while Leesal stared at something distant.

Sheela, though, scowled, and her voice matched the look. "You should never have agreed to an assignment like that!" She slapped my shoulder again, and frowned as she shook her hand like it stung. "What were you thinking? You had a hard enough time forgetting about her. Why would they want you, of all people, to return to that part of your life?"

I shrugged as I stared at the remaining delicious and frothy concoction within my own mug. Poison or not, I'd enjoy the ale. After finishing it off I said, "Because The Misters have the most twisted sense of humor."

Reckard nodded. "Or they knew you would know where to find her or be able to learn where she's hiding." He eyed me from under his brow. "I don't envy you this one, old chap. Not in the least."

Sheela said, "You should've told them no. You should've told them where they could shove their powers and their business." She stood and folded her arms. "I worry about – did they consider the danger to you? Or to those around you?"

"What does it matter," I asked, "when I'm the walking dead? So this assignment kills me sooner than the magic does." I shrugged before tipping the mug to catch the last few drops.

To die, to live, to suffer, to be redeemed? What did it matter? What did it matter in the grand scheme of history? I only asked that my end be quick and painless.

The voice growled, "Do not be so bitter. Savor the life you have."

Sheela planted her fists on her hips. "There are ways to break your magic addiction." She spoke as if she knew that for a fact. "The gnomes have methods. Why not talk to your friend Cavendish about arranging something?"

I held a hand up. "I like Cavendish, but that doesn't mean I trust him with my life. He is a gnome. Besides, I didn't come here this evening because I wanted to argue the same arguments we've had a dozen times. I came here because I need to drink. I need to forget Aimee." And her betrayal, and her attempts to kill me. Part of me wanted to scream, part of me wanted to cry, and the remaining part questioned whether or not I could convince her to let me court her again.

The thoughts of a mad man, or of one slipping into madness.

The beautiful woman in my lap studied the invitation. Her hair glistened in the distant firelight, lending a softness to her strength. The effect filed the canon with an unnecessary longing. "You know, I haven't been inside the Schaever's walls in years. Maybe I'll forgive you this once just because you brought me such a nice surprise."

Before I stopped myself, I asked, "When were you at the Schaevers?"

You? A bar maid?

Reckard stared at her with an intensity that spoke of adoration. "Tell us, love, who you'll be taking to the Ball? I happen to know a gentleman with time available. He knows all the latest dances and would show you an evening of perpetual bliss." His fingers danced across the table.

She ignored my question as she peered at Reckard over the top of the invitation. With a raised brow she said, "I shall give the matter my utmost consideration, sir."

Sweet Sheela. She was a woman whose past remained a wonderful mystery. She claimed to be twenty-two, and that she was from a most ordinary family of simple means. While she played the part well, I had caught her on several occasions carrying herself with a certain refinement that spoke of proper society. More telling, though, were her eyes. While her face often shone with happiness, her eyes always remained sad. They held the wisdom brought about by a hard life and much pain. The signs were familiar, for I saw them each time I peered into a mirror. Yes, she kept secrets that were likely terrible. She would probably share them if I but asked, as I just mistakenly had. I wouldn't do that to her, though. Out of respect for a kindred soul, I couldn't. It would be most unfair to her and me, to make her think I fancied her as more than a friend.

"So, Ash, what are you scheming?" Reckard asked as he continued watching Sheela. "About how to confront Aimee?"

"Allow me to tell you," Cavendish said as he hopped onto the table. Reckard and Sheela both instinctively shied away from the strange creature. And Leesal? She departed with a loud sniff.

"I don't need help, but thank you," I said in a tone to indicate the topic wasn't debatable. "This is a matter of honor and pride and is something I must do alone."

Cavendish ignored me as he bowed to Sheela and swept his red hat off his head as he did so, revealing a bald circle in the middle of his black, curly hair. The little man appeared like a typical gnome in almost every way, aside from the large, silver-rimmed goggles that made his eyes look twice as big as they really were. He stood just under two feet tall, he wore a split beard ending in two points at the base of his neck, he had black eyes, and an easy smile. His clothing consisted of a white shirt with a green vest, both of which were open halfway down his chest, revealing a broad expanse of curly, black hair. His pants were black, as were his knee-high boots. Hair covered the backs of his hands and his arms as well. Many called gnomes the hairy little monsters, but if you so accused them, you'd often find yourself in a fight with a dozen of them.

While Cavendish appeared the typical gnome, he was an extraordinary exception. The creatures always traveled in packs of five or six, but never Cavendish. They often enjoyed drinking to excess, but a drop rarely touched Cavendish's lips. Most spoke with a high-pitched tone, but Cavendish's voice was as deep and gruff as a dwarf's. They also shunned anything to do with science, but Cavendish went to extremes to learn about the latest inventions and theories.

He also fancied watches, never wearing less than two on each arm. Given his relatively small arms as compared to a human's, it made quite the odd statement of fashion.

He replaced his hat before saying, "You're after the Head of Forneil, which is needed to complete the statue."

Surprise filled my tone. "How did you—"

"What? Know? When the matter concerns events on the other side of the Gateway, then word spreads quickly. This room already knows that's what you seek. That would be why you have weapons pointing at you, the kind with a nasty poison that makes dying very unpleasant." When Sheela squeaked, he jumped like he just noticed her. He tried to grin, but his expression better resembled a snarl.

It caused me no little annoyance when he knew more about my assignments than I did, though it only made matters worse if I let him know of my displeasure. The damnable creature enjoyed lording such information over me. He reminded me of The Misters in that regard.

The gnome sat cross-legged in the middle of the table. He pulled out a pocket watch and studied it. The gold finish on the cover sparkled. He flipped it over to reveal a clear casing through which could be viewed every gear.

The creature owned more watches than everyone between London and Paris and Amsterdam combined. He wanted me to comment on his latest acquisition, but I refused to give him the satisfaction.

After a moment, one where he looked at me out of the corner of his bug-eyed goggles, he sighed and tucked the watch into his vest pocket. "Your life is in great danger, here, at this moment. Only because I agreed to discuss the matter with you have the others refrained from trying to kill you." He nodded to the reptilians gathered three tables over. "They have a poisoned arrow ready." He pointed to the troll on the other side. "He was sent specifically to crush your skull."

I motioned for another ale. "So why are you here? To warn me? If so, then you succeeded. I consider myself warned. Go away."

The gnome rubbed his lips. "I'm here to do more than warn you. I'm here to help you find the Head."

Reckard leaned on the table with one forearm firmly planted on it. "Look, chap, did you not hear Ash? He doesn't want help. And he doesn't need the help of a gnome."

Something the gnome said earlier suddenly stirred my curiosity, so I held a hand up for Reckard to stop. "Tell me, Cavendish, what the Head has to do with your world? And how is it that everyone knows I'm trying to get the piece?"

The gnome glanced left and right before whispering, "They know. They are the ones who broke the statue in order to limit its power."

"They?" I asked with no little sarcasm. "The Elders?"

"Hush!" He motioned for quiet. "I never mentioned them. If they really exist." He glanced to each side again. "They put a bounty on your head."

They. The Elders. The mysterious group who ruled the magical realm, the ones whose name was spoken with more reverence than most humans spoke God's name. They used fear to assure that only certain information about their world made it through the Gateway. Many speculated it was they who either killed or enslaved any human who passed through the portal. The two who returned paid the price of their lives. Not that the threat of death kept some humans from taking the risk. The promise of fame and fortune drove many to try. Life's desperations encouraged others. The two hundred and thirty scratches on the bricks to the right of the Gateway kept tally on the attempts.

Many humans viewed the arrangements as unfair. At least once a year, Parliament debated whether or not to impose restrictions on the magical creatures' travels. What kept them from doing so was the Gateway Treaty itself. In return to unhindered access to this world by the magical realm, the Gateway Secretary was given access to magic at a reduced cost as compared to everyone else. The arrangement profited the British Empire in untold ways: new weapons, new medical discoveries, new mining techniques, and new methods of increasing textile production were but a few. In short, the Gateway assured the continuation of British power in the world at a time just after it had been successfully challenged.

The fact that The Elders could be involved only complicated matters, so I asked, "Why do they care about the Head of Forneil?"

Cavendish still spoke with a hushed tone. "The statue, if whole, is powerful...powerful enough to decide the war for one side or the other."

Reckard shook his head. "Let me try to understand what you're saying." He leaned closer as he eyed Cavendish with distrust. "The Elders had the statue, could have used it against the orcs to end the war, but chose to break it in half? And then they lost the pieces?" He looked at me, and his tone matched his disbelief. "Am I the only one who sees a problem?"

Cavendish frowned. He started to answer, stopped, cleared his throat, then said, "They wanted to pieces to come into this world. They had people assigned to track them, to learn where they went. They needed to know."

"So what happened?" I asked, glancing at Reckard, who nodded in approval.

"You happened," Cavendish said as he looked straight into my eyes. "And now you're trying to unite the pieces, which cannot be allowed."

"Why not?" Reckard asked, "let Ash collect the Head, then take both pieces from The Misters?"

Cavendish chewed on his lip as he regarded my fellow thief. "And what if The Misters were hired by the orcs to find both pieces?"

My fellow thief leaned back in his chair. "I don't envy you, Ash. Wars, a former wife, and creatures wanting to kill you? This is a mess."

Yes, it was, and I needed more ale to settle the growing unease in my belly. "So what are they wanting to learn? Why go through all this trouble?" I motioned for another mug. "And why do so many want me dead?"

The gnome took a deep breath. "Even though you deserve an answer to the first question, all I can say is there's something happening in your world they are concerned about. I am not allowed to give you specifics." He held his hand up before I could reply. "It's not fair, but I value my own life so I'll say nothing more about the matter. As for your second question, they put a price on your head to keep you from succeeding in your assignment. It's enough to make sure someone tries."

The newly arrived mug offered something to dull the growing ache in the back of my skull. Too many intrigues. Too much to worry about when all I wanted was to capture Aimee and learn the truth about our life together. Did life not owe me such a simple task?

The little voice laughed. "You're neither guaranteed nor owed a simple, care-free life."

"Yes, I am!" I said with a little too much insistence. When the others looked at me, I continued on as if I meant to speak. "I will find the Head and give it to The Misters."

Cavendish waved his hands for quiet. As he peered around for the third time, he crumpled his hat in his hands. "For the sake of your own life, you had best listen to what I have to say. First off, keep your voice down."

Sheela whispered, "You might want to consider his words." She eyed the gnome in a strange way, as if she knew something about why he had been sent to help. "Though I've never cared for him, I would at least hear what he has to say." When I gave her a surprised look, she shrugged. "I want you to live. Is that wrong? I heard all the talk before you arrived and it frightened me." She paused. "I do care for you, Ash."

Why? You deserve a better man who can give you a better life.

Before she could go further I asked, "So why are you going to help me recover something that no one wants me to recover?"

He tried to smile again, but didn't laugh. He rarely laughed. "Because The Gatherers aren't remaining idle in this affair. Even as your Company seeks the Head, they seek to regain the rest of the statue which you stole with amazing timing. My employers would like the assurance of knowing the Head is safe from either group. The only reason no one has killed you is because I asked for time to talk to you, to try to make you see reason in giving me the Head so it can disappear through the Gateway forever."

Sheela glared at the gnome. "But if Ash turns it over to you, then his masters will kill him." She pointed at him. "And if that happens..."

Cavendish shifted in his vest as he peered at me with his black eyes. "I don't want anything to happen to him, either.

There are few that Cavendish calls friend and he is one of them. That's why I am here, now, giving Ash a chance."

Reckard spewed his ale into his mug. When the rest of the table stared, he wiped his mouth and said, "How touching, gnome. We're so much more comforted by your loyalty." He frowned. "If this Head is so important, why not buy it from The Gatherers? Or send your own people to steal it?"

The gnome said, "Because Ash is already involved. For good or for ill, he is our man."

My fellow thief leaned forward and his tone seethed with loathing. "How convenient to make a human risk his life for non-humans. Let red blood be spilled instead of green or purple or whatever flows through you."

Cavendish leveled a gaze on him that spoke of either a serious disturbance or a deep hatred. Since it was never good to see friends bicker I said, "You have an idea of what I should do...if I should agree?"

Cavendish's glare melted into the snarl-smile. "Do you have a choice?" The look on his face was one of immense satisfaction, and it made me want to say I'd take my chances with the room full of assassins just to spite him. But I held my tongue as he continued, "The difficult part in what we have to do is finding someone who can make a convincing counterfeit of the Head. To make matters more complicated, the fake Head will require some level of magic ability." He stroked both points of his beard, one with each hand. "Otherwise, your masters will recognize it for the counterfeit that it is."

Sheela spoke as if the matter was settled. "While Cavendish works on that, I'll help you at the Ball tomorrow night and we'll get the real Head from," she swallowed hard, "Aimee. I'm looking forward to slapping the woman who caused you so much pain and trouble."

She warmed my cold heart, did Sheela. She'd defend my honor and my pride for no other reason than knowing Aimee had ripped my heart into so many pieces it could never hope to be mended.

Unless Aimee mends it for you.

Reckard placed his mug on the table a little too hard, distracting me from the dark and dangerous thoughts. "I thought you were going to allow me the honor of escorting you." He motioned to me in a dismissive manner. "He doesn't deserve to take you. I, on the other hand, will treat you like the lady you are." When Sheela made no reply, he added, "I'll find Aimee, too, if that makes you feel better. She won't expect me."

I asked, "What if she tries to blow you away?"

He looked at Sheela with an intensity reserved for religious zealots and shunned lovers. "If I die for a beautiful woman, my life will have had the ultimate fulfillment."

What if he was killed by an equally beautiful woman? What would he say then?

Cavendish edged forward. "What is this about a party? Are you referring to the Duke's Ball?" After a quick glance around, he continued, "I might be able to locate an invitation, but it'll require a substantial amount of coin."

As she held up the invitation, Sheela said, "Ash is one step ahead of you, gnome."

"Oh?" Cavendish tried to take the invitation to examine it, but Sheela refused to release it. After a moment of tugging, he gave up. "It sounds like you have a plan, Ash. Care to share it with me so I can assure those who are here to kill you that they should be a little more patient?" He rubbed his lips with the back of his hand. "I'm listening."

A plan? Yes, I suppose I needed one. At least a better one than going to the Ball, surprising Aimee, grabbing her, and forcing her to give me the Head while admitting she was wrong...no, that's not it.

My soon-to-be companion to the Ball said, "He's already told us about his plan. We are going to the Ball dressed in such finery that no one will recognize us. As we dance, we'll observe the crowd. We'll locate Aimee, and watch to see what she does. Then I'll isolate her. Ash will grab her, and I'll take the Head. We'll return here before anyone can stop us."

Cavendish tilted his head. "You have the beginnings of a plan, but have you considered the possibility that she won't have the item on her?" His voice went lower, more contemplative. "So many details. You are dealing with a delicate situation, and we need to plan this to the smallest move."

All I wanted at the moment was more ale, to drown myself in its blissful wetness. Though it pained me to do so I said, "I'll trust the details to you, Cavendish."

Trust? A gnome? Had it come to that?

"So you agree to my proposal?"

Sheela squeezed my arm, and Reckard nodded slowly, so I said, "Yes."

"Now that is what I needed to hear!" He eyed the invitation. "The fact that you managed to snag one of those is impressive, and makes our work easier." As he leaned forward he whispered, "Listen close, and I'll tell you exactly how we are going to do this and why it will work."

I listened to how we were going to the Ball, how he would arrange for our clothing to be just right, which scared me as much as anything, for all I could picture was having to wear one of those awful gnome vests and in blue sparkles or some other atrocious color. Sheela saved me from such a fate, though. She argued with him until he relented and agreed to let her arrange the clothing, as well as the transportation.

Once we were announced as the Greenhews, according to the invitation, we were to separate to cover the room and locate Aimee. Sheela would be responsible for finding out who escorted my former wife, a fact for which I was grateful. Sheela was to work her feminine charms to pull Aimee's beau away. Only then would I approach her and demand a word in private.

"But she knows I'm searching for her," I said and told him about the explosion at the Bank.

He remained quiet for a moment. "That is a problem. Would she be willing to kill innocent men and women if she saw you approaching?"

"No," I said quickly. "She isn't capable of such a horrendous act."

"Yet she killed others the first time she tried to kill you. She sacrificed the Bank to try to kill you a second time." He stroked his beards as the truth of his observations settled uneasy. "Surprise. That is our main advantage, along with the threat of death. I have an idea which knife to use but I might not have time to locate it." After a deep breath he continued with the rest of the plan.

Once her beau was safely away, I would move in. I'd use the knife to insist that she go with me. Once we moved her from the crowd, he would use a special magic to convince her that she needed to give us the Head. Then we would flee back here, where he would have a counterfeit Head made.

The gnome said, "Of course, there is one detail that we must get correct. It will be necessary in order to convince your masters that your Head is genuine. Once they hear of the deed, they'll not doubt you. They'd have no reason to."

The tone in his voice made me sit straighter and made the voice growl a warning. "Cavendish, what are you talking about?"

"In order to keep your masters from guessing you are giving them a counterfeit, you'll have to kill Aimee." Did he notice the blood draining from my face? "You can kill her?"

I swallowed hard. "Of course."

I already agreed to.

Still, why was everyone so determined to see me do just that? Everyone except the canon's voice, which howled like a cornered and wounded dog.

CHAPTER 6

Life can be ugly. There are moments when we must deal with unpleasant consequences that are a part of our curse. Attending a funeral gives a not-so-subtle reminder of our mortality. No joy can be found in watching a child, especially a small one, struggle with influenza or scarlet fever or dysentery. Divorcing one's spouse, one whom you adore and worship and would do almost anything for, can be the darkest of moments.

So it is that when life presents a moment of beauty, it should be savored all the more.

Sheela wasn't a perfect woman by any means. She worried about what appeared to be the most inconsequential matters, she could let her opinions be known on a range of social issues, and she snorted when she laughed. But she had many admirable qualities. As I saw her standing in the fading light of the day, she radiated a perfection no others could match. Her unflinching loyalty to her friends, her servant's heart, and her willingness to see the good in many situations all joined to make her that much more. Perfect.

The what-if debate could be played with her in the same way I played it with Rebecca Donnavan and Lauree. Her devotion was freely offered. I could have accepted. But to what end? So I could torture myself more? So I could burden her with my disgrace?

I was an evil and sinful man, and she deserved better. She needed someone who could appreciate her, who would love her the way she ought to be loved: with selflessness and devotion.

For once, the canon's voice agreed.

She wore a red, strapless dress that hugged her belly before spreading in waves from her hips, down her legs, and to her feet. A gold necklace dipped towards her bosom. On the end hung a diamond-shaped pendant the width of my thumbnail. In its center was a red stone so translucent as to be almost clear. From each ear hung a gold chain ending in a red stone polished and shaped like a pearl. Her hair was pulled tight on each side. Red clips held it together on the back where it hung free and brushed the base of her neck. Leaving her shoulders bare was a nice touch, for it highlighted her delicate bone structure and allowed her face to display the better features: a strong jaw line ending in a sharp chin that somehow wasn't too sharp, cheekbones complimenting the jaw by not being too sharp either, and a nose that was just right for such a shape. Had she belonged to a family of means, she wouldn't have lacked for suitors from old, established families.

She stood at the corner and seemed oblivious to the stares given by many passing gentlemen. As I approached, the corsage in my hand shook.

The voice said, "You don't deserve a woman like her. Don't give her false hope."

The moment slowed as she turned towards me and smiled such a smile that she glowed even brighter, appearing more angelic. "You look like quite the lord."

I gave her a deep bow, one reserved for a king or queen, for no other greeting seemed appropriate in her presence. "Then it's unfortunate I'm neither a lord nor a gentleman."

I kissed her gloved hand. "But I dare not leave such a stunning lady without an escort to the Duke's Ball, so I will offer my services. Will you allow me the honor?"

She took my own gloved hand and drew me close. "Ash, you are more than worthy to take me..." Her face turned flush as she cleared her throat. "To the Ball. Take me to the Ball." She brushed lint from my lapels. Her hands moved to straighten my red scarf, which was the exact shade of her dress and of her pendant. Once finished, she peered at me with an expression that warmed my belly. "I never thought I'd see you in such finery."

And I never imagined her in such a dress. Rather, I imagined her in much, much less. In nothing, actually, despite the voice's disapproval.

To distract her from my own flushed face, I presented her with a small bouquet of flowers. A single red rose was surrounded by white heather with red lace running both through and around.

Her voice was one of playful sarcasm. "Tell me you picked the flowers special for this occasion."

I offered my arm. "Of course, my lady."

Actually, she chose the arrangement like she chose our clothing with the precision and expertise of a lady of refinement. The flowers held a special meaning, but I had long ago lost interest in keeping up with flower dictionaries.

By coincidence, though, the rose's color matched the red-handled dagger inside my boot, which was the weapon Cavendish had spoken of when putting his plan together. He claimed it would obey the will of the one possessing it, that a mere thought would propel it into action. When I tried to test it after he bonded it to my hand, he held it tight and scowled.

Sheela snuggled close. "Thank you, Ash. Even though I know what we're walking into, I feel like this will be the first perfect evening I've had since..." Silence was followed by a sigh. "In quite some time." She rested her head on my shoulder, but squeezed my hands.

We didn't have to wait long for the brougham, the two-wheeled type that was the perfect size for our party, to arrive. A cream color with engraved swirls of silver covered it. Reckard drove from a small platform on the back. When he saw Sheela, he smiled. After he stopped the pair of horses, he helped her onto the seat. He then tipped his hat as I stepped inside. My foot made the carriage tilt and Sheela yelled in surprise. Reckard caught the side and whispered, "I don't care for this business. You are placing her in danger and I promise if anything happens to her, I will hold you responsible."

In reaction to his warning, I said in a dismissive tone, "You have my word as a gentleman that I won't let anyone harm her."

He scoffed. "A gentleman? Is that what you consider yourself?"

This time his words struck deep and his concern for Sheela stirred a strange feeling of anger. Because he was a friend, I let the offense pass.

I slid into the seat next to Sheela as the boards beneath my foot creaked. The brougham gave little bounce as Reckard stepped onto his platform. With a snap of the reins, we were on our way.

Sheela smiled and her face spoke of genuine joy as she stared at something distant. For just a moment, her usual guarded eyes of pain and burdens eased into those of an innocent girl just coming of age. She sat straight, with her hands in her lap. Her appearance was of perfect ease, in contrast to my nervousness at attending the Ball and confronting Aimee.

Who are you, Sheela?

The question sat at the end of my tongue. I almost asked. I almost uttered those dangerous words. What stopped me was Sheela shaking her head as if to release whatever tried to make her truly happy. Her voice carried a hint of regret and loss as she said, "I cannot believe you allowed yourself to get involved in such a dangerous situation, Ash. Going after your former wife? Raising the ire of those on the other side of the Gateway? Having no choice but to trust a gnome to bring you through this alive?" She gave a long sigh. "I don't know how you're able to do it. If it was me, it'd make me scream."

Who said I didn't want to do just that? Especially with such a beautiful woman so close, yet so far removed?

This time, I squeezed her hands. "This is a business arrangement. Nothing more. This is what I have to do. If The Company wanted me to march straight into a demon's lair, I would have to do it. And believe me, dealing with Aimee won't be much different." Her eyes reflected the pain within me. "As for Cavendish? Yes, he's a gnome at heart and he will use this situation to his own gain. He will get all the honor for pulling this off with those on the other side of the Gateway. I can't blame him though. I don't know what I would do if all of my people rejected me. And I won't be responsible for hurting others on the other side of the Gateway."

A long, steady look made me uncomfortable, as if I spoke nonsense. "Your actions have consequences, Ash. Your decisions affect others whether or not you want them to."

I gave a short laugh. "This wasn't my decision, and I had no choice."

"You always have choices. You may not like them, but you have choices. Sometimes you must make the hard choice, the one that changes your life forever." A tear fell from her right eye and I caught it at the edge of her cheek.

It sat on the tip of my finger, then soaked into the cloth of my glove.

She pulled away. "Cavendish isn't the one who has to convince his masters he is giving them the genuine item. He isn't the one risking his life for some silly magic thingy." Wrinkles in her dress provided a convenient distraction. "I promised myself I wouldn't say anything because I knew we would argue and it would ruin the Ball. When I was a girl, I used to dream about going to this. I pretended I was the wife of a great lord." She laughed too forcefully, like she tried to hide something obvious. "Imagine that. Me. The wife of a lord, when all I am is a serving maid working in the worst beerhouse in the city, one that caters to the non-humans." Her voice fell to a whisper, again, with a tone full of pain, "How far the proud can fall."

Did she refer to herself or to me? Surely the latter, for no one had fallen as far as I.

Still, I tried to encourage her by squeezing her hands. "You will be the most beautiful woman at the Ball. You'll draw the eyes of every wealthy merchant and handsome aristocrat. I'm blessed to be the one to take you. You'll be more radiant than the Duke's betrothed."

Her eyes grew big and full of fear. "Did I do too much with our clothes? I tried to be careful. Nothing too simple. Nothing too dramatic. We must be normal, like any other person there." A shadow passed over her face. It spoke of her painful secret. "I didn't want to start like this." The shadow remained as she pulled her hands away. "We will deal with your former wife, and then we will enjoy the rest of the evening."

I, too, turned, unable to continue watching her suffer.

The question again waited at the tip of my tongue.

Who are you, Sheela?

The halls of Campden University passed. They loomed large as they sat on the corner of the Schaever's estate. The current duke planned it after he returned from Cambridge. He presented it to the town both as a gift and to establish his own legacy. Its mission was to study the magical arts and pursue understanding of similar mysteries for the benefit of mankind.

So far, he had constructed two buildings. The first was square, with a clock tower on the front and windows covering all four sides. The second was round with a grassy courtyard in the center. Both were of red brick and white trim. They were said to be connected to the Schaever home by a complex of underground tunnels.

Despite its modest and relatively recent existence, many stories already circulated about strange lights seen in the wee hours of the morning, of strange experiments gone awry, and of unusual creatures seen scampering about the campus under the light of the moon. The more macabre stories spoke of experiments involving human, non-human, and animal combinations: men with webbed fingers and toes, a cyclops with three cat eyes, a woman covered in ape hair, an elf with bird-like feathers and wings. Though elixirs were the likely cause, if true, the Duke made no attempt to dispel the rumors, which made me wonder if he didn't enjoy his school's notoriety.

Sheela and I said nothing more as we reached the Duke's estate, a fact for which I was both pleased and sad. I didn't want to hear more of Sheela's concerns for my well-being, yet I enjoyed listening to her voice.

Women will drive you mad. They'll be the death of your sanity.

A pair of Guardsmen stood outside the gate, directing the progression of carriages onto the grounds. So we waited while far larger and fancier carriages than our own passed. There were at least six with a six-horse team, each adorned with colorful feathers on their harnesses, indicating nobility. The merchants displayed their own signs:

harnesses decorated with jewels, silk-dyed cloths hanging from the edges of the roof, and ornate statues on the corners, ones imported from various parts of the world. One had a periscope rising from its roof. It twisted all about, like a cyclops eye, taking in the details of the evening. Another, likely a partner at the Merchant Exchange, had capillary-like tubes running along its engravings. Different colors flowed through the tubes, creating a constant change of patterns and hues.

As we began the ascent up the hill, in a group of four other broughams, I asked as much to spite Reckard as anything, "You will do me the honor of dancing, won't you?"

Immediate regret arose, for how could I dance with a lead foot?

"Perhaps. I might condescend to let myself be seen with a thief." She hid her snorting laugh behind the back of her hand. "Smarter people than me would find...what's the word?"

"Irony."

"Umm, hmm, much irony in this, I'm sure."

"It appears you already have." I pointed to my foot. "Especially with this thing. Curse Pienne and his elixirs."

She stroked my arm in a familiar, soothing manner. "Oh, be grateful Pienne's magic saved you from the last explosion." She touched the scars on my cheek with tenderness. "I prefer slow dances, anyway. You can get so much...closer." The twinkle in her eye made me take a quick breath. I looked out the window to take my mind away from her suggestion, away from the longing and desire that tried to stir.

We approached the twenty-foot outer stone wall separating the Schaevers from the rest of the world. One had to admire them despite their eccentric and overbearing airs. As a family, they used the creation of the Gateway to their fullest advantage. In the days following the discovery, the widow of the scientist gathered her forces. She used her family's vast influences to exert pressure on Parliament to both declare the Gateway a national treasure and to gain a seat for the family on the House of Lords, at the Church of England's expense. As more creatures crossed into our world, she recognized the need for neutrality for the Gateway. She worked behind the scenes of the treaty negotiations. Legend said she was the one who suggested exchanging the well-hidden secrets of her husband's research for most of the land around Chipping Campden and Broad Campden. The Prime Minister agreed, thus assuring governmental control of the Gateway and easing a major point of contention in the treaty.

Her fortunes thus secured, Duchess Schaever brought in architects from France and Germany and organized her lands into the town of Campden. They developed new streets and built new houses and businesses, which she either sold for a nice profit or rented for an even nicer sum. And with Campden being the single source of magic in the world, demand grew as people discovered new opportunities to exploit the power as it challenged the foundations of science itself.

The succeeding Schaevers used their financial gains to build a home to rival that of the oldest, most established families in England. They spared no expense, and their subsequent rise in wealth and influence earned them quite a few enemies.

We entered the grounds proper and Sheela laughed when she saw the decorations within. Along the wall, red, blue, and white banners hung from the top to the bottom. Between them hovered magical lights that created white sparkling circles on the grass. The main house, built before the others and expanded through the years, glowed blue, then red, then green, then purple, then pink, then white.

Each color change lasted a minute before giving way to the next.

Colored lights with tiny feet lined the carriage path. They all danced in circles as the carriages passed.

From the grounds themselves drifted the music of a string quartet. Sheela asked, "Where are the musicians? I don't see them."

Such magic was new and often used at other, more intimate gatherings. The quartet was inside the house, but stones carried their sounds. That bit of magic was difficult and cost more than most people earned in a lifetime. Those who employed it tried to project an air of wealth and greatness, but for the good Duke not to do so would have been an affront to his obvious position.

I told Sheela about the rocks. She nodded in approval and understanding. "Can we look at them this evening? I want to walk the grounds." She pointed to the sparkling lights. "That's where I want to dance. A slow, slow one, away from everyone else, where we can pretend we are the only people in the world."

The desire for her stirred again. It compelled me to take her hands and say, "We will."

"Promise?"

"I promise." *So long as everything goes as planned.*

We stopped at the entrance. Floating lights above created a warm, almost creamy glow. Reckard opened the door and said, "Are the lady and the gentleman ready?" He held a hand out to help Sheela.

I climbed out on my own, and as he closed the door he whispered, "I will see you around back, old chap. Don't tarry long." He squeezed my arm and his voice seethed. "Don't let anything happen to Sheela, old chap."

I pulled my arm from him as Sheela took my other one, and her touch soothed the nervousness trying to take greater hold. Reckard's jealous stare followed us down the purple carpet. I tried to disguise my heavy foot as a limp. The music grew louder as we approached the steps, and butterfly lights flittered to and fro above. We walked past the great stone lions which had been brought to life through magic. They strained at their bases and roared though no sounds emerged. They shook their manes and pawed at the ground as they watched us at eye-level.

As we approached the entrance, laughter enveloped us. The music of a chamber orchestra filled the air. Heat radiated from within. A man dressed in a black tux with a white scarf and white gloves stepped in the way. He held out his right hand. "Your invitation if you please."

After I presented it, he studied it in the light above us, a green one that stopped projecting its color about seven feet up. He moved out of our way with a flourish of his coattails. "A good evening to you, Mr. and Mrs. Greenhew. The Duke and his betrothed extend their appreciation for your attendance."

Sheela couldn't seem to help but squeeze my arm tighter as we passed into the foyer. The room had a red marble floor, and on each wall, a row of small, gray busts of long-passed family members displayed on white pedestals. From there, we moved into the ballroom proper.

Hundreds of people filled the grand room. They stood and talked and moved from one side to the other in an orchestrated swell of chaos. Dresses of all shapes and sizes and colors afforded a feast for the eyes. There were white dresses reminiscent of a bride's gown in honor of the announced engagement, with lace and flowing trains. There were black dresses that hugged the bodies and accented every curve and sometimes every bulge. Whether that was good or bad depended on the perspective of the viewer. There were dresses reminiscent of medieval armor, with steel bodices cupping the bosom just so. To a one, they also had colored stones embedded in the metal, with a web of wires running from one to the others. There were green dresses with a low-cut 'V' in the front that almost exposed the naval, a Campden fashion rage of late and one that challenged the sensibilities of the rest of the empire. But such was the influence of magical creatures on this little part of the world. It already caused a scandal in Parliament where the Gateway Secretary had been asked to review decency standards for magic. The Archbishop himself was said to have made an impassioned plea in the House of Lords to control the corrupting influence of the magical creatures.

I cannot say I disagreed with him, for my own eyes were drawn to more than one well-endowed, magically enhanced wearer of the style.

Almost all the gentlemen wore the classic style of tuxedos though a few challenged sensibility and taste. Vests and lace ruffles on the cuffs were the latest fashion twist. Many took advantage, matching their vest color to their lady's dress. Several wore white in an obvious statement against the preferred attire. Some wore tails while some wore gloves. A few eschewed jackets and kept with the vests though they all wore shirts with more frills and puffy sleeves to offset the less formal look. A few wore metal vambraces with open faced clocks, two inches in diameter, lined like buttons. They also wore hard leather pauldrons with colored stones to match their lady's dress.

As magnificent a scene as all those people provided, they were nothing when compared to the room itself. The ceiling stood at least twenty feet high with square tiles alternating between engravings of flowers and solid, polished silver. In the center, twenty tiles had been removed so the room opened to the evening sky.

Banners hung in ten rows across the width of the room. They sparkled with silver and gold, and transitioned from solid to translucent in rhythm to the music. Torch-like light blazed along the sides of the room. Elves painted a creamy, marble color held the fires in the cups of their bare hands.

Sheela motioned to them. "I have never seen so many at once on this side. Either the Duke paid them well or he has quite the influence with their leaders."

Indeed. And either spoke of greater importance. The man obviously wanted to flaunt the power of magic over that of science.

The orchestra played at the opposite end of the room, behind a row of hedges grown for the occasion. Through the gaps I could see their instruments sparkle. Their music was carried throughout the room and magnified above the noise of the guests by the magic stones which were cleverly disguised as small columns perfect for using as a table for snacks or as a place for the weary to lean between dances.

Two rows of tables lined the left side and on them sat an assortment of breads, meats, cheeses, pies, cakes, puddings, and drinks, all waiting for the formal dinner. I pointed to them. "I don't know what half of those are."

As I led Sheela down the five steps and onto the ball room floor she said, "The rule is to pretend you like whatever is served, whether you do or don't, then gossip about what was good and bad in the following days." An older couple, a pair in their late forties, received a smile and nod as they passed. The husband, in a simple black tux, returned the nod, while the wife, in a blue dress that appeared to be trying to choke her neck and wrists, kept her eyes to the wonders above.

"How are we going to find her in all of these people?" Sheela asked with concern. "It could take us hours."

The same thought had crossed my mind. I had no idea if Aimee moved along the main floor, if she walked in the gardens outside, or if she had even arrived. But there was one thing I did know. "We will find her. Make no mistake."

We must.

I took Sheela to the tables and said, "I need a drink. After that, we'll dance."

She pulled back.

"Is something wrong? I know I won't be as graceful as I should be, but..." My words died as they earned a potent scowl.

She put her hands on her hips. "Why do you want to dance when our first priority is to find Aimee? Surprise, remember? That's our advantage."

Though she was correct, and Aimee was our business, spending a moment with Sheela seemed more important. For troubling herself with the preparations, she deserved a bit of enjoyment, an opportunity to forget her problems. I motioned to all the room. "We have an evening to locate her. I won't let pass the opportunity to dance with you. Please?"

"I don't know..." She looked towards the dance floor, where they had already dispensed with the formal progression of dances and given way to a freer style. "I...I cannot..."

"Of course you can." I patted her hand. "These people might adhere more to traditional dancing than they do at Branagh's, but they are still just people."

Just like the people at Branagh's who drank or used magic to escape their troubles, some of these people did the same, though always in private. They might appear cleaner and neater on the outside, but often their lives were just as dirty and messy and...

A cup of rum-laced punch burned my throat. The sensation was deserved. It helped to chase away the voice and the memories.

Sheela said, "It's too risky. Dancing with everyone."

Part of me felt relief, but the more sensible part urged me to say, "I refuse to let this opportunity slip by. We will find Aimee afterwards."

"You don't understand." She leaned close like she wanted to tell a secret, but she grabbed a cup and drained it straight away. Though she was every bit the lady, she could drink like a man. While the one drink satisfied my desire, she took another and quickly emptied it. When she noted my look she said, "I need something to calm my nerves."

I pulled her close, placing my hand in the small of her back. "I need your nerves and your alertness just the way they are. I need your good senses and your good judgment." I smiled to give her some reassurance. "And besides, I understand. I'm nervous, too." When I tried to lead her away, she held back.

Her voice was full of fear. "I can't do this, Ash."

"Yes, you can." I held my arms wide. "If I'm willing to try, if I go out there, then you can do it. Inside is that little girl who wants to enjoy this Ball for all its worth. Inside is that girl who always wanted to dance the night away, bathed in magic lights with the swell of the music filling her."

She hung her head. "I'm sorry, Ash." Under her breath she added, "I can't."

"What's going on, Sheela?" I then asked, before better sense prevailed, "What are you not telling me?"

Her bosom rose and fell with heavy breaths, indicating either anger or fear. "Just like you face the ghosts of your past, so I'm facing my own. I thought I could do this, but it's too much."

Now curiosity drove me beyond the point of stopping. "What ghosts?"

She bit her lip and kept her head down. "Things best left undisturbed, things capable of great danger."

The voice said, "You have no right to know. The way you treat her gives you no right to know who she was or what she tries to keep secret."

True, but then why did the fact that she didn't trust me sting so? Why did it make me mad enough to hold her hand tight, and hobble towards the dance floor, pulling her behind despite her attempts to resist? "You are the most beautiful woman here. It would be shameful if you didn't add that beauty to the dancing. As I said before, the eyes of every gentleman will be on you."

She pulled hard enough to make me stop. "I don't want the eyes of all these men watching." Tears filled her eyes. "There's simply too much at risk."

"Trust me."

Did I actually say that? To her? What had taken hold of me?

She bit her lower lip again as she stared at me. "Do you know what you ask? Do you appreciate the risks?" Her gaze went over my shoulder, to the dance floor. "Would it matter if you did? You wouldn't care, would you?" She gave not a hard look, but a broken one, like she learned of a betrayal.

It caused my own broken heart to feel a slight ache. "Sheela—"

"No, you're correct, Ash. I will face the consequences of my choices like a woman should." She pulled me toward the dance floor. "I wanted you to know this is one of the hard ones. I hope we survive the consequences."

A song had just ended. We passed several couples who forewent the next. For all of her sudden bravado, though, Sheela stopped at the edge.

Still, we stood under the open roof. The stars above appeared close enough to touch and their lights twinkled all about the dance floor. Of the floor itself, the stone had given way to images of cloud-like white puffs and a light fog that separated about our feet. Together, it all gave the sense of dancing in the heavens themselves. A nice touch. What manner of magic created such an atmosphere?

The next song began and radiated from the clouds beneath us. I put Sheela's right hand on my shoulder, then held her left hand. "Follow my lead and don't worry about anything else or anybody."

How could one when enveloped in such a sense of otherworldly wonders?

I hoped I could move my left foot, at least enough to give the semblance of dancing. We began slow to let her, and me, gain confidence. She squeezed my hand tight, but she did better than could have been expected, much better than I did. She danced like she had done so at least a hundred times before and relaxed enough to move with the flow of the song and with the other dancers. A smile appeared, despite the single tear that ran down her cheek.

Sheela. So strong and sassy, so kind and loyal. Yet so mysterious. She appeared the part of the angel at that moment, with the stars reflecting in her eyes and the light of the heavens glowing about her. She was the most beautiful woman on that floor.

My heart ached again. It stirred the longing I never wanted to experience again.

Could I be?

No. I couldn't. I wouldn't.

Yet my soul yearned all the worse for the delicate woman in my arms. Despite myself, I pulled her closer so I could feel her heat.

I was cruel. To her. To me.

I could not love again. I could not suffer the potential pain of heartache. I was not that strong. Aimee had—

I sucked in a quick breath, for twenty feet past Sheela's shoulder, Aimee danced. She looked even more radiant than I remembered. Her glow shone brighter than the heavens as she took beauty to another realm, one higher than the stars themselves.

She had curled her hair. The ringlets cascaded in waves and danced their own dance. She, too, wore a strapless dress that had to have been held up by nothing except magic. The short and black bodice cupped her bosom and displayed the top of its fullness. Layers upon layers of tight, white lace along her waist rippled with her movements and revealed hints of flesh beneath. Those gave way to layers of a light, sheer blue reminiscent of an older fashion that swirled about her hips and legs.

She smiled that smile, the one that told her dance partner he was the only man in the world, the one that melted any resolve to stand firm against her.

I had not seen that smile directed at me in a long time. And while it sometimes scared me, it always increased my desire for her.

All at once, I saw flashes of moments when I watched her from a distance: from the first time at the Bank, to when she stood with pride at the top of the steps outside the Bank's door and looked across the city with satisfaction, to when she stood at the end of the aisle with the lace covering her face, to the time she spoke to Bishop Donnavan and hid a laugh behind her hand. With the flashes came the same spontaneous joy I felt then. It filled every part of my body, down to the pores of my skin.

I stepped on Sheela's foot and made her stumble. "Ouch," she whispered. "Pay attention."

"My apologies. At least it was my good foot." My eyes refused to leave the goddess who dared to kiss the one she danced with. "I see her."

Sheela tried to turn, but I said, "Wait. Follow my lead."

Surprise, Ash. You must surprise her.

Aimee swung around with her partner and she laughed. Her tone carried through the music and noise as if she stood as close as Sheela. It both soothed and mocked.

I loved her laugh, which I never heard often enough.

Do you love it still?

We maneuvered through other dancing couples to keep her in view, but were too slow.

Curse Pienne, again.

We bumped into one couple, a lord of some military rank as indicated by the ribbons hanging about his neck. The man said, just loud enough for us to hear, "I wish the Duke would consider including a dance floor where we avoid the necessity of mingling so much with the lesser born."

Sheela's brow narrowed and her face turned red.

"Ignore him," I said as I recognized the look of resolve. Many patrons at Branagh's received the same expression just before she put them in their place. "He's a highborn fool. Nothing worth worrying about."

Still her nostrils flared. "Baron Desmend has always been a—" She took a sudden and deep breath. After a moment, she whispered, "Do you still see her?"

I glanced at her. "How do you know—"

Her tone matched her glare. "Do you still see her?"

"No, there are too many between us." And oh, how my eyes longed to feast on her beauty again.

The song swelled in its climax as every instrument in the orchestra played. We spun between two couples, then slide-stepped around another.

And still I didn't see Aimee.

Yet Aimee wasn't as important as Sheela's knowledge of the Baron. "So how did you know—"

She spun around three more couples as the song concluded.

My leg ached at the knee and in the thigh. My lungs burned, and my eyes searched for Aimee.

Everyone stopped to acknowledge his or her partner. Sheela and I did the same though I stretched my neck to locate my former wife while doing so. I nudged aside several couples as they left the floor. One, a man as round as he was tall, and adorned in a black tux with pink lace on his cuffs said, "You'd think some people were dancing their last dance."

"What is she wearing?" Sheela asked. After I described the dress, she said, "Let's go separate ways so we can cover more of the room." She pointed to the back. "You work your way there and let Reckard in." She pointed to the front. "I'll work my way over there and make sure she doesn't slip out to the yard."

I nodded before giving her a light kiss on the cheek.

She grabbed my shoulders and pulled me closer. "Don't think you can escape with just that." And then she kissed me deep as the next song started, and the dancers moved about us, some gasping at the display of affection. She tasted sweeter than ever at that moment. Her perfume overwhelmed with its hints of flowers combined with a dash of fresh sea air.

Despite the canon's voice, I grabbed her hips and returned the moment of passion, there within the heavens. When I pulled away, she swayed and touched her mouth. "Watch yourself, Ash. You might decide you love me."

Yes, had we met in a different time, before the old Ash died, before he was replaced by the new, contemptible one.

Speaking of the past I said, "You still haven't told me how you know Baron - what's his name - Desperate?"

A couple bumped into us and stumbled. The woman, who wore a red dress that reached her knees and gave her a school-girl like appearance on a fifty year-old frame, glared like I caused all the misery of her life, for daring to ruin such a special moment.

I caught her and said, "My apologies. I have lead feet when it concerns dancing."

Her partner snatched her away. He, with gray hair swept back and white wrinkles lining his well-tanned face, said, "Keep your hands to yourself, sir."

I held both of mine up, then reached for Sheela and said, "Bonni, never let it be said that we Greenhews caused a disturbance in the Duke's home." We walked from the floor, avoiding more dancers, and Sheela gave my arm a light slap. She hid a laughing snort behind her other hand and still avoided answering my question.

Who are you, Sheela? Better yet, why do I care so much?

The voice said, "Because she is worth caring for that much."

Maybe bringing her to the Ball was a mistake. The otherworldly atmosphere made my emotions unstable. That had to be the explanation. I should have asked Leesal, or Lauree.

"Meet at the tables," I said, then watched her slide between couples with all the grace of a great dancer. Her work at Branagh's proved its worth again. I longed for such agility, especially considering the hundreds standing between me and the back.

As a server passed with a tray of drinks, I took one and sipped on it as I went. I kept an eye out for Aimee as I moved towards the orchestra, who at this distance no longer needed music stones to deliver their sounds. My neck ached as I looked from side to side. While there were many women who deserved a second glance, I had to remain focused on the one.

When she stepped in front of me, I almost dropped my glass in surprise. My belly flipped twice.

"Alexander," she said as if the name tasted like poison. "Why am I not surprised to find you here of all places?"

That familiar haughtiness, that cold snake-like, business-like, stature that helped her to advance in her position. She peered down her nose. She folded her arms across her bosom, covering it like it was an honor to view that which I knew the flesh and fullness and tenderness of so well. Her hips were cocked just so, like she meant every word she said. Which she did.

"Aimee," I said and stopped myself from smiling. "It has been many years. You look as beautiful as always."

"And you look as if you aged thirty years." She sniffed. "But such is the price of magic addiction."

"To some of us, yes. Others are more blessed. I'm sure you can appreciate that."

A single eyebrow arose. "Indeed. What brings you here?"

I motioned to the room and proclaimed, "The Duke's Ball, of course! Why would I want to miss such an extravaganza? It's the talk of the town, the biggest event of the year, at least until the premier at Chen's. Why, it's an honor to see who the good Duke has chosen for his bride."

Her eyebrow remained in place. "And just the opposite of where you would rather be. I know you. And how useless, how disappointing, is such knowledge? You would rather be in a quiet place with your nose stuck in one of your theology books, studying about us humans while letting life pass you by."

This time, I smiled. And for that, her eyebrow dropped, her entire brow grew sharper, and her eyes darker. The effect made her look all the more beautiful.

She was a goddess among mortals. My heart skipped one beat.

The voice said, "But she doesn't know you so well. Not anymore. Not that she ever did."

"Would you care for a drink?" I asked as I lifted my glass.

"With you? I hear you took to the bottle after the divorce. I thought you understood us humans well enough to deal with any of your own emotional difficulties. Though I must admit I was surprised, for I thought you could have dealt with the situation so much better. I thought you would rely on your beliefs and convictions and your god. Did you not tell me how he could help you through any situation?" She tossed her hair back. "But that wasn't enough, was it? You had to take to drinking for relief. Which never gave you enough, did it? So you took to the magic elixirs."

I nodded slowly. "True, I grew addicted to the magic." My next words were some of the most important I had spoken. "Because I needed relief from the pain after the explosion. You remember the incident, don't you? The one that almost killed me? The one you hoped would kill me?"

Her gaze grew more intense, her mouth just a little tighter. Had I not known her so well, the changes would've been unnoticeable. What they said was I spoke the truth.

The canon within sobbed as the knowledge pierced my heart and soul just as bad as the day she told me she wanted a divorce. Yet the thief within smoldered with anger, urging revenge.

She held a hand out. "So would you like to give me your invitation or should I call a Guardsman over?"

My mouth turned dry, so I finished my drink. After placing the empty glass on a passing tray I said, "Whatever do you mean? You don't believe it's a counterfeit, do you?"

"It belongs to the Greenhews."

No secrets between her and Bonni. The Greenhews would have searched for it among their ruins.

Think of the dagger. Think of the dagger.

"I am a man of honest means," I said as if she offended me. "It's my invitation."

Her hand remained outstretched. "Then let me examine it."

"Of course." I reached inside my coat.

At once, a blade flashed in the light. It sliced through my trousers at the thigh, then through my lapel as it slid, sharp-edge first, into my hand.

Praise you, Pienne, and your elixirs.

Aimee reached for me. A tendril of purple smoke escaped between her fingers.

I grabbed her hand and squeezed it shut as I pressed the dagger against the soft flesh of her flat stomach. It took every bit of self-control not to push it all the way in. "I have a matter to discuss with you in private."

She smirked. "Yes, why don't we talk? I'll turn around, and you can keep the dagger in my back while I take us to another room."

For once, we agreed. "Let me set the pace."

We seemed to crawl through the crowd, towards the side opposite from the preparation tables. The dagger remained planted in the small of her back as I continued to squeeze her hand shut.

"Aimee," a man said as he approached. He was tall, a good four inches above me, and he had a full head of black hair that swooped low over his eyes. His face had a softness to it, like he had been raised in a life of luxury. He carried two drinks, one of which he handed to her.

She took it, then kissed his cheek and looked at me. "This is my escort for the evening."

If she thought seeing him would make me jealous, she was wrong. On the contrary, I felt sorry for the chap. "So does this poor, unsuspecting man have a name or do you prefer to forego the trouble of learning about a fellow human these days?"

As she scowled, the man offered his free hand. "I'm Henry. And you are?"

"Alexander." I dared not release Aimee's hand, so I nodded to his. He gave no sign of recognition of my name, so I added, "Aimee's first husband."

At that, he gave her a startled look.

Aimee asked, "Was that necessary?"

"It is part of who you are, dear. He needs to know the woman he's dealing with." I prodded her with the dagger. "After all, he needs to watch himself, else an accident might happen."

The untouched drink in the shocked man's hand appeared forgotten, so I took it and said, "It's a pleasure to meet you, Henry. If you think you love her, you had best flee. She'll break your heart and keep a thousand secrets." I drank the punch in one, long draught, then handed the empty glass to him.

Aimee walked again. After we moved out of earshot she said, "That was unnecessary, Alexander. There was no need to involve the man in our history."

"And why not? Is he a client you're seeking to impress for the Bank? Does he have large sums of money he wishes to invest?"

She offered no reply, so I was likely correct. She would never have stooped so low to bring just anyone to such an important occasion. No, if Henry was a poor, working-class fellow, she might have, at best, allowed him to take her to a cafe after waiting for several hours after regular Bank time.

We continued to work our way through the crowd, and five more people stopped Aimee. Two were work associates I didn't recognize, meaning they belonged in the row of offices on the first floor. Two others were personal acquaintances I didn't know. But the last was someone I knew well: old Lady Havens, escorted by her always-present grandson.

The woman's stooped back forced her to look down. Wrinkles lined her face. White, curly hair thinned on her head. She leaned on a cane with her right hand and held onto her grandson with her left. She tilted her head to the side to look at Aimee. "My dear, it is always a pleasure to see you. How have you kept yourself? I saw you with that dashing young man as you entered. Finally putting that nasty marriage behind you?"

Aimee smiled at the old lady. "I am pleased to tell you that I'm engaged. The marriage will be in three months, and I couldn't be more delighted."

I whispered, "Then Henry has my sympathies. Does he know what he's committing to?"

She continued to smile, but her lips tightened.

Old Lady Havens said, "And is this..." She eyed me close and her brow raised slightly. "That glow about you appears familiar, sir. Have we met before?"

The old woman had gone blind many, many years ago. She turned to magic elixirs to try to cure her problem and for her efforts, had developed the ability to see an aura about a person. She once told me there were as many as there were colors in the rainbow and each had a shape based on the person's heart. While the colors sometimes changed, the shapes always remained the same.

The way her eyes darted back and forth meant she tried to connect the shape of my heart with my name.

I poked the dagger into Aimee's back and she said, "It's always a pleasure to see you, Lady Havens. Perhaps we can talk more, later?" She kissed the old woman's hand before we walked away.

The old woman watched us go with blank, but focused eyes that sent a shiver through my back.

The sound of a glass shattering drew our attention as it did everyone in the immediate area.

A server, a pale woman dressed in a long-sleeved black dress and wearing a black hat into which her hair was tucked, dropped to her knees to gather the glass with her bare hands. A young man loomed over her and bellowed, "You careless worm. Look what you've done!" He peered down his coat, which had absorbed a good deal of drink.

"I'll make sure you pay for this. I'll have my uncle take care of you for good."

"My apologies, sir," the lady said. Her voice sounded much like Sheela's. "I didn't see you, I was just—"

"Being clumsy? You're supposed to blend in like the poor thing you are, not stumble into me." He kicked a shard out of her reach.

The lady continued to gather the pieces.

Aimee tried to go on, but I said, "Wait."

She smirked. "Still acting the part of the bishop, aren't you?"

"Whatever do you mean?"

She nodded towards the server. "You're going to help her." That was a statement and not a question.

"What makes you—"

The server said something that made the man roar and grab her by the top of the head, hat and hair both. He lifted her up. "Please," she whimpered as she held onto his arm.

Though Guardsmen watched, not a one tried to interfere.

"The Duke's nephew," Aimee said, amused. "Not a pleasant man to cross. He has a most persistent anger to compliment his cruel nature."

He shook the much smaller woman as she cried out and held up both hands. Shards of glass protruded from her palms. The sight stirred the canon and gave rise to anger.

If I went, I would lose Aimee. I would lose my advantage. I might risk the lives of those around me if Aimee tried to blow me away.

If I didn't help, though, the lady would be hurt, or killed.

"Go help," Aimee said with a wave of her free hand. "I'm not going anywhere."

I was already moving towards the scene and the voice said, "Defend us thy humble servants in all assaults of our enemies."

"Please," the server said. "I was trying..."

The man reared back to strike her again, but I took hold of his fist. He spun, and the smell of rum overwhelmed my nose, making the back of my throat burn. He equaled me in height and his frame showed the sturdiness and stoutness of a noble raised in the arts of combat. Under normal circumstances, he could've beaten me into a bloody mess.

But when were circumstances ever normal?

He said, "How dare you—"

"Frank Greenhew," I said, then smiled.

"How dare you, whoever you are, for interfering in my affairs." A red-tipped nose on a long face separated blood-shot eyes. He also wore vambraces and pauldrons. On the former, small diamonds outlined the Duke's badger.

"You have proven your point," I said like I addressed a reasonable man. "Let the lady be. Go clean yourself off."

He pushed me. "You dare threaten me, sir? Back away now, and I'll let this insult pass."

I pointed to the server. "I'll leave as soon as you leave her be."

"Oh, I've only begun on it." He grabbed my coat and drew me close to whisper, "When I'm done it will be a pile of mechanical rubbish."

The stink coming from his breath made my belly lurch. I pushed him back and said, "What—"

He punched me. Square across the jaw.

The crunch of bones sounded in my ear.

The man howled in pain as he held his hand out. Two fingers hung at unnatural angles.

After pushing him aside, I bent down to help the server. She continued to scoop the glass with her bare hands. But something was unnatural about her. A faint click-whir sounded from her arms, not unlike the noise in Pienne's lab. They also moved in the same, almost stiff way the Guardsman with the marble eyes had on the night I rescued

Rebecca Donnavan from her attackers. As I lifted her hands, she said, "Don't. Please." I picked three slivers from the bottom of her right palm. There was no blood, just like the Guardsman. But beneath the skin, there was black metal.

I stared at the woman. What did it mean? What—

The Duke's nephew roared as he tackled me from the side. We slid across the floor, knocking a couple down. Somehow, the intoxicated man ended up on top of me. He tried to choke me with his good hand.

A punch to the nose sent him backwards as blood spewed over my vest and coat. His type understood only one form of persuasion. I punched again, but my hand struck a solid wall of air. The room shimmered in waves as I gasped for breath. I reached up and my hand stopped a good three inches short of my face.

A blast of air pinned me to the floor as Aimee and Bonni loomed overhead. Next to them stood the same man I passed on the Greenhew's path. Unlike the previous time, I now earned his full attention. "My nephew has found trouble again." He regarded me with an expression that could be taken as either pity or scorn as he tapped his cane on the floor. "Unfortunately, you should never have encouraged him, sir. And you should never have insisted on helping."

With a respectful tone Bonni asked, "What do you want me to do with him?"

My chest burned as I tried to draw in air, and the ceiling seemed to spin.

Aimee took my dagger. "I told you I wouldn't leave, Alexander. Duke Schaever has something special in mind for you." She looked at Bonni like they shared yet another secret. "Let's teach him a lesson. If he survives, maybe he will learn not to cross paths with The Gatherers. If he doesn't, which is most probable, then I finally rid the world of his wasted existence." She smiled and motioned. "Follow me."

My ears roared. My eyes watered. My chest burned even more. Hands lifted me.

Think about the dagger. Think about the dagger. Not about Aimee's beauty. Not about the time she bought me a gold watch, with the magic stones that chimed on the quarter hours. Think about...

What?

Frank Greenhew spoke with a delighted, triumphant tone. "Stay with us a moment longer. You'll want to see this." Under his breath he added, "Good riddance you meddling weasel. I ought to kill you for burning down our home." He said, louder, "Can you allow him a little air, darling? He is quite heavy."

"No," she snapped, "this is payment for what he did. I want him to suffer. I want him to die."

Her husband answered, "Remember, love, we could have so much more fun and satisfaction if he but lives a little longer."

What felt like a smothering blanket lifted and allowed a gasping breath before returning.

The dagger. Need the dagger. Concentrate. Focus on it, not on the spinning. Not on the image of Aimee on our wedding day when she walked down the center aisle of Saint James.

Her white gown, as pure as fresh fallen snow, made her appear radiant. Full sleeves ran from middle finger to her shoulders, where the cut dropped, in modesty, to the top of her bosom. So secretive. So promising. So tantalizing.

Aimee. Beautiful. Lovely.

Now we entered a stairwell and ascended the steps. Frank huffed and wobbled on his wounded leg as he tried to pull my leaden body up. I gave him no help. Not that I could do much besides try not to pass out. He struggled as best he could.

The Duke said, "Lady Aimee, all is prepared according to our plans."

"Thank you," she said with a pleased tone. "You've always been a wise man. I never would have thought of the catapult."

He laughed. "We should send a message to our rivals, should we not? And what better way to show them how we deal with their underlings? After all, when our enemies besiege us, we sometimes launch our rubbish at them."

The Duke continued, "Frank, I expected the next shipment of gnomes this morning, as you promised I would receive them. Is there a problem with the money?" He paused. "Don't forget to let him breath."

I managed two good breaths, just enough to keep me aware of something besides a burning chest and a light head.

The dagger. Need the dagger.

No, better to wait. Only get one chance.

Frank spoke with a nervousness I had never heard from him as if he feared the consequences of his words. "No, Duke Schaever, the problem is with the supplier. He said the gnomes have grown suspicious of every situation and they travel in larger packs. I will need a few more days." He took a deep breath. "I won't release the money until I know they are in your possession."

For the first time since I knew him, Frank added nothing under his breath.

Gnomes had been disappearing of late and had become skittish, even in Branagh's. They called themselves a family, which included anyone of pure gnome blood. They distrusted most outside of the family, but of late had taken the distrust to an extreme end.

"I will find a proper incentive to assure the contract is honored and we get our delivery," the Duke said with irritation. "Just take proper care of my money."

We reached the top, some five stories up. Here, the good Duke would mark the culmination of his festivities with works of fire imported from the Far East. He had two golden-colored cannons with Chinese dragons engraved on the sides, which would shake the hearts of all who watched. He would dazzle the countryside with a display of lights this part of the empire had not seen the likes of since the last Ball. Throughout the town, those not socially important enough to deserve an invitation remained awake as they anticipated the heavenly spectacle.

"An impressive display," a voice said from the shadows on the right. The accent was familiar, but I couldn't place it. The burning in my chest made it impossible to think. "Your creations are every bit what was promised."

The Duke replied, "And we have an unfortunate incident we must deal with." He glanced at his nephew.

The voice sounded eager as it answered, "We are pleased, and trust you to deal with any incidents."

I heard similar accents at Branagh's. Was it elf? No, for it wasn't light enough. Troll? No, it was scratchy, but not gruff. Reptilian was more of a hiss with a slurred 's.'

"Remember," the Duke said as Frank sat me against the wall, "this is a variation on the first model, one meant to blend better. We are still working on other capabilities using different combinations based on our research."

An orc stepped into the light, and if not for the smothering shield I would've suck in a quick breath of surprise. This one was unlike any orc I encountered in Branagh's. Where those had the severe under bites, with boney faces, this one's features were smoother, his head longer, his under bite almost non-existent. Only one of his eyes bulged, for a scar ran across the empty socket of the other eye. He wore fine clothes: trousers and a shirt, both a burgundy color. He was bald, save for a two-foot long braid on the back of his head.

The strange orc eyed me. "This is the one seeking our object?"

The Duke nodded once. "Lady Aimee will deal with the matter. Let me show you."

He led the orc to the two catapults, medieval replicas that'd be used in tribute to our ancestors. In those, he would launch ordinance that would explode in a ball of light as bright as the noon sun. He motioned for Aimee to join them, then showed her how to pull the lever on the already prepared catapult on the left side.

"And what might this be?" a soft-spoken, gentle, and reassuring voice asked from behind us. The sound almost extinguished the anger and tension in the air, except I thought I saw the Duke bristle. "The time is approaching when the introductions must be made. Are we delayed?"

Everyone turned to a woman adorned in a white dress with pink roses embroidered along the neck and sleeves. It covered her bosom, except for a small circle just between them. It then hugged her small waist before spreading out in crinoline-like fashion, except much smaller and more practical.

She stood with her chin slightly up so that she appeared to look to the stars. A round chin gave way to full cheeks and matching lips begging to be kissed, over and over. A slender, pointed nose divided eyes with just a hint of elven narrowness. Black hair fell over and covered one side of her face, and she let it remain in place as she peered upon all of us.

I never dreamed it possible, but both Sheela and Aimee's beauty paled in comparison. Yet something more surprising drew my eyes away – the one who stepped from behind Lady Elizabeth.

Rebecca Donnavan?

She wore a simpler red dress of more modest taste though a golden dragon embroidered across the right shoulder drew the eyes to her bosom and neck. A single pearl in a silver web-like setting hung on a silver chain and rested in the dragon's claw at the center of her bosom.

Our eyes met, and she gave me a look of curiosity mixed with surprise. She whispered to Lady Elizabeth, who said, "I was showing my dear friend some of your preparations for the evening. Are we interrupting?"

If Rebecca noted my red face or the fact that I leaned against the wall and made no effort to rise in greeting, she gave no sign. Rather, she gave me a warm and familiar smile as if she were oblivious to my situation.

I returned the smile and hoped it appeared as if I was pleased to see her even if shame cut through me like I had not felt since the early days of my elixir addiction. She now saw me as I truly was: a pitiful thief playing a game where the stakes were life and death, a magic addict living at the beck and call of cruel masters, not a rescuer in a dark alley.

Duke Schaever approached the pair and, after sweeping his cane under his left arm, said, "Lady Elizabeth, Miss Donnavan, I apologize for this, but a matter of business arose that required my prompt attention."

The lady nodded to the orc. "Frengarn, it is a pleasure to see you again. I'm glad to see you could attend our gathering."

The orc bowed. "Though I must remain in the shadows, I am pleased to be here." He looked at the Duke. "You understand how I must keep track of Reginald, else I will be forgotten amidst his plans and his schemes."

Lady Elizabeth's smile was not unlike the sun parting the clouds on a gloomy, overcast day. "And he sometimes needs to be reminded of his previous obligations." She raised her brow. "I assume this matter required your personal attention?"

If I wanted to call for Rebecca to help me, I couldn't have managed more than a gurgle. Truthfully, though, I wanted her to leave so I didn't have to bear more shame.

The Duke kissed Elizabeth's gloved hand, then Rebecca's. "I fear it does." He motioned to the stairs. "If you would be pleased to wait below, I shall not be but a moment longer. Once I finish, then our evening shall proceed without further interruption, and I will introduce you both to new wonders."

"Do you promise?"

"Of course," he said as if nothing else mattered.

She smiled and patted his hand. "Then we shall be patient." She nodded to Aimee. "Please excuse the interruption, Lady Aimee. I am glad you joined us this evening, too. I've missed our conversations. Should I trust all is well and that you'll resume your duties soon?"

Aimee gave a short curtsy. "I've never been better, Your Grace. And I'm looking forward to getting back to our lessons." She glanced at me. "After certain business is finished."

Elizabeth smiled again. "Then let us detain you no longer." She turned with a sweep of her dress, and after taking Rebecca's hand, floated back to the stairs.

For her part, Rebecca tilted her head as if finally noticing my pitiful state. She spoke to Elizabeth as they departed, but I couldn't hear the words for the roaring in my ears.

Everyone continued to stare at the departed forms as if we knew we gazed upon beauty's perfection for the last time. Bonni had forgotten all about me, which meant my head floated away to join the Duke's betrothed and my body passed into the state where breathing no longer mattered.

"He's turning purple," the Duke's nephew said, as if the prospect of my suffocating delighted him.

The others looked at me, and within a moment, air burned my lungs. I coughed. My eyes watered. I wanted to yell, but Bonni choked me again.

"Let me have the honor of killing him," the Duke's nephew said with eagerness.

"No," the Duke answered, "this is more personal than your trying to beat one of my mechanical servants. Lady Aimee should do this."

"He broke my hand!"

"He did worse to Lady Aimee. Now stand aside!"

Everything turned into a smear of browns and reds and blues. As my lungs screamed, my head felt like it rose to a place of peace and rest. It was at that moment when a blur floated behind the party. It was much smaller than the others, almost gnome-sized. I tried to make the colors sharpen, but it disappeared into the shadows.

Cavendish?

Had he come to save me?

Duke Schaever stared down. "Aimee, you are much improved on your choice of husband. Lord Henry is a much more distinguished gentleman. I understand why they ordered you to rid yourself of this one."

She looked down at me too as she stood beside the esteemed host. "I grew bored with him. When they told me it was time to remove him from my life, I gave no argument. Was I sad? For a moment, perhaps. But now I see the wisdom in their decision. He has proven to be a thorn in my side. But no more. Not after this." She paused. "Bonni, won't you let him breathe?"

"Must I?" she asked as if the thought pained her.

"Yes," Duke Schaever said. "Let him breathe on his own. He has no hope for escape. No one will hear him if he cries for help."

Fresh air again burned my chest. The feeling rivaled any pleasure I had ever experienced.

Frank and the Duke placed me in the catapult's cup. They secured my legs and tied my hands behind my back.

Where was Cavendish? Why did he wait to save me?

Perhaps I imagined him?

"What are you doing?" the orc asked.

Before the Duke replied, a crack, like a rock striking stone, sounded from the stairwell. Everyone turned as the Duke said, "Elizabeth, I must insist that you wait below."

No one answered.

The party looked at one another. Frank moved towards the door, followed by Bonni.

The Duke, his nephew, the orc, and Aimee remained in place, but with their backs to me.

Cavendish whispered, "What have you done?" His voice sounded like it resonated through the catapult's cup.

"Cut me free," I whispered. "Quickly."

"You ruined everything. You didn't follow the plan."

What was he doing? Or not doing? "I walked into a trap. Now cut me free."

Frank said from within the stairwell, "She's not here. No one is here."

Cavendish said, "I'll be lucky to salvage this mess. I'll give Sheela your regrets."

"What do you mean?" I asked as the tightness of fear gripped my chest. "Hurry!"

"Check again," the Duke said, then turned. With all the gentleness of a father directing a daughter he motioned for Aimee to go to the lever. "Finish this business. I want the assurance he doesn't live to tell the secrets he saw. I want to enjoy the rest of the evening." He motioned to me. "This is how I deal with those who put themselves in my business, Frengarn."

Where was Cavendish? The conniving, hairy little monster! Was he betraying me so soon?

Aimee moved to the lever. She held my dagger in her right hand. "Do you have any last words, Alexander? Anything you want to say?"

I wanted to say so many things to her since the divorce. Many times I imagined exacting the revenge of my pain and suffering on her, so she would understand what she did. I had prepared speeches elaborate enough to impress the Queen's court.

But at that moment, words failed me. All I could think of was, "I hate you."

The voice agreed. To a point.

She smiled. "Good. Then we understand each other better than we ever did." She gave a forced laugh. "You always wanted to fly, Alexander. Now you'll get your wish."

Think of the dagger. Picture its form. Will it into your hand.

It flew from her hand and into mine. As she looked at me in astonishment, I cut through the rope around my wrists.

I reached for her.

She pushed the lever. The catapult arm sprung forward.

I sailed through the night, flapping my arms like that might assist my flight. The Duke's estate disappeared far below. Campden and the spires of Saint James receded in the distance. The eastern estates disappeared, too, as I sailed high towards the farms.

Aimee was wrong.

This wasn't flying.

And the landing would hurt.

CHAPTER 7

"...he is alive...better...dead..."

"...make...he is ready..."

"...yes...answer...failure..."

Bones ached. My arms felt twisted. My skull pounded as my chest throbbed.

"...waking...that is...congratulations..."

A cloth kept my eyes closed.

My lungs rattled as I breathed, like fluid had entered them. A knot sat in the back of my throat.

"...prepare...hour..."

A hard prick on my right arm made me gasp, then warmth spread through my shoulder and into my head.

Pienne?

Another hard prick on my arm woke me, and bulbous cheeks and the familiar sharp, protruding brow appeared far closer than necessary. A smile spread across his face and Pienne said, "Returned to us? That is good. Very good. Pienne thought he lost Alexander this time. Well, he did lose Alexander for a bit, but he worked diligently to bring him back. Often there's less magic in healing and more science. Getting that combination correct can be the real challenge."

Each beat of my heart shot waves of pain through my body. I couldn't help but moan. "Where am I?" My tongue stuck to the roof of my mouth. "What happened?"

"Alexander is in Pienne's room though not in the usual chair. No, this time Pienne had to use his table and his different elixirs." He motioned to the array of tubes and beakers above, each filled with a different colored liquid that either swirled or bubbled. "As for what happened, Alexander arrived dying and broken and Pienne worked on him for another four days." He held up a bent and twisted needle. "With Alexander's toughened skin, he had a difficult time finding a needle sharp enough to pierce it. Ruined twenty before he succeeded. And even then, he had to warm Alexander's skin. He's very sorry for the burns."

"What?" I tried to sit up, but my body protested the movement by throbbing all the faster. Three spots on each arm felt like a hot poker had been applied.

Pienne pushed me down with the gentleness of a mother. "Now, Alexander, let's not be impatient to see the Masters. The elixir he is attached to will restore strength, but it will require a few more minutes."

A tube protruded from my right arm, in the middle of blistered skin, and a clear liquid flowed. "But if I'm getting an elixir, then why am I not—"

"Passed out? Dreaming? Enjoying the experience?" His brows rose, but his eyes still remained hidden. "Because this one requires much more science and little magic and Alexander's body is responding to the fact he has slept for so long."

The throbbing and the headache eased. I gave it a moment longer to settle before asking, "What happened? The last thing I remember was..."

Flying over the countryside with the wind whipping at my face, and the birds keeping me company.

"Where did I land?" I asked, dreading the answer.

"Land?" Pienne asked in an amused tone. "Oh, Alexander will have to ask him." He motioned to the right.

Reckard stepped out of the shadows. He folded his arms and didn't smile. "You don't remember, old chap? No, I suppose any of us would prefer to forget." His voice sounded as if it pained him to recall the details. "We found you in a hole four feet deep in the middle of a farmer's field. You bled from your ears and nose and mouth and eyes and you were very much unconscious. But you lived if barely. It took an hour just to dig you out."

There wasn't a need to hide my surprise. Not among friends. "Us?"

"Sheela, Cavendish, and me." He pointed in a threatening fashion. "You were stupid, old chap. Stupid beyond anything you have ever done that was stupid. What were you thinking? Trying to capture Aimee on your own? You forgot about me, and you didn't give Cavendish the opportunity to inject his elixir. You cost us all dearly." He threw his hands up. "It was as if Aimee knew you better than you know yourself. It was as if she knew you'd try a foolish trick. And did you get any closer to getting the Head? No, of course not. In fact, you let her escape, and who knows where she's hiding."

This was one of those unpleasant moments, when I felt like something lower than a worm, even if I wasn't completely responsible. "I'm sorry. But she—"

He scoffed. "Sorry? I don't think you're ever sorry anymore. Not truly. You're too numb to emotion and the world and have isolated yourself too much. You've withdrawn from everything but the magic. Do you know what you've put Sheela through? Have you thought about how much she cried while we tried to save you?"

I tried to raise a hand to get him to stop, but my strength drained away when I reached halfway.

The voice seemed to laugh as if it thought I needed to listen to such as this.

Reckard continued, "She cried all the way back to town. Then we had to sneak you past a company of Guardsmen. That took some doing, let me tell you." He leaned forward. "You know I would do anything to make her care for me half as much as she cares for you. Yet for a reason that escapes sense or logic, she all but compromises her good sense to earn your attention and affection." His face turned red. "What does she see in you? What does she—"

I spoke with a flat tone. "Cavendish followed me. To the roof."

"—hope to—" He blinked twice, then stood back as if surprised. "What?"

"I talked to the bastard after they loaded me onto the catapult. He could've freed me." I paused. "But he chose not to."

Reckard looked at me from under his brow. "That is a serious accusation, but not surprising. You cannot trust those creatures, so it's your own fault for thinking he's your friend." His voice dipped lower still. "Did you know Leesal held Sheela down so she wouldn't try to follow me here? What sort of disaster might that have caused if she discovered this place? The Misters would've administered the third elixir to both of us. And her."

Sheela. Why can you not find another man? You deserve better. Reckard adores you. Why refuse his advances with such determination?

A deep breath hurt enough to make sweat break out on my forehead. "But you stopped her."

He scoffed again. "Sure...after I promised a dozen times I'd take care of you and return you to her. She really lo—"

Pienne pushed between us and pulled the needle from my arm, which felt like a crab's pincers grabbing my skin, followed by a sharp pain of release. He wrapped a cloth around the bleeding hole. "Pienne gave Alexander the ability to withstand an explosion, but not the force of striking the ground like he did. While his skin is toughened that doesn't mean his insides are as hard." He helped me to sit up and said, as a nauseous wave moved through me, "Pienne wanted to heal Alexander better, but our Masters grow impatient." He pulled me off the table. "They have summoned both thieves. And they did not sound pleased. No, not at all. In fact, Pienne thinks he will lose himself in a quiet place where he can study his elixirs. He'll make sure they can't locate him for a while. That will assure Alexander of more time to live if they decide he needs the third elixir."

He shoved me out, and I had to balance against the wall to keep from falling. As Pienne closed the door he said, "May the one above have mercy on—" The lock clicked and the enveloping darkness seemed more oppressive than before.

"Let's get this behind us," Reckard said with the same dread weighing heavy on my shoulders. He walked down the hallway to the waiting room and audience, and offered no assistance as I continued to lean against the wall, dragging my foot along. My foot seemed to grow heavier the closer I came to the door.

Just before I reached it, the door opened. Together we entered the familiar light. Reckard stepped to the left while I hobbled to the right. The room spun, but closed eyes and a deep breath calmed it. We stood in agonizing silence.

Remain calm, Ash. Think about anything other than the third elixir.

The faster my heart beat, the more pain I felt.

Mister Mercy said, "Our intrepid assassin stands again, yes? Feeling better, yes?"

"Somewhat," I said, trying not to let pain or fear rattle my voice.

"Hmmm," Mister Important said, "it would appear that Pienne has worked another miracle. You should be more grateful to him." He paused. "And to us."

Grateful to them? For getting me into this affair? Was the man serious?

Well yes, he is.

I said, with as much sincerity as I could muster, "I am grateful. More than you can know."

"We know a lot, yes?" Mister Mercy said with an extra measure of haughtiness, and the tone raised the hairs on my neck. "Certainly more than you. Infinitely more. We know you believe we are blind to your ways, yes? You believe you are a righteous man, deep within. Perhaps a good man in a bad situation, yes? Then I want to reveal to you exactly what you are." As he paused I imagined he wrung his hands in anticipation. "I want you to prove your gratitude. Show us. Enlighten us on the great man who stands before us."

Though his words were confusing, surely Reckard could offer a sign of better understanding of what they wanted. Yet he stood straight with his eyes fixed on the voices ahead. So I gave a safe response. "You have my word, good sirs."

They both laughed. The sound didn't echo. It died and the foreboding sensation made my belly flip twice. Mister Mercy said with much amusement, "The word of a thief? The word of a man who lives because we say he lives? Tell me, what good is that? What good is the word of a magic addict? How can anything you do be good? There is nothing good left in you unless we say there is."

Nothing good? Perhaps, but I had always been a man of my word. Yes, I had flaws and imperfections like any other, but I always honored my word. Even now.

Mister Important spoke without humor. "You can do better, thief and murderer. You can and you will show us. You can grovel. Hmmm?"

Grovel? Did they mean beg? That was their game? They thought I had some dignity remaining that could be stripped away? Well, then I would reveal just what a fine actor I could be. I'd give a performance worthy of Lauree.

The canon's voice tried to quote an evening prayer, but the thief within took liberties with the words and changed them to say, to myself of course, "Dearly beloved brethren, The Misters moveth us in sundry places to acknowledge and confess our manifold sins and wickedness."

I bowed my head to hide a smile as I held my arms wide. My legs hurt too much to bend them or I might've provided a better show. The words of another evening prayer were appropriate, but with some changes to better accommodate the situation. "I have erred and strayed from your ways like a lost sheep. I have followed too much the devices of my heart." Then I added, "You are both greater than I, a mere mortal doomed to die in the streets like a feral dog. You are full of grace and mercy. I am nothing."

Mister Important continued, "He flatters us, hmmm? But he does not sound sincere enough. We have wasted too much effort on this mongrel, for a dog he is. We will deal with him like we would an unwelcomed stray."

"Yes," Mister Mercy took the queue, "perhaps we should tell Pienne to administer the third elixir." There was a sound, like a deep breath or a sigh of satisfaction, "Reckard. Escort your friend to his death, yes?"

My heart pounded in my head.

They healed me. They invested time and effort to save me. Why would they kill me now?

Did death bring them such pleasure? If so, they were madder than I believed, and I was a fool for ever agreeing to work for them.

Before Reckard moved, I fell to my knees. My thighs sent a wave of protest through my belly and chest. The bright light grew very dim to my aching eyes.

"How touching," Mister Mercy said with venom in his tone. "At the threat of death he takes our words seriously."

I bit my lower lip, for this would be a most unpleasant moment. Apparently, I still maintained a small amount of dignity and it fought every thought, every word. It proved The Misters knew me better than I believed possible. The voice tried to summon more half-forgotten prayers, but I ignored it and said, "Please, sirs, I ask you to grant me another chance. You are a most gracious employer and I deserve your scorn and ridicule. But I have always been cooperative and loyal. I have always worked diligently to accomplish your assignments."

Mister Important said, "You mock us. You think we play some type of game, hmmm?"

My dry tongue refused to move, so all I could do was shake my head.

How—why—But, I—

Was I that poor of an actor?

I whispered, "No, sir. Never. Magic is serious. Magic is the power to take control of the world."

The man laughed a humorless laugh. "I doubt his sincerity and do not believe he respects what we do. I do not believe he respects us. He never has, has he? And what good is someone we cannot trust? He will never kill Aimee, though she deserves his hatred and scorn, though he was the one who saved her from our assassin's blade the first time."

"A mistake, sirs," I said as I prostrated myself. "I didn't know."

Yet they revealed another truth.

"Please, sirs," I continued as the time of my death approached with each passing second, "grant me another chance. I'll correct the mistake I made that night. Had I not interfered, you would have saved me much heartache and grief. How can I repay that, but to remain loyal to you?"

Neither said a word. I touched my forehead to the floor.

How close to the edge of death did I walk?

Only they knew…they whose whims and desires controlled my life.

Bile rose in my mouth.

I said in a voice just above a whisper, "Did you know that Duke Schaever is aligned with The Gatherers?" When the silence continued, I added, "He helped Aimee and the Greenhews load me onto the catapult. He had it prepared ahead of time in expectation of one of your men."

The silence continued a moment longer until Mister Mercy interrupted it with, "We suspected, yes?" Did he speak with a hint of eagerness?

To feed his sudden desire I said, "And I confirmed. He has also been collecting gnomes."

The silence stretched again until Mister Important said, "She must be killed. I do not believe we can trust him. I believe we made a mistake in assigning him to this duty and there is one way to rectify our mistakes, to assure we do not repeat them."

The opportunity for mercy slipped from my hand. There was but one more bit of information to share though it might seal my death. Still it had to be tried, and the words had to be spoken with the utmost sincerity. "He is creating mechanical people, ones with real skin, ones who can blend with hundreds of people and no one ever suspects. And he is making them for an orc." If I remembered the creature's name, I would've added it.

The silence stretched long again.

Did they believe me? I wouldn't blame them if they didn't. I still couldn't quite believe my own eyes even though I twice witnessed the creations. Yes, more than one scientist theorized on the possibility of people composed of metal and gears and flesh and hair, but no one had solved the problem of maintaining a constant flow of electrical power. Neither had they solved the issue of intelligence.

Had the Duke done both? How? And what did he plan to do with such secrets? Sell it to the orc so his people could overthrow The Elders and finish the war? But—

Reckard said, making me start in surprise, "Sirs, if I may? I'd like to offer my assistance for this assignment."

Silence filled the room yet again. I held my breath.

What are you doing, Reckard?

"Continue, yes?" Mister Mercy said. I had the distinct impression he gripped the third elixir tight.

My friend said, "You are correct in the fact that Ash may not be able to kill Aimee. Though he has every right to do so, he is not a killer. Not yet. But I am. I've killed for you before. Let me join him in finding the Head, and I will make sure she tastes the sharp end of a blade."

Mister Mercy spoke in a near-whisper. "He speaks true. He is loyal is our Reckard. Never questions us. Never mocks us, yes? Never plays games."

Mister Important said, "It is touching how he cares for his friend. But would he value that friendship as much if he shared in Mister Asherton's fate? If Mister Asherton fails to bring us the Head, should they both die? Hmmm?"

"No," I said as the thought of Reckard's death gave me renewed strength. "Let me do this. Alone. Reckard need not risk his own life on my behalf."

My friend said, "I accept your decisions, sirs. Let our fates be twisted together in this endeavor."

"No!"

The Misters laughed again. After their laughter died in unison, silence filled the room.

I whispered, "Don't do this, Reckard." My words somehow sounded like I yelled.

Mister Mercy said, "How touching. What a show of devotion on both their behalves. It almost moves me to sympathy, yes? But what would keep us from disposing of our dear Mister Asherton and giving Mister Reckard the assignment?"

"Let me—"

Reckard said, "Ash knows her best. We will need that knowledge to find her again."

"And why does he need to find her again, hmmm?" There was yet another pause, one more deafening than before. "Because he failed! Because he did not believe us! Once more, I will ask what good is he, if we cannot trust him?"

What could I say? What apologia, what defense, could I give? They were right in the fact that I was a miserable creature. Not only was I weak and given to the temptations of magic, I was also ignorant and foolish, else I would've seen Aimee for what she was: a cunning fox disguised as a human, or a demon sent to torture me.

How Reckard maintained his composure and voice, I wasn't sure. For myself, anger and frustration battled within. My friend said, "Even in his failure, he did something worthwhile. He confirmed that Duke Schaever is a member of The Gatherers and that he is building...mechanical people?" He glanced at me with skepticism. "Is that not worth something? Can you not reward him for that?"

Mister Important said, "But there would have been better ways to learn, yes? We could have made arrangements. And besides, there is the matter of confirming the truth of what he claims."

With a sense that perhaps they backed away from the edge of light, that the third elixir might be forgotten I said, "I know what I saw, sirs, as mad as it sounds. Duke Schaever is dangerous. He—"

Reckard cleared his throat and said, "From what I've heard, all of your previous attempts to infiltrate Duke Schaever's household have failed. The Duke employs powerful magic of his own." He took a step forward. "In fact, the only reason Ash entered the Duke's estate without being detected was because there was already so much magic on the grounds. The Duke spent a small fortune on his Ball."

"Hmmm, but this one grows bold. Should we tolerate his assumption that he can tell us what we already know? Look. He even steps forward like he might be worthy of our attention."

"Or on an equal footing, yes?"

Reckard backed away, bowing as if he addressed the Queen herself. "Your decision is your own, sirs. I only wish to remind you that even in his failure, Ash has been of value."

The silence stretched long again. Too long. I had to do something, say something.

"I was the one who failed." My voice sounded like a roar and it echoed in my head, reiterating the words. "Let me suffer the punishment alone. If you grant me another chance, then I'll suffer the consequences, good or bad, alone."

Mister Mercy said, "Will you kill her this time? Are you capable of killing her? Or do you still love her?"

A good question, and a fair one. Where did my heart lie? Did part of me still hope for reconciliation? Could I ever truly hate her?

Yes.

No?

I swallowed hard. "I will do what I must, sir."

"And avoid answering my question, yes? Always a slippery one. Always a righteous one."

Reckard glared at me like I said too much. "I can kill her, sir. If Ash fails, I'll be there to do it."

"What if his love is so great that he tricks you, yes? What if he keeps you from killing her?"

My fellow thief didn't need to kill anyone. I didn't care for all of this talk. "I'll kill her myself." While the canon mocked me, I added, "I don't love her. Not anymore."

Reckard motioned to me. "I trust Ash enough to think he will help me do it."

"Trust?" Mister Important said. "Again, I ask why should we trust one who had her in his grasp and failed to complete his assignment? Why should we trust one who has already demonstrated that he cannot be trusted? Hmmm?"

"Because she will go into hiding and he is the one who can find her. He knows her mannerisms. He knows her friends."

They laughed again and Mister Mercy spoke as if he addressed a fool. "But he did not really know her, yes? I grow weary of this pointless debate. I grow weary of dealing with this matter."

My mouth turned drier. It begged for a Branagh's Ale. I hated enduring this, having to play their game. I hated that my life wasn't my own.

Is this what Aimee and her explosion had driven me to? Did she deserve the credit or the blame? Or had I done this to myself?

Mister Important, who surely dangled the dreaded elixir before me, said, "If this were any other object besides the Head of Forneil, we would kill you both for your presumptions about us. Hmmm, but the Head is important enough for us to grant a final attempt. We will bind the both of you together. Fail and you both die. Succeed and you both live. Expect no other reward for success or punishment for failure."

Mister Mercy added, "We will inform Pienne that he is to finish healing you, Mister Asherton. Yes, we will restore you to health, and we will strengthen your own magic while giving your loyal friend a power of his own."

"What does that say for your former wife, hmmm? Is she so strong and cunning to require two of our people to both find and kill her?"

I wanted to say, "That is more of an indication of the power of her friends," but I kept my mouth closed for once.

The room went dark and Mister Important spoke in such a way that the hairs on my arms stood straight. "Do not fail us. If you do, we will make your death quite painful. And quite long. Not hours. Not days. Weeks. Maybe months. You will beg for death and we will refuse."

Reckard helped me from the floor as a cold sweat covered me. As we walked towards Pienne's door I said, "You didn't need to involve yourself in this. I'll not be responsible for your death."

He gave a 'harumph', then said, "If you think I'm doing this for you, then you truly are a fool."

When we reached the door I asked, "Then why—"

The man spun me around to face him. "Because of the woman who cried and screamed over your broken and twisted and buried body. Because of the woman whose heart broke because she feared you were dead in the crater you made in that field." Breath that smelled of bile washed over me. "Are you so cold as to put her through such pain and anguish and not care? If so, then I pity you. I, obviously, have a weakness when it comes to seeing Sheela in tears. I'm doing this for her and for no other reason besides." He paused. "And you complicated matters by lying about that mechanical person. Did you think such nonsense would impress them?"

"But I—"

Pienne's door opened and the squatty man greeted us with a smile and a clap.

CHAPTER 8

Pienne was a true master of his craft. He administered another dose of his second elixir, which further strengthened my skin and made my foot even heavier. It also turned the skin up to my ankle silver.

The toady little man appeared pleased with the change. He smiled so big the shadows of his eyes disappeared into his cheeks. "Pienne doesn't know if he can help Alexander again if he is launched from another catapult." He peered at me, leaning close. "Though he must say he has not heard of anything like that before. He would venture to guess that Alexander is the only one who has ever survived such an experience." His breath smelled of fish. "So what is it like? To fly through the sky like that?"

"That wasn't flying," I said with an irritated tone. "I'll let you know what it is like when you give me the flying elixir."

Pienne gave me a look like I had lupins sticking out of my ears.

I continued, "And speaking of dangerous elixirs, it seems our Duke has created mechanical life."

Reckard rolled his eyes. His side-effect was a high-pitched voice that sounded ridiculous. I couldn't decide whether it reminded me of a lady or a small girl. So I had to stifle a laugh when he said, "You fought an elixired Guardsman. Nothing more."

It took a moment to compose myself before telling him about the server and to that he said, "Probably another elixir, maybe to give her stamina to make it through the night." He glared when a grin escaped my self-control. "Pienne, this voice is annoying!"

The toady man ignored him and leaned closer like he wanted to catch my every word before it escaped my mouth. He spoke in a whisper. "Describe what Alexander saw. Spare Pienne no detail."

I did so, even mentioning the click-whir sound that reminded me of his lab. For his part, the man didn't seem to breathe. His brows twitched, but he made no other movement. "That makes sense to Pienne. That fits with his problem."

"What problem?" Reckard and I asked at the same time.

He motioned to the tubes. "Pienne sometimes requires help with new magic. He must go to those who know and learn from them." He paced as he continued, "Pienne's sources have been quiet of late. No one responds to his questions. Pienne thought..."

"Thought what? They stopped appreciating you?"

His cheeks turned red and looked like radishes sticking out of his flesh. "Perhaps they had a better offer of money than Pienne could make? Such a possibility makes Pienne feel better."

"You two think the Duke is making mechanical people?" Reckard asked. He had a half-laugh, half-mad kind of expression. "Do you not hear what you're saying?"

Pienne rubbed his ear. "Pienne sees one potential problem. All theories on making mechanical people believe they must be made of metal refined by the hottest fire possible. Hotter than what is needed for steam engines or a blacksmith." He shrugged. "Pienne believes only a dragon's flames can produce such heat. But Pienne hasn't heard about a dragon being around here in many years."

"Could he use the Merchant's Exchange to import what he needs?" I asked. "What if there were dragons elsewhere?"

Reckard grabbed my arm. "Let's go, Ash. We are not breaking into that place unless The Misters force us. Since they're not, well, then let's start on this assignment."

I let him pull me because in one respect he was right. Yet something Pienne said had set off the voice. Something about dragons fit with something else I had heard. But what was it? There was something there...something important...but what?

Pienne followed us to the door. He scratched one of his chins, but didn't say good-bye as he closed the door.

Reckard asked, "So where to now? Where do you think she's hiding?"

"I need to mull that over and I need a drink to help me do so." Branagh's called as strong as ever. "And I need to apologize to someone, it would seem."

"Branagh's, then? Are you sure? It will take us all night for you to walk there and besides, most of that room still wants to see you dead."

I said, with as calm a voice as possible, "I want to kill Cavendish, the back-stabbing little trickster. He used me."

The voice said such an act was wrong.

True, it would be, but it would also be oh, so satisfying.

I tipped my imaginary hat to the cyclops. "Evening, Lord Mayor."

He grunted as the door swung open. The night and the warm glow of the gas light rushed in.

"Aimee expected me at the Ball," I said.

"And she knew what to do to make you panic, old chap. She played you like a cello. And because you still love her, you couldn't think straight."

I tried to punch him, but the man disappeared. In the most literal sense.

He said, from the right, "Admit the obvious. You still love her."

I tried to punch him again, and he said from the left, "It's true, is it not? That's why you treat Sheela as you do. You never stopped loving Aimee."

"Would you at least offer me the dignity of seeing who it is I'm trying to strike? I don't like hitting a lady, but in your case..." Laughter bubbled up. I bent double as the sound echoed down the alley. Reckard's voice wasn't so humorous as to earn such a round of laughter. Instead this was born of something more: a near-death experience, a ludicrous assignment, Sheela angry with me, and a supposed friend betraying me. If I didn't laugh, I'd yell until my throat was raw.

Reckard appeared several feet ahead with arms crossed. He scowled. "Do you think I want someone with your thick skin to hit me? You need to hear the truth. You need to accept the fact that you can't kill her. No matter what she does to you, you still love her."

My laughter faded. "Not anymore."

This time, he laughed. "I'm supposed to believe you?"

"Yes, I admit that deep inside I held onto some small piece of love, but after the object of such affection tosses you over the town it quenches the remaining embers of love."

Doesn't it?

"A day too late to grow up enough to realize that, don't you think, old chap? She put you through hell. No woman is worth that." He tapped his chin in thought. "Except Sheela. Look, you cannot make this business so personal. You must remain a professional." He fell in beside me as we walked, but remained out of arm's reach.

How easy for him to lecture like one of my professors at Oxford. How could I not make this affair personal on some level? There were too many emotions invested in the woman for me not to feel something...even the loathing filling me at the moment. I needed a magic elixir to let me forget, like the days after the divorce. That, or I could use a good drink. Since I couldn't seek the comforts of the first, what with Pienne's magic flowing through my veins, I'd have to take solace in the second.

Why did life have to be so damn difficult? Why was it so full of problems and pain? Not just here or there, but all the time?

The answer to that, of course, was clear. The canon tried to tell me what I didn't want to hear. I refused to acknowledge his righteous condemnation.

I said, "Don't think the business of the mechanical person is complete. I know what I saw. When someone has glass sticking in her hands or a knife sticking into his belly and there's no blood...well, that's proof enough."

Reckard waved the comment away. "The moment got to you, old chap. Nothing more."

As I turned the corner to enter the shadows of the Merchant's Exchange I said, "Then why did the Duke—"

My friend put a hand on my chest and whispered, "Stop." The high-pitched urgency in his voice restrained me from grabbing him.

Down the street waited the small company of Guardsmen. Three sat on the front steps of the Exchange while two others faced them. Their voices carried over the quiet street.

"Give me a moment," Reckard said. He had already disappeared.

As soon as I withdrew into the shadows a voice said, "What've we here?" A pair of Guardsmen faced me. Both had their swords drawn.

This was getting better every moment. Perhaps I should've felt more concerned about encountering the pair, but the lingering effects of the elixir renewed the sense of invincibility and immortality

I held my hands up. "Just trying to take a shorter route to there." I pointed towards the next intersection.

The men looked me up and down. Neither had a distinguishing feature. They resembled any other Guardsmen, like the Duke bred the same man for just such a service.

If men they were. What if he...

The way the one on the right squinted made my belly churn. He said, "This one looks familiar." He leaned forward. "Do I know you? Been to The George lately?"

"No," I answered, "I was on my way to The Gnome. Have a taste for their fish and chips. Best there is."

The Guardsmen shook his head. "You don't look The George's type, now I think about it. You look more like an Eight Bells man."

The other spoke as if irritated by our banter. "This here's a restricted area. You're trespassing."

I lowered my hands. "Once you've tasted The Gnome's fresh catch, there's nothing better. And I heard the train whistle not more than a few hours ago, meaning they should have their fish ready by now." A shrug added emphasis to my dilemma. "My choice to get there quickly was to either go this way or fly or jump over buildings. Since the last two aren't choices, well..." I smiled.

The first one's eyes grew bigger. He shook his sword at me. "That's it! That's it!" His voice went high. "The one we chased last week! The one who jumped away from the airship."

Me and my fool of a mouth.

"Not me," I said as I backed away, waving my hands. "Sorry. Must've been someone else."

The Guardsmen charged, both yelling for their captain while waving their swords about. They gave me just enough time to take a deep breath and turn my profile to them. The one who recognized me missed, stumbled forward, and received a hard fist to the back that sent him tumbling.

A sword from the other caught me in the ribs. The weapon stopped like it struck a brick wall. The jarring impact knocked it out of the man's hand.

Now I released the frustration brought about by The Misters and Reckard. Here was the opportunity for relief. I grabbed the blade and swung. Blood shot out from the man's shattered nose and splattered against the Exchange wall.

At least he was real.

"What's that?" a Guardsman in the front called. "Did you two bring the rum like we asked? Or are you louts drinking it all?"

"Hel—" the first Guardsmen's plea ended when I caught his side with the cross-guard of the bloodied sword. He rolled over and tried to defend himself by waving his own weapon about even faster. I grabbed it with my free hand, then smashed the other down, creating another spray of blood.

Both Guardsmen sobbed as they rolled around. They tried to push me away as I searched their pockets for the rum. The one who recognized me carried the bottle.

Mount Gay brand. The men knew their rum and must have pooled quite a bit of coin to buy such a quality drink. Were they celebrating, perhaps? A birthday or promotion?

"Thank you, gentlemen," I said as I twisted the top off. The smell of spices burned my nose.

"...make you pay..." the one who recognized me said. He tried to grab my foot, but I stepped out of reach.

An invisible Reckard asked, making me jump in surprise, "What are you doing?"

"Sharing a drink with my new friends." After toasting them, I drank.

An invisible hand grabbed my arm and spilled some of the rum. "We don't have time for such nonsense."

I tipped my imaginary hat. "A pleasure, gentlemen." As we rounded the corner, the other Guardsmen were nowhere to be found. "Did you have to fight them, too?"

Reckard's high-pitched voice sounded pleased. "No, but I gave them a reason to be angry enough to. I broke open a side entrance to the Exchange. That will keep them busy."

"Did you look inside to see—"

"No," he said as he continued to lead.

We passed the front steps, and I topped the rum, then left it on the bottom step. The Guardsmen would need a good drink after they explained to their superiors how they failed to keep the building secured.

Even though he was invisible, I imagined Reckard rolled his eyes as he said, "Leave you alone for two minutes and you have to find someone to fight."

"It appears I'm developing a reputation with the Guardsmen." That was not good considering The Misters' standards.

We continued on our way in silence. With my reduced speed it took an agonizingly long time to reach Branagh's. The longer it took, the more I wanted to wash the taste of the rum from my mouth. I needed an ale. A cold one. A real one.

Hansan greeted us and said, "A rough couple of days, sirs? Heard what happened at the Duke's. I must say Sheela almost convinced me to forbid you entrance. She's mighty upset and mad."

With equal parts dread and anticipation I asked, "She's here?"

"Worked non-stop since you almost died," he continued with his jovial tone. "She seems to go from thinking she saved you to thinking you died after all and she hasn't received word of it yet." He motioned to the corridor. "Well, have a good evening. Hope you survive the experience."

"What?" I asked a now-visible Reckard as he shook his head.

"You should apologize. You should do everything you can to make it up to her."

"She knows the risks of my job. She knows the dangers."

He put a hand on my shoulder. "Look, you heartless bastard, you would risk your life trying to prove to Aimee that you still love her - a cold and evil woman - and you are so nonchalant with a good woman who loves and adores you." His voice went higher. "What's wrong with you?" He disappeared. "Don't try to hit me again, either."

He didn't want to hear everything that was wrong with me. He didn't need to hear how I couldn't open my heart to the potential of breaking like that again. Aimee's betrayal showed just how dangerous love was. I couldn't risk it again.

Still I said, "I will apologize to Sheela if that's what you want."

He said from far to the right, "Yes, it is."

I started down the hall again. "Fine."

"That's the appreciation I receive for saving your life?" he asked from behind. "Do you not realize just how close you were to dying? Or is that what you wanted the whole time?"

This conversation grew as tiresome as the one with The Misters. Because Reckard was a friend, I refrained from lashing out, from speaking my mind.

"Evening, sir," Jansan said with a tone matching Hansan's. "Glad to see you up and about again. Cavendish said to send word he's looking for you. He said to wait at the door until he saw you. Said something about a nasty crowd, and the price on your head." He opened the door to the smells and sights of the room. "Have a pleasant evening, sir."

The cyclops' jovial warning followed us into the familiar room, where the familiar noise greeted us. The smell of ale tickled my nose and my mouth watered. I hurried towards an empty seat, but stopped when those at the nearest table looked over and quit talking. The table next to them looked up to see what was going on and when they saw me, they also quit talking. The surrounding tables did the same. And the ones around them sensed the sudden quiet and followed suit. A wave of silence spread throughout the room until everyone stopped to stare.

Was that how every entrance into the place would go from here on?

I yawned to show them how much I cared, and to mask the sudden urge to forget the ale and leave.

The gnome appeared, walking backwards from the tables while waving his hands. "I have this under control. You all have my assurance." As he moved closer, the crowd returned to a more moderate level of conversation, though many continued to watch. Cavendish gave a dramatic sigh as he turned around. He said, "It's about time—"

I snatched the hairy little creature up by the throat. "You lying, conniving, betraying little gnome." I pinned him against the wall. "So what's the real reason you're helping me? Or not helping, depending on the moment? Depending on your own needs? How could you salvage the disaster at the Ball? What did you mean?"

He kicked as he tried to pry my hand loose. His face turned red as he blabbered, "No—it's not like—you don't—"

Reckard moved next to the gnome. He tried to sound threatening, but his voice betrayed his intent. "Ash said you watched while they loaded him on the catapult. Is that true?"

Cavendish tried to smile. "Yes, but—"

His flesh dug beneath my nails as I squeezed harder. The tendons in his neck and the muscles contracted as he tried to take a breath. "So what game are you playing? Tell me!" I reached into his vest and pulled out a gold watch. As it spun on its chain, the Duke's badger flashed in the light. "A nice addition to your collection. Is this what you were after? You wanted a chance to pick the Duke's pocket?"

"Look out!" Reckard disappeared.

A club shattered off my back. I turned, with Cavendish still in hand, and faced three reptilians. Their tongues flicked in and out while their red eyes radiated hatred. They wore the typical lizard garb: leather straps in an 'x' across their chest, studded choker collars three inches wide around their necks, a buckle around their waist adorned in rubies and pearls, and a red or yellow or purple loincloth, depending on their clan. They all carried the spiked clubs, the ones as big around as a small tree.

Their leader, who wore a red loincloth and who held the splintered remains of his weapon, spoke with a whispery-raspy voice, "Let the gnome go."

"This thing?" I asked as I shook Cavendish. "What does he mean to you?"

"The assssuranssssse of your life."

"I have a private conversation I intend to finish. When we're done, I will be more than pleased to have a round with you."

The other two reptilians slapped their clubs in their three-fingered hands. Their leader said, "Let Cavendisssssh go."

Stupid lizards. Once they thought they would fight, there was no talking them out of it. What was it about their nature that they loved violence so much?

"I don't know what he promised you," I said, "but I know he is a liar and a betrayer. You can neither trust nor believe anything he says."

The reptilian on the end swung his club. I flinched even though he was well out of range.

Reckard grunted and sounded like he fell to the ground with a thump. I could imagine how much that hurt.

The reptilian leader - how was he different? They all looked the same - said, "We'll kill your friend unlesssss you let Cavendissssh go."

I shrugged. "What friend?"

The reptilian at the end pointed down with his club. He pushed against an invisible Reckard, who moaned. "Did your friend forget we can sssssee through hissss magic?"

Their leader said, "Let Cavendissssh go and your friend livessss."

Though it pained me to do so, I dropped the purple-faced gnome. He caught himself with his hands and knees, and coughed. "Ash...I swear I wasn't....trying to hurt you." He held his throat and coughed more. "Or get you hurt."

I shook the watch at him. "You had a chance to cut me free, but you refused. Maybe you wanted them to pull the lever. I ought to turn you over to the Guardsmen."

Stupid gnome. And to think he almost made me mad enough to kill him.

He looked at me from the corners of his eyes. "Tell me what I could have done? Really? Me? A gnome against what? Five humans, and three of them magic users, in addition to an orc?"

"You always have your own magic. You are always prepared. And you stole the watch. Cutting my bonds would have been a far simpler task."

He nodded as he glared. "But you didn't follow the plan."

My knuckles turned white as I squeezed the watch. "I tried to tell you at the catapult that I walked into a trap. She expected me. We never had surprise on our side."

More coughs rattled his small frame as he stood. "Then you're lucky to be alive." He straightened his vest, then stomped both feet. His eyes locked on the watch, but he had enough sense to refrain from asking for it. "I'm sorry, Ash. I should have helped you. Now can we have a civilized conversation?"

He didn't sound sincere enough, and I was about to question him further when Reckard moaned again. I pointed to the reptilian who pinned my friend down. "We will be civilized when your friend releases my friend." I placed a special emphasis on the word friend.

Cavendish nodded.

The lizard man's tongue flicked twice before he rested the club on his shoulder.

That was the moment when Sheela swept in. She ran straight for Cavendish and fell to her knees before the little man. She took him in both hands, much like she would a crying child, and looked him up and down. "Are you injured? Are you hurt?"

"He's fine," I said. *And lucky the lizard men are here.*

She touched his neck. "Let me get something cold to put on that. Some ice, maybe?"

As she stood, I said, "He is fine, Sheela. Leave him be." I regretted the words almost immediately.

With both fists planted on her hips, she stalked towards me, and stopped just a few inches short. She waved her finger and said, "You...you...I should...do you know..."

I made the mistake of smiling.

She slapped me. Not once, but twice. The slightest tingle arose on my cheek, but she whimpered as her hand turned the same color as the fire in the hearth.

"Sheela," I said as I reached out.

She pushed me away. "You're a bastard, Alexander Asherton." Tears ran down her cheeks as she held her hand again. "You believe you can walk in here and act as if nothing happened? Do you believe yourself so righteous and mighty that you can get away with what you did? With trying to talk to that woman?" She pushed me further away. "Leave! And never come back. I don't want to see you again."

I don't want to see you again. The same words Aimee used on the day she announced she wanted a divorce. Did she do it in private, between the two of us? No, she waited until we were with the Greenhews, those dear, dear friends. We ate dinner at their house. Aimee gave no sign of her impending declaration. She waited until Kevin cleared the dessert dishes, then spoke.

Sheela stomped away. "I need to find ice for Cavendish."

It would've been better to have kept my mouth closed. I should have let her go and saved her more pain. But thanks to the insistence of the voice I said, "Sheela, wait." When she paused and turned her head I said, "I'm sorry."

"Sorry doesn't do much. Not this time." She continued walking.

No, it might not do much, but it did enough. Didn't it?

Cavendish spoke with a tone of respect. "She was there when we found you. When the rest of us were ready to give you up for dead, she almost single-handedly carried your twisted and broken body back to town." He rubbed his throat again. "So I would say you owe her more than an apology unless you wanted to die."

Ah yes, death. That which had sought me more often of late. Despite its insistence, "I die when my masters tell me."

The gnome nodded. "Of course. The Company is all isn't it? A benevolent and merciful master." He motioned to the reptilians. "These gentlemen are but a small delegation of those in this room who would like to see you dead, regardless of The Company's desires. I spent two days trying to convince The Elders not to lose faith in you."

The fact that he spoke their name meant he was serious.

Still, I snorted as I squatted in front of him. "You sold me out. And for what? A watch."

He held his hands before him in a plea of innocence. Something in his look said he hid the truth.

For that, he received a hard poke on the chest. "It wasn't the watch, was it? You needed more information. You wanted to learn something." I poked him again, and he stepped into a reptilian's leg. "Tell me what you were after, Cavendish, or you will never see the Head of Forneil. Or this watch."

The gnome grinned in his mischievous fashion, with a glint in his eye. "To follow through on your first threat would be your death. The second would be a threat only if you survived the first one."

"What are threats among friends? Call it a warning of potential disaster." I motioned to the lizard men. "Besides, I could handle these 'gentleman.' And I use that term in the loosest sense. As for your watch?" When I feigned to throw it across the room, the gnome lunged forward, squealing at the same time. I caught him as the reptilians tried to insert themselves between us. We stood, frozen, in a dare for someone to make the first move.

Cavendish did so by stepping back and folding his arms. He rocked on his heels as he said, "Say you survive my three friends here. What about the next group? Or the next? Or this entire room? What if someone hired a dragon? I hear heat is a weakness for your particular magic, and you can't move fast enough to elude such a nasty beast."

His tone earned a glare. My hands twitched and tried to move for his throat again. "Is that a threat?"

The gnome gave a half-shrug. "What are threats among friends? Call it a warning of potential disaster."

I wanted to hit the hairy little creature and knock the smug look off his face. He deserved it.

My expression must have betrayed my intent, for the reptilian leader lowered his splintered club until it rested between Cavendish and me.

As I glared at the lizard man I asked the gnome, "What did you want at the Ball? What were you really after?"

He closed his eyes as if he contemplated a deep, profound thought. After a moment he asked, "What does it matter what I might need so long as you acquire the Head?"

The implications of his answer made me stand straighter. "It matters. It matters because I need to know the extent of your loyalty. I have defended you and your name. Perhaps I was wrong to do so." I tried to push by the reptilians, but they stood their ground. Their leader and I locked eyes. "I've always wanted a nice pair of reptile-skinned boots."

His tongue flicked three times before he said, "I haven't feasssssted on human flessssh in dayssss."

Threats on top of threats. Maybe the time had arrived to settle all these differences with fists. That might be the simplest of ways. It might be the most satisfying, too.

I folded my arms. "Chew on my tough skin, snake-boy."

When the reptilian took a step towards me, Cavendish jumped between us and said, "Stop. Both of you. Stop!" When we looked down, he put his hands on his waist and said, "Fine, Ash. I'll tell you what I wanted if you give me the watch."

I held it out and when he took it, I didn't let go of the chain. "The truth. All of it."

The hairy little creature sighed. "I was going to help you escape. I followed you and slipped in behind them." He wrung his hands. "But...they mentioned the gnome delivery. And you know my brothers have a problem with kidnappings and disappearances. And..."

"And you wanted to hear more. You decided I was worth the sacrifice to learn who has taken your brothers?" I took a deep breath to hold back the anger threatening to explode. "I need a drink."

He spoke louder. "I did what I had to. And then there was Frengarn. He is no ordinary orc. His involvement with Duke Schaever is significant." He tried to stand taller, which looked humorous on such a short frame. "Besides, I knew you'd survive."

Again, I wanted to strike the smug look from his face. I wanted to fight the reptilians. I wanted to be free from the tangles of the intrigues binding me. Yet instead of doing any of those, I released the chain. As Cavendish tucked the watch into his vest I asked, "Don't you realize what I had to go through just to live?" I snarled. "You—"

He shrank back and squealed. "I learned valuable information!"

The reptilians leaned forward in anticipation. Every eye in the room watched us, except for Sheela, who cleared a table with her back turned.

Could I take them all on? Did I want to?

If I tried, I'd be banned from Branagh's forever. Then where would I go to get a decent drink?

Could I blame Cavendish for his predicament? For reasons I didn't completely understand, his family refused to let him associate with them. I believed it due to his fascination with all things mechanical, but he never said. It was one matter to be shunned by friends. It was an entirely different one to be exiled from your own race. I could sympathize with the hairy little creature.

To a point.

The voice told me to take another deep breath and exhale slow. After doing so, I asked in a less accusatory tone, "What information, Cavendish? And who is Frengarn?"

He blinked several times, then tugged his beards. "Frengarn is an orc, but as I said, he is not an ordinary one. He is one of their leaders, one of their strategists. He's supposed to be the mastermind behind their defeat of Reganas Five." He stopped as his face turned red, then quickly added, "And he is dangerous."

"What's Reganas Five?" I asked.

"Nothing you need to know, human," the reptilian leader answered. "Nothing consssserning you."

"I learned much that is of interest to us. To you," Cavendish said to change the subject. "The Duke himself has taken an interest in these affairs. He shelters the Greenhews in one of his homes on George Lane, which is a safe house for The Gatherers. He offered to let Aimee stay with them and assured her it has the utmost security." The gnome scratched his chin.

So the game had begun again. I held the question about Reganas Five for now. To pursue an answer would waste time and effort, so I'd be patient. Besides, I needed to know why my heart beat faster at the mention of Aimee? I asked, trying not to look at Sheela, "She accepted the Duke's invitation?"

"Of course," Cavendish answered, "though she expressed concern about her duties at the Bank. The Duke assured her that with the building half-destroyed he could convince her superiors to allow her a holiday."

"Any word of the Head?"

He bit his lip, then said, "Unfortunately, no. I wish she had spoken of it, but they passed back into the crowd and I heard nothing else."

"Nothing of your brothers?"

He shook his head.

I sneered. "Now that is a real pity."

Reckard, who had reappeared, stepped beside me. He placed a restraining hand on my shoulder. "The Misters have given us one chance. We shouldn't risk it for any reason."

"Don't worry," I said with an accusatory tone. "Cavendish always has a plan. Correct? You will work twice as hard to help me because I might help you get more information about your brothers in return, and maybe something about this Frengarn." I paused. "Correct?"

The gnome nodded. "Of course. Can a friend do otherwise?"

Borrowing Frank Greenhew's annoying mannerism, I said under my breath, "They don't sell out their friends when faced with death."

My fellow Company thief motioned to the lizards. "Tell your snakes to leave, gnome. They have no reason to hear any of this."

Cavendish rubbed his throat, but didn't look at the reptilians. Instead, he waved them away. "Thank you, gentlemen, for lending a hand. I believe Ash comprehends the situation."

The leader said, "Are you ssssure? He'sssss a tricky one thissss one."

"If you see him attacking me again, you'll be at my side, right?" He waved them away a second time.

The lizard men took one long look at me, and the leader shook his broken club in warning. Their tongues darted in and out before they headed for the nearest fireplace. As they went, the noise of the tavern returned to its normal level again.

Still, many either watched or glared.

All except for Sheela, who continued to ignore me altogether.

A sharp pain of guilt shot through my chest.

Why?

The voice answered, "Because you're a fool."

Cavendish cleared his throat. "Your masters have assigned both of you to this? What an intriguing development."

Reckard motioned to me with his thumb. "It was the only way I could save him. The Misters were ready to administer the third potion."

I let my continued frustration fill my voice. "And look at what you've gotten yourself involved with. You were foolish, Reckard."

The man nodded. He stared at Cavendish as he said, "Sure, but it's also what I do for a friend."

But only if the friend is a lady whom you adore.

The gnome gave him a blank expression. "A fine gesture, I'm sure. But let's return to the business at hand, which is getting into the townhome and giving this to our dear Aimee." He held a small vial of purple elixir between his thumb and index finger.

Since he waited for one of us to do so, I indulged his dramatic pause and asked, "Pray tell, what is that?"

"Something to compel her to tell us the truth," he said, not bothering to hide his delight, "to tell us where the Head is located. It will work so well she'll tell us anything we want to know."

My heart beat faster and I felt my face go flush with excitement. I asked, with perhaps a little too much eagerness, "Everything?"

Cavendish pulled back and tucked the vial into a vest pocket. "Yes, everything. I've used it several times and always to the best effect. Now listen, and I will tell you what our plan is."

Our plan? Or my plan?

This could be the opportunity I dreamt of all of those countless nights during the recovery. This could be the opportunity to learn the truth about our past, the truth about why she left, and the truth of why she tried to kill me.

And whether she ever loved me.

CHAPTER 9

I waited at the corner of George Lane and Pear Tree Close, almost in the heart of Campden itself. Two streets to the north, Saint James' spires loomed like sentinels of hope in a world gone mad with magic and science. Two streets to the east, the broken hull of the Bank stood as a reminder of the dangers surrounding my person. Before me stood a town home similar to thirty along the way. It rose three stories and was an architectural beauty. Bay windows on the first floor and balconies at every window of the second floor allowed for views over the neighbors. A chimney stood at each end. The bottom was no less modest, with engravings around each window frame. The brown stones had been painted white, and the trim a sky blue. However, the only mark that told of its distinguished ownership was the small crest on top of the front door. It was the coat of arms of the Duke: a shield with the lightning bolt diagonally across its face and a fist in the upper left corner and the badger in the lower right.

No one had entered or left in the last three hours, and the windows were so well curtained as to keep movement within from being detected. To the casual passerby, it would have appeared either quiet or empty. But as night fell, light escaped from the edges of the windows, indicating someone was home.

Too bad Pienne removed my jumping ability. I could have leapt onto the rooftop, entered an upper window, and no one would have known.

Instead, I had to wait. With my lead foot, there would be no jumping, there'd be no running. There would only be waiting. And waiting. And waiting.

I watched an airship circle the town near Branagh's entrance. Its bright light glowed in the dark sky as it searched for the errant refugees or roving orcs. It reminded me of the larger stakes involved in my mission. Yes, it was personal, but it went beyond the problems and past history of two people. Who was I, a miserable man, to determine the destiny of the magical realm? Yet dwelling on such thoughts, on the bigger problems, added more urgency to myself, and a greater desire to untangle myself from the web of intrigues.

What took Cavendish so long? And Reckard? Had they been captured already? Did they not realize I had questions ready for Aimee? Questions that gnawed at me for years? And I was about to be presented with perhaps the only chance to have them answered?

The gnome said the Duke kept at least one reptilian and one cyclops at each of his residences. The man took no chances on having his enemies use magic against him. Yet Cavendish assured me that his friends had taken care of the reptilian. The cyclops, though, he promised to save for me.

So I continued to wait as night descended on the street. I kept to the shadows as the streetlights were lit by two boys of twelve or thirteen. Their light poles turned the gas on for each lamp, then lit them with the flick of a flame.

The last of the workers, merchants mostly and some of the wealthiest in the city, ended their days in pursuit of the comforts of their homes. Some returned to the streets with their wife or mistress or lady friend, all dressed in their finest and destined, most likely, to one of the theaters or the music hall. Some went by carriage and some preferred to walk.

I couldn't blame the latter, for the evening had turned comfortable. While the warmth of the day still lingered, the promise of a cool night awaited and the air rested in the pleasant middle state, undecided as to which side it preferred. For those destined for their favorite cafe or inn, the temperature would be perfect for sitting outside to enjoy their meal.

Those had always been savored moments with Aimee. The real woman revealed herself layer-by-layer, bite-by-bite, and course-by-course. It was always as if a magical transformation took hold of her, like a caterpillar taking the last step to becoming a majestic butterfly, with yellows and gold, and flying free.

The light in the door of the townhome shifted just before the door itself opened. Cavendish stepped onto the landing and motioned for me.

I hurried as fast as possible, and the little man all but jumped up and down. Pulling my foot up all six of the steps forced me to stop to catch my breath at the top.

The gnome grabbed my hand and whispered, "I thought you could move quicker."

I thought about telling him Pienne's additional dose of elixir made my foot even heavier, but decided silence was the better option since we entered the house proper.

The foyer was just wide enough for a single person to walk through. A rug ran its length and in the middle of it was the Duke's crest, woven in gold in all of its glory. A narrow chandelier hung from the high ceiling. Few of its candles had been lit. The only other feature worth noting was the nook on the right just as we entered. In it rested a wooden stool where the doorman would be stationed, hiding from view from those within the house, but strategically situated for new arrivals. The fact that the stool rose to a height equal with my chest said it had been specially crafted for the attending cyclops.

When Cavendish closed the door, he stopped to whisper, "I have the layout of the house. There are three floors. On this one, there's the kitchen, the dining room, a saloon for sitting, one for smoking, and a library. On the first floor is the drawing room, with chambers beyond and a small area for the servants." He held up three fingers. "The second floor holds the Duke's chamber and a chamber for his significant other. There is a sitting room between them. There's also a game saloon, and two smaller servant chambers."

"So Aimee will be on the first floor." At least I wouldn't have to climb two flights of stairs. A small blessing in and of itself. "Let's be off."

The gnome grabbed my arm. "Wait. We located the cyclops."

I nodded to the nook. "That much I figured out already. Where is he?"

At that moment, we heard a thud, like a foot striking a wall, followed by a grunt.

Cavendish said, "Reckard distracted the creature for you, though how long he can keep it away I don't know. I don't plan to wait around to find out." He started to pull me, but paused. "Oh, and there's no sign of the reptilian, as promised."

I would have to remember just how loyal a reptilian could be. Useful information.

The first room was empty, save for the light haze of smoke from a recently enjoyed pipe. The full, rich scent of Latikia still hung in the air, stirring a desire to throw myself in a chair to enjoy a cigar. If ever the Greenhews had something about them to appreciate, it was Frank's smoking room. He always kept a well-stocked humidor. Even though Aimee frowned on such excesses and claimed smoking was the same as burning money, she indulged me on occasion.

We passed the sitting saloon, which also sat empty. A lone lamp burned, giving just enough light to guide a restless soul seeking a different locale in the middle of the night.

At the end of the hallway awaited the dining room. Already the table had been set for the next meal. Golden rings engraved with the badger held cloth-wrapped forks and knives. They rested next to white plates with a design along the rim of a twisting rope of blue interlaced with a gold thread. In the middle of the table sat a bouquet of roses and carnations and decorative green leaves and the little white flower I always forgot the name of.

After making sure the room was clear, we turned to the left, and climbed up the stairs. Cavendish helped me, or tried to, by lifting my leg. I let him do so even though his small frame could do little.

Halfway up he huffed and puffed and grew more determined. At three-fourths of the way he said, "This is slowing us down. The longer we're in this house, the more danger we're in."

"I'm doing the best I can." My thigh burned like Frank Greenhew had set fire to it.

Finally we reached the top and entered the first floor proper where the drawing room greeted us. Four chairs sat along the edge of a circular rug eight feet in diameter. A pattern of twisting rose vines and petals covered it. A fifth chair sat in front of a small wooden desk with a cherry stain. Two portraits hung on the wall, one on each side. The left one was a young gentleman wearing an officer's uniform with two golden eagles on each shoulder. Duke Schaever's great grandfather if my memory served. Then the opposite portrait of the portly woman with golden pears on her earrings and necklace was, I assumed, his wife.

Cavendish pulled on my hand and led me into another hallway with six doors.

Eagerness filled my voice as I asked, "So which one is she behind?" The quicker we found her, the quicker my questions would be answered.

He shrugged. "We'll find out soon enough. Are you ready?"

Reckard's high-pitched voice said, "I am." He appeared in front of us.

I gasped despite myself, and Cavendish fumbled a cylinder he had just removed from his pocket. The company of my friend made me look across the room. "So where is the cyclops?"

A smile broke across his face. "Enjoying a nice slumber in the kitchen though he will have a big lump on his head come morning. For some reason, I enjoyed that."

"Quiet!" the gnome said. "We must be as silent as the mouse, for the slightest sound could bring the house down on top of us." He reached into another pocket and removed a clear lens, which he fit into the right eye of his goggles. It magnified his eye to three times the size of his other. Appropriately enough, the device was called a magic eye. Using the cylinders, a person could inspect another place without physically being there. I had used such magic on several occasions.

Cavendish looked at me and blinked, then rolled the cylinder, attached to a string, under the door.

As I loomed over him I whispered, "What do you see?"

He turned his head left and right. He looked up and down. The magic eye would follow his movements. "This room is empty. I must commend the Duke on his choice of furnishings. Quite lush, with a four-poster bed, a reading table, a wall of books, a washing table where it appears he has a magic fountain for fresh water." With the cylinder in hand again, he nodded to the next room.

There, he repeated the process of rolling the cylinder under the door, and looking all about. "There is someone here, but not your former wife. It's a lady. An elf dressed in black. She—" He gasped as he yanked the cylinder out. He motioned to the first door as he pulled me by the arm.

Reckard opened it and took my other arm just as the second door opened. They pulled me in the same moment the occupant of the other room stepped into the hallway. A woman asked with the light twilly, bird-like accent of an elf, "Who's there? I will not have spies watching my every move." She walked down the hallway towards us. "I will not stand for this. Do you hear me?"

As she approached our door, Cavendish and I pressed ourselves into the shadows. Reckard disappeared.

The woman peered within the room. She stood six feet tall, and straight, blonde hair fell to her waist in contrast to her black leather clothing. She was as lithe and angular as most elves, a fact highlighted by the snug fitting bodice and the tight leggings. Her face held the same angles, the same flat nose, the same sunken eyes, and protruding brow. What stood out, though, were her blood red lips, and her white irised eyes. I had seen that combination only once.

Then, I had reached the peak of my magic addiction, just weeks prior to joining The Company. I needed the numbing magic like a suckling babe needed milk. My body shook without control as it craved the release from the phantom pain of the burns.

In desperation, I offered myself to one such as she: a living embodiment of magic. What were they called? Treyo Duthkus if I recall the name. The literal translation from elfish meant 'one who is a fountain of energy.' The practical application of such a person meant they controlled an unending source of magic, to the point they were the essence of magic. They held great powers and could do almost anything they desired. They were usually surrounded by a group of men or women, depending on their pleasures, who did anything they were bid in exchange for receiving a constant magic high.

Yes, I stooped low enough to offer myself to one such as she. Even though serving one meant no longer having any dignity left, for such elves were not kind to their subjects, not unless you became a favored pet.

They were dangerous were the Treyo Duthkus.

Powerful. Cold. Deadly.

She stepped into the room and held up her left hand. A light blazed on top of her palm, throwing lights as bright as that of the noon sun across the room.

I shielded my eyes and waited for her to blast us with her powers.

Something in her room crashed to the floor. She rolled her tongue in the back of her throat, an elfish sign of anger, and hurried away. "I know you're there. You cannot hide from me." Her voice disappeared as she entered her room and closed the door.

Cavendish let out a long breath. "If Reckard survives, we must thank him. I don't like being in the same house as one of them."

As the hairs on my arms relaxed, I asked, "Why would the Duke be keeping her here?"

"Did you notice the bracelet on her wrist?" When I shook my head, he frowned. "Be more attentive, Ash. The smallest details can determine success or failure." He held his arm up, then wrapped his fingers around his wrist. "An ivory bracelet inlaid with six pearls in perfect symmetry. What does that tell you?"

"Someone is courting her and buying expensive gifts?"

He rolled his eyes. "A bonded slave. And I'm sure she is none too happy about her condition. The Duke is a more powerful man than we thought. He had to do something we don't want to know about to capture her. I don't want to think of what use she will be put to."

I tried to follow him back to the hallway, but he held his hand out. "No. You wait here. I'll signal when I find her." He continued on, and I watched from around the corner.

Something struck the elf's door. She said, "I locked it. Do you think I would be foolish enough not to cover your escape?"

Cavendish all but ran past the elf's room. He stopped at the next door and rolled his cylinder beneath it. He looked left, then right, then up, then down. After a quick look left again, he pulled his cylinder out.

He motioned for me to return to the room as he darted down the way.

The door opened, and my good friends the Greenhews stepped out. They both wore white robes, which exposed bare feet and bare legs up to their knees.

Bonni hurried to the elf's room. "I told you I heard what sounded like fighting next door."

Frank said, "But we were...why don't we..." He threw his hands up. "She's powerful enough to deal with her own problems." Under his breath, he added, "Though I wonder if she might join us."

Something heavy struck the wall within the elf's room. The impact shook the floor.

Bonni pointed. "See? She might need help."

Behind them, Cavendish worked at investigating the next room. He blended with the shadows so well I had a hard time spotting him. He faced the Greenhews, keeping his free eye on them, as he moved his head all around.

Frank sighed. "If it will make you feel better and keep your mind from wandering so much, then we will see what's happening." He knocked on the door. "Yasminn, do you require any assistance?" When no one answered, he knocked louder. "Yasminn?"

Cavendish finished with the third room and moved across the hallway to the fourth. He rolled his cylinder beneath it.

Frank knocked again, then tried the knob.

Another crash sounded from within and the elf said, "I see you now. Yes, I do. You're a man. Did you expect to catch me unawares? Did you believe me defenseless? Or does your master desire to break me? How does this feel?"

Reckard gave a high-pitched yell, and there was another sound of something heavy, like a person, striking the wall.

He couldn't be left alone in there to be hurt or to die. I owed him that much. But what could I do?

Bonni rapped on the door. "Yasminn! Let us in and we'll help you capture the intruder." She knocked again. "Please."

Cavendish finished at the fourth door. He looked between the Greenhews, who blocked his way to the fifth door. He weighed the cylinder in his hand.

The elf asked, "What do you want?"

Reckard yelled again, and the wall beside me shook.

The fifth door opened, and Aimee stepped out. When it concerned sleeping, she always eschewed social modesty for freedom, meaning she believed in a minimum amount of clothing. However, she would attempt to practice politeness in strange surroundings. So the fact that she wore a thin gown meant she was not completely comfortable in the house. I could still see her bare legs, though, all the way to her naked hips and buttocks. She had some of the most beautiful legs ever bestowed upon a woman. They were long and slender, yet had a smooth shape from thigh to calf. Nothing bulged and there were no sharp angles, like a knee might have.

She was such a beautiful woman.

Yet you are so evil, the depths of which I will soon learn.

"What's the matter?" she asked as she rubbed her eyes.

Bonni put her hands on her hips. "Someone has broken into the house and attacked Yasminn. She refuses to answer the door."

"She's an elf." Aimee shrugged as she folded her arms. "She can take care of herself."

Yasminn screamed as Reckard yelled.

"Do not come any closer," the elf said. "This is a final warning."

"Can you not do something?" Bonni asked. "Blow the door open?"

"Please?" Frank said, holding his hands in a mocking plea. Under his breath, he added, "We were in the middle of..."

Aimee gave them both a knowing look as she motioned them back. "This will take a moment." She squatted next to the door and cupped her hands together over the floor.

Reckard would never survive all four attacking him. Something had to be done, but what? Attack all three outside the door?

This smelled of the Galley Slave affair. Cavendish had worked out an elaborate scheme that fell apart after ten minutes. And how did he compensate? By running away, only to return after I knocked four people senseless.

I need to get us out of this mess.

I hit my fist in my palm, then stared at my hands, then at the wall separating me from the elf's room.

Perhaps?

I stepped into the room and pressed my back against the wall opposite from Yasminn. I took a deep breath and glanced down at my foot.

Big steps, Ash. The biggest you can muster.

With high leg lifts, I set out. My left foot hit the floor with a 'whoomp' sound. Once, twice, three times. I lowered my shoulder and slammed into the wall. The impact was enough to shake a bit of the plaster loose. It also made a loud thump. But other than that?

Nothing.

At least until a painting fell to the floor. The cracking of the frame sounded like two pistols firing at once.

"What was that?" Frank asked. "It came from the other room."

My shoulder throbbed just the slightest bit.

So I knew what a ball from a catapult felt like when it struck a stone wall and bounced off. I never imagined I would be so kin to such a weapon. A sword? Yes. A catapult ball? No.

Frank moved closer to the room. "Do you remember this door being open?"

The elf yelled, "I have you now!"

I couldn't break through the wall fast enough to reach Reckard. What else could I do?

Frank moved into the doorway. "I don't know who is here, but you had best give yourself up. You won't escape." Under his breath he added, "You will burn like paper."

I took the first round from him when his home burned in his determination to kill me. He claimed the second when he carried me to the catapult. Now it was time to make it the best of three decision. I wouldn't lose to the likes of Frank Greenhew. He wouldn't know the satisfaction of besting me for good.

I grabbed a decorative pitcher from the dresser. As Frank created one of his flames to light the room, I threw it and followed behind.

He never saw the projectile. His own flames obscured it until it smashed him in the face. The impact sounded like a rotten board cracking. He moaned as he stumbled backwards into the hall.

"Love?" Bonni asked.

A second later I slammed into him, and we crashed into the wall. He had been holding his nose, so his belly took the full brunt of the impact. He grunted in pain and doubled-over.

I rolled off him, and moved towards Bonni, who backed away with eyes wide. "You! You! How—"

"Stay back!" Aimee said as she stood. A black ball smoldered with purple smoke where her hands had been. She grabbed Bonni and pulled her to the side. "Watch what you're doing!"

The air shimmered in waves from Bonni's fingertips. I ducked beneath the blow and the impact struck Frank, rolling him over and over and over until he reached the drawing room.

"Love!" Bonni reached for her husband while Aimee spun her away.

Smoke poured from the black ball at a frenzied pace.

I reached the two ladies and grabbed Aimee by the hair before she could turn around. She shrieked and said, "Who—"

"Take a guess," I said as I jerked her head back so she could see me. "Surprised?"

If she was, all signs of it quickly disappeared.

Oh, how you change airs from one moment to the next.

She sneered. "You are about to be the one surprised, dear."

"If you're talking about the bomb...well, I've already survived two of yours. Have I not?"

She glared, then spit in my face.

Bonni reached behind and released one of her air blasts. It spun me around, which caused Aimee to turn and face her own creation. As she still had Bonni in hand, it caused that lady to be the closest.

"Bonni, no—"

The explosion drowned Aimee's remaining words. I tried to draw both women away. Why? Because of the instinct to protect the fairer sex? Or because it was the right thing to do? Maybe because the voice approved?

Bonni proved she still had some wits about her. She hit the explosion with an equal force of air, driving the brunt of the blast into the door, which shattered into hundreds of splinters that flew into the room as quick as crossbow bolts. Still, the reaction of the air and the blast knocked us onto the floor.

A clump of Aimee's hair tore off in my fist.

My former wife pulled Bonni up and said, "Hit him with everything you can." The venom in her voice went beyond mere hatred.

The force of the subsequent air rolled me down the hallway. Only when I struck something hard did I stop. That something happened to be a face I had seen once before. And that once was enough to burn it in my mind forever.

The mechanical serving lady at the Duke's Ball.

She gave me a long look before turning her gaze upon the others. She wore the same black outfit with the white apron on which was stitched the Duke's badger. After planting her fists on her hips she spoke with as natural a tone as any person. "What is the meaning of this disturbance? You are guests! Can you not respect my master's property?"

Aimee and Bonni leaned on each other as they faced the creature. It was Aimee who said, "We have intruders in the house, Roberta." She pointed to me. "There is one of them. I suggest you secure him first."

The woman reached for me, but I scrambled backwards. Her hands showed no signs of damage. They appeared to be completely healed as she grabbed me by the shirt and lifted me like I weighed little more than an insect.

"Wait," I said. "I tried to help you. Remember? At the Ball?"

Aimee pointed to the elf's room. "Another is in there though it appears Yasminn is gaining control of the situation."

The serving creature hurried to the room. Both Aimee and Bonni shied from it as it passed them.

"Let me go," I said. Besides the problem that a woman no taller that five and one half feet carried me over her shoulder like a sack of potatoes was the iron-like hold she had on me. "This isn't what you think."

"Do you require assistance?" the creature asked the elf.

"No," she answered as she held Reckard, who choked and gagged, by the neck.

The elf raised one brow while the other remained in place. "Another has come to kill me?"

"No." *Will anyone listen?* "I've come to kill her." I pointed at Aimee.

At that moment, Cavendish made his reappearance. The sight of him made the elf draw back and hiss. "What do you want?"

"Just this one," the gnome said as he buried a needle in Aimee's calf.

Aimee cried out. She sank to the floor as she turned.

The mechanical creature said, still with a neutral voice undisturbed by the surrounding chaos, "These are guests within my master's home and therefore are under my protection."

The thought of striking a woman settled uneasy in my belly. To hurt one of the fairer sex? The canon refused to consider the possibility.

Yet the creature holding me was not a woman. She—it—was—

Not a real person, Ash. Do what you must.

I beat the back of its head and it felt as if I struck solid metal. As I continued, my blows did little besides make her head twitch. I grabbed her hair and pulled with all my strength. At first, nothing happened, but then her hair shifted. The creature's head leaned back as the skin moved with the hair. Thus encouraged, I pulled all the harder. A rip sounded, like a sheet tearing in half.

Most of the hair came off in my hand, along with most of her face. What it revealed was a skull made of black metal. A small opening with a screen sat where the ear should have been. The eyes moved about in a random fashion and she moaned through a mouth with too natural looking teeth. A chill ran up my back at the sight.

"The eyes," Cavendish said with a voice on the edge of panic. "Take out her eyes."

If he called the creature 'it' or 'thing' or 'horror' or anything but 'her', I would've obeyed without hesitation. But calling it a woman made me pause.

That's when the creature threw me across the elf's room. I landed against the bed, cracking the footboard. A cloud of feathers and goose down filled the surrounding air. As quick as I tried to clear them out of my face, a thought entered my mind.

I grabbed the bedding and threw it at the elf.

It didn't result in the hoped-for effect. Instead of covering the room, they obscured me further. Even that did little good as I arose from the bed, in the grip of an elven spell. My left foot lifted off the floor last. My head bumped against the ceiling, then I flew across the way and struck the serving lady, who lashed out in every direction. It didn't arise, though, as I did.

The elf raised her one brow again. "Full of surprises, aren't we?"

I stepped over Aimee. "Let me take this woman and we'll bother you no more. Our quarrel isn't with you."

I refuse to let you deny me this opportunity. Nothing will stand between me and the answers that have eluded me for so long.

The elf laughed a deep, throaty laugh very unbecoming of a lady. "Do you believe the magic of an elixir can compare to that which I command? Yours is but a parlor trick, a jester's amusement for the king, compared to what I can do." She moved forward with her head lowered, watching from beneath her brow. "Learn what it means to fear."

My skin itched and burned all over. Spiders appeared from the air. As they materialized, they covered my body. I swatted at them, but couldn't knock them off. I yelled and danced around as my legs and arms burned from a thousand bites.

The elf laughed again.

I closed my mouth, but the spiders pried my lips open and crawled inside. Then between my teeth. Then over my tongue, hundreds of tiny legs tickling my taste buds. They crawled into my ears and into my nose. I spit and snorted and tried to smash my ears against my shoulders. Still they crawled and stung. They moved up my nose and filled my head with the scent of dirt and the acrid smell of venom. They moved down my throat, making me gasp for air.

The elf took hold of my chin and forced me to look at her. Her face melted and contorted into a demon with black eyes and a tongue of fire. Her angles turned sharper and stretched until she stood ten feet in height. She spoke with the roaring of flames. "Do you fear now, human? Do you understand what real magic can do?"

My lungs screamed. My belly bulged with the spiders. The hallway spun behind the elf and all I wanted to do was cry. My knees buckled, but she held me up.

She drew my face to hers. I wanted to kiss her, to caress her. I needed to be full of her sensation. My lips pleaded for her.

The elf brought my mouth to hers and instead of quenching the desire, my mouth burned and my head became engulfed in flames. Her fire seared, yet I wanted more. It consumed, yet I couldn't get enough. Should I cry or should I scream or should I moan?

A voice pierced the confusion. "I understand what a good weapon can do."

The elf cried out. I fell to my knees and immediately, the burning and stinging ceased. The spiders disappeared, and the hallway returned to normal.

She moaned and crumpled into a heap. Over her stood Reckard with a bloody dagger in his hand. He still held his throat with the other. "Let's go, Ash. Gather Aimee and I'll take Cavendish."

I stood and did as told.

"You. Cannot." The elf held her hand out and Reckard kicked it. A pop and crack sounded as the woman's wrist went limp.

Reckard's tone carried a deep loathing. "Lie still if you want to live." He cradled Cavendish in his arms like he might a baby.

I threw Aimee over my shoulder. Her heat and her breathing were much like they were on those many nights we shared a bed. They reminded me of better moments.

We stepped around the mechanical creature, with its metal face and marble-like eyes rolling in their sockets. It sounded as if it cried, but it had no tears. It only twitched its head left and right.

We moved towards the drawing room, with Reckard in the lead.

The elf gave us no more trouble. No one tried to stop us, not even Bonni, who attended her bleeding husband. And so, we departed the Duke's home and entered the streets of Campden, victorious at last.

CHAPTER 10

The moment had arrived. All the questions that ran through my mind, all the doubts that kept me awake on slow and painful nights, and all the worries that I could have done more were about to be put to rest. How many times had I dreamt of the chance to ask just one of the many questions?

Aimee sat in a wooden, straight-backed chair with worn stain both on the seat and the back of the same type I imagined a Guardsman would place a suspected individual in for an interrogation. There was something about the simplicity of the design of such a piece of furnishing that begged for someone to be strapped down and be forced into questioning. With its thick legs, it allowed us to strap her wrists to them, well away from the other. We also took the extra measure of tying each finger to the chair so she couldn't form one of her explosive surprises. With its board across the top and the rest open, it allowed us to strap her upper body into place. The only piece it lacked was a taller back to let us secure her head.

She sat there, enveloped in a bright light emanating from a two-foot high lamp on a table. Its strength cut through her gown and exposed every detail of her body. Some I had forgotten, like the mole on the left side of her naval and the dimple just above her hips. The small tattoo, no larger than a shilling, of a rose on her right hip was new.

The sight stirred long dormant desires. All I had to do was reach out and touch her flesh, feel its smoothness again. She was so close. Yet she was as far away as ever.

If Reckard and the gnome noticed her beauty, they disguised it with scowls.

And speaking of angry, Aimee glared into the darkness where the three of us waited. The Misters would've approved of our arrangements. It felt strange being in their position. Could I make my voice as cold and distant as theirs?

Aimee all but spit. "I know you're watching, Alexander. I know you're hoping to learn something new. But let me assure you that you will regret this. I will track you down and kill you. I will make your death slow and painful. That, I promise."

"You have already tried to kill me twice, yes?" I glanced at Reckard and couldn't help but grin. My voice went higher and raspier. "What makes you believe you shall succeed a third time? Two were enough, yes?"

Reckard shook his head as his scowl gave way to a grin.

She squirmed, testing her bonds. "All it takes is for one attempt to succeed. You know I never make a promise I cannot keep."

That earned a laugh. "Except for the promise to remain married until death and through both good times and bad, yes? Or was that not really a promise?"

The woman glared in my general direction.

So cold. So proud. So achingly beautiful.

Cavendish held a syringe with a long needle and a purple liquid within. What I failed to notice before were black swirls twisting and curling and giving it a rather sinister appearance. He tapped the needle, releasing the bubbles of air. "If you gentlemen don't mind, I'll administer the elixir."

"Hmmmm," Reckard said with an even bigger grin. "You should make it as painful as you can. We all owe her much."

Cavendish stepped into the circle of light. "Oh, I assure you it will be most painful."

At the sight of the elixir, Aimee's eyes grew wide as if she recognized it. She spit at the gnome. "Get away you disgusting creature. Don't touch me with that. If you do, I promise you'll regret it."

I said, "Perhaps we should make sure you don't live long enough to keep all of these valuable promises, yes? Do you want to make another one?" The more I talked, the less I found imitating The Misters so amusing. Instead, all the old anger arose. All the resentment and pain followed behind that, all the emotions and confusion that drove me to seek the peace of escape offered by the magic.

To make it worse, the scars on my face throbbed.

"Mock me, Alexander. Torture me. But know this truth." Aimee licked her lips. "I have friends in places more powerful than you can imagine. If anything happens to me, if I cannot make you pay for this, then they will. You will never know peace. You will never be able to escape."

I started into the light, but Reckard grabbed my arm. He whispered, "She's trying to drive you mad. She's trying to force you into a mistake. Keep your wits about you, old chap."

He was right, and the voice agreed. I would keep my composure. I wouldn't let her control me.

You are always the manipulator, Aimee. How easy I make it for you.

Cavendish moved beside her and said, "You won't enjoy this, I assure you."

As he lifted the syringe, she threw herself at him with such force that her chair jumped a foot in the air. She slammed into him and he sprawled backwards. The syringe rolled across the floor and stopped at the edge of the light.

Aimee gasped as her chair teetered. She crashed to the floor and moaned when she fell on her left arm. Yet she still tried to bite Cavendish, only inches from her.

The gnome scrambled away with an expression between loathing and fear.

I pushed past Reckard and into the circle of light. With the syringe in hand, I approached Aimee.

"I was wondering if you'd be brave enough to face me." She tried to spit at me, too, but with her face almost against the floor, she could do so little. "You're a coward and a liar, Alexander. And a hypocrite."

"In what way?" I asked as I bent over her. "Like the time I took the assassin's blade for you? Yes, what a cowardly and hypocritical act. I should have let him kill you. That would have been braver. Not actually living with you." Like I had often done while we lay next to each other, I stroked her arm.

Our eyes locked. Where I used to see love reflected in those beautiful circles, I now saw contempt.

"Oh, you had your moments," she said, her voice still seething. "You could be warm and sociable. You could charm like a modern Romeo. But more often than not, you hid behind the bishop's garb and lied to yourself about who you were. Now you hide behind the false powers of your masters, and you lie to yourself about what you want. You sold all of your precious ideals and notions of righteousness for the temporary escape of the elixirs."

I held my arms wide as much for the act as to keep them away from her. "Then enlighten me further. You know what I want? Tell me. During our time together, you were always quick to tell me what to do and when to do it."

She took a deep breath to let the moment of anticipation last even longer. "What you really want is to forget me." She laughed softly at first, then louder. "And here I am returned to ruin your life further, you pathetic fool of a man. You'll never be able to forget me, will you? Visions of my naked body are burned in your mind. You stare at me even now, remembering the times we shared. You wish we could do that again." Her grin was like that on a cat about to pounce on an unsuspecting mouse. "You and your stupid notion of moments. You act like each special second should be savored. You believed your love was a moment worth treasuring, so you escape into its memory over and over. The truth is, you were a pawn. Nothing more."

Her words struck deep, resonating like the final note of a symphony.

I was stronger than mere words though. She couldn't hurt me. Not anymore.

"I shall enjoy this more than you, I promise." I covered my mouth in mock surprise. "Why, I made a promise, too. And I keep mine far better than you."

"What is truth, Alexander? Have you learned yet? When your mind floated away on the magic, did you find a higher purpose?" She tried to lean forward. "Or did you dream of me in bed? Was your every thought consumed by me? Your lovely and dear wife whom you lost by your own stupidity." Her voice took on a sumptuous tone. "You want me. Admit it. You long to touch me again. To kiss me. To feel my thighs squeezing you."

"Don't listen to her," Reckard said.

"So you have another friend here?" she asked. "Am I too much woman for you? Hiding behind others? Just like you hid behind that whore at the Duke's Ball? She was so clumsy when you danced. I saw you. I saw how she put her feet in your way. She flinched when you stepped on her toes. So tell me...where did you find her? At some forgotten alehouse? At one of those places I would never be caught dead within ten yards of?"

"That's enough," I said as the canon growled within.

She continued without pausing. "Did you have to inject her with magic so she would escort you? Or does she prefer fools like you? How much did you pay her? What is the hourly rate for such women?"

I grabbed her hair and pulled her upright.

She uttered neither word nor moan nor groan. She only laughed, and so hard tears ran down her cheeks.

The face was the same one I used to see in the light of the moon as she slept. I'd trace every line as I gave thanks that such a woman could love me, would marry me. I kissed those lips countless times. I stroked those cheeks. So soft. So perfect in their smoothness.

Her eyes opened. "So what now, Alexander? Will you keep holding my hair? Or will you kiss me? You want to. You know you do."

"Careful," Cavendish said.

"Let's see if the whore taught you anything worth learning. What tricks are popular with those women these days?"

It is one matter to insult me. But to insult Sheela?

I didn't hesitate to jab the needle into her upper arm, on the meaty part just before the arm gives way to the shoulder.

"Wait—" Cavendish tried to grab the syringe.

He was too late. I pushed the elixir into her.

She shuddered once, then twice. "I hate—" Her head fell forward as foam appeared between her lips.

Cavendish pulled me away. "What did you—you might have killed her! The elixir must be administered slow. Too much, too fast will send the recipient into immediate shock."

I dropped the empty syringe into his hand. "Good." So it appeared I could kill her after all. Why did such knowledge make me feel sick, and make me feel like I stood on the edge of a magic escape, both at the same time?

Because I loved her.

And I hated her.

Reckard grabbed my shoulders. "Damn it, Ash." He looked at Cavendish. "Did he just condemn us?"

The gnome nodded.

Aimee convulsed. Her head tossed back and forth. Her eyes squeezed tight, then opened, revealing the whites.

I needed to help her.

But didn't she receive what she deserved?

The voice said, "When the wicked man turneth away from his wickedness that he hath committed." So who was I to judge?

Reckard continued, "You've killed us both? Why can you not control yourself around her?" He shook me. "She isn't worth anything!"

My former wife moaned and threw her head back. The arteries in her neck pulsed. Foam covered her lips as she choked.

I wanted to cry at the possibility of who she should have been.

I wanted to laugh at the fact she would truly be removed from my life.

Reckard's high-pitched pleading sounded silly. "Is there anything you can do, Cavendish?"

The gnome stared at Aimee. "The convulsions will give way to chills, starting at the wound. That will mark the final stages of her death."

True to his word, Aimee's arm shook. As the movements passed into her shoulder, such was the force that her chair bounced.

We watched. For all of his concern, Reckard offered no help.

The shaking moved down her bosom, down her belly, into her hips, then her legs. Her chair danced from one side to another as her teeth clacked together. Foam sprayed in all directions.

Cavendish moved away and said, "When she stops moving, she'll be dead." His shoulders drooped. "All of our work and worry and it amounts to nothing."

"At least your Head will be out of The Company's reach," I said. "You and all the others from the Gateway can rest assured again." As for myself, I would never have my questions answered. Such was the price for my impulsiveness.

Murderer could be added to my titles, too. The old Ash was well and truly dead.

Reckard pushed me though I didn't budge. "Going through the Gateway is the only hope I have of living." He tried to push me again. "She manipulated you. She knew exactly what to say and do. And you allowed her." When he tried to push me a third time, I knocked his hand away.

My voice sounded dead. Cold seeped through me. "Turn invisible and move to another country, another continent. You can start over."

As for me? What did it matter? Why bother fighting the inevitable?

Aimee's shaking stopped as suddenly as it started.

Cavendish squeezed his hat. "That's it, then." He held his right hand out. "This is farewell. I hope you avoid your masters for as long as you can. But if they don't get you, your magic addiction will, I suppose."

I knocked the gnome's hand away.

Reckard disappeared. "My only chance will be to sell my body to one of those elves like the one at the Duke's home. Those creatures are powerful enough to keep The Misters from exacting their vengeance. Thanks for nothing, Alexander." He paused before adding, "Old chap."

Aimee's head drooped towards her bosom. Her sweat-drenched hair hung about her face. I moved some out of the way and as I did, her arm twitched.

"What was that?" I asked as the seeping cold ceased.

The gnome replaced his hat. "A residual effect of the magic."

"No, I don't believe so."

I hope not.

I leaned close and heard a low moan. Her neck showed a light pulse. Unwilling to disturb her, I whispered, "She lives."

"What?" Cavendish squeezed between us. He felt her wrist, then held his hand in front of her mouth. His half-scowl, half-grin appeared. "Ash, you must be the luckiest man who ever lived. Reckard, bring water. There might be hope for us yet."

Reckard reappeared on the other side of her with a cup in hand. The gnome took it and pressed it against Aimee's lips. He poured a little in, then wiped her lips. "Both of you, back to the darkness. I'll take care of the questions."

"No," I said, for I wouldn't let this chance pass. "I will question her."

The gnome poured a little more water. "I won't risk you ruining everything because of your emotional state. One effect of this magic is that you're never sure how the one being questioned will perform. Sometimes they can be so nice they answer every question with more information than you need or want. Other times they can be so mad they give you enough to answer the question and nothing else. Either way, to get anything useful from them, you must ask the correct questions." He handed me the cup as she moaned. "Do you think you'd be able to ask the right ones?

Do you think you'd be able to react to her in an appropriate manner?"

"Yes, I do," I said in a tone that let him know he offended me.

Reckard took my arm. "I agree with Cavendish. I don't think you can. Come along."

When I hesitated, Reckard pulled harder.

Aimee was so close. The answers of a hundred nights of tossing and turning, of worrying and wondering, were closer.

I said, "I can tell you what to ask."

He pointed and frowned. "Go. Quickly. She's coming back to us, no thanks to you. And both of you remain quiet. It confuses the subject if more than one asks the questions, and the answers you get are less likely to be useful."

Aimee's head rolled to the right as her eyes fluttered open.

Reckard whispered, "Come on, Ash. Let the gnome do this."

But what if this moment never returns? What if I lose this one chance?

Both men eyed me with anger and concern. Why would I expect a different reaction from them? They could not comprehend the situation. They could not appreciate the significance. This was like Paul's moment on the road to Damascus when he learned the truth and was forever changed.

Aimee whispered, "Where am I? What's happening?"

Her voice made me start, enough that Reckard succeeded in pulling me towards the darkness. For the moment, I gave into his insistence. The veil of darkness seemed to imply more than just remaining hidden, though, and I cared little for the feeling.

Cavendish spoke in a cordial way. "You are Aimee, an accountant at the Bank of Campden. Is that correct?"

Her lids drooped. "Yes, that is true. I work in an office on the first floor. Do you know how hard it is for a woman to attain such a position? Most men labor thirty years and never move off the second or third floors. But Duke Schaever can identify natural talent and abilities. He arranged for my opportunity when so many others wouldn't dare to so much as listen to or acknowledge me."

Really? You never mentioned that. You claimed you helped one of the trustees when his rival tried to have him arrested for embezzlement. You found the true accounting books and handed them over to the authorities. In return, he hired you to help him with further audits.

She continued, "Do you know how many men laughed at me when I told them I wanted a job? That's why they—"

"You are a talented lady with many gifts." Cavendish smiled at me. "You deserve all the honors you receive. In fact, you deserve more. The trustees should add you to their ranks, should they not?"

Adoring eyes regarded the gnome. "I have long thought they are keeping me from reaching the height of my true potential. Oh, I could be so much more for the Bank. I could manage parts of it better than those old bastards. But they enjoy lording over us lesser employees. They enjoy watching me scurry as quick as I can between rooms, trying to broker deals on loans, trying to placate some important ambassador from the United States just so they can own him and extract information from him. I always negotiate the best deal possible, for when someone needs to borrow money, they're at the mercy of the lender. Yet I know I could have made an even better deal if I had been the one in charge of certain negotiations. Take the Baron of Longstreet as an example. He suffered through a nasty divorce. It seems he dabbled in magic a little too much and drained their coffers dry. When his wife discovered his misdeeds, she exploded. He had to come to us to borrow enough money to pay for her lawyer. And now we own a vast collection of property, including paintings and items long suspected to be magical in nature." She whispered. "Tell no one else, but I've been working to procure those very items for my other employers."

The gnome put a hand on her arm. "You do a fine job, dear. You are a good and hard worker."

She giggled. "I don't know why I'm telling this to a gnome. You all are dirty little creatures. You are despicable little toadies. I wish there were more dragons around to eat you out of existence." She giggled more. "And you look so ridiculous in those goggles. You resemble a fish. What does a gnome need with fish goggles, anyway? Trying to look important? Or smart? Or both?"

The knuckles on Cavendish's free hand turned white.

There was great satisfaction in knowing she could manipulate someone besides me. I whispered, "Don't become emotionally involved."

The gnome took a shuddering breath. He tugged at his beards and said, "Yes, we all must work with those we despise from time-to-time. Since you mentioned magical items, tell me where I can find the Head of Forneil. You possess it, do you not?"

Her giggles stopped. "Did you know my former husband has been looking for it? He, of all people, tried to force me to give it to him. But he is such a bumbling oaf he walked right into my trap. Oh, we knew he would try to find me at the Ball. So we set a grand trap for him. I thought the catapult to be a nice touch. He always wanted to fly, so I granted his wish. And do you think he was grateful?"

That wasn't flying!

"No," the gnome said, "but on the subject of the Head. Do you still possess it?"

Her eyes fluttered again. "Of course not. I had to hide it in a safer place after I learned Alexander wanted it. He works for the others, you know. He let himself be degraded to where he had to sell himself just to live, or so I heard. I always knew I held power over him, but I never imagined I could drive him to the brink of death. How pathetic it is to let someone do that to you. Why would anyone let himself depend on another so much? You're setting yourself up for disappointment and heartache when you do."

"Some people call such attachment unconditional love." The gnome sounded like he approved of the notion. He glanced in my direction. "But we digress. I want to know more about the Head."

"I hid it. I don't want my former husband to find it. Why would he need it? He never had much use for magic when we were married, except for those people he tried to break from their magic addictions." She smiled like she had stolen candy from a merchant and got away with it. "Did you know he never suspected my power or my past? Oh, he was always far more interested in his Bible and his studies and what he called the fallen human condition. He was supposed to understand people to help them and he couldn't even understand the one person he claimed to love."

That isn't true. I tried to make you happy. I tried to show you my love and devotion.

Cavendish said, "Yes, but where is the Head? Where did you hide it?"

She shrugged. "Well, I didn't really hide it, now did I? But I don't have it in my possession anymore. No, I don't want Alexander to get it. He once told me he thought it was a mistake that the Gateway was ever opened, that introducing magic into our world helped to disguise the truth of our lives, that the magic gave us a means of false escape and false security. And then he seeks that very thing. What a hypocrite. He makes me ill."

Reckard squeezed my arm and whispered, "She is evil and vile. Do not listen to her."

Oh, I knew what she was. I had heard her talk about some of her peers in much the same tone and with much the same judgments.

But that didn't make it any easier to hear, especially since I agreed with her. I was a hypocrite of the worst type.

Cavendish sighed to show his obvious boredom. "Aimee, you are straying from the questions."

"Am I? You're asking and I'm answering. I'm telling you the reason I hid the Head."

"But you said you didn't hide it. What did you do with it?"

"Oh.." She smirked in a shy way that spoke of innocence waiting to be claimed. "I gave it away. For a time."

Reckard and I both started towards her, but caught ourselves. We looked at each other, then at her.

Cavendish appeared as pale as I felt. He wiped his forehead with a lace cloth. "You gave it away? To whom? Why?"

"After consulting with my superiors, we felt it was best to give it to Duke Schaever. We knew he could guard it much better than myself, at least until Alexander was dealt with. Then, I will deliver the Head and finish what I am supposed to do with it."

The Duke. The man who had more magical protection and detectors and resources than anyone else in the city. The man who commanded the most power, outside of The Company and The Gatherers.

Reckard whispered, "This is bad."

"I know," Aimee continued with her matter-of-fact tone, "my former husband will refuse to stop until either he has it or has died trying to get it, so I gave it to Reginald so he could hide it. I don't think Alexander will ever be able to locate it. He could spend years searching and never find it."

Cavendish wiped his forehead again. "Do you have any idea where the Duke would keep such a treasured possession?"

She nodded and spoke with delight. "Oh, he has a vault where he stores important items for my superiors. The real ones you understand, not the ones at the Bank. It lies beneath his lands. He keeps an assortment of oddities there. It is the most heavily protected secret in Europe. Neither the Prime Minister nor his Gateway Secretary knows about it."

Cavendish scratched his head.

I whispered, "Ask her where the room is. And ask her if Frengarn is involved."

Aimee looked about as if discovering her whereabouts for the first time. "I must go, you know. I'm to meet my superiors this evening." She leaned forward. "They've had someone tracking me ever since Alexander attacked the Greenhews. They watch my every move. Not even Reginald knows that, bless his good heart. He helps me, but there are matters even he cannot control."

The gnome patted her arm. "We will let you go when the time is right. Now back to the Head."

Reckard whispered, "Do you think we were followed?"

"You doubled back," I said. "You would have seen someone unless they were invisible, too."

Reckard disappeared as my belly sunk below my knees. "I'll have another look about the building."

Aimee said, "I know nothing else about the Head."

When Cavendish cleared his throat to get Aimee's attention, she stopped rolling her head to look down at him. "I told you everything you could possibly want to know about the Head of Forneil. To approach the storehouses without permission is certain death. Reginald doesn't deal with formalities. He claims he has enough of those in his public life. He is direct, is our dear Duke. He lets you know where you stand when it comes to magical matters. I respect that."

"Yes, well, where is the exact location of this storage room?"

"Beneath his home."

"Where?"

"Underground." She strained like she wanted to reach out to touch Cavendish. "You're a queer little man, did you know that? Cute for a gnome and those ridiculous goggles make you more so. I like how your cheeks turn red when you appear confused. It makes me want to squeeze them like I would a baby's. I imagine a dragon would enjoy chewing on the fat in them."

The gnome pulled on his beards as his face turned redder than normal. "Yes, well, just tell me how to get to this...vault...this storage room."

She shook her head as she moaned. "I shouldn't tell you, should I?" She scrunched her face, like she did when she felt flustered, which was a rare occurrence. "But I must, I fear. I must tell you that you reach it by the underground sewage tunnels, the ones they built when they brought the trains in, the ones they used those machines to build, the ones with the drill on the front as big as giants." She moaned again. "What have you done to me?"

Cavendish's face turned even redder if that was possible. "And what guards the—"

A crash sounded in the room overhead, followed by a loud thump.

The gnome stared at me as I entered the circle of light. "Check on Reckard. See if he needs help. I'll finish the questions."

"She is coming out of it much too soon," he said as he removed his hat and scratched his curly hair. "We haven't much time left. Something's wrong. Maybe they sold me a diluted potion. That would explain how she survived your carelessness."

I pushed Cavendish to the door and tried to keep the rising excitement from my tone. "Then I will make this quick. Now go help Reckard."

The gnome said, "You're bigger than me. You go help."

I pointed to my silver foot. "By the time I reach him, Reckard could be dead. If he needs help, he won't be getting it from me."

Praise Pienne and his elixirs.

Cavendish looked between Aimee and me. When I pushed him again, he relented. As he hurried from the light, I turned my attention to the dear lady in the chair, the one who glared at me and said, "So you're involved in this matter, are you? Can you believe I used to adore that face of yours and now all I want to do is kick your nose into your head? I want to feel the crunch of bone beneath my heel and see your blood splatter."

The image reminded me of the evil sitting before me and not of the beautiful and tender woman. That helped me remain calm. "You have always been so pleasant, Aimee. And it's always just so exciting to talk to you."

Her tirade continued. "Stupid little imaginary vicar, lording over the people with your righteous attitude, like you knew better than they did, like you were worthy enough to judge them. Now we know you really weren't. Now we know you are just like them."

"If you want to make this unpleasant, then let's get down to the business before us. The business of truth."

"Unplea—"

My lips almost didn't move fast enough to say, "Were you the one who caused the explosion the day I signed the divorce papers?"

"Of course," she said like I asked the most obvious of questions, and was a fool to do so. "Who else could craft such a beautiful magic but me? Who else could control it as I do? It has taken years to perfect my gift, but it was well worth the trials and errors. Why, the one that was meant to kill you was my test of ultimate perfection." She squirmed her hips as if she enjoyed a particularly personal thought. "The Gatherers required it as part of my training, to show what I was capable of. And the fireball it unleashed was a picture of perfection." Her squirming continued in much the same way she did when—

I took a deep breath to calm my reaction. "Only it didn't work as planned. You failed to kill me."

She glowered and arched her head back. "What are you doing to me, Alexander? What have you done?"

Before I could answer, the sound of a fight erupted at the top of the stairs. Reckard yelled at Cavendish, and two shots were fired.

Aimee's face lightened. "See? The Gatherers come for me even now."

Too little time. Too many questions remained.

"Why did you want to kill me?"

She threw her head forward, and whispered like she talked to herself, "Best to keep that one a secret and yet..." She shook her head. "Ordered to do it. Didn't want to. Still adored you. My superiors told me to kill you, just like they told me to marry you."

A numbing cold washed through me all at once. I had the sudden urge to seek the escape of a good elixir. With a dry mouth I replied, "They told you to marry me. And you obeyed. That is the only reason you stood beside me at the altar?"

"My superiors thought you provided a good cover. The Co...The Co..." She cleared her throat. "The Company grew suspicious of me and they feared how well placed I had become at the Bank. So they sent the assassin whom you stopped. My superiors ordered me to marry you because who would suspect the wife of a canon of being in league with a group of magic users? Who would suspect I had my own abilities? Certainly not my dear devoted husband."

I have to ask you. I have to know.

"Did you love me?"

She nodded.

My mouth turned drier and I had to lick my lips twice before I could ask, "Are you sure?"

"Of course," she said with assurance. "How could I not love you after you saved me? I'm not that cold. Before the incident, no man had ever shown he cared for me other than desiring my body. But you were different. From the beginning you were different. You were my equal in many ways, yet you were so ignorant of that which was before you. You were so strong and sure of yourself, yet so trapped in your own little world you never peered outside it. If you had, I might not have lost that love. I might love you still. I think I would. And I might have left The Gatherers to be with you. In the first months of our marriage, I was so happy. I didn't believe I deserved your love and couldn't wait to spend time with you, the man I respected. I...I considered resigning from the Bank just to be with you more. I..."

What did I do wrong? What could I have changed? We could still be married. None of this had to happen. None of this...

The sounds of the struggle moved down the stairs.

I asked, "Did you want to marry me?"

She, too, licked her lips. "Yes." She said the word like it was simple and easy, like I was foolish to have doubted her.

"And you were willing to kill me?"

She shrugged. "The superiors ordered it. I tried to convince them otherwise, but they were most insistent. They didn't want to risk you discovering the truth and selling the information to The Company."

I snorted. "You make it sound like I owe you my life."

"No, we owe nothing to each other anymore. I owed you a debt of my life, but I paid that when I didn't kill you."

"But you said—"

"I was ordered to kill you. Do you think you could have walked away unless I wanted you to? I thought I helped you. I thought you would seek a new parish in another town and start over with a new life. I hoped you would find another woman to marry, that she would be just the one you deserved." She looked me in the eyes. The venom was absent from her tone as she continued, "I've never been a good person. I was so bad that both of my parents abandoned me when I was still but a babe. I have never believed in your god or higher callings. All I want in life is to get what I can force it to give. I was..." Hair fell about her face as she shook her head.

I asked with a dry mouth, "You were?"

"You almost convinced me I could change. You always brought out the best in me. Often times I felt free with you. But other times I felt trapped. Why?"

The canon answered aloud before I could stop him. "Because there is one in whom we can hope. He is—"

"Spare me your righteous sermon." She peered from between strands. "Do not pretend you're a better person than me. At least I recognized I would never be different. You, though, became a magic addict. You threw everything away and now you haunt me in my own town with shades of a past I'd rather forget. You are a waste of a person, Alexander, especially considering how much potential you had with the Church. You could have been a bishop with a seat in the House of Lords. Instead, you've become..." Her voice trailed off, and I thought I heard a quiet sob. "You were a good and noble man, Ash. When you became what you are now...it killed what you nurtured in me. How could I believe anything you ever told me? I lost my respect for you. I lost any reason to believe you." She paused. "I hate you for that. Above all else, I hate you for killing that small happiness."

Her words made me feel old and tired, worn and frayed. They gave me a heavy feeling, like my soul struggled to make one second connect to the next. She was right. I threw it all away. I didn't want that life anymore or the memories or the happiness.

The door crashed open, spilling a visible Reckard onto the floor with a cyclops on top of him. Cavendish rushed in with a troll on his heels.

This isn't finished. I need to know more, and they interrupted.

I stomped over to the tangled mass of Reckard and cyclops. I grabbed the magical creature by the scruff of his shirt.

He slashed with a knife. It bounced off my skin and before he recovered from his own surprise, I smashed my fist in his face. His glass shield shattered. He howled like a cat in a fight.

Cavendish darted between my legs. As I looked up, a troll's fist struck across my right cheek with enough force to break teeth and shatter the cheekbone of a typical human. As it snapped my head to the side, for the slightest instant, pain shot through my face and into my neck. The sound of breaking bones filled my ears.

The troll groaned as it doubled over its crooked hand.

I gave the creature no pause, but kicked up and across. His nose exploded in a gusher of blood.

The mighty creature howled. The sound of his pain brought more footsteps over our heads.

"There's a small army descending on this place," Reckard said as he leaned on his knees and took deep breaths. "We had best be leaving."

Aimee watched the proceedings with great interest. Despite her disheveled appearance, with matted hair and dried foam, she remained just as beautiful. Regal, even.

As I went to her, the cyclops took a swing. I blocked his fist with my elbow. The creature whimpered as a tingling moved down to my hand and fingers. I shook my arm out as I stood before my former wife.

The venom returned to her voice. "You are a dead man, Alexander Asherton. If I don't kill you, the Duke will. I promise."

Reckard said, "We got the information. Let's go."

I looked at Aimee. "You tried to save me even as you tried to kill me?"

How strange, how demented, is that?

No more strange and demented than what I did next.

I grabbed her hair and forced her head back.

I kissed her.

She resisted, of course, but her resistance melted like a lump of sugar in a cup of fresh tea.

Reckard tugged at me. "Are you insane? Let's go!"

Her lips tasted as sweet as that sugar, and my head twirled with a mix of love, lust, anger, betrayal, and pain. When I pulled away, we looked at each other like we did when we exchanged vows.

Her laughter brought an abrupt end to the moment. "You still love me, Alexander." She laughed harder, but with a tinge of madness.

Cavendish joined Reckard in pulling at me. As more footsteps raced down the stairs, I let them move me.

Aimee's mocking laughter followed.

CHAPTER 11

We entered Back Ends Street when the night showed signs of relenting in its battle against the day. Shadows stretched long, and the stars disappeared one-by-one. No sooner had we cleared the confines of the building than Cavendish cried out and hugged my leg.

"Are you mad?" I asked as I tried to pry him off.

And in that second, that seemingly insignificant moment of time, something sharp raked across my back. It burned like a hot poker pressed hard against my skin. I turned and saw a long shadow disappear behind a roof. Its form suggested—

"A dragon?" Reckard asked. His face turned pale just before he disappeared. "They sent a dragon after us?" His voice was full of the same surprise and fear making my heart beat faster.

"Look out!" Cavendish said, and I turned just in time to knock the outstretched talons of the dark green creature away. It made no sound as it swooped back into the air with wings stretched in a forward arch. Its head was shaped like a spade, with stumps of horns lining the outer edges.

The silent death, the swooping plague, and the quiet end were all names for the dragons. They were formidable foes. A full grown one could kill twenty soldiers in the span of a breath. Though this one was young, as evidenced by its six-foot length, it was no less dangerous.

"How did it get through Branagh's without being spotted?" I asked as it circled about for an additional go.

Reckard said, "I don't know, old chap. I don't want to wait around to ask. Split up and meet at Branagh's."

"No, wait." Where was he? "It's best if we stay together."

"Why?" he asked from down the road. "So it can burn us at the same time?"

Cavendish quivered on my leg.

"Look," I said as I lifted the little man, "I have a difficult enough time walking about without you. Quit cowering and help find a way out of this mess."

The dragon was beautiful in a deadly sense. Sleek and majestic, it presented an air of strength and power that made me want to watch in wonder while running in fear.

Two loud pops were followed by a pair of lead balls stinging my chest. As they bounced off and brought me out of my trance, men with rifles emerged from the building. While they didn't wear the uniform of the Guardsmen, they had the look about them: stocky build, short-cropped hair and a face that said they would obey orders without question. They moved to the side in unison as they reloaded their weapons.

Are you real or a machine? There is only one way to find out.

I stalked towards them as they raised their guns. They released their death in unison. Both balls bounced off my head, creating a dull ache on either side.

As the men stood with dumbfounded looks, I wrenched the rifles away, then knocked the men across the jaws. They fell to the side, but arose together with knives in hand. One spit blood.

So at least I dealt with a real person.

I shook the rifles at them. "Really, do you think that will work after seeing how effective these were?"

They looked at each other.

I threw the rifles down, then motioned to them. "You might as well try."

They obliged, and I grabbed one blade bare handed while deflecting another. I twisted the one around, but the man refused to let go. For his stubbornness, he was forced to his knees and had the tip of the blade pointed at his throat.

Something knocked me across the back. As I fell into the man, talons scratched at my head. They grabbed my hair and ripped out the roots.

Now that hurt...to the point I had to concentrate on fending off the creature as it tried to grab more.

It swooped just above me, its head darting back and forth as it prepared to snap.

The second man struck again. I took the brunt of his impact, wrenched his weapon away, then lunged for the dragon. My foot did little more than budge. The creature flew out of reach as I sprawled to the ground.

Cavendish squealed as he ran down the street. The dragon glanced at him. It seemed to hesitate on indecision before it answered a primal desire and swooped towards the little man.

I tried to rise and run towards them in one motion, but my foot held me in place. "Cavendish, behind you!"

The little man looked over his shoulder, to where the dragon's snout snapped once, then twice. He squealed again as he tripped over his own feet.

The dragon lunged as Cavendish rolled along the ground.

The gnome stopped against the side of a building, and the dragon disengaged to avoid crashing. It circled high as the gnome pressed himself flat.

I had covered half the distance to him, with knee and thigh burning, when she spoke from the doorway. "Alexander, you will pay for what you have done."

Aimee.

A blast of air sent me sprawling forward.

Bonni Greenhew, too?

She was becoming too much like a bad toothache, one that flared up just after a bite of bread pudding.

As I turned over, the two men jumped me.

"Hold him there," Aimee said as she moved down the street, supported by Bonni.

Cavendish yelled, "Ash, help me! Save me!"

As the dragon moved low across the way, a scream pierced the air. It wasn't the gnome's.

Curious onlookers had gathered in the street to watch the strange spectacle taking place. But they ran in every direction as the dragon cut a straight path through them, heading for the shaking body of Cavendish.

Two men, one heavy-set and wearing the apron of a cook, and a lady, who also wore an apron, but with a dusting of flour across her, knocked the gentlemen off me as they fled the horrors of the magical creature. A bit of flour fell into my eyes, making them burn and water. I tried to wipe them as I faced the determined wrath of Aimee, but my tears flowed as she cupped her palms together. "What's wrong, Alexander?" she asked as purple smoke arose. "Are you crying because you realize the futility of defying me? This time I won't save you. This time I will make you pay for all the misery you just put me through." She wore a robe now, one with the Duke's crest.

As I retreated, I managed a glance at Cavendish, who had risen to his knees. He held his arms before his face like he didn't want to see the approaching, inevitable death.

The dragon hovered over the gnome and raised its head for the final snap.

Through all of this I managed to end up with only one weapon: the dagger. I could throw it at Aimee and try to kill her. Or I could throw it at the dragon and try to give Cavendish the chance to escape.

Kill my former wife who put me through earthly hell, or save a friend who refused to do the same when faced with a similar decision.

The voice said I had no choice. And it was right. I just hoped Aimee's explosion wouldn't hurt too much.

The dagger flew towards the dragon. Because of the creature's youth, its scales had yet to harden fully, meaning it remained vulnerable to blades and arrows and bullets. Unfortunately, the knife didn't carry enough force to do more than scratch its back.

Still, the creature turned. Its black eyes blazed hatred as it spotted me hurrying forward. Teeth flashed as it raced to meet me.

Of all the foolish acts, Ash...you are charging a dragon?

It snapped, and I flinched as I punched. My fist grazed its nose, and it gave a high-pitched scream of anger. Before it recovered, I grabbed hold of its body and held as tight as I could.

The creature twisted and contorted and snapped and snorted. It wriggled worse than a worm at the end of a fisherman's hook, and lashed my back with its tail, which stung like an army of ants.

I turned back to Aimee, who stopped. Smoke enveloped her hands. Some dripped towards the ground as the rest drifted upwards.

"Give me your best, love," I said as I squeezed the dragon with all of my might. It slipped and squirmed all the harder.

Aimee's face turned whiter than Reckard's. Bonni didn't move, either.

Why?

The dragon screamed its rage, then bit my arm. The teeth didn't break my skin, but they left deep pockmarks that burned. As a matter-of-fact, they burned so bad I smacked the creature on the head to make it release me.

It returned the favor by biting my calf, which sent a sharp pain into my thigh.

Still Aimee withheld her explosion.

"Stop!" a man called from behind. The true Guardsmen arrived on the scene, forty of them.

The dragon bit a third time, this one on my thigh. For that, I pulled on its wings.

It responded by letting out a whimper.

The Guardsmen moved towards me and as I faced them, Aimee and Bonni both disappeared back through the door.

"Look," I said with relief at not having to endure another of Aimee's bombs. "I've captured a dragon. I wonder who has disregarded the law and allowed one to fly free in our lands?"

The Captain of the Guardsmen, with his golden rope around each shoulder, motioned to his left and his right. "Surround him, men. Take him alive if you can. Kill him if you must."

The dragon looked into my eyes as it hissed. It snapped at my face and my neck. I released it to defend myself, and it flew free with a sound that could best be described as a maniacal, high-pitched laugh.

Twenty of the Guardsmen surrounded me by that time. Fifteen held pikes at the ready while another five aimed their pistols.

"I'm unarmed," I said as I held my arms up. There was no hiding my frustration. "And you just allowed the evidence to escape."

The Captain said, "On the ground." He pointed for emphasis.

Too much effort and hard work had been expended on too many nights to avoid them. Why would I want such effort to be wasted by allowing them to take me captive now?

There was but one strategy when faced with overwhelming numbers: neutralize the leader. So I stepped towards the Captain. Not only did my weighty left leg hurt, but my right almost echoed it where the dragon had bitten.

"I told you to lie on the ground. Now!" He motioned for his men to tighten the circle. "I'll not warn you again."

"Good." I knocked the nearest pike away. It snapped back into place as the Captain retreated. The look on his face spoke of either fear or that he saw the depths of madness for the first time.

"Kill him," the man said without hesitation.

Like the good soldiers they were, they obeyed in an instant. Almost as one, they pulled back with looks of astonishment and fear and anger, for their pikes had bounced off their target. At least the ones with the pistols spared me their annoying stings.

"I'll not be your punch and judy today," I said as I grabbed the nearest pike, then forced the soldier holding onto it into the one next to him. When the soldier released the pike, I flipped it round, and charged the Captain.

The man stumbled out of the way, and my blow glanced off his shoulder. I turned to keep him on the defensive. They wouldn't stop while even one still stood. Could I beat them senseless? Could they beat me senseless? Or was this all just senseless?

The sound of galloping horses filled the street. Around the corner, a carriage half-painted white raced so fast it tilted onto two wheels. For a moment, it appeared that it might fall, but the horses broke into a full run and the carriage straightened after several bounces.

Someone worked the reins with invisible hands. He pulled hard and the horses' heads reared back. Their shoes scraped so sharp on the cobblestone that sparks shot from beneath them.

The carriage swept the Captain and his men aside as it stopped beside me. The door flew open and a familiar gnome reached out.

I threw the pike at the nearest Guardsman, then pulled myself halfway in. "Go! Now!"

The carriage started out again, and I held onto the base of the seats to keep from flying out. My lead foot must've hit someone as I swung around, for I heard a distinct 'oof' and felt a thump.

The pop of pistols sounded, and Cavendish covered his head. Three balls bounced off my legs. Two others passed through the side of the carriage and missed the gnome. I pulled myself all the way in. Cavendish slammed the door shut before he slid to the floor. He breathed heavy as he wiped his forehead.

Two shudders moved through me before the full measure of the dragon's teeth and the full measure of my madness set in.

Not only had I challenge a dragon, but I grabbed it?

My arm and leg and thigh burned like a hundred ants tried to enjoy a feast. I ripped my sleeve off and the naked flesh pulsed with every heartbeat. Small red bumps, arranged in order like the teeth one would expect to find inside a dragon's maw, ran across my upper arm. The skin swelled.

"Either Pienne's elixir is wearing off," I said with weariness, "or I discovered its weakness."

Cavendish whispered, "Before dragons mature and gain their fire-breath, they have a spit not unlike acid. I doubt even your magic elixir provides you with an immunity."

Acid? "You mean I'm being eaten alive?"

The gnome nodded.

I pushed myself up and beat on the front of the carriage. "Reckard, to the Royal Fountains. Quickly!"

"Are you insane?" he called back. "The entire force of Guardsmen will be following us as well as their airships. We need to go underground if we're going to escape."

"We'll go underground, but I need to get to the Fountains first. Dump me into them and continue on."

"No. I won't leave you and I won't take you to the Fountains. Someone is always there."

"Listen to me," I yelled as I beat harder on the front. The burns grew worse. "I don't have time to explain! Just get me there!"

Reckard mumbled words best left unsaid, but he turned the carriage. We raced towards the northern part of the town where a lush park awaited. It was one of the jewels of the county, having been donated on behalf of the Schaevers in recognition of the empire's generosity. It covered several acres and contained open fields of lush, green grass. Special flowers lined the perimeter and at least some of them were in bloom at any time of the year. There was also the Royal Fountain, where a statue by Bertel Thorvaldsen of a tall and lovely woman, some say she was supposed to be Athena, dipped her hands into the water. Around her stood statues of cherubim, each holding a bucket from which water spouted over the top of the fair lady and landed untouched in the fountain itself.

My wounds throbbed even more.

Cavendish said, "Thank you for saving me. I thought the dragon would eat me."

I said, between gritted teeth, "You're welcome. That is what friends do for each other." Did he catch my special emphasis on friends? "But next time show your gratitude by helping me fight instead of cowering and making yourself easy prey."

A lady screamed just before the carriage bounced high enough to toss me into the air. I landed against the front chair, with my face wedged in the corner.

More voices arose in protest. Several dogs barked.

I kicked the door open before we stopped. As Reckard pulled up to the Fountain, I tumbled onto the ground.

The wounds burned to the point that my neck and head ached, and my leg and arm felt like they roasted. I pulled myself up, taking deep breaths. My foot dug a trench through a flowerbed as I reached the concrete lip of the pool.

"What are you doing?" Reckard asked.

I didn't answer, for the world spun around once before turning into a wet darkness.

"Are you sure he will live?" Sheela asked, concern and compassion in her voice.

Cavendish said, "Water acts the same on the dragon acid as it does on the dragon fire. Extinguishes it immediately. Other than some residual burns, he should be fine."

I pushed a hand away.

"See?" the gnome said with a pleased tone. "He's moving about already."

The faint light of a burning lamp illuminated a dozen crates arranged against the walls. The smell of stale ale and old wine filled the air. Mixed with it was the smell of dust and ammonia, which meant I was in one of Branagh's storage rooms.

Sheela kissed my forehead. "How are you feeling?"

How to answer such a simple question? With the truth: my body ached like never before, save for the days after Aimee's attempted murder? Or the safer version that wouldn't make Sheela so worried? The latter seemed more reasonable, so I said, "Like I was inside a furnace."

"Good." She slapped me, but lightly. "I know you won't feel that, and I'm not willing to hurt my hand again to prove a worthless point to you." She shook her finger in my face. "All you do is get yourself into trouble, then run here half-dead. It's bad enough most of the tavern wants to finish the job. So what do I do but allow you back? I hide you and protect you and worry about you." Tears flowed down her cheeks, and she wiped them with the hem of her serving apron.

Cavendish looked away as the voice laughed at me.

I caught her wrist and said, "Sheela…"

"Don't say it, Ash. Don't say anything." She pulled her hand away and stood. "Don't tell me you are sorry. Don't tell me you wish things were different. I either want to kiss you or kick you. You infuriate me. You make me want to hate you."

When she turned, I caught her foot. The movement hurt my arm, but this had to be done. "Sheela, I am truly sorry. I cannot say how sorry I am."

Her hair obscured her expression. "Then don't."

Reckard cleared his throat and said, "It's about time you told her." He appeared beside us. "Now why don't the two of you kiss and be happy friends again?"

Sheela shook her head. "He isn't capable of happiness. Will not allow himself to enjoy anything."

My fellow thief sighed. "Must women be so attracted to lost causes?" He held his arms wide, and he tried to speak with a lower tone, which made his words seem all the more ridiculous. "Love me, Sheela. Take a chance with someone who will do anything for you."

She planted her hands on her hips. "You dare to ask that of me now? After what you already asked? You can go jump in a lake. A large and deep one. And take Ash with you. That way you will both sink."

My partner in crime rocked back-and-forth on a wooden stool. "I'm not going to jump in a lake, but Ash came as close as possible." He tilted his head as he looked at me. "Pray tell, old chap, how you got chewed up by the dragon?"

My arm and leg were still red, but no longer swollen. Teeth marks lined both. "This is what happens when you grab one and wrestle it."

Sheela spun around. She wore a look of absolute horror. Her voice was almost as high as Reckard's. "You. Did. What?"

"What I had to do to save his worthless skin," I said as I pointed to Cavendish. "When the dragon tried to bite me, I did the only reasonable thing: I grabbed it and held tight. Strangely enough when I did, Aimee stopped trying to kill me. She had a nice explosive ready, too. I bet she hated releasing it." I held my hands out to show how big it was. "Probably would have hurt. But she refused to risk injuring the dragon. Why? She has never been fond of the creatures that I can recall."

Cavendish said, "The bigger question is how the dragon got into the city. Has someone opened another Gateway? My brothers have been searching the city over, but have found nothing. And I was almost the next one of them to disappear." A visible shudder ran through him.

Disappearing gnomes. A dragon. Guardsmen who appeared undazed and unconcerned when they saw it. Mechanical people. Aimee. A renowned orc named Frengarn. How did it all fit together? And I could not forget the Greenhews, an enslaved elf, and Reganas Five. What was going on? There were too many pieces to a puzzle for which I had no picture to guide me to the answer.

"Ash," Sheela said, then waited until I looked in her eyes. "Are you serious when you say you fought a dragon?"

"I didn't poke myself with a knife." To add emphasis to my words, I held my pock-marked arm out. "You haven't seen any come through Branagh's lately have you?"

She examined my arm by lightly touching it. The feel of her fingers was enough to warm my belly. "Not in a year and that one caused such a commotion they were banned even from Branagh's for six months. No, we'd all know if one tried." As she put a finger on the bigger mark she asked, "Will that heal?"

"Eventually," Cavendish said with a knowing tone. "It takes longer to recover from dragon acid, much like it takes longer to recover from their fire. There might be some scarring."

As if I need more?

I caught myself rubbing the side of my face. Sheela did, too. She took my hand, and stepped close to whisper, "I think you look handsome. The dragon marks make you more so. Battle scarred. Refined by fire."

She was a good woman, too good and kind for the likes of a hypocrite like me. Aimee spoke true when she assessed what I had become in light of what I used to be.

Sheela said, "Before Ash woke, you asked about the tunnels, Reckard." When he nodded, she took on a look of wariness.

The man gave an exaggerated shrug. "The Duke is keeping the Head of Forneil in a storeroom beneath his estate and the only way to get to it is through the tunnels. You once mentioned how you used to go in them."

"I won't tell you anything," she said as she shook her finger at him. "I am not returning to that part of my life." She pushed him aside as she headed for the door. "I have put up with enough foolishness for one day from the both of you."

Reckard grabbed her arm and whispered something. Whatever it was, she turned pale and bowed her head. Her voice went low. "You take our friendship too far. You've no idea what you ask."

"I know my life depends on what you know. And you know something of value."

She smoldered like a cinder in the fire, pulsing different shades of red as she looked at me. "I might just hate you for this."

I feigned surprise. "Me? What did I do?"

"Yes, you." She looked at Reckard. "I do hate you."

"I'd rather you hate me alive than adore me dead." Despite his nonchalant attitude, the spark of excitement in his eyes dimmed. He almost frowned, but before he could do so he said, "Tell us about the tunnels."

Her eyes narrowed and she spoke with a resignation I had never heard from her. "Fine." She pressed her lips together, like she couldn't quite decide how to begin. After a moment, she started with, "I played in them when I was a girl. My friends and I would sneak away when our parents were too busy to notice. It's best to stay away from them. Those tunnels are bad. They are collapsing or on the verge of doing so. One wrong move and you'll send an entire section down on top of your head." She put her hands on her hips. "Some double on top of themselves, meaning you can fall to your death just as easy."

Reckard said, "So either teach us what to look for or go with us."

I sat straighter. "No—"

He continued, "That way you won't worry."

This wasn't right, and I refused to allow such a notion to be considered. "Sheela doesn't need to be involved in this anymore."

"I'm already involved more than I wanted to be, Ash. I'm always involved in your foolishness whether you like it or not, whether you realize it or not. Each time The Misters give you an assignment, I'm involved. I worry about you. I try to help you." She eyed Reckard with the determined look I had seen before, the one she used when a table became rambunctious and she had to put a creature in its place. When she wore the expression, it always bode ill for the receiver. "Maybe I will go. I put in enough time lately trying to forget about Ash that they cannot complain about me taking time away."

"No, Sheela." My tone needed to be forceful, my words decisive. "I don't want you to go."

My actions had hurt her enough. I wouldn't let her become involved in whatever we faced. A dance at the Ball was one matter, but the dangers awaiting in the Duke's underground realm was altogether different.

"I don't want to." She looked between us. "But you will go, won't you? You will go no matter how much I warn you not to, no matter how much I beg or threaten."

"We have no choice. But you do." I tried to make my tone more forceful. "Don't go."

"Careful, Ash. I might mistake your concern to mean you care for me."

The accusation bit deeper than it should have. Before I stopped myself, the voice took hold. I said, "I do care for you. I do not want to see you hurt."

She directed the same determined look at me, and my hope sank to my feet. There would be no talking her out of her decision even though she didn't yet admit she had already decided. Still, I had to try something.

Since forcefulness didn't work, I tried begging, complete with folded hands held before me. "Please don't go."

"Why not? So you don't have to put yourself in my place for once?" She folded her arms over her bosom. "Maybe you need to worry about me. Maybe you need to learn what it is you put me through every time you go on one of your foolish errands for The Company."

My leg burned as I stood. I gave her a good, long look to let her know how disappointed I was. "Reckard, you know better than to ask her to help."

He half-shrugged. "Call it self-preservation. She knows the tunnels. I want to live and I will do what I need to do to make sure I do. This business is getting nastier by the hour."

"Which is why you should tell her not to come. She might listen to you."

He snorted. "She has that look. You know the one. Her mind is decided."

Sheela looked between us and glared. "What does that mean? What look?"

The voice urged me to fight them further, but it was pointless. I'd have to do my best to protect Sheela. Which meant, "We will need weapons and some basic supplies."

Sheela said, "You didn't ans—"

"We must go soon," Reckard added. "Aimee knows we know where the Head is. She will alert the Duke and he will reinforce his defenses. The sooner we reach his storage chamber, the better the chance we'll be able to steal the Head."

Cavendish, who had been too quiet during the debate, gave me a curious look. "Did you find out what type of defenses he has?"

"No," I said in a way that meant I didn't want to discuss the matter further. "I was getting to that when someone brought a fight to the room."

Reckard stood and faced me. "You didn't waste your time asking her other questions, did you?"

"I was getting to the point of asking her about the defenses."

He nodded in a knowing fashion. "That should have been your first question. Or were you too busy indulging your curiosity?"

Sheela moved between us. "What happened?" She pointed at me. "You were alone with her? Why?" She looked at Reckard. "Tell me they weren't alone."

My fellow thief motioned my way. "Ask him yourself. We had her tied to a chair and drugged with an elixir of truth."

Sheela shook her finger and her jaw moved up and down, but she said nothing. She stopped, looked at Reckard, then me, then Reckard again. Her expression changed from shock to amused to anger. She leaned close. I thought she was about to slap me. Instead she whispered, "So what did you learn?"

Reckard rolled his eyes and frowned. "Don't encourage him." He turned for the door.

I asked, "Where are you going?"

"To find an ale."

I tried to stand. "I'll join you."

Sheela grabbed my arm. "Not so quick. You must remain out of sight. Remember those people who want you dead? They're still out there."

"But..." Besides the fact that my mouth felt as parched as a farmer's field at the end of a summer drought, I needed to relax, to mull over Aimee's revelations, and to consider what we were walking towards. I needed time to myself. I needed an elixir to escape all the troubles.

The voice said, "No, you only need grace, for it is sufficient."

True, but I used my share long ago.

"She's right," Reckard said. "After I finish my drink, I will try to remember to bring you one, old chap."

"Sheela, would you—"

Reckard said, "She'll be too busy helping collect what we need for our journey."

Cavendish moved for the door, too. "And I need time to gather items that might be useful. And we need to plan our attack."

"Not enough time, gnome. Gather items we can use against trolls, cyclopes and elves. We know the Duke employs them and he will guard his store room with the best he commands." Reckard paused with his hand on the door. "Lean on your reptilian friends to make sure we don't have to deal with their kind."

Cavendish pulled on his beard. "Favors cost money. So do magical items. I need at least four hours to do everything."

As he revealed the room beyond, with its noises and smell of ale and sweat, Reckard said, "Sell a watch for money. You only have an hour."

CHAPTER 12

We stood over an iron grate not more than a hundred yards from Branagh's main entrance. A steel lock with not one, or two, but three keyholes held a single latch in place.

Cavendish examined it by almost laying on top of and pressing his right lens against it. "Impressive. Most impressive. They don't want anyone down there, do they?" He flipped a red lens over his eyes and leaned closer still. "I see traces of oil. The mechanisms have been maintained, like someone expects to use it anytime."

Reckard said, "Good. That confirms we are on the correct path." He motioned to the lock. "So open it, gnome. Make yourself useful."

The creature looked at Reckard and the red lenses gave him a sinister appearance, enough to make my fellow Company thief clear his throat and add, "If you please."

"This is intricate work," Cavendish said as he produced a set of picks. "It will take time."

Sheela moved in front of Reckard and me. "Then I have the opportunity to explain something to all of you." Her eyes appeared strained and her mouth was tight. "I shouldn't say anything, but I need you to understand and this is the only way." She looked at me as if the others didn't exist. "I won't repeat myself, and I expect you to keep this to yourself. Otherwise, I will speak to Hansan and Jansan about keeping you out of Branagh's forever." While continuing to stare at me she added, "Agreed?"

"Yes," I said as the canon's voice grumbled a warning. What was this about? Why did I have the sudden feeling that my day would become even worse?

"Of course," Cavendish said in a disinterested manner, almost as if he knew what she would say.

When Reckard remained silent, she tore her eyes away so she could bore them into him. "Agreed?"

The man hesitated before asking, "Can I tell Leesal?"

"Leesal already knows, but that doesn't mean you two can discuss it."

The man took a step back. "She already knows?"

Such was the shaking of Sheela's lamp and her scowl that I said, "You had best agree, Reckard."

He looked at me as if I might help plead his case. "Why can I not say anything to Leesal?"

"Reckard!"

"I agree. I agree." He paused. "Do you want me to swear an oath of silence?"

Sheela's lamp settled a little. She took a deep breath and said, as she returned her gaze to me, "No, I will take you at your word. I shouldn't, but I will." She bit her lower lip as pain filled her eyes. "I...I..." She closed her eyes just before the words tumbled out. "I know these tunnels...because my friends and I used to play here. We had so much fun it was impossible to keep us away. We played hide-and-seek, we chased one another, we tested each other to see how long we could stand complete darkness and you'd be surprised at how long we went sometimes. We played all types of variations on those games. At first, we kept to the few sections that are open and in use, but they grew boring as they became more familiar. When we stumbled across an unlocked entrance to the forbidden sections, the opportunity to explore something new and strange opened to us." She studied her feet like she could see through the floor to the land below.

"I had a friend named Gaelen, an Irish girl the same age as I. Our birthdays were only days apart. We were complete opposites in almost every way. Where I was always tall for my age, she was short. Where my hair was long and straight and brown, hers was short and curly and red. I was thin, and she was a bit on the heavy side. I loved mischief, and she always took the safest way out. We drove each other crazy, but we were the best and the closest of friends you could imagine." Her voice grew quieter. "But being Irish, Gaelen never backed down when she set her mind to doing something. The others teased her all the time because she refused to race the forbidden sections. We..." She took another deep breath, then exhaled slowly. She cleared her throat and continued, "We played one game where we entered the tunnels at different points, then raced to see who could reach the middle first. Gaelen never played. She always waited at the designated spot to declare the winner."

A feeling of certain doom filled me as I guessed where this tale would lead. I dared not interrupt, though, for this was a new part of Sheela being revealed, a fascinating one.

She continued, "Well, we had just turned thirteen, and Gaelen decided she was tired of being teased. Since our birthdays, she declared she was becoming a woman and becoming a woman meant she would put aside girlish fears." Sheela cleared her throat. "So she took my place in a race. I went to the meeting spot, and Gaelen raced the tunnels alone." Her hands covered her face as she broke down into sobs.

Seeing her in such pain wasn't worth satisfying my curiosity. I put a hand on her arm. "You don't have to finish."

"Yes," she whispered, still covering her face, "I do. I do so you might understand. You want to know who I am?

Well, this is a part of me." She let her hands fall, exposing watery eyes and a red nose. "This is one of my moments. One of the big ones, like when Aimee tried to kill you after your divorce."

Despite myself, I leaned forward. Even Cavendish paused, with two picks sticking out of two locks and a third sticking from between his teeth. He pulled on both ends of his beard.

Sheela's voice grew quieter. "Everyone arrived at the meeting place except for Gaelen. She didn't know the tunnels as well as we did, so we allowed her extra time, but after half an hour I insisted we search for her. All five of us set out down her passage. We called and called. We split when the tunnel forked. We covered the entire area."

"Did you find her?" Cavendish asked. He looked at me and stopped pulling his beard. "Where was she? Did she quit and go home?"

No. She never made it.

Sheela shook her head. "Better for her if she had. No, we found where she fell through the bottom of a tunnel not more than fifty yards from the start. As I said, she was on the heavy side and she ran across a weak spot that couldn't support her weight. She fell through not just that tunnel, but also one beneath it. She died the instant she hit. Her head was split open." When she shivered, I took her in my arms. "I will never forget the image. And I won't let that happen to you." She poked me in the chest for good effect.

Reckard eyed us with something close to jealousy.

Cavendish mumbled with the pick in his mouth, "You can get him through with that heavy foot, right?"

"I hope so." The lamp still shook in her hand.

As he resumed his work, Cavendish whispered, "She sure loves you."

Yes, she did, and I wasn't about to argue with myself over the point any further. What to do about it was another matter. I wanted to do more than hug her while she was in such pain, but that would expose misplaced feelings. It would hurt Reckard, too, and I owed him for saving me from The Misters.

This was yet another reason I refused to care about love. It was too damn complicated.

Faint clicks sounded from the locks and saved me from indecision and a descent into the darker recesses of my emotions. Cavendish pulled the latch back. He grinned as he changed to clear lenses on his goggles. With a twirl of his arms, he motioned to the darkness. "After you, Ash."

We climbed down a ladder and entered the true underground of Campden, where legends spoke of monstrous rats, snakes larger than men are tall, feral pigs, half-dead sheep with teeth as sharp as knives, and strange groans heard in the deepest hours of the night.

If any of those stories bothered Sheela, she gave no indication as she led the way with her lamp held high, with all the assurance of someone who had faced that place a hundred times, even if her last visit had been so disastrous. We walked through a brick and mortar land that smelled much like the sewer one would expect. At least the builders had been considerate enough to include a narrow walkway on the left side so we were not forced to wade through the murky, foul water. Instead, we kicked rats out of our way, and avoided the endless number of cobwebs waiting to entangle the face of an unsuspecting intruder.

I followed behind Sheela while Cavendish stuck close to me. Reckard brought up the rear, unseen and as silent as the assassin he had been ordered to be.

For the journey, the gnome had collected several magical items. He gave Sheela a ring of protection, which he said would help should she be struck by any type of magical force. For himself, he found what he called the Medallion of Pureness, which was stained by the blood of elves. He claimed it would reduce any effects of elven magic directed at him. For me, he found what he called an Anklet of Speed, which was attached to my left leg. It supposedly assisted the wearer in moving faster.

Two magical daggers he kept for himself. He claimed not even a cyclops was impervious to their edges. He doubted I was, either, but I refused his request to test the theory.

He found nothing for Reckard, who showed sincere gratitude for not having to wear something he considered all but useless.

As for other weapons, Reckard and I both carried a sword along with an assortment of knives. Sheela opted for a brace of pistols, which she kept strapped to her back. She claimed a bullet often worked best when dealing with a magical creature.

"How far do we go before we find the forbidden sections?" Cavendish asked as Sheela stopped at an intersection.

She held her lamp higher as she looked left and right. "We have a way. This path is not as direct, but it should be safer."

"Safety isn't our concern," I said as she pulled her dress up, exposing her calves, and waded across the knee-deep murk.

When she reached the other side, where another walkway led into darkness, she said, "But your safety is my only concern. Besides, what good would we do by entering the tunnels now, only to be stopped at a collapsed section? We'd just have to double-back and come this way." She helped me out of the putrid slime. "This way has fewer weak spots."

Cavendish, who had ridden on my back, slipped off my shoulders.

We continued on and crossed three more intersections. At each, Sheela stopped to inspect the paths, almost like she tried to orient herself before continuing on. She moved with a purpose and a knowledge I had to respect.

"How many years did you play down here?" I asked, and the voice chided me for asking her to reveal more disturbing memories.

She said, not glancing back, "For the better part of five. We couldn't always slip away, and you can only return home smelling like this place every so often, else you will be asked questions you don't want to answer."

All I could envision was Sheela's friend lying dead at my feet, with her head cracked open amidst a tangle of red, curly hair. What did she go through, to have lost her best friend at such a young and impressionable age?

I asked, "Have you been down here since the...accident?"

"No," she said with finality. "I vowed never to come back. Not that I had a choice, for our games were finished. My parents almost locked me in the house for two months. And I cannot begin to describe the horror that Gaelen's parents suffered. The tragedy struck them so hard that her father left the family six months later. The last we heard, he signed on with a ship bound for the East Indies."

At least he didn't turn to the elixirs for help.

Cavendish asked, "So do you know where the Duke's place is?"

"No, but I have a good idea. There was one section of the tunnels we couldn't reach. The ceiling had collapsed long ago. I'm guessing the Duke might have cleared it out."

"So we are going to a place you don't know?" the gnome asked, echoing my same question.

"Yes." She forced a laugh. "But don't worry. I know these tunnels well enough to recognize certain signs of impending danger."

Her words did nothing to reassure me. "Such as?"

"Piles of crumbling mortar, bricks that stick out too far or are pressed in a little too much if they are on the floor, vines are always a sign of trouble, things like that. Gaelen didn't know the old tunnels well enough to recognize the signs of the impending collapse. The rest of us ran over that same spot a hundred times and knew to avoid it." She stopped at a grate that was raised a good five inches above the water. "We're here."

We gathered around and peered into the darkness below. Cavendish pulled out his picks and worked on the five-hole lock.

The sewers had been built during an early construction boom in the town. Two enterprising companies out of London bid for the work. Both proposed using new steam-drilling machines they claimed chewed through rock and dirt like a submersible sliced through the water. On the first, it took two men constantly shoveling coal into a furnace hungrier than a newborn babe. On the second, they used a new form of coal that was combined with other additives to make it burn slow and hot, with the need for someone to monitor a series of gauges to keep the machine from melting itself.

The first Duke Schaever decided it was in Campden's best interest to let them race for the prize of the top asking price in gold. The only condition was they had to hire locals from the workhouses. That set in motion a near-disastrous competition as both companies worked day and night, and shook the ground beneath the town for six months straight. Being greedy bastards, they tried to sabotage their competitor's machines. Failing that, they shot at each other's workers as they came to and from their respective construction sites. When the Guardsmen were formed to protect each side, the rivalry spilled over to the alehouses, where ambushes were planned, and any slight offense was likely to end in a furniture-busting debacle. When the first Duke threatened to throw them both out of town without pay, he did more harm than good.

Each side left the other alone, but they tunneled too fast and without concern for safety or functionality or where other tunnels had been dug. The result, discovered years later, was that over half of the tunnels were unusable because of the threat of collapse. And the sewage stagnated, causing many areas of town to smell worse than London before the high tide swept the Thames clean. The few good tunnels, built during the first month of the effort, were put into service while the others were sealed until such time as someone decided it was worth the effort and expense to repair them.

When the latch fell away, Sheela pulled the grate back. She dropped into the hole, taking the lamp with her. I handed her Cavendish before swinging my feet over the opening. The surrounding darkness inspired me to ask, "So what was your record for staying in the dark?"

As I dropped, and faster than I should have because of my lead foot, she answered. But the crunch of the brick beneath my heel drowned her words. "What?" I asked.

"Six hours was as far as we went. That was a tie between me and a boy named John. We refused to let the other win and stopped by mutual agreement because we needed to go home for dinner."

Reckard followed last. He appeared for an instant when he hit the floor.

Sheela held the lamp high again. "As much as I like to hear your voice, Ash, we had best be quiet from here. We don't know what might wait ahead."

She told me, a professional thief, how to sneak around? "Are you sure you haven't worked for The Misters?"

A different darkness settled on her face. "If I ever meet The Misters—"

"You'll be dead," Reckard said, "and I'll be sad. Sadder, perhaps, than Ash. Now quiet and let the lady lead the way."

Sheela smiled at Reckard as she stood a little taller and set out.

The tunnels were round, save for the one-foot wide, flat floor. Their height was a good four feet above my head, putting them at about ten feet. They were made of brown brick. Otherwise, nothing seemed strange or unusual about them. They smelled different than the sewers though. They had a definite musty and earthy scent and lacked much of the pungent stink. They reminded me of one of my grandmother's quilts after it sat in the wardrobe for too long.

After twenty feet, Sheela pointed to a place on the floor, a rough circle of three feet with recessed bricks. "Avoid that, Ash. Go around as far as you can."

I did as told, all but pressing my back against the opposite wall. Still, the bricks beneath my left foot shifted. Only after I cleared the area and my chest burned did I remember to breathe.

Sheela nodded in satisfaction before continuing on. The tunnel stopped when it intersected with another. She turned right and pointed at the vines growing from the ceiling. Crushed bricks were scattered on the floor after ten more feet. Dirt was piled two feet high on the right, next to the spot where the bricks fell.

I took a broken one to examine it. Cavendish gave it a quick glance as he passed. He didn't notice something big and heavy stepped on it. I put it down, then hurried to keep up with the group.

Sheela identified another weak spot, one with two recessed bricks. Cavendish, out of curiosity and doubt, pushed on them. They gave way beneath him and I had to catch him by the collar to keep him from following headfirst. When I set him back in place, he adjusted his goggles and whispered, "Thank you, Ash."

Sheela raised her brow, and her face appeared a mix between amused and irritated. She kept going without a word until we reached another dead end at another crossing tunnel. "Around this turn, about thirty feet down, was the point at which we could go no further."

As Reckard passed he said, "Let me look. Cavendish, you might have proven yourself useful if you had found something to help us see in the dark."

The gnome flipped green lenses over his eyes. "I can see well enough. I even know where you are." He tugged on his beards. "You don't need to make that gesture, sir!"

Sheela motioned Reckard along. "Be careful and watch your step."

"How about a kiss for luck?" he asked.

She answered with a squeal and held her hand to her cheek. "Reckard! I refuse to believe—"

"You are long overdue for that, love," the thief said. "At least I know when a lady expects one. Whether or not she wants it from me is another matter."

I'm certain he looked at me, but I refused to take his bait.

What did you think of it, Sheela? Did you enjoy it? Do you want more?

Those questions hung over me as we began a moment of waiting, one that seemed to last an eternity. Sheela spent the entire time watching me. I returned her look, but grew uncomfortable as it felt as if she memorized what I looked like for posterity's sake.

Finally Reckard whispered, "Two cyclopes. Both carrying rather large, wide swords. They are wearing some type of black, shiny armor."

"Is the passage open?" Sheela asked.

"Yes. There are reinforcing braces beginning behind the creatures. The Duke appears to have been a busy man. And for many, many years if I had to guess. Wonder what all he is keeping for The Gatherers?"

"Something good and worth our trouble," I said, all but feeling the Head within reach.

The voice whispered there could be more than we imagined as if it saw the complete picture of the puzzle.

What is it, then?

Cavendish held out his two daggers. "Take these and move behind the cyclopes. Bury each to the hilt in the base of their necks."

When Reckard took the weapons they disappeared.

"That's bizarre," I said in an admiring tone, "how you can make whatever you touch disappear, too?"

"At least it means I don't have to run about naked." He laughed. "Now wait here while I try to dispose of our friends."

"Do you have to kill them?" I asked. "Why not disable them or knock them unconscious?"

Reckard answered, "I won't risk their powers against us. And don't worry your righteous heart, Ash. This is on me, not you." He paused. "I'll do whatever it takes to keep Sheela safe."

"And I won't?" I answered quickly. Reckard didn't reply.

You will let him kill them? You'll stand here and do nothing?

One look at Sheela answered the question. I wouldn't let anything happen to her, either, even if it meant doing what Reckard was about to do.

Thus began another moment of waiting, one more unbearable than the last. Sheela pulled me away from the corner at one point and she whispered, "If you lean too far out, they'll see you."

At that same moment, we heard a grunt, followed by the deep bellow of a cyclops. A second joined him.

Both killed without warning.

We waited for Reckard to return and tell of his success. Instead, a breeze stirred, as if someone passed. My friend said from far behind, "Cavendish, the daggers only pricked them. What did you give me?"

The gnome's mouth opened and closed three times.

As fear shot through me I said, "You mean—"

And then the cyclopes were on top of us.

I pushed Sheela out of the way of the first one. The creature roared as it swung its large sword. I met its challenge by foolishly sticking my arm in the way. The impact of its blow knocked me sideways, into the second cyclops, which landed a blow hard enough to sever a man in half. But all he did was make my shoulder throb as his blade broke.

The creature snarled as he tried to grab me, but Reckard pulled me away. "Run as fast as you can. They've been enhanced beyond anything I've ever seen or dealt with."

"Then how—"

He hissed, "Just run."

I turned to do as told, but moved as slow as ever.

The nearest cyclops reached for me, but grunted when something - Reckard's sword? - knocked his hands away. The creature swung and smashed the side of the tunnel, knocking loose a half-dozen bricks. A spray of dirt covered his face shield, forcing him to pause to wipe it off.

I continued to run with my looping, gimpy strides.

I need to go faster. Reckard can't keep them occupied forever.

One cyclops grabbed my shoulder and spun me about. I tried to poke his eye, but my hand bounced off his shield. He growled in rage anyway, like I mortally offended him for trying such a tactic, and threw me against the wall. My body pushed the bricks in. They stayed in place as I fell to the floor.

The creature picked me up and threw me down the way, towards Sheela, whose eyes were wide with horror.

After five rolls, I regained my feet. I dusted off my somewhat tattered clothes.

The creature ran for me, gaining momentum like a train engine, but Reckard tripped him. The cyclops fell forward with the sound of breaking bricks echoing through the tunnel.

I ran again, expecting to be as slow as before, but a tingling sensation started at the anklet, then moved into my foot, calf, and thigh. My leg felt lighter than my right…much lighter. I passed Sheela, and Cavendish. I had to slow so they could join me.

Both cyclopes bellowed and roared behind. They swung at the air, then lowered their shoulders and charged as a pair. They stopped suddenly and smashed the floor with their fists.

"Watch it, you bumbling oafs," Reckard said.

The cyclops on the right grunted as a brick bounced off his face shield. The left one swung again, and Reckard said, "You oafs can do better. I know you can."

"Sheela," I said, "lead us to one of those weak places in the floor. Quickly."

She nodded and ran ahead. She turned left, then paused to see if I followed.

I motioned for her to wait. These cyclopes needed to be as mad as possible, mad enough to lose their simple minds.

Both creatures charged, swatting at the air in front of them as they went. I sheathed my sword, lowered my shoulder, and met them full-speed with the assistance of the anklet. The right one and I collided with an impact not unlike one of Aimee's explosions. The force rippled through skin and muscle and into the bone, throwing me backwards like I tried to move a stone wall.

The cyclops, for his part, fell back as well.

The other cyclops grabbed me. He squeezed me between his hands. My skin held, but my shoulders threatened to break. How strong were these creatures? What type of elixirs flowed in them?

I kicked the creature in the chin, then planted a foot on his mask. For a moment, we remained at a standstill, locked in a battle of wills. The moment ended when his shield shattered.

That allowed Reckard to poke him in the eye.

The creature dropped me as he roared and covered his eye. Despite the blood seeping between his fingers, he charged again. The other followed.

"To the left," I said as I ran, hoping Reckard remained with me.

Down the tunnel, Sheela's lamp swung back and forth like a beacon of safe harbor. Bricks crunched beneath my heels as I ran.

Sheela came into full view. Cavendish stood beside and behind her. She pointed to the floor before her. "Jump, Ash. Jump!"

That was the spot where Cavendish pushed the bricks and almost fell through. It appeared Sheela had loosened several others. She stood well back from the spot, and I leapt over it.

But the anklet helped with running, not jumping. I struck the floor in a full sprawl, far short of my intended target.

The bricks beneath me crumpled.

I scrambled to reach surer footing. The cyclopes bellowed with delight when they saw me stretched out. They slowed to snatch me up, and I closed my eyes in anticipation of the beating I was about to receive.

But the floor gave way beneath them. And me, too.

Sheela screamed as my left foot dragged the rest of my body with it. I scratched and clawed at the bricks trying to hold onto anything.

I wouldn't end my life like Sheela's childhood friend. To put her through such horrors a second time? The thought made me dig my fingers deep in spite of the jagged edges of broken rocks.

"Hold tight," Reckard said as he grabbed my arm. He secured me by the elbow.

The cyclopes hit the floor on the level below with such force that both tunnels shook. A dusting of mortar showered us as Sheela and Cavendish shielded their heads to prepare for an impending collapse.

The creatures roared as they reached for my feet.

I kicked one hand away and avoided another.

Reckard pulled with all of his strength, inch-by-inch. Cavendish joined him and did little. The effort was appreciated nonetheless.

I grabbed hold of the edge.

A cyclops grabbed my left leg and crushed the anklet. I tried to twist away, but he pulled me back down, inch-by-inch.

A now visible Reckard strained as he fought the weight. His face turned red as his neck muscles tightened.

That was the moment Sheela stepped to the edge and spoke with fury. "Let him go!" She fired a pistol. The sound echoed three times. A thud followed, then a howl of pain, and a release of my foot.

I crawled out of reach before stopping to catch my breath.

Too close, Ash. Much too close.

An inspection of the anklet showed indentions left by the cyclops' fingers and thumb.

Cavendish pulled on his beard. "Does that hurt?"

I shook my head. "The better question is whether it still works."

When he leaned close I thought about giving him a swift kick for all of his troubles. But I resisted, and for my reward the gnome said, "It's not broken, so it should work. I cannot guarantee it though." He scratched beneath his cap.

"But you could guarantee the daggers," an invisible Reckard said. He probably shook his fist at the gnome. "They almost killed us instead of killing them. At least Ash can be satisfied they aren't dead."

Sheela stood between Cavendish and Reckard's voice. She nodded at the enraged cyclopes below, one of which nursed a bleeding cheek where the bullet grazed. "There's no getting across the hole. We must go a different way."

Reckard said, with a still-seething voice, "Then show us where to go. Please."

Sheela took Cavendish by the hand, like he was a favored child, and set off as before. This time, though, she kept glancing back like she wanted to make sure I still followed.

I did so without complaint, though between the remains of the dragon bites and the cyclopes' pounding, my belly hurt, my arms hurt, and my legs hurt. Yet I had come too far, endured too much, and had too much at stake to turn back. I had to push through the moment, and strive for the next, when I might gain a second burst of strength.

Soon enough, we went down the tunnel where the cyclopes once stood guard. We stopped at a square opening about eight-feet by eight-feet. It went straight up, much like a shaft in a coal mine. Cables and chains hung overhead, awaiting someone to enter the cage in the darkness above. Metal bands along the bottom edge of the shaft would hold the cage in place while a cart was loaded on or off. That cart would then attach to the steel pipe following each side at the widest points and run on a set of tracks along the bottom of the tunnel.

Besides those improvements, every five feet, a ring of steel six inches wide had been embedded in the bricks. Impressive. I said, "The Duke has been busy. What else do we have waiting for us?"

Reckard spoke from ahead. "I'll stay at the forward edge of the light to keep watch for whatever we're about to encounter. Sheela, keep the lantern held high."

"I will," she said as she lifted it above her head.

As we went, she pointed to a place with new bricks. "Probably a hole they repaired." She pointed to a similar spot in the ceiling.

How much money did you invest in the place, Duke Schaever? Not only buying the magic to protect it, but also the physical labor and machinery needed to build it. And paying the workers to remain silent.

Or do you pay them?

I whispered, "Maybe this is why the Duke needs the gnomes. Maybe he works them to death before bringing in a fresh batch."

Cavendish gave a low whistle. "No one cares about my brothers, so what does it matter if either world misses a few? By killing them, he guarantees the secrecy of this place." He pulled on his beard. "I think you might be onto something, Ash."

Maybe. But it didn't feel right, and the voice sounded uneasy. I had enough experience dealing with human nature to recognize those men who always schemed and planned, who plotted and maneuvered. They never stopped working to gain the upper hand on everyone. Based on what I witnessed, the Duke appeared to be that type of man. No, he didn't appear to be that type. He was unquestionably that type.

He was dangerous.

So what did he want? What was his goal?

The tunnel forked two hundred feet in and Reckard said, "The tracks and tubes follow the left tunnel. That's the way I'm going."

Sheela stared at the ceiling. "There's something different here." She pointed to all the patches. "The bricks are not set the same as in the previous tunnel."

"Different workers?" I asked. "A different quarry for the brick, maybe?"

She bit her lower lip. "Maybe."

We made our way fifty feet, when Reckard called, "I tripped over something! A thick stri—"

The tunnel shook. Out of an instinctive need to protect that which I cared for, I grabbed Sheela while Cavendish darted back.

I reached out like I could take hold of Reckard wherever he was.

A deep boom sounded as the ceiling collapsed. A blast of air followed, carrying bits of dirt and rocks with it. Many pieces bounced off me as I shielded Sheela.

After a moment, it settled. We found ourselves knee-deep in earth.

"A trap. You were right, Sheela." I dusted her hair and felt its silkiness. For a reason I didn't want to consider, the feeling lasted far longer than was proper.

Where Reckard had been, a wall of dirt clogged the way.

Sheela said, "Do you think..." She choked as her eyes filled with tears. Mine almost did the same.

Time was precious, so I started digging. She stepped beside me, and together we threw mounds of dirt behind. Even Cavendish reappeared and joined the effort.

"He cannot survive long," I said, trying to keep my voice calm. I didn't want the fear and panic welling within me to affect the others. "We must find him." My arms ached more, but I wouldn't cease. Not until I reached him.

Unfortunately, the more dirt we moved, the more took its place from above. The longer we went, the more defeated I felt. After a good twenty minutes, we made little progress other than making the dirt behind all the higher, and giving me a feeling of complete hopelessness.

Sheela fell to her knees. She pounded the dirt. "Damn it, Ash. I promised myself never to come back to this place. There is nothing but death here. And it's always my friends." She beat the dirt so hard, she buried her hands each time. "Damn this place to a thousand hells!"

Indeed. Not knowing what else to do, I hugged her. She beat on my chest before giving way to sobs.

Coldness seeped through me, of the type that indicates a giving up, of a failure. I spoke, but it sounded like a stranger talking. "The Duke and Aimee will pay for this. Reckard was a good friend."

The best. Loyal in spite of our profession and your supposed battle for Sheela's affections. Why did she not love you instead of me?

Cavendish, who continued digging, said, "I feel something!" He all but stuck his head and shoulders into the soft earth.

Sheela hurried to his side. She pushed her arms into the dirt as deep as she could manage. "I feel something, too!"

The gnome, with his arse sticking up, grunted as he pulled. Sheela helped.

I tried to reach in and add my strength, but seemed to get in the way. Sheela bumped me to the right. Cavendish squirmed left and right. When they exposed Reckard's visible arm, I grabbed it and pulled.

The dirt fought to keep its limp captive. It gathered about us like it threatened to bury us, too, if we continued the rescue. Yet Reckard's elbow appeared in spite of it. Then his shoulder.

Do you live, old chap? Or have you already suffocated?

I pushed Cavendish down as I took hold of Reckard's shoulder and planted my feet. My arms burned and my shoulders protested as I pulled with every bit of strength I could muster. Reckard emerged inch-by-inch.

Cavendish brushed dirt out of Reckard's hair and pushed it from his eyes and nose and mouth.

I continued to pull, but cramps took hold and burned like Frank Greenhew's flames engulfed my limbs.

"Rest, Ash," Sheela said as she moved in front, almost smothering Reckard. She put her mouth on his and while she did it to make him breathe, my heart beat faster and the voice grumbled.

Why?

The voice said, "Because you refuse to admit the truth."

The unease within my chest grew the longer she pressed her lips onto his.

If only Reckard knew what she did...it was the very essence of his dream.

Cavendish continued digging.

Sheela said, "Come on, old chap. Don't do this." She breathed into his mouth again.

Cavendish paused to clean the dirt from his goggles and said, "He might be too far gone."

Sheela grabbed Reckard's shoulders and pulled. She grimaced and grunted, and the earth gave up its prisoner with a sucking sound. More dirt fell in one last play. With my assistance, she pulled Reckard free all the way to his toes. "Step on his chest, Ash."

With my foot? "I'll break his ribs."

"What does a broken rib mean to a dead man? If he lives, the pain will remind him of his blessing." When I made no move, she planted her fists on her hips. "Ash!"

I pressed down with my left foot until she waved for me to stop. She breathed into his mouth again.

Cavendish leaned on Reckard, taking deep breaths. "He's dead. He couldn't survive this long."

There was no pleasure in admitting it, but the gnome was right. And I felt what? Sadness? Disappointment? Anger? Or nothing at all? Had my mind fully comprehended the reality of death or had I simply turned numb to it? He was a Company thief, after all, and that meant he should have died several times over. It had caught up to him was all.

Still he was a good and loyal friend. He deserved tears and a toast of Branagh's Ale. He deserved Sheela's continued attempts to save him.

Cavendish took his silly hat off and held it over his chest. He bowed three times in quick succession in the gnomish way of saying farewell. As he replaced the hat he said, "I don't want to interrupt the crying and the grief, but we need to keep moving. Our time is no less urgent for the loss. More so, I would say."

"Shut up," Sheela said as she beat Reckard's chest one last time. She stood and pointed at the gnome. "Shut up!"

I pulled her hand back. "Shhh! He's right. We will have to mourn Reckard when we return to Branagh's. We will drink a round in his memory. But for now, we need to keep going." I wrapped my arms about her again. "Stay strong. We don't know what else we will face. Keep yourself together."

"Shut up...and...and let me cry."

I did as told although it hurt to see her in so much pain. She shouldn't have to bury her face in my coat, or have her tears wash her face clean.

She whispered, "I hate this forsaken place. I hate being here." She wiped her cheeks, smearing mud across them. "I don't want to remember my past."

"Why?" I asked even though I felt the same concerning my own.

She had the same look on her face as she did when we were at the Ball when she fought the urge to tell me her secrets. This time, though, her eyes darted left and right as if she lost the fight. All at once she said, "Because I'm running from my past just like you are. I used to be married, too, and my husband was a difficult man. His indiscretions were legendary, but I had to live with them."

I put a finger over her lips and said, "You don't have to tell me this." I didn't deserve to know.

"I'm a Gateway survivor."

Had such a pronouncement not come from her with such a serious tone in such a tragic situation, I would've laughed. Instead, I stood in stunned silence.

Cavendish echoed my unspoken thoughts when he asked, "You mean you've been through?"

She glared at me like I asked the question. "Yes. I lived and survived on the other side for two very long years. When I returned to this world, I was allowed to survive the spell on the Gateway, but at the cost of being fifteen years younger in appearance." She planted her hands on her hips. "So now you know. Sheela's big secret is revealed."

What could I say? How could I respond?

"It's about time you admitted as much," Reckard said, then coughed. "You are Lady Carrigan, aren't you? The one who ran away, and many thought had died in London?" We all faced him as he sat up and rubbed his chest. "Did a boulder land on top of me?" His high-pitched tone had never sounded so good.

The voice laughed and the sadness that burdened my shoulders lifted.

Sheela threw her arms around him. "How long—"

"Long enough to realize I wasn't dreaming. I think I knew I lived when I smelled the gnome."

Cavendish quit pulling on his beards. "That's—"

"He saved you," Sheela said as she slapped Reckard's arm. "He refused to quit digging until we pulled you free."

Reckard flinched and mumbled, "Thank you, Cavendish." He peered at Sheela from under his brow. "That is what you want me to say?"

She nodded. "And mean it."

I held a hand out and when he took it, I pulled him to his feet. "I'm glad you returned to us." When he wobbled, I held him steady.

He rubbed his forehead. "Sometimes I think life is too valued by the living. Still, I seem to owe you all my thanks." He took a step and almost fell.

"We should rest a bit," Sheela said as she motioned for us to sit.

Reckard said, "No, we keep moving, m'Lady."

"Lady Carrigan?" I asked as the full realization of what she said struck. "You're Lady Carrigan?"

Her tale was famous around Campden. She married Lord Arthur Carrigan when she was but fifteen. Her beauty attracted gentlemen from across three counties and legend said two would-be suitors dueled to the death over the privilege to call on her. Unfortunately for the young lady, her father lost most of the family fortune playing games of chance. Lord Carrigan offered to pay the debts before Sheela's father was arrested, but at the price of her hand in marriage.

"Lady Anne Carrigan?" I asked, trying to imagine Sheela — a bar maid! — as a lady of distinguished society. Yet such imagining was not so difficult as it might have been. In fact, given the Ball and the other times I had observed her behavior, it made a strange sort of sense.

"Anne?" I asked.

She folded her arms. "I'm no longer the person to whom you keep referring. I am Sheela, now."

Reckard coughed and spit. "There was quite the reward for you. I wonder if it's still good." He eyed her from beneath his brow. "What proof do you have of your word, anyway?"

She lifted the pendant she always wore, the diamond-shaped one. "This belonged to my mother. My father gave it to her as a wedding present. If you look into the stone, you will see my family's crest." She held it up so Reckard and I could verify her claim.

Indeed, a crest of a fox and a sword was etched into the metal.

Before we could say anything, she pulled a pistol from its holster and pushed the barrel against Reckard's chest. "Anne Carrigan died. This pendant is all that remains of her. It's best we remember her with fondness in her deceased state." She looked at me and her lips were tight. "Not a word of this to anyone." The gun moved to Cavendish. "If you so much as breathe this secret, I will make sure you pay a price you're not willing to pay." She paused before pushing the barrel against Reckard's chest again. "Understand?" When he nodded, she pushed it into my chest. The barrel shook. "Understand?"

I nodded, too. "Was it that bad? Your former life?"

She hesitated before replacing the pistol. "Do you think you saw the dark side of a fallen world when you were a canon? Then you know nothing. My former husband was a monster with powerful and influential friends. I will not go into the sordid details of his private life. Suffice to say he admired a certain Donatien Alphonse Francois." She shuddered. "I'll die before I return to that life." Her shoulders appeared to slump a little as she turned away.

A lady, noble born, and a Gateway survivor.

Reckard asked, "So what is on the other side? You are the only human who really—"

263

She pointed the pistol at him for the third time. "I keep those secrets on the threat of my life. I work at Branagh's at The Elders' pleasure."

Cavendish cringed. "Don't speak their name!"

I grinned, glad to have the opportunity to make the gnome uncomfortable. "You've mentioned them before, gnome. I knew it was The Elders who sent you to help me."

Cavendish turned pale. "Don't speak their name, Ash!"

Sheela took my hand. "The gnome's fears are not unfounded. While speaking their name is not dangerous in and of itself, if they knew I told you this much, they would kill us all." She spoke with such assurance it brokered neither argument nor further questions, save for one.

"How have you kept anyone from recognizing you?" Only then did I realize the danger she put herself in by going to the Ball. It was no surprise she was so nervous. Why would she risk so much?

Because of me?

As if she read my thoughts she said, "I have subtle means of disguise. I almost gave myself away when we went to the Ball. Yet I had no choice. After the Ball, I was told to do anything necessary to help you find the Head." She looked at each of us as if deciding whether she should shoot us. After letting out a slow breath, she put the pistol back in its holster. "No one is looking for a younger version of myself. The others who have come back through were much, much older."

Reckard asked, "How did you get through without being noticed? Someone would have seen and reported it."

"Not if shape shifting spells are involved, and their side-effect is to leave you with slight alterations to your features." Before we could say anything else, she added, "You've attracted the attention of powerful forces, Ash, ones on both sides of the terrible war. I hope we all survive them."

I asked, "So who is Frengarn, and what is Reganas Five?"

She gave the gnome, who shook his head vehemently, a measuring look. He all but squeaked when she said, "Frengarn is dangerous. He is high in the rigid social structure of the orcs. As for Reganas Five—"

"They don't need to know!" Cavendish said. "Say nothing else, please!"

She closed her eyes, and the tightness at the corners indicated pain. "I was at Reganas Five in the last days. I saw it fall." Sadness filled her voice, and a tear ran down her right cheek. "It was beautiful, an oasis of art and nature combined, where magic made colors more vibrant, smells sharper, sounds soother, and tastes sweeter. It was one of the elf's homes, the most splendid of all the Reganas."

Cavendish tried to shake Sheela's leg. "Please...if they know you're saying this—"

"Pity the survivors, Cavendish. Say a prayer for them. I speak for them because we do a great disservice to their memories by forgetting their sacrifice." She resumed the journey, and the three of us followed without a word, save for Cavendish whispering, "Not a word of this to anyone."

I disregarded his words as I watched Sheela, Anne, and felt like I didn't really know her.

The voice said such thoughts were nonsense. She remained the same beautiful, loyal, and loving woman, even if I saw her with a new perspective, and had a new appreciation for her.

When we reached the other tunnel, Cavendish recovered enough of his wits to run his foot across the dirt. It flickered. When he touched the side it flickered, too, giving a glimpse of the track and rails.

The gnome flipped purple lenses on his goggles. He changed them to orange, and he spoke like he was pleased to discuss something more agreeable. "Ah, an illusion. Very clever. I see through it, now."

"A little late," Sheela murmured.

He ignored her as he motioned for us to follow. After forty feet, the illusion ended. The track and tubes reappeared. A clever disguise. The Duke was proving to be as cunning as he was rich.

We moved carefully, and I said, "Cavendish, you're small. Scout ahead like Reckard did."

The gnome turned pale. "Me? End up buried? No. I'll stay with you."

When I tried to push the little man, he refused to budge. "The Duke would not collapse both tunnels. He wouldn't be able to reach his treasure horde."

"Maybe he has a third entrance."

"I am sure he paid those cyclopes to guard a fake entrance."

The gnome crossed his arms. "I refuse to go." He waved a hand. "After you."

I pointed to his eyes. "Use your goggles to look for traps."

"I would miss them without the correct filter." He cocked his head. "So lead the way."

"I'll go," Reckard said.

He ran into my outstretched arm. I wouldn't allow him to risk his life like that again. So I snarled at the hairy little creature and took the lead. As such, our progress slowed, especially when the tunnel took a turn or a bend or descended lower. But we saw nothing else, except the regular bands and the replaced bricks and the tracks and the tubes, until we approached a doorway. Before it stood four lizard men. They all wore the red loincloths and carried metal swords of the same color as the cyclopes' armor. They readied them when they saw us.

"Cavendish," I said with disappointment, "I thought you made sure these creatures wouldn't bother us."

"Someone didn't give me enough time." He moved forward without looking in Reckard's direction. "I will talk with them. I will find out which side they're on."

Reckard whispered, "I'm in no condition to fight them no matter how much I'd like to."

I took one of Sheela's pistols. "The creatures aren't bullet proof, so we can even the odds."

"Let me take it." An invisible hand tugged on it. "You won't kill them. You don't have it in you."

"Who said anything about killing?" I asked as I held tight. "A wound should be good enough."

"A wound could poison them if the bullet remains. That might lead to their death." He tugged harder. "Keep your conscience clear of such acts. For now."

I gave in and released the pistol, which disappeared.

"Those are unusual swords," Reckard said as Cavendish approached the group. "I didn't think the reptilians could even carry metal. I thought they had a reaction to it. What kind of magic is working on them?"

"The kind that gets you killed," I said. "Let me worry about them." When Sheela readied her second pistol, I continued, "Don't fight and use that as a last defense." I almost added, "M'Lady," but decided against making an armed lady angry with me.

Cavendish stood before the lizard men. He gestured as he spoke. His words didn't reach us, and the lizard's faces were unreadable so I couldn't guess as to what to expect.

One lizard pointed first at us, then at the doorway behind them. It shook its sword and the jagged blade absorbed all light from around it. The hisses and slurs didn't sound friendly. It helped little when Cavendish glanced at us. His face was as red as the queen's robes and sweat ran to his goggles.

Sheela started forward. "I should talk to them."

"No," I said, grabbing her arm. She wouldn't face such danger needlessly. "Let Cavendish take care of the matter. I will convince them of the wisdom of his request at the first sign of trouble."

She spoke in a knowing tone. "I think we're beyond that."

Two lizards picked Cavendish up, holding him by each arm, and stalked towards us. The gnome struggled and kicked at the air, but the lizards ignored him.

I stepped into the light with sword ready.

The creature on the left said, "Unwisssse for you to do that, human."

"Harming the gnome would be more unwise," I answered, "if you value your cold-blooded existence."

The lizards dropped Cavendish, and he fell to his knees. The one that had spoken continued, "We had no intenssssion of hurting the gnome. Out of ressssspect for him, we allow him to leave. We will alsssso allow you."

I nodded to the door. "We need to go in there."

"We cannot allow you in."

"Cannot or will not?"

Their tongues flickered twice before the same one said, "Cannot."

Cavendish pointed to their necks. "They are slaves, Ash. Like the elf at the house where we kidnapped your wife. Same type of band. Remember? The ivory one inlaid with six pearls in perfect symmetry? They have no choice."

I shrugged and said, "Then remove the bands and free them."

The lizards looked at each other, then at me. In their unblinking eyes was a certain surprise, like they hadn't considered doing that very thing. Foolish reptiles.

Cavendish motioned for the left one to bend down. He used his lock-pick set to work on the clasp. After a moment, the band dropped to the floor. The lizard rubbed his neck as the gnome grinned and set about working on the second lizard. While he worked, an angry scream echoed through the tunnel.

Cavendish dropped a pick and as he retrieved it, asked, "What was that?"

In answer, the other lizards charged while the one Cavendish worked on tried to push him away.

His recently freed friend held him fast and said, "Hold your weapon." He motioned to the others. "Sssstop!"

Not a one listened. They bore down on us as the free one struggled to contain the second.

Once a reptilian decided to fight, there was no convincing it otherwise, even when he wasn't a slave.

Reckard fired and a charging reptilian fell. Blood oozed from a hole in his shoulder, which he clutched with his hand.

His comrade took his discarded sword and ran faster.

I stepped around the one Cavendish worked on and met the attack. The lizard swung with such force that my weapon broke. The upper half clanged against the rail as I tried to lock cross-guards to check his momentum. But his sword sliced through my broken blade.

He brought the other around, and I blocked with my forearm. Sharp pain raced up and into my shoulder as the blade cut. Not deep, but deep enough to draw blood.

Sheela said, "Ash, give me a clear shot."

While I wanted to, the creature moved too fast. Not knowing what else to do, I threw the hilt of my useless sword and hit him square on the nose. He hissed and drew up short. A hand pulled me away, then Cavendish's freed friends jumped on their comrade. They pinned his arms to the floor. Cavendish sat on the creature's chest and worked on the collar as he squirmed and twisted.

Sheela pushed my sleeve back and wrapped my wound with a cloth. She didn't say a word and didn't need to. Her tender touch spoke loud enough.

"That is it, then," Cavendish said as he held up a sparkling band at the same moment another scream pierced the tunnel. His eyes grew larger in his goggles. "What is that anyway?"

"A mad elf," the nearest reptilian said. "One that issss not pleassssed with our freedom." He helped the one up from the floor.

"So you will help us defeat him, correct?" I asked. After all, the enemy of my enemy had to be my friend, or so I thought.

The lizard pointed to his wounded and now unconscious comrade. "You will pay for that by fighting alone. Thissss doessss not conssssern ussss. Maybe you kill each other. Do ussss all good."

I pointed to the fallen lizard. "He would've killed you, too."

"Perhapssss. Now we will never know." His tongue darted in and out. "We have to get help. Your bullet issss poisssson."

Sheela stepped up to them, and looked each in the eyes, "You are marked. I had best never see you in Branagh's."

The lizard showed no reaction other than flicking its tongue. It pushed past. The others picked their wounded comrade up and followed. While we could have used their help, I wasn't too disappointed. Still I had to ask them, "What's down there?"

"Death," the lizard said, and all three hissed in a sign of amusement.

Reckard said, "Stupid snakes."

"Be thankful we don't have to fight them," Cavendish said. He nodded to my arm. "Their swords are made of a special and powerful metal. They said it was the same as what the mechanical people are made from." He scratched under his cap. "And that bodes ill for us."

For us or for me?

Reckard spoke with weariness as he returned Sheela's pistol. "Let's finish this." He turned invisible.

Sheela took my hand as we went towards the waiting doorway. Together, we stepped into a room that could best be described as cavernous.

"Where did this come from?" she asked with the same awe I felt.

The room was at least a hundred feet high and a hundred feet across. The tracks led to the center, where a giant forge awaited a re-awakening, but with no source of fuel. At the top of the forge hung an enormous pot made of the same black metal as the cyclopes' armor and the reptilians' swords. It was suspended by a chain connected to a track of wooden beams. Where the track led were vats six-feet tall, four-feet wide, and two-feet thick, reminiscent of coffins in both shape and size. A complex maze of scaffolding, not unlike the supports of a bridge, held each in place. A chute ran to the floor with screws and bolts and pins and other metal objects scattered about. Well-worn trails led to the other side, where a twelve-foot high doorway, rounded at the top, awaited.

As for the rest of the room, mounds of dirt and piles of crushed rock covered the floor. Bricks and reinforcing timbers ran eight feet up the walls, and there were stacks of each waiting to be used. Above the line was raw earth, dirt, and scared rock where something had blasted and chipped it away.

"The perfect job for someone who has a talent with explosives," I said, my tone echoing Sheela's. "It's no wonder Aimee knows the Duke so well. She has been helping him."

A streak of white light shot through the maze of scaffolding and beams, and struck at Sheela and me. It made a sound like the crack of a whip.

We both fell backwards. A burning sensation ran through me as I sat. I reached for Sheela and she coughed as she pushed herself onto her hands and knees. Her ring glowed a bright white.

I took her lamp and held it high.

Another blast and whip-crack followed, one strong enough to lift me off my feet and throw me against the brick wall.

Sheela, with better sense, scrambled behind a pile of bricks.

Another blast sounded, and Cavendish yelped.

A voice said, "You are trespassing on forbidden ground."

"Are you okay?" I asked Sheela.

She nodded. A clump of earth fell from her nose. With her dirt-caked cheeks and tousled hair, she had a unique, natural type of beauty I found appealing. "What of you?"

"I'm fine," I said, which was a lie. I hurt all over, and I was exhausted. But... "I will draw the magic away while Reckard works his way around." Before she could protest, I stuck my head into full view and darted, or tried to, for a pile of rocks. I received the reward of a blast of light that struck the ground behind and kicked up a cloud of dirt.

"Go no further," the voice said. It had that high-twilly pitch like an elven woman.

The light cracked again on the side where Sheela tried to move. The voice said, "Remain there, girl. I will not send another warning."

The expression Sheela wore spoke of fear and panic and worry. That alone made me decide what to do.

It would hurt, but it couldn't be any worse than the catapult landing. And if Pienne was worth what The Misters paid him, I'd survive, even if I wished I were dead.

I picked out two rocks from the pile next to me. Each was just big enough to hold in my palms. I threw one before half-running, half-limping to another pile.

The first rock exploded in a blast.

The second sailed through the air as I slid behind a much smaller pile.

Light caught my foot, which sent a burning sensation up my calf, into my thigh, and into my belly. I coughed as I squeezed my eyes tight to focus on the moment, to focus on breathing. A roaring filled my ears.

Keep moving, Ash. Keep moving. Ignore the protests of your body.

As the burning subsided, I grabbed two more rocks. After a deep breath to gather my courage, I moved towards another pile. This time I threw both rocks together in the general direction of the light's source.

They exploded in mid-air before reaching the scaffolding. Another blast followed. It struck me square in the chest.

My heart felt as if it exploded in my chest, like it wanted to escape out of my ears. Another blast struck across the shoulder and knocked me flat on my back.

I thought I heard Sheela scream, but my ears rang like I stood in the middle of Saint James' largest bell while it tolled. I burned like Frank Greenhew's flames engulfed every inch of me.

The air cracked and more light flashed.

Sheela screamed again, but more out of pain. The sound cut through me worse than any blade could hope to.

"She...Sheela?" I asked as I fought the pounding as I pushed an encompassing blackness from my mind. I had to reach her. My pain didn't matter even if breathing hurt as I turned over. "Sheela...are...you okay?" I crawled towards another dirt pile.

"She is dead," the elf said, then laughed a triumphant laugh. "You are next."

Dead? No, she isn't dead. Not here. Not now. To lose her would...

What? Hurt too much?

I expected another burning blast, but as soon as the light flashed, someone jumped on my back. "Try that again," Cavendish shouted with glee. "You are no match for gnome magic."

The elf obliged by sending a crackling barrage of light that spun the gnome around three times, lifted him up, and knocked him into a pile of bricks. Both the pile and the gnome tumbled into a heap.

The distraction gave me enough time to crawl to a safe haven. My heart had slowed a little. And enough.

What is taking so long, Reckard? You should have reached her by now.

Cavendish laughed as he jumped out of the bricks. "See? See?" He danced about as if nothing had happened. "You are useless and pathetic, lady. You cannot hope to match the greatness of the gnomes."

"You people are the ones who are small and pathetic," the elf said with the same loathing Aimee had when speaking to me. "You will forever seek to regain the true power you once held, but never find it. You will always strive to master forgotten secrets. You will forever fail."

"Sheela?" I called as quietly as I could, yet still loud enough to be heard.

A moan answered, much to my relief and dismay. She lived, but was she hurt? How bad?

Cavendish stood with his hands on his hips. He sounded offended when he said, "Gnomes are true power. We know secrets you can only imagine."

The elf said, "I do not know what magic you think you know, little man, but I will show you what true power means."

I crawled towards Sheela's moaning and spotted her crumpled against the wall. Her eyes were half-open. Blood trickled from her mouth.

"Then show me how mighty you think you are," Cavendish said as he held his arms wide. "We are waiting. Do your best!"

The elf whistled a high-pitched, long whistle that echoed around the room and resonated with the ringing of my ears. They hurt to the point that I had to cover them.

Cavendish danced on the brick pile. "That's all? Why, I can whistle, too." He demonstrated by whistling, *Jared's Ballad*, a popular tune at Branagh's about a less-than upstanding elf.

When I reached Sheela, I pulled her into my lap.

Her eyes opened more. She reached up to touch my cheek. "As...Ash...are you...okay?"

"Don't worry about me. Where are you hurt?"

She gave a quiet chuckle. "All over. But I'll survive. For the moment. Just winded and bruised." She blinked, then managed a beautiful smile that eased the lines of pain etched around her eyes and softened the ache of worry in my chest. She wiped her mouth. "Bit my cheek though. Hurts."

The elf whistled again.

"We need to bring her down," I said, then silently gave thanks that Sheela was alive. "Where is Reckard?"

Cavendish whistled again, mocking the elf. He danced a circle, then turned and stuck his arse in the air. His hat fell off. He grabbed it as he laughed louder. He stood, with arms wide. "I'm still waiting. You cannot do anything to me, elf."

He stopped and squealed the same squeal as when we fought the dragon in the street. The sound made my heart beat faster.

I peered over the bricks and watched as a head emerged from the other doorway. It was large. Huge. Enormous. Covered in scales blacker than the moonless nights. With feather-like scales rising from behind each eye. And on top of its head, long, pale horns ended in sharp tips near its ears.

The voice whispered, "Deliver us in all time of our tribulation."

"What...is wrong?" Sheela asked as she pushed herself up.

I tried to speak, but no sound emerged.

I tried again and failed.

She peered over the bricks and said what I couldn't. "That's one...damn big dragon."

CHAPTER 13

"Sheela," I said in a voice calmer than I expected. "Leave."

"What of you?" She grabbed my arm, but with a weak grip. "You...need to leave, too."

I pulled her behind the bricks. "No. I still have to get the Head of Forneil."

"But that dragon will kill you." She gave a weak tug. "I'm not going to let you die in here. I'm not..."

I took her in my arms. Concern filled her eyes. Mud was smeared across her left cheek. Her nose twitched like she held back tears. Her lips had a slight quiver. To stop them, I kissed her long and deep.

What am I doing? Here, in the midst of madness?

Ignoring all consequences, and giving myself over to an assurance of heartache and pain, of betrayal and resentment. That's where love always led.

I was cruel to Sheela. I gave her hope where hope shouldn't be, but given current prospects what else could I do?

Yet I savored the taste of her lips and the copper bitterness of her blood. The smell of her cheek with its sweat and earth-tinged scent felt more real than anything had in years. Of their own accord, my fingers ran through her hair, gripped the back of her head, and pressed all the tighter.

She responded in kind as she pressed her body against mine.

In that moment my ears stopped ringing, my aches and pains dissipated into nothingness, and I felt young again. The effect was not so unlike that of an elixir.

This is love's power.

Sheela pulled away, but continued to hold me. "A kiss won't make this better. I don't want you to stay."

As the kiss faded, all the aches returned as well as the ear ringing. I couldn't look at her — why had I dared to kiss her? — as I motioned to the exit. "You had best leave before the dragon finds us. Something happened to Reckard. He might be hurt. Or worse."

For emphasis, the beast shot out flames that sent a wave of heat overhead, just behind Cavendish as he ran out the door.

"Please go," I said as I squeezed Sheela's hands. "Follow the gnome. I will not risk your dying."

She wiped blood from her chin. "I don't want to leave you, but I might consider it on one condition."

The tone of her voice and the look in her eyes told me what she was about to say. I put a finger over her lips. There was no hesitating, for her life meant more than anything else. "Yes, Sheela, I love you."

"You don't mean it," she said, looking into, and through, my eyes. "But it's a start. That is the first time I've heard you actually speak those words." Her brow narrowed. "But it doesn't mean I'm leaving."

"But you—"

"Said I might consider it." She held the pistols up. "I still have these. Last I checked, a bullet killed elves as easy as men."

"I will not let you risk your life." The bullets wouldn't do much more than scratch the dragon.

One brow arose in question. "Just like I don't want you risking yours? We are in this together, Ash. You and me. Whether or not you accept the fact." Both pistols clicked as she cocked them. "And you best stay low while you try to distract her." When I laughed at the absurdity of our situation and her orders, she added, "I'm glad you're amused. Me? I'm as mad as I am when a Branagh's patron tries to slip away without paying."

My smile melted away. I had witnessed her challenge a group of reptilians over a half-pence and force them to pay.

Did I feel more sorry for the elf or for me?

I moved from behind the barrier as quietly as possible, towards another pile of bricks. By keeping along the edge, I might be able to work underneath the elf and behind the dragon.

She didn't see me as I reached the first pile. Her voice carried through the chamber, uttering a strange tongue.

Dragon-speak.

She was one who could talk to the beasts. Such elves were as rare as the Treyo Duthkus. They were named Ghiren Karkens, I believe.

They were expensive employees, the most expensive of any from the Gateway.

The dragon answered the elf's words by blowing flames over our heads. For a moment, the heat sucked away all the air, making me gasp and choke. As soon as the flames ended, the air returned in a rush.

That was the moment I moved from behind my heated barrier, but the elf released a bolt of lightning to keep me contained. Another wave of heat followed.

As soon as that ended, the dragon's head rose high enough to see over the platforms and the massive pot. But it hadn't fully entered the room. Why? Too big, perhaps?

As it swung its head back and forth, the elf spoke her strange words again.

This time, the dragon struck the pile to the left. The bricks melted under the sustained onslaught.

What if Sheela hid there? It would have burned her alive. And then I—

Again, what? What will I be? Sad? Angry? Heartbroken?

The dragon unleashed a wall of flames that spread over half the room. Again, it sucked the air out from all about me, not unlike Bonni's power. I gasped and choked until the flames subsided.

Then I ran for the pile of melted bricks, trying to ignore the protest of my lungs.

The elf struck with a blast of her light. It knocked me sideways.

She spoke, and the dragon released another wall of flames. Despite scrambling as fast as possible, the fire consumed me. I rolled across the dirt floor to smother my clothes and reached the safety of another pile of bricks. My burned arm and leg hurt even more, but other than blackened clothes I survived.

The elf spoke with a pleasant-sounding tone. She perched high on a ledge that appeared to have been built for the workers. The shadows obscured the details of her features, but she stood tall. Proud.

Sheela's face appeared as ashen as the remains in the Verentain Mausoleum. Her pistols shook. She bit her lower lip as she peered over her pile of rubble, and aimed one of the weapons with a steadier, but still shaking, hand.

The elf needed to be distracted. She couldn't see Sheela.

I hefted a brick as I moved back from the pile, then released it in mimic of the catapult I was slowly becoming. Another followed.

Both sailed over all the contraptions in the center of the room. They just cleared the wooden beams as they descended. The first one hit the wall above the elf's perch and released a clump of dirt that fell on top of her. The second sailed low and hit something that flickered for an instant. My mind took its time to decipher the familiar figure.

Reckard?

I motioned for Sheela not to fire. "Wait—"

The pistol popped at the same time the elf blasted her light. The latter struck my shoulder and filled my chest with a burning that reached deep into my belly. I took quick breaths as my lungs screamed. Numbing pain moved into my head.

Think of Sheela's kiss and her caress, of the night we met at Branagh's.

She faced a giant, ironically enough, who refused to pay for his drinks, and I made the mistake of thinking she required some assistance.

The elf spoke to her pet. The dragon responded by unleashing another round.

As the flames subsided, Sheela raised her second pistol. "Wait!" I said and doubled over as I shivered. A tingling sensation moved across my shoulders, then down my arms.

The elf said, "I see you both, and now you shall die." She pointed to each of us. Lights flickered down her arms. They gathered in sparkling balls at the end of her hands, with blue and gray bolts jumping around the white center. She spoke her dragon tongue, and the beast faced us.

If I could reach Sheela, I could shield her. I could make sure she survived the coming rain of hellfire.

Surprise filled the elf's voice for the first time. "What—"

Her arms and legs flailed like she tried to grab hold of empty air. The sparkling light shot in all directions, releasing crackles and pops like Duke Schaever's exploding lights. She floated at the edge of nothingness for a moment as her scream echoed through the chamber. Then she fell. She hit with a sickening crunch.

The dragon bellowed in rage and what sounded like pain. It shook its head.

Reckard appeared on the ledge. He waved.

The sight of him eased the lingering pain within. I yelled, "Taking your time, eh?"

He pointed to the wall below. "Show me how I'm supposed to get up here quickly, especially with a dragon shaking everything." He made a show of rubbing his shoulder. "It didn't help that you nearly knocked me off, old chap. That wasn't a bullet that whistled by my ear, was it?"

Sheela and I looked at each other. Our lips quivered just before we laughed in unison. Why?

Because we came that close to dying.

The dragon tilted its head back and forth as if it listened. After a moment, it retreated through the doorway.

Sheela and I met Reckard as he reached the floor. He nodded towards the door. "Not to interrupt this tender reunion among friends, but shouldn't we be quick to see what awaits us? A dragon and the infamous Head of Forneil, do you think?"

Think? "I'm afraid to speculate on any possibilities with the way this has been going. I wouldn't be surprised to find a room full of dragons."

Reckard slapped me on the back. "There's a pleasant thought, old chap. Now why don't I distract our large friend while you try to find the Head?"

"Sheela," I said, "remain here and guard our exit." My tone was too harsh, too demanding for what she just survived. I let out a long breath to soothe the feel of dread. "Please."

She nodded once as she reloaded her pistols. "Only because the dragon is immune to bullets. Be careful, Ash.

Be quick." As I followed Reckard she added, "Wait." She removed the ring Cavendish gave her. "Take this. You might need it more than me."

When she held her hand out, I curled her fingers around the ring. "Keep it. I don't want to leave you unprotected. You don't know what might happen."

She pulled her hand away, then grabbed mine. "Which is why you need it more." She slid the ring over my smallest finger. "I have the pistols, and I'll use them to kill if I must. I'll be fine." She released my hand. "Again...be careful."

I gave her a reassuring smile and almost followed with a reassuring kiss. Almost.

Reckard and I walked to the doorway. He kicked several bricks that had fallen during the dragon's rampage. I paused to take a couple just in case I might need them. As he entered, my fellow-thief whispered, "This isn't good, old chap. I do sometimes hate it when you're right."

As I stopped next to him, my belly flipped at least three times.

This room was larger than the previous one, at least twice as big. Ledges lined the sides, at least a hundred of them, and on every one rested a dragon. Small or medium all, they appeared to be babies as compared to the dragon we already had the pleasure of meeting.

Speaking of which, in the middle of the room, perched on a vault with a door made of the same metal as the reptilian swords, was the dragon itself. Its body was as black as its head, but white scars ran across its back, like it had been beaten into submission. Both of its rear legs were chained to large blocks bolted to the top of the vault.

Scattered about the floor were small bones. Some appeared to belong to animals such as rabbits and squirrels, but some appeared all too human-like.

"Now we know where all the disappearing gnomes have been going," I said as the pieces of the puzzle formed a clearer and sickening picture.

"A dragon nursery?" Reckard asked with a great deal of awe. "The Duke is breeding his own army of the beasts? How has he kept it such a secret?"

A voice from behind said, "Because I am careful. I trust few with the knowledge of this matter. Those I do not trust who are fortunate enough to learn? They are killed."

Duke Schaever.

He stood on the same mound of dirt where Cavendish danced. He wore a white, double-breasted coat that reached to his knees, with two rows of large, gold buttons on the front. His trousers were white as well and he wore dark red boots that appeared to be reptile skin. He leaned on an ivory cane into which had been carved a twisting dragon along its length. The tip was silver and appeared sharp.

To his right stood Bonni and Frank. To his left stood Aimee. And in front of him was Sheela, crumpled in a heap and unconscious. She bled from a blow to the side of the head.

Aimee spoke with triumphant satisfaction. "This is the end, Alexander. You've caused the Duke enough trouble. We already have your woman." She kicked Sheela down the pile of dirt.

The canon growled, and Reckard caught me by the shoulder. He whispered, "I still have Cavendish's daggers. Say the word. I'll take the Duke and Aimee. You'll have to shield me from that point."

No, I needed to shield Sheela, but it's impossible to reach her in time. Think, Ash. Devise a plan. Something. Anything.

I looked at the ring on my finger. If Sheela still wore it, she'd be safe from Frank's flames and Bonni's air tricks.

Why did she insist on my taking it? Why did I let her give it to me?

The Duke tapped his cane on a stone. "I must thank you, Mister Asherton." He made his words sound as if I should be honored that he spoke my name. "Due to your continued persistence, you revealed some of the flaws in my creations. The servant at my home was quite the mess. I expect the next version to be much more realistic. Her skin will not be so easy to remove." He gave a single, approving nod. "In spite of this, however, I find that you waste my precious time. You require essential resources to deal with you. I say enough." He swept his cane around. "Kill them all."

The blood rushed from my head. The Duke's ultimatum meant killing Sheela, and I could not allow that. Not while I still drew breath.

I held my hands up. "Wait. I'm the one you want. Release the lady and take me."

The Duke stared at me for a long moment before he laughed a humorless laugh. He removed a white cloth from an inside pocket and wiped his eyes for dramatic effect. No one joined his laughter, though, and after replacing the cloth he said, "I find it incomprehensible that Lady Aimee could marry an imbecile. So I will assume you did not hear me the first time. I shall endeavour to be more specific. This is not a negotiation for your life. Your two friends, as well as yourself, are dead." He raised his right brow as if he expected a reply.

"Do something," Reckard whispered with a tone of desperation. "Don't let them kill Sheela."

I won't. Yet what can I do?

After a moment, the Duke sighed. "I hoped for more from the man who survived my catapult and both of Lady Aimee's attempts to kill him. I came here to see just what such a man could do, and all I find is an apparent fool staring at me with indecision and confusion. How disappointing."

What is he saying? That he wants me to fight?

"Kill them," he said, "and when you finish, take the bodies to the sanctum. We might yet infiltrate The Company and destroy them from within."

Aimee and Bonni moved towards me while Frank stepped over Sheela. Fire covered his hands as he asked, "How quick do you want her to die?" Under his breath, he added, "Allow me to make it slow for Asherton's sake."

I held my hand out as if I could stop him. "Wait!"

"Quickly," Duke Schaever said. "I will not see a lady suffer."

Think, Ash, think!

Reckard started forward with a yell, but I grabbed his arm.

I knew what needed to be done. And it hurt so much more than it should have. This was the reason I didn't want her to love me. Aimee was correct in her assessment of my life. I was a disappointment to those who loved me, who trusted me with their secrets.

Reckard yelled at me, but I only saw his lips move. The canon's voice babbled something that sounded wise, but was lost in the pounding within my head. I almost choked. My chest tightened.

Reckard's face turned red and spittle flew from his mouth just before he disappeared.

As Frank's flames increased, I uttered words that sounded as if a stranger spoke. Somehow, I spoke loud enough to be heard over the commotion. "Don't worry, Reckard, he won't kill Lady Carrigan!" My mouth was dry and the bitterness of betrayal filled it.

Frank pointed to Sheela, but the Duke knocked his arms away with a sweep of his cane. Flames shot through the air at the same moment that a discernable crack of ivory on bone sounded.

Duke Schaever pointed his cane at me. "Repeat yourself."

Forgive me, Sheela. For what you will endure, forgive me. For what I condemn you to, forgive me.

I said, with all the assurance I could give, "That is Lady Carrigan. She didn't die in London as her husband surely knows. I believe he has a rather large reward to offer her rescuer though I am sure he could give a gentleman of your means something else as a sign of gratitude for restoring the one closest to his heart."

"What are you doing?" Reckard all but hissed. "Fool! You'll exile her to a fate worse than death."

Perhaps.

I prayed and hoped I didn't, but perhaps he was correct. But at least she would live.

The Duke studied me as Aimee and Bonni watched. He asked, "What proof do you have of this claim?"

"She wears a pendant with her family's crest. Not Lord Carrigan's, but her father's, Lord Murphy."

Duke Schaever reached into her bosom and broke the chain as he lifted the pendant. He held it close to his right eye as he examined both sides. "This is not infallible evidence of your claim, sir. She could have bought this or stolen it." He gave me a look as if he tried to decide whether to grant her mercy.

One choice could assure that he made the correct decision. The betrayal would be completed. "She is also a Gateway survivor. The only known Gateway survivor."

"Alexander is lying," Aimee said as she moved towards me with smoking hands. "He is trying to save someone he loves. He will do anything, say anything, to keep you from killing her."

"True enough," I said, "but why risk killing her before confirming my claim further? Question her once she wakes, then decide whether to kill her. You have nothing to lose and much to gain, including secrets you have desired for so long."

"She'll hate you," Reckard whispered. "She'll never forgive you."

His words caused a stirring in my belly as I whispered, "I hope I live to endure such hatred." And to rescue her. "Besides, if she hates me, maybe then she'll love you."

He snorted. "She'll just as likely blame me for assisting you."

Aimee gave me a look that spoke of contempt. "You do love her. I recognize the glimmer in your eyes."

"I won't deny it," I said and that made my actions all the worse. "The way you speak makes me wonder if you might be envious of her."

"On the contrary, Alexander, I pity her, especially if what you claim is true." She smiled, but there was little humor in the expression. "I look forward to the interrogation. I will make sure she suffers the humiliation you put me through in the examination when you learned of this place."

"Enough," Duke Schaever said with a tone commanding complete and immediate obedience. He studied Sheela as the pendant twisted on its chain. He looked at me. "Tell me, sir, why you would turn a lady whom you love over to a man such as myself?"

The answer deserved the utmost of dignity, so I stood taller. "If you have ever loved, then you understand the extremes we go to protect the one most precious to us."

He nodded, and I thought I saw his shoulders droop the slightest bit. "Indeed, Mister Asherton. Indeed. I understand better than you might believe." He took Sheela in his arms, much to my relief and dismay. "Give me the assurance those two are dead." The man carried her away.

Aimee, Bonni and Frank advanced, the latter limping as he rubbed his forearm.

"Leave Alexander for me," Aimee said. "The two of you see if you can find his suddenly invisible friend."

"Go to the vault," I said in the hope Reckard could hear me. "Collect whatever you think looks interesting. Find the Head. Then leave this place. I'll delay these three for as long as possible."

"What are you going to do?" he asked from behind, his high-pitched voice adding to the sense of urgency.

"Something very stupid. Go." I backed away from the approaching trio, and in doing so I backed away from Sheela, from the possibility of rescuing her. I entered the dragon nursery.

The vault door opened with a long creak of the hinges.

Aimee's glare went beyond mere hatred. It spoke of a loathing that chilled any notion of hope and was the look she held on me as she headed for the vault's door. "Keep Alexander busy, but save his death for me. I'm responsible for the safety of the Head and I will make sure no one else acquires it."

I scooped up several bones and threw them at her to draw her attention away. One struck her shoulder. Another hit her shin. A third would've hit her stomach had she not covered it in time. She stumbled back, then cupped her hands together. Smoke escaped between her fingers.

"Go," Bonni said as she held her hand up, "I'll keep him occupied."

Aimee nodded to her friend and continued to the door.

As I backed away, Bonni struck with her favorite trick. The surrounding air vanished. Almost. I could still breathe, compliments of Sheela's ring, though it felt like I did so through a small hole. When I rounded the corner of the vault and disappeared from her view, the spell ceased and I breathed again.

Just before I turned the next corner, Bonni appeared. I took a deep breath, expecting her same trick. This time, she squeezed the air around my ankles to the point it felt like I moved through thick mud. I skidded across the dirt floor, out of her view, and stopped just inches from a pile of dragon dung.

Running around the vault in circles wasn't the way to deal with the Greenhews. What more could be done?

A long, satisfied sigh by the dragon above and a ladder carved into the side of the vault gave me the answer. The voice said, "This is certain death."

True, but certain death is continuing to do what I'm doing. And I won't die without a good fight.

"You cannot escape that way," Frank said as I climbed. "In here, there is no place to run. There is no place to hide."

When I reached the top I said, "That should make your job of killing me all the easier." My subsequent grin was meant to annoy him all the more. "So why haven't you done so?"

"You're a bastard. I wanted to kill you every time you ever sullied my home by setting foot in it."

The dragon had settled on its bed of stone. Its front legs were curled beneath it, and its chest and neck rested on the vault's top. Its eyes were closed as it took the heavy breaths of a deep sleep, in an enviable moment of peace. A pity it would soon be disturbed.

I hoped.

The air grew thick around my legs and thin around my head. A wink at Bonni made her scowl even more. Her face turned red as she pointed at me, but the air didn't change thanks to Sheela's ring.

Thinking of her name brought a pang of guilt, which made my aches and pains hurt all the worse. I would find her. I would save her from the Duke...but first I needed to survive.

The dragon's scales were as hard as steel. From deep within, they reflected the light of the lamps. They felt as smooth as a polished rock.

Dragons were such beautiful creatures. Yet they were so deadly and so terribly unpredictable.

I took hold of a scale at the beast's haunches and pulled myself up. My feet slipped, and I fell against it. My left foot hit hard enough to make a loud, cracking sound.

A ripple moved down the creature's neck, through its body, and to its tail. Otherwise, it remained undisturbed.

Frank peered over the top of the vault. "What do you think you're doing?" Under his breath, he added, "Why do I have to deal with such fools?"

He didn't receive an answer. Instead, I concentrated on planting my feet better as I reached into the crevice of a scar and pulled myself up. The going went faster as I neared the top where the creature's body flattened. When I reached the spot between its front legs, where a natural seat formed between its muscles, I pried back a scale to expose the leathery skin beneath.

"I apologize for this," I whispered, "but I need your assistance."

The flesh resisted the blade. I pushed harder until the tip drew blood. One drop followed another and another. As the blade bit deeper, a steady stream flowed. With a final shove, the blade sank to the handle.

The dragon shuddered, and its scales rippled again.

I grabbed the handle with both hands and twisted.

The dragon's eyelids opened. Then its neck rose, which made me fall back and grab hold of scales on each side. It bellowed in pain, a pitiful noise that echoed around the chamber. It swung its head from side to side before trying to twist around to find the source of its discomfort.

Frank yelled, "What are you trying to do? Kill us all?"

Well, yes, that is the general idea.

The dragon stood as the vault shook from an explosion. The beast bellowed again before it sniffed.

A blast of fire passed over my head, but was close enough that I felt it. A second wave struck, and I tried to avoid it by flattening myself on the dragon's back. Flames took hold of my scorched and tattered clothing. I patted them out.

Frank sent another wave, and I took the full brunt of it.

He released a fourth wave I couldn't avoid, either, unless I wanted to abandon my post.

The dragon turned to stare at Frank, who visibly gulped. The creature's body expanded just before it released its own flames.

Frank held his arms up to protect his head, and to keep from seeing his approaching and inevitable death. But the flames diverted before him as if they struck an invisible corner.

The visibly shaken man said, "Thank you, darling."

The dragon shifted as it swung its head back and forth in the familiar pattern.

"You didn't hurt him," I said. "Don't give up." To make sure it understood, I beat on the scale that trapped the knife.

It bellowed as it shuddered twice more.

The vault shook as more explosions sounded within. Did Reckard continue to hold his own, or was he dead?

Bonni stood next to her husband on top of the vault. Her hair, fallen loose from its ties, hung about her face in crinkled strands. She pushed it to the side with one hand as she pointed to me with the other. "I don't care if I'm supposed to save you for Aimee. This time, you die."

Thick air pinned me against the dragon with enough force to squeeze my breath out.

The dragon tried for at least the sixth time to twist its head around. It bellowed frustration yet again.

And it echoed my own as I slowly pushed against Bonni's air. I squirmed and inched my way forward. There wasn't enough air to counter such an exertion, so my lungs burned. The scales should have scraped my stomach, but if they did, I didn't feel it. I moved towards the beast's neck as my body screamed for more air. My arms and legs tingled, and my head spun.

The dragon jumped from its perch. When it landed, a cloud of dust lifted high, and the floor cracked length-wise. One side appeared to shift an inch lower than the other. The beast turned to the vault and released a wall of flames that forced the Greenhews to abandon their position. They, too, jumped from the top. As they did, Bonni's spell ended.

Never had stale chamber air, mixed with the sharp tang of dragon, tasted so good, or felt so good. Unfortunately, as I enjoyed the deep breath, the dragon shifted.

I joined the others on the floor.

The dragon bellowed again before going suddenly quiet. Too quiet. It sniffed as it grew very still.

Bonni and Frank picked themselves up and checked on each other.

The dragon turned to the door. There stood something that gave me hope even as it frightened me.

Cavendish!

I hobbled towards him as the beast loomed overhead. Its shadow cast an impending doom. "Go back," I said. "Go back."

Why is the anklet not working when I need it the most?

Why had the gnome returned? He should be pursuing Duke Schaever and Sheela.

Bonni ran for the gnome, too. She wore a smile that spoke of ill tidings for Cavendish's future.

"Stop!" Frank said.

For a moment, silence followed. For a moment, all was still, save for Bonni and I converging on the gnome.

And then everything turned into a blur.

CHAPTER 14

Ledges and dragons and bricks all blurred into a smear of shapes and colors as the chamber rushed by. The smell of blood and scorched flesh filled my nose as it settled on my tongue.

Bonni screamed in my ear, a helpless and fear-filled noise.

The black dragon held both of us in its giant maw, with Bonni wedged between me and an eyetooth as long as I was tall. The fact that she was beside me was the reason she wasn't dead. The dragon tried to close its teeth, but my thick skin kept it from doing so.

The surrounding air warmed a considerable degree. Flames shot past. As the dragon swept us around, Frank blasted the beast over and over and over. He yelled as he did so.

"Help me," I said as I pushed against the dragon's mouth. "Pull the air from its lungs or push one of your balls of air down its throat. Choke it. Hurt it."

Bonni did neither. Instead, she tried to wriggle out of her place, and she tried to kick me while doing so.

"What are you doing?" I asked, even as I understood her intentions, though I prayed I was wrong.

She sneered. "I hate you, Alexander Asherton."

"The feeling is mutual. You can hate me more when we're both free." I pushed hard and pried the teeth apart just a little and just enough...for her to slip free.

She spoke with something close to unbridled joy. "Good-bye Alexander. I hope you rot in your supposed hell." And with that, she slipped off the creature's lip.

Frank yelled, "Bonni, no—"

She fell at least twenty feet. I tried to see if she still moved, but the black dragon shook its head again and blurred everything.

The sensation was not unlike the peak of a magic-high, except for the chest-crushing sensation, and the horrid breath of rotting gnome. It also taught me what a child's doll felt like in the midst of a tantrum.

"Look," I said, "I am not a tasty delight. And I am not worth all the effort you're exerting to eat me." Its flapping tongue provided an opportunity, so I squeezed and pulled as hard as I could. "I'll make this as unenjoyable as possible." I pulled again on the dry and thin, reptilian-like tongue and twisted it for good measure.

The dragon lunged forward. It spit me onto a ledge a good twenty feet above the floor.

The beast then jumped towards Cavendish, who ran as fast as his short legs could manage. It slammed into the side of the cavern where a dozen of its brood slept. Three of the creatures fell from their perches. When they landed hard, they awoke with squeals and high-pitched moans. One, no more than two feet long, flapped still unformed wings as it flopped to either side in an attempt to gain its feet. Two others wobbled on their hind legs.

As one, they all let out a piercing scream-like cry. All three heads turned towards the gnome.

That gave me an idea.

A gray-scaled dragon about four feet in length, lay curled beside me. With my back against the wall, and my feet in its side, one heave sent it over the edge.

It spun through the air with its head waving on a loose neck, oblivious of its impending impact. When it hit, it gave a high-pitched bellow and rolled onto its feet.

The big dragon turned to the Greenhews. Frank stopped trying to lift Bonni when he saw the beast eyeing them. He reached forward and released a column of flames that struck the dragon in the face.

The beast responded by releasing its own flames.

Bonni raised a shaking hand to shield them with her thickened air, shaped like a giant's shield. The flames covered its breadth and licked the edges as it dispersed about them. The dragon continued to breathe its death. Bonni's shield buckled under the onslaught. The dragon might have won had Frank not released his own flames at the smallest dragon, which had the misfortune of passing in front of the Greenhews as it lopped towards Cavendish. When Frank's flames struck, the little beast screamed. It flailed as its wings smoldered. It flapped and flopped in circles.

The black dragon stopped and sniffed to locate its small child. It picked the little one up in its front talons to cradle it in the curve of its neck to provide comfort in the baby dragon's last, painful and mournful moments.

To watch the sad ending felt wrong, so I turned from the display of tenderness, and faced my current predicament. If I still had the jumping power, I would've had the perfect ability for facing such an insurmountable amount of space between the floor and myself.

"No chance, no glory, eh, Ash?" I asked, then leapt. My belly and chest caught the next lower ledge, and my foot pulled me down. The resident dragon's tail provided support, but it swung around, making me slip down to my neck.

Hold on. One hand-at-a-time. That's all it takes.

The task was easier than it sounded considering how fast I needed to move. Once I made it to the top, though, the temptation to lie on the ledge and rest almost compelled me to forget my friends. It took the roar of flames and the heat filling the chamber to convince me to keep going, to keep striving for the prize in the vault. So another heave sent another dragon to the floor. This one hit with a thud, and the floor beneath it gave way, not unlike the weak spots in the tunnels. It struggled to free itself.

Frank protected his wife as he faced off with the black dragon. Both poured flames at each other, which met in the middle and created a solid wall of yellow and red that spread to both the floor and the ceiling. The flames swept over a dozen dragons, disturbing their peace. All twelve heads looked up.

They caught Cavendish's scent almost at once and either hopped off their beds or took to flight. One circled twice in silence before dropping straight down.

Chaos was growing, and I needed more. The Greenhews had to be in the heart of it, too busy with survival to pay me any mind. Then I could slip into the vault and help Reckard.

I leapt to another lower ledge and slammed into it with such force I almost bounced off. My lead foot dragged me down as my fingers scrapped the rock. I hung on the edge. One twitch could send me plummeting.

Hold on again. One—

My fingers slipped, and I fell. Why I flapped my arms like I might fly, I don't know. Panic, maybe? A need to try something? Anything? Because I hadn't properly learned that lesson while hurtling over Campden?

A mighty thump sounded when I struck. Waves of pain shot through my back, belly, and chest. The ground sank like it attempted to bury me.

So why not let it?

I didn't want to move. I was tired and hurt beyond belief. I had done all that I could. Hadn't I?

No, not quite. Sheela had to be rescued from the Duke, and I needed to protect what I held dearest, no matter the danger to myself.

The voice approved of the sacrificial nature of the thought, but it wasn't the one who had to find the strength to carry on.

By the time I removed myself from the floor, Frank had placed Bonni over his shoulder. He stood almost side-by-side with Cavendish in a circle of dragons.

I could escape into the vault, but I wouldn't leave Cavendish. Despite our differences, he was a friend. Besides, he could go after Sheela and the Duke while I faced Aimee.

The gnome's cheeks appeared a darker shade of red against his pale skin. Yet, despite his shaking hand, he held a dagger at the ready.

Sensing easy prey, the dragons converged for the kill. In their determination, they climbed over, bit, and clawed one another. Not a one of them took notice of me until I slammed my shoulder into the nearest one, a dragon ten feet long. I pushed it aside, then punched the one ahead on its front shoulder, cracking a still-forming scale. That must have hurt, for the dragon shuddered and bellowed in rage.

Both beasts lunged at me.

I caught the bigger one by the jaw and pulled him into the gaping maw of the second, which bit hard and made the bigger one bellow again.

Both stepped away, stunned at the strange turn of events.

Something latched onto my leg. I forced a laugh and said, "This is your kind of place, Cavendish."

Needle-like pricks told me it wasn't the gnome. Rather, it was a two-foot dragon determined to eat my calf. The sight of its snout and its teeth and the sound of its snarling delight made me want to smash it to bits. So I stomped on the little dragon's head with my lead foot. The bone between its eyes crunched beneath my heel. My foot sunk into its head a good five inches as blood oozed around my ankle. The dragon shuddered twice before going motionless.

Cavendish squealed as two dragons snapped at him. He managed to avoid them while slashing open the snout of each.

The big, black one bellowed loud enough to shake the chamber again. All the dragons stopped to look at their queen, giving me the opportunity to grab Cavendish by the scruff of his neck. I dragged the frightened gnome across the dirt floor by his heels and knocked a five-foot dragon aside. Where it once stood, awaited an opening, an escape.

Don't hesitate. Go. Run. Find Sheela.

A wall of solid air stopped me with enough force to knock me back.

Bonni loomed over us, supported by her husband. Bloodied strands of hair fell about her face. Dirt, mixed with blood, caked her clothes and her skin. When she pointed, a clump of red mud fell from her elbow. "You're not going anywhere."

The black dragon bellowed again, and the smaller dragons scattered.

"We don't have time to argue," I said as I pushed against her wall.

Bonni snarled. "You wanted Aimee, but involved my husband and me. You destroyed our home even though we had nothing to do with your obsession over a woman who never loved you.”

“Nice try, Bonni, but I know the truth. Aimee loved me.”

She pressed her air harder. “Did you know I tried to talk her out of marrying you?”

“Spare me the details,” I said as I continued my slow push against her magic. “You’ve always hated me. Since the time we first met, and I knocked over a goblet of wine and stained your favorite table cloth, you’ve despised me.”

“She only married you because she felt obligated after you saved her.”

“And because your master thought it would provide a good disguise.”

Her eyes grew wide. “How did you—” She cried out as a dragon clamped onto her shin.

Frank blasted the dragon. “You will pay for this you stupid beasts.” He pointed. “I’ll hunt you down and kill you, Asherton. You and everyone you care about.”

Fine. If that’s the way you want to play it, Frank, then…fine. Just…fine.

“Let’s finish it,” I said as I pushed Cavendish behind me. “Here and now. Let’s see who the best man is.”

His hands clenched in and out of fists. He had a determined look, with his chin jutted out and his brow drawn low. He took one step towards me, but stopped when Bonni moaned. His expression softened at the moment he looked at her, but changed to hatred at the moment he returned to me. “It will have to wait.” Under his breath he added, “And I will catch you when you don’t have magic flowing in your blood. And I will burn you apart, limb by limb.”

“If I see you again, Frank, I’ll kill you.” Well…probably not, but he didn’t need to know I lied. “If you ever try to do anything to me, I’ll make sure something happens to Bonni.” I paused. “If she survives this day.”

He stepped towards me. "Don't threaten my wife. I should kill you here and now."

"Then do it." I motioned for him to attack. "Let's settle our differences."

He released a shaft of flames. There was no avoiding them.

The best option was to embrace the fire, to let my power protect me. I closed my eyes and held my breath as the fire engulfed my body. My skin heated like metal and glowed like a sword in the blacksmith's forge as I stepped forward, pushing against the flames. I knocked Frank's hand away, then punched him in the belly. As he bent double, I struck down across his jaw.

He stumbled forward towards Bonni. He waved his free hand, releasing spurts of flames in every direction. Some struck the wall, some struck dragons, and one passed close enough to Cavendish to make him squeal.

Another struck the black dragon, earning its renewed interest.

Frank regained his footing. He glared at me through an eye that swelled.

I could finish him. Forever. The dragons could feast on him and Bonni.

But I didn't throw the final punch. I couldn't. The sight of a desperate husband defending and saving his wife was a reminder that Frank was human somewhere in the depths of his dark heart.

He pointed again, but a dragon swept down and clawed at his head. He tried to knock the beast away with a blast.

Another dragon tried to bite me, but I buried my fist between its eyes. The impact shook it to the end of its tail.

A second beast snagged my left hand and for that, I punched it once and again, also between the eyes. It released, and twisted first left and then right, as blood ran from its eyes.

My hand bled from where its teeth punctured my still-hot skin. It burned, along with the bites on my calf. They would swell if I didn't find water soon.

Again, I grabbed Cavendish by the scruff of his neck and ran. A sudden tingling filled my ankle, foot, and thigh as the damaged anklet decided to work. Into the other chamber I went, not unlike a rabbit bounding across a field of grass. I didn't stop until we reached the opposite doorway. There, I set my friend on the ground. "Listen, gnome, I don't understand why you returned, but Duke Schaever has Sheela. Find him and free her and tell her I'm sorry."

The gnome pulled at his beard. "I came back to help you. Remember? That's what a friend is supposed to do?"

His words gave me pause. In another time and place, they would've been savored for their honesty. But not here. Not now. "Then be the best of friends and find Sheela!" How could I make him understand the urgency? "Go!" I pointed to the tunnel. "What are you waiting for?"

My words startled him. He blinked once, and again, as if he was unsure of where or who he was. After a moment, he removed a bracelet. "Take this."

Diamonds the size of a small spider sparkled all around a gold band. "What does it do?"

"Protects you from fire."

The act of caring and friendship extinguished some of the anger and fear within me. "Thank you," I said as I nodded to him. "Find her. Please."

He nodded, too, and said, "Good luck. If we survive, you can find me at Branagh's with Sheela." He bowed three times, then disappeared in the darkness.

I made no move, preferring to remain in the fragileness of the moment, of the time when all possibilities were before me. Cavendish would rescue Sheela. He could track anything with those foolish goggles. I left her in good and capable hands, ones that would set right the wrong. I would take the Head from Aimee if Reckard didn't already possess it. Everything would work out for the best.

Would it not?

The voice remained silent, neither approving nor admonishing my decisions.

Had I condemned Sheela to a worse fate than I knew?

Either way... "Let's get this over with, Ash." I turned back to the dragon nursery as a dozen of the creatures spilled into this chamber, following Cavendish's scent. They ran on their hind legs, their torsos lopping back and forth.

Their bites echoed the pain within my heart.

A brown dragon six feet from nose to tail, turned towards me. Spit flew from its mouth in anticipation of a coming feast. Its black eyes appeared as dark as the shadows on a moonless night.

I was tired of dragons. And of Aimee. And of this entire affair. The Misters sent me on a fool's errand. Did they want me dead? Did I know too much, and they feared I might turn?

Or did they not care? Was I nothing more than an expendable commodity to them?

Absolutely.

I grabbed the dragon by the snout and pounded on its head to release no little amount of frustration. The action surprised it and after I landed four blows, it groaned as it turned back for the nursery.

I followed it and expected to have to battle another of the beasts, but a wall of flames greeted me. It washed over and enveloped me in its heat. But my skin didn't warm as much or as fast this time as the diamonds on the bracelet glowed.

Halfway through the doorway, I faced a bloodied Frank, still supporting his wife. He appeared as surprised to see me as I was to see him.

"Once we clear this place, then I'll finish you," he said.

I walked past, having neither the strength nor the desire to argue.

"Did you hear me?" he asked with a mad desperation. "I'll hunt you down! I'll kill you! If it's the last thing I do!"

His was a threat best dealt with if I survived the waiting moments.

"You're a dead man, Asherton!"

I entered the nursery and faced the dragons anew.

Another explosion sounded from the vault.

So Reckard still fought. But was he as beaten and bloodied as I?

As I passed a dragon, it sniffed the air, then bellowed like it caught Cavendish's scent.

Which it did because of the bracelet.

I tossed it to the right, far away.

The dragon followed the scent as did at least ten others. They cleared a path between the vault and me, between Aimee and me.

The black dragon settled onto its bed and didn't appear inclined to want to move. It did, though, shift its head from side to side in the direction the bracelet had flown.

"Thank you, Cavendish," I said.

It was good to have friends, especially as I now faced the hardest part of this affair.

CHAPTER 15

Within the vault awaited a room against which the dragon nursery couldn't compare in terms of scope or grandeur. Given how much I knew about the Duke, the fact he created a place such as this wasn't surprising. No, too much had surprised me already to give me any more sense of wonder or fear.

What I saw, what I stood in, was the ultimate dream of a scientist who specialized in solving problems involving time and space dimensions. I read articles many years ago that speculated about using a great power source to open a rip in time, thus creating an infinite area existing in neither real time nor actual space. The scientists based their theories on the same ones used for the Gateway, but concluded no single power source on the planet was large enough to create the rip. Obviously, Duke Schaever solved the dilemma and he did so by using a complex merging of magic and science.

The room gave an otherworldly sense of not quite belonging as I could see it before me, yet had no sense of its true size. After all, how can the mortal mind comprehend the infinite? I also had the feeling that shadows moved in the corners of my eyes as if someone moved about just out of sight. There was nothing, though, other than a slight haze that remained too still if I moved my eyes too fast.

This place added to my admiration of Duke Schaever. The Misters were well advised to deal with him carefully.

As I turned my gaze from the far reaches to what waited before me, cold seeped into my arms and legs. My heart beat faster, and the burns from the dragon bites flared stronger. I almost sobbed in anguish and fear.

Was I surprised?

Admittedly so. And overawed.

Why?

Because of what was revealed in a blue light floating at the top of the room, the one bathing everything within in a chilling luminescence. That everything happened to be row upon row of mechanical people, not quite like the serving lady at the Ball, the servant at the townhome, or the Guardsman with the marble eyes. Rather, these were metal skeletons lying on wooden tables as if they slept a peaceful slumber. Some appeared complete, from the top of their skull to the tips of their toes. Many were in various stages of assembly, and a few were but parts arranged in order. What stood out on them all was that the metal was the same type worn by the cyclopes guarding the tunnel, the same metal the large pot in the first chamber was made from, the same metal of the reptilians' swords.

The metal that cut me easily enough.

Tubes similar to the ones Pienne used for his elixirs connected a number of complete skeletons. Fluids, from red to green to white to blue, flowed into them.

There were fifteen rows of tables, from left to right, and each row disappeared in the distance.

A moan from the right made the hairs on my arms stand straight while making my chest ache.

An elf was suspended face down from the ceiling in a spread-eagle fashion like the Michelangelo drawing of the man in the circle. Wires held him up by the skin of his arms, shoulders, waist, and Achilles tendons. Tubes ran from both his forearms and inner thighs. The former drew his blood away while the latter replaced it with a clear liquid. Around his wrist appeared to be an ivory bracelet. Was it the same as the one worn by the Treyo Duthku at the Duke's townhome? Was he a slave forced to give his life in the name of....what? Science gone mad? Magic turned evil? A combination of both?

To add to the disturbing scene were six others suspended in similar fashion, all with a dozen tubes attached to them. Two of the elves appeared almost translucent in the light. Below each one, the tubes met at a wooden table with a rack of beakers and vials that bubbled and smoked. There, other elves attended the flow and made adjustments as needed. They all wore the same white coat as Duke Schaever, with the gold buttons on the front. They also wore black gloves that sparkled even in the strange light. At least one at each table wore a metal plate that covered the face from the nose to the left ear. At the left eye was a red lens the size of a schilling. On the cheek was a series of small tubes that converged at a screened cylinder, no more than two inches high and two inches in diameter, on the shoulder. Most disturbingly, they wore a bracelet and as close as they were, I could see the white of the ivory and the inlaid pearls.

There was no sound, other than the occasional moans of the pitiful creatures above. It felt as if the room sucked away anything one might dare to say.

I descended the ten steps at the door as quietly as possible. While my lead foot should have sounded like thunder striking the metal steps, instead it made a dull thud.

A complete skeleton rested on the nearest table. Skin grew on its hands and feet. Vessel-like strings extended four to five inches from the edge of the skin to the surface of the metal. Each pulsed as if a beating heart moved the red fluid within. Morbid curiosity moved me to touch one hand. The skin felt as real as any living person's.

Except it was cold, almost frigid.

I drew back and blew on my fingers to warm them, to chase away the sense of death crawling up my arm.

What was Duke Schaever planning? What purpose did an army of things such as these serve?

The possibilities...were numerous.

Conquest? Power?

Not subtle enough for the likes of such a man.

Manipulation? Replacement?

Possible. But why? To what end?

For once, the voice remained silent, much like the metal face. Its empty eye sockets stared into nothing, yet looked straight through me. Dead, but alive. As lifeless as a rock, yet slumbering.

The pieces of the puzzle fit together much better, but the picture remained elusive and unfocused. I needed more answers and time.

That, of course, was the one commodity I didn't have.

I hobbled down the way and passed one cluster of tubes where two elves worked in unison. Their arms reached and moved, neither slowing nor pausing. They wove a symphony of strange angles and odd contortions through the beakers and vials and complex webbing of tubes. Both wore the strange faceplate and examined a beaker or dial as they moved.

Pienne would've been jealous of the scope and the display of power, of innovation. I wanted to ask them how the elixirs granted life if that was what they did to the mechanical skeletons.

By taking it from the living, perhaps?

The thought made the canon gasp and gave release to a single sob.

Find Reckard, and the Head. Don't think about the horrors surrounding you. Don't imagine them rising or reaching out or of being suspended from on high.

As I hurried through, I passed beneath four more of the hanging elves, each in various states of decay and death, each wearing a bracelet. No one tried to stop me. The workers were far too involved in their task at hand to pay me any mind. Once clear of the area, I took deep breaths to collect myself, for as impressive and disturbing as the mechanical farm of life was behind, what lay ahead was no less intimidating.

A maze of storage drawers spread out in the next section of the vault. It was an expanse of treasures untold, rows upon rows of drawers, interspersed with statues big and small, and with objects from columns to lamp stands decorated with gold and jewels. From the right, a brown light rippled through the haze and an explosion followed, though muted.

Reckard and Aimee had wrought untold devastation while the oblivious managers of life and death continued their labors behind us.

Shear exhaustion, both physical and mental, forced me to my knees. The dragon bites burned as their acid ate my skin. My wounds ached. At least a dozen bruises covered me. Yet there would be no stopping. Not now, when I journeyed so far, and the Head was so close. But what could keep me going?

The answer, of course, was found in the woman I betrayed. I would keep going for her. I needed the assurance that Cavendish rescued her. I would make amends for the way I treated her in the cavern.

Why?

Because I—

"Admit it, Ash," I said as the air made the words flat and lifeless. "I do love her."

There. I said it. The canon's voice, which laughed with no little fervor, was appeased.

Yes, I loved her even though the love could, and did, hurt, deeper than anything else. But it was also a powerful fuel, and the heart was a strange engine consuming it. It could give me the power to continue if only for a bit longer. The hope of seeing Sheela again, whether or not she wanted to see me, moved me to my feet.

You can do this. You can finish the assignment. Just take one step, then another.

I did so, pushing away the aches and pains, remembering the power and passion of Sheela's kiss in the cavern. I followed a long hallway lined on both sides with rows upon rows of drawers ranging in size from four-inches wide by two-inches high to two-feet wide by two-feet high. Many were thrown to the floor, littering the polished stone with an assortment of goods, from jewels to coins to wands to books with covers scorched by the recent explosions.

I picked one up and dusted its cover. The title read, 'Surrey County Families and Genealogy.' Within were pages upon pages of names and illustrations of homes and towns.

I tossed the book on top of several others as I proceeded on. The light above seemed to follow, projecting the same amount both in front and behind, never changing.

Aimee's voice sounded like a distant whisper in the vault's air. "Give me the Head, and I'll let you live."

Reckard answered, "You'll have to take it out of my dead grasp since the Duke has already decided my sentence."

She laughed at him in a way that spoke of patience coming to an end, like the time she laughed at me for trying to explain the problems with separation and divorce.

As I hurried to reach my friend, the anklet worked every-other step, and sent shots of warmth up my leg. The passage ended at a statue of a bearded man with wrinkled cheeks and eyes. He looked heavenward, and stretched his right hand out, pointing to something distant. In his left hand, he held a sword etched with runes. A sense of cold emanated from the weapon, and I kept my distance as I followed the smoke and empty drawers to the right.

Aimee said, "It's a shame my former husband made you a part of this. I wish it was him standing in front of me."

"Why?" Reckard asked in a scoffing tone. "So you could try to blow him apart again?"

Reckard faced certain death, but he defended me? Or did he try to delay the inevitable? Or was he a truer friend than I deserved?

"He always was a foolish idealist," Aimee said, echoing Reckard's voice. "He could never accept that people never change."

You are wrong. People change for many reasons.

I kicked boxes out of the way, and crushed stones and pottery beneath my lead foot as I hurried towards them. In the center of the next intersection stood a twisted column of black and white rock. The black absorbed all the light around it while the white pulsed with a heartbeat, filling me with both laughter and sadness.

An explosion shook the vault and a cloud of smoke roiled through the passage straight ahead. I fell to one knee and caught myself trying to block the smoke with my arms, just like the first time she tried to kill me.

Was I so afraid? Did the scar from those wounds run so deep?

Then perhaps it was time to find true healing by settling the matter and putting her out of our collective misery. I would do the world a favor by ridding it of her presence.

And in that one act, I would mark the end of the old Alexander Asherton forever. How fitting that she would be the one responsible for such a feat. What little I stitched together after the divorce and the explosion would be forever torn asunder. I hoped The Misters appreciated what they did. I hoped someone appreciated what I was about to become.

A monster no better than Duke Schaever, a killer of that which God made in His image.

The knife in my hand felt as cold as my heart was becoming, as cold as the mechanical hand. Maybe Reckard was right. Maybe I loved nothing. Maybe I fooled myself into thinking I loved Sheela.

I gripped the small weapon tight, and walked around the strange pole, into the swirling dust and ash, into the heart of evil.

The smoke twisted in a different pattern as a familiar breeze brushed past. "Reckard?"

The man appeared, and the sight of him made me gasp. The hair on the left side of his head was scorched, and the side of his face was as black as night, except for the streaks of blood running from two gashes across his skull. His shirt was more of a rag hanging limp over his shoulders. What it didn't cover were at least a half-dozen cuts and scrapes. His right hand was twisted in an unnatural angle and hung loose. His legs fared no better as two large splinters protruded from his right thigh.

Still he grinned as he held a grotesque lump of a twisted face in his good hand. "I have it, old chap. And she won't take it from me." His voice contained a slight edge of madness.

I pointed down the way. "Don't stop until you reach Branagh's. Understand?"

He nodded and continued to grin. "What are you going to do?"

My voice sounded as dead as I felt. "I will make sure Aimee doesn't follow."

His grin faded as his eyes showed a flicker of sanity. "Do you need help, then? I'll do it, old chap, if you distract her long enough for me to get close."

"I'll kill her," I said as I pointed. "You? Go! Now."

"You're going to kill me?" Aimee asked with all the disgust and loathing she could muster in her voice. It was the same tone she used for poor folks who tried to convince her to let the Bank lend them money. "You don't have it in you. You don't have the courage." She approached through the swirling dust and smoke. At first she appeared to be a ghoul or fiend with ever-shifting form. As she moved closer, the details grew sharper and, step-by-step, revealed her own wounds: scratches on her cheeks, a bruise on her right shoulder beneath a ripped sleeve, smudges of soot along her belly, the shredded lengths of her skirt.

Reckard had held his own, but it wasn't enough.

I said, "Go, Reckard."

"Stay, Reckard," she answered, still with the loathing. All the hatred in the world filled her bloodshot eyes. "Watch me kill him." She started towards me and her hands smoldered. "But then again, I could just kill you both."

I moved between her and Reckard. "No."

She eyed me like she did one of her ledgers. The same flicker shot across her face, like she discovered a mistake in the figures. She held her smoking bomb at the ready, but made no move to throw it. "My dear Alexander, my dearest Ash, we never finished our talk when I was under the truth elixir, did we? Do you not want to ask me more questions? Do you not want to know all the details of how I learned to despise you?"

I stepped forward and with a hand behind my back, motioned for Reckard to go. "You let me share your bed because you felt affection for me after I saved you from the assassin. You pretended to care for me because your superiors wanted you to." I tried to speak in an honest way in the hope I appealed to the woman I once knew, the one who might still exist somewhere within. "But you married me because you loved me."

"No," she replied much too fast, "I married you because I thought I loved you. But what is love? It isn't what you imagined it to be. It isn't what you thought I was capable of."

"I saw who you are." She had to be given one more chance, didn't she? A final plea? "I saw the person inside who escaped the lie you built around yourself. I saw the beautiful woman who became more radiant than the moon, even as she learned what care and trust and love mean."

Her brow narrowed as smoke poured faster from between her hands. "You saw what you wanted to see and you imagined me to be the woman you wanted me to be. You always placed me on a pedestal. You never really saw me as I was. As I am. As I stand here, ready to kill you." The bomb grew larger by the second. "Yet I respected you. I thought you had great promise in life. You were charming, you were loving and devoted. You could have done most anything you wanted. But you tossed it all into the rubbish. You squandered every opportunity and destroyed what hope you built inside me." She paused, then whispered, "You're a bastard."

She threw the bomb, and I swatted it far across the vault. When it exploded, it rocked the room to its core. The ceiling groaned as it cracked from left to right.

Aimee held her hands out to either side. Small bombs as dark as night and no bigger than three-inches across, appeared in each. She threw them and created more almost immediately.

I knocked the first one to the side. It exploded, opening a hole in a large drawer. Two silver necklaces depicting intertwined snakes fell to the floor. I knocked the second aside and it, too, shattered a drawer. A third I swatted back at her, which made her fall to her knees to avoid her own explosion.

Stop her, Ash. Stop her before she destroys you or herself.

As I stepped forward, I deflected two more. She sneered as if she smelled something sour, then interlocked her thumbs and let her palms face me. The bombs raced out twice as fast, much too quick for my reflexes.

The first one struck my left shoulder and exploded. It didn't hurt, but stood me up. The second struck my belly, forcing the breath from me. The third struck my right thigh, and almost immediately the fourth hit the top of my head as I doubled-over. The fifth exploded on my left forearm as I tried to cover myself. The sixth hit my left shoulder, which knocked me on my back.

She gave no time to recover, but jumped on top of me. "I hate you. I hate what you've become. I hate that you work for them." Her hands covered my mouth like she wanted to suffocate me, but a smoking ball grew between my lips. She tried to pry my teeth apart, but I pushed her over my head.

The bomb exploded. Its impact knocked my front teeth loose and made the others ache. Blood spilled from between my fingers as I covered my mouth. The gums throbbed.

I pushed myself to my knees. If I didn't stop her—

Another ball struck, knocking me backwards with such force that I landed on my head.

She jumped on me again and tried to shove another ball into my mouth.

I knocked her on the side of the head, and she fell off. As soon as I spit the ball out, it exploded. The bright flash left white streaks across my vision.

Another explosion knocked me into the wall itself.

It was too much. She was too quick, and even my hardened skin couldn't take much more.

I lost the knife long ago. So I picked up a chunk of marble fallen from above and threw it where I thought she might be.

She gave a quick grunt.

Encouraged by the first success, I ran with arms wide, and caught her with my left forearm. She twisted away.

Another explosion knocked my legs out. I smacked the floor with my face and lost a front tooth. Blood poured down my chin. My lips and gums pounded with every beat of my heart.

You're losing, Ash. You will let her bury you in a forgotten hole in time, the lady who has caused so much pain.

My vision remained streaked with white light, despite efforts to blink to clear it, as I searched for another chunk of marble. A foot pinned my arm.

"You won't do that again." She grabbed my hair, pulled my head back, and tried to stuff another bomb into my mouth.

"And you won't do that again." I twisted, then threw my head forward.

She moaned as she fell.

I pulled her close, then put my hands on her throat.

She whispered, "You always thought you were better than me, Ash. In many ways you were. Not now. Years ago. Would you be a killer, too?"

"If I must be. If you force me to be." I squeezed her flesh between my fingers.

I wanted to kill her. I wanted to...

No, I couldn't. I—

The sound of flames and fire filled my ears, and the smell of smoke filled my nose as I flew. Aimee's bomb felt as if it was a ball from a catapult that struck me in the belly.

I broke through the vault's ceiling, flew through the dragon nursery, and bounced off the side before falling to the ground.

Breathing hurt. My insides felt like they had been rearranged.

Am I dying?

I could neither move, nor hear anything. I couldn't see anything. All I could do was remain on the floor with a single moment of clarity rising as if it sensed my end.

Our lives are made of a series of moments...of laughing, loving, caring, screaming and yes, even dying. I faced that final moment. The fact I did so because of Aimee made it less glorious than I would've preferred. How much better to go out in a dragon's flame or in battle against twenty cyclopes? But to lie on a floor in the deepest bowels of the town? Helpless and alone? With every bone and every muscle burning with pain? With my skin swelling from the bites? Never knowing if Sheela was safe?

The canon's voice sensed the approach of those final breaths, for it whispered, "Good Lord, deliver us. From lightning and tempest; from plague, pestilence, and famine; from battle and murder, and from sudden death."

My feet moved, but not of my accord. Someone dragged me across the floor.

I tried to twist free, but my body refused to do much more than twitch.

"Don't struggle." Reckard's high-pitched voice penetrated the noise in my head. "I'll get you out of here. Sheela will kill me if I don't."

Sheela? Is she free?

The floor shook, and a rumble echoed through the cavern. The black dragon roared in defiance.

Everything went quiet. Too quiet.

"Good-bye, Alexander!" Aimee called from behind us.

"No, you don't," Reckard said as he dropped my feet.

What he did, I'm not sure since I saw nothing more than shadows and movements. He might have thrown the daggers Cavendish had given him.

"What's happening?" I asked.

Aimee cried out, and Reckard said, "Now she—" He stopped and his high-pitched voice went even higher with unbridled fear. "Oh, my..."

"What? What's happening?"

He started to say something about an explosion, but thunder and the roar of a great force of air and fire swallowed his words. Aimee had indeed released one of her bombs, but not just any bomb. This was the biggest by far, the grandest, most complex weaving of magical explosiveness she had ever created.

It was her moment, the one I denied her on the streets of Campden. This was her time of triumph.

The force threw Reckard away. It washed over me and rolled me against the wall. My skin warmed as heat pressed against me like I bore the weight of ten grindstones on my chest.

Following that, the floor shuddered, and another rumble echoed through the cavern. This time, though, the rumbling and shaking didn't stop. Dragons fell from their ledges. The black dragon roared its defiance again.

One beast landed on top of me. I struggled to push it off. It tried to bite, but neither of us could get an adequate grip on the other as the shaking grew more intense. The thunder grew louder.

I was beaten. I was bruised. Surely I would die from my internal wounds. Yet I would not let Aimee escape a final act of justice, not while breath remained.

The dragon fell off, and I scrambled on hands and knees to catch the movement headed for the doorway. I lost sight of her in the streaks of white, but kept moving.

The floor tilted to the side, away from the escape. I flattened myself as I tried to find something to grab hold of.

"Let me go," Aimee said as I wrapped my hands around her ankle. She kicked me in the face, but I felt only a light push on the cheek.

The floor tilted more as the roaring grew louder. The smell of water filled the air.

Animal cries filled the room as the dragons panicked.

Aimee continued to kick at me as we both slid towards the point where the vault should've been. It sounded as if water bubbled and boiled below us.

Desperation filled her voice as she said, "Let. Me. Go!"

I laughed at her as we struck water and it enveloped us. I dragged her down. Where that down was, I wasn't sure. Knowing she went with me was enough.

Something smacked me, crushed me, and tore my hands away.

I grabbed hold of large scales.

The black dragon.

The beast flailed, but I held tight as it lifted out of the water.

Fresh air, complete with its smoke and dragon-tainted scent, burned my lungs.

I wished I could've seen well enough to better know what was happening, other than the room seeming to sink.

The dragon lurched upwards, and I heard someone say, "Ash, grab my arm!"

As I flailed, fingers wrapped around my forearm. I released the dragon and struck the dirt again.

"Why did Pienne have to make you so damn heavy, old chap?" Reckard asked through the sounds of the water and the dragons. After a moment, he pulled me over an edge, and onto solid ground.

"This is terrible," Reckard whispered. "Are you seeing this, Ash?"

No, I wasn't seeing anything. I simply laid there, taking deep breaths. Sleep is what I wanted. And an elixir to escape the pain of death. I wanted to let it all end.

So it was that I welcomed the peace of the darkness that settled over me.

CHAPTER 16

Branagh's Ale. Its malty tang slid down my parched throat and tickled my empty belly. It stung my gums where I had lost the front tooth. Never had it tasted so smooth, yet settled so bitter. The noise of hundreds of people talking and enjoying a similar drink had never sounded so comforting, yet so hollow.

Life was worth savoring. Yet without Sheela, it felt like much less than it should have.

The canon tried to say something about the only source of true fulfillment, but I drowned it with another drink.

I lived. I loved. That should satisfy the voice's urgings, for I was more than before.

And...less.

Cavendish never caught Duke Schaever. The man simply disappeared, and for all the gnome's gadgets and lenses, he couldn't locate the trail.

So Sheela remained a captive. She was in the town somewhere, most likely at the Duke's estate. I needed to plan a way to reach her and right the wrong I had done.

But only so long as I lived through my wounds.

At least two ribs were broken. And I might have ruptured my belly or some other organ. As good as the ale tasted, it made me ache deep within.

It hurt to breathe, to move, to laugh, to cry, to move my arm when I needed a drink. But the pleasure and the promise of the ale more than made up for the effort and the pain.

Reckard looked as bad as I felt. Though he cleaned off the dried and caked blood, he wore bandages across almost his entire body. One ran across the corner of his left eye and gave him the look of a pirate or a scoundrel. He still maintained a shadow of madness in his expressions, too.

"So what happened at the chamber?" he asked, still with his high-pitched tone. "Why did the entire place collapse?"

Before answering, I took another sip. "I have asked myself that same question too many times already, and all I can conclude is the Duke built a safety mechanism in case the dragons proved too unwieldy or in the case someone discovered what he was doing. It's no coincidence he built the vault over an underground reservoir. I saw the floor buckle several times during the battle. At the time I gave it little thought, but in hindsight, it looked like the signs Sheela told us to look for in the sewers."

The mention of her name made Reckard pause as he lifted his mug. "That's a bad business, old chap. Are you sure you shouldn't have allowed her to die? I think she would've preferred that fate over what you condemned her to."

The ale settled even worse as my belly churned. To avoid further ill feelings, I changed the conversation by asking, "Why did the Duke have so many dragons? What was he planning for them? Did you notice there was no coal in the first chamber? The one with the forge? There was no coal dust, either. And no tar caking the ceiling. It was all clean. Too clean."

Reckard's jaw almost dropped. "The dragons were producing the fire for him?"

"Believe me when I say it's hotter than a normal fire." I caught myself rubbing my legs. "They also provided added security for those occasions when someone like us happened along. But sinking the vault was the real stroke of genius. Once he puts aside any threats to it, he can raise it again using the power of the enslaved elves trapped inside. No one else can get to it without his knowing."

Reckard snorted. "I'm guessing the Duke will not appreciate the fact that we discovered his plans for world domination. Is that not what he wants? To build an army of mechanical people powered by magic? Who could stop him?" He looked at me, then rolled his eyes. "Fine. You were right, old chap. I never should have doubted your word. I'll never do so again."

He received a tip of the mug. "At least not today, eh?"

My friend returned the gesture. "I wonder what he will do? The Duke, I mean."

What he always does. Complicate matters. Double the Guardsmen. As soon as he learns we survived, he will put a bounty on my head and your head and the head of every person associated with The Company. He will escalate the war, and he will fight to win. He has the assets and power to do so. Campden will become very, very dangerous.

"For all of that," Reckard said, his voice growing quieter, "the better question is whether your former wife is dead. I saw her disappear below the foaming water. She struggled for several minutes, but the thrashing dragons and the force of the vault pulled her under. No one can survive that, eh?" He raised his mug. "A toast then, to the end of a woman who deserved to die worse deaths."

I raised my mug, but there was a hollowness within me at the thought that she was gone. In some ways, Reckard was right. She deserved worse, but didn't we all? Without grace and mercy, the world would be unbearable. And because of that very grace and mercy, I did still care. A little.

The thought of Aimee dead filled me with a sick feeling of loss and emptiness. It made the voice sad.

I thought of the nights we walked the streets and lanes, walking hand-in-hand, talking about our past and our dreams. I thought of the nights we spent in each other's arms, of the operas we watched together, of the intensity on her face as she studied each scene unfolding before her. There was the moment when she shared a laugh with Bonni Greenhew, then turned to see if I watched and, catching my eye, smiled the most mischievous smile I had seen. And there was the night she swam in the fountain and convinced me to join her. We ran from the Guardsmen, our clothes left behind.

Why did death soften the pain of the bad times and make the best of times seem better?

Reckard took a long drink to end his toast, but I didn't join him. When he finished, he wiped his mouth with a loose bandage. "So did that couple make it out? What were their names? Bread and Frankincense?"

I laughed in spite of the pain shooting through my belly. "Bonni and Frank Greenhew. They were beat up bad, but they escaped. Maybe we won't have to worry with them again."

"There are still too many lingering questions. I won't feel safe on the streets again." He scratched under his bandage, just above his eyebrow. "I...I just wish..." He shrugged. "Well, it's not worth mentioning. I don't know what I want except for some of Pienne's healing, along with a warm bath."

We had done enough on this little mission for The Misters to treat us like nobility though they would do nothing of the sort. We deserved a healing and a substantial monetary reward. The quarter on my apartment would be due soon, and I hadn't a single shilling to my name.

Sheela deserved the healing, too, as she deserved double everything I'd received so long as Cavendish's counterfeit didn't get me a rewarding death.

Speaking of the little man, he climbed onto the table. All three of his reptilian guards stood behind him, all carrying their oversized weapons.

I ignored the trio of tongue-flickers as I studied the gnome, who had replaced his dirty and torn clothes for a cleaner and more sensible outfit, complete with ruffled sleeves and shoes that curled at the toes. The yellow shirt with the purple leggings made quite the statement as contrasted with his ever-present goggles.

"Ash, I—" He shook his head. "I...I'm..."

I put a hand on his shoulder. "You tried and you can keep trying. You can help me find her and free her."

Fog filled his goggles. He removed them to wipe them clear. "I'll do what I can for you. Given who she is and what you have done with the Head of Forneil, some on the other side might help, too." He adjusted the goggles, then said with a more somber tone than usual, "I have it ready, sirs, and I present it to you." In his right hand sat the grotesque suggestion of a head with its protruding teeth and deep eye sockets. There was no nose, but the mouth stretched an abnormally large amount so it resembled an expression of pain. To complete the effect, the color was the same grayish-green color.

"Where is the original?" I asked, not hiding my disgust.

The gnome looked left, and right. The reptilian leader put a three-fingered hand on his shoulder. "Don't. We cannot trusssst him."

"Yes, we can." Cavendish shrugged the reptilian hand off, then pulled the actual Head of Forneil out of his vest pocket.

"Your assurance is touching, gnome," Reckard said. "Especially when you have everything to gain, and we have everything to lose."

I stared hard at Reckard. "The gnome fought just as bravely as we did down there. He saved you in the tunnel collapse. He came back to help us. For all that he deserves our respect."

It was your finest hour, Cavendish.

Doubt and anger flickered across Reckard's eyes, but he nodded once before settling back.

I pushed Cavendish's hands together to make a better comparison. When I tried to take the original, he pulled back slightly.

"So much for me being trustworthy, eh?" I looked at the reptilians, who all took a step forward and pressed against the table. The leader's club twitched. "I won't steal it. I could have done that a dozen times already."

Cavendish looked as ashamed as a gnome could. He motioned the reptilians back.

Despite the canon warning me not to touch it, I turned the original over and over. I held it in the light. I studied the edge where it had been broken from the rest of the abomination. Then I gave it back to Cavendish and took the counterfeit, which I examined in the same way. Impressive. "This has been given some magical abilities?"

The gnome nodded. "Just enough to make it appear real, but not enough to do any true damage."

I placed the counterfeit in the gnome's hands and pushed the pair towards Reckard. "What is your opinion?"

My fellow thief made a thorough examination of the set. "Fine craftsmanship." He glanced at the reptilians, then pointed at Cavendish. "Hear me well, gnome. If my masters discover this trick and they kill me, I will haunt you for the rest of your life and beyond. You will never know a peaceful night's rest. That goes for your friends, too." The little man stepped away. His face turned a darker shade of red as Reckard added, "And I will find a way to get through the Gateway." He poked the gnome in the chest for good measure.

Cavendish gulped as he returned the original to his pocket. The counterfeit he gave to me as he kept one eye on Reckard. He tipped his hat. "A pleasure doing business with you, Ash. I wish the same could be said of your friends." Before Reckard could respond, the gnome hurried off with his entourage. They headed straight for the Gateway.

I couldn't help but laugh.

"He mocks death," Reckard said as he leaned forward. "Are you mad, Ash?"

Perhaps.

I shrugged and took another sip of the ale, paused, then drained the mug of the rest of its contents. That finished, I made one painful movement after another as I stood. The table kept me from falling over. "Well, it's best we put you out of your misery, and see The Misters. I believe our time grows short."

Reckard grimaced as he stood. "I forgot they gave us a week. And it has been, what?"

"A week."

We stood, shoulder-to-shoulder, at the door to the lawyer's building. The usual knock opened the door.

"Evening Lord Mayor," I said to the doorman, who still hid in the shadows. "A lovely evening, is it not?"

"If it ends with your death," the cyclops said with his deep voice.

I tipped my imaginary hat to him. "It's always a pleasure to see you, too, governor."

Reckard pushed me forward, and the door swung shut. He whispered, "How can you make light of this? You've done nothing but laugh and joke since we left Branagh's."

"The Misters have done almost all they can to me and I live still," I said despite the truth I was frightened. Now that I put my first love in the past and opened myself to the possibility of a new one, I lived for something again. But if The Misters ever found out I now had a new weakness in Sheela, they would use it against me.

Reckard mumbled to himself as he pushed past and led the way to the far door, which swung open as we approached. The usual bright light embraced us.

Ah yes, The Misters' little game.

We entered, and Mister Important said with an accusatory tone, "You are late, yes?" However, his voice eased as he continued, "Yet by the looks of your condition, I trust you succeeded in your little quest? Or did it prove too dangerous for two of our best employees? Did you fail and wish to collect your third elixir?"

I placed the counterfeit Head on the table, next to an object covered by a purple cloth. The rest of the statue probably waited underneath. "We did all that was asked."

"Hmmm," Mister Mercy said with a hint of delight, "then you killed your former wife?" Did he move towards the edge of the light? Did a large grin spread across his face?

Anger tinged my answer. "As far as we know, she is dead."

Mister Important said, "Elaborate, yes? Tell us of your adventures."

I informed them of all that happened, but left out the parts with Sheela and Cavendish. I embellished the fight in the dragon nursery with a telling of the great feats of Reckard and myself when faced with such incredible odds with no one and nothing to help us. I spoke of the mechanical abominations, and gave Aimee a torturous death by drowning as she fought a doomed fight against the inevitable. The story was so touching I almost let a tear escape.

Reckard, for his part, never looked at me. He never poked or kicked me. Instead, he kept his head bowed and his eyes to the ground. However, I thought I heard a chuckle escape when I described how he killed the elf after an intense struggle that could have ended with both of their deaths.

Mister Mercy sounded reserved. "This is disturbing news. It seems Duke Schaever has kept himself occupied in far too many endeavors. Hmmm, I wonder if we have not underestimated the man."

They had best not continue underestimating him. But they would.

"That is for another discussion, yes?" Mister Important said, probably waving his hands in dismissal. "Now is the moment when you unite the Head with the body, Mister Asherton."

I placed my hand on my chest and didn't have to feign surprise. "Me? Surely I am not worthy to perform such a task. Surely one of you good masters deserves the opportunity."

"Perhaps we do, but we need to make sure you brought us the real Head. Or did you sell the original, hmmm?" He paused, and quiet settled over the room.

Reckard gulped.

"Show us, yes?" Mister Important said, too eager and too sure of himself.

The voice warned me to step with caution, to be aware. It reinforced the feel of dread creeping through me.

With a shaking hand, I removed the purple cloth and revealed the statue in all of its hideous form. It seemed to welcome a familiar face. I drew my eyes from it even though all I wanted to do was stare at it and learn what it wanted me to do. The bright lights dimmed a little, as if the statue itself consumed the goodness in the room.

Wanting to get this unpleasantness over with, I didn't hesitate to place the Head on the body. In hindsight, I should've heeded the voice's warning.

A black light shot out, cutting across me. It sliced through my thick skin. When I stumbled back, Reckard caught me.

Blood appeared across the width of my belly. The wound was deep enough that it felt like a heavy sword severed my insides. I doubled-over to keep myself together, and to keep anything from spilling out.

"What did you do?" Reckard asked, his madness showing in his voice and his face.

Mister Mercy laughed. "Now you understand why we had no intention of rejoining the pieces ourselves, hmmm?"

Pain filled my chest and abdomen. Blood poured from around my fingers.

Am I dying?

Reckard started to say something else, but stopped. He stared at the monstrosity.

"Cover..." Speaking sent a sharp pain through my chest, and a surge of blood soaking into my shirt.

The light in the room grew darker still.

I couldn't look...shouldn't look. I must keep my eyes closed tight.

I saw a vision of Sheela wearing the dress she chose for the Duke's Ball. She looked stunning, like an angelic being bringing beauty and hope to a wasteland of filth and ugliness.

How could I let The Misters and this horrible statue take that away?

Reckard released me, and I caught myself with one hand as I clamped my skin together with the other.

The room tilted to the right.

I nudged the table, fumbling for anything with my numb hand. I felt the pressure of something in my fist.

This was my only chance. I had to do it correct the first time.

I took a quick breath.

And opened my eyes.

In the dimming light, I saw the cloth in my hand. I took another short, pain-filled breath, then covered the statue. My strength failed, and I fell forward against the table. It skipped backwards. The statue wobbled. It stood on its edge for a moment.

And then it settled back into place.

The bright lights returned, and Reckard bent over me as the edges of my vision turned black and moved to the center.

Mister Important said, "I believe you should take your friend to Pienne, yes? Healing elixirs await."

The room went dark as The Misters ended the Head of Forneil assignment. They did so on their own terms. Again.

One of these days, if I lived through the next moments, I would play their game against them.

Reckard called for Pienne's assistance. Light from the toady-man's door filled the hallway. He ran to us with two beakers in his chubby hands. The contents of one he poured into my mouth.

In an instant, my aches and pains eased as numbness settled over me. I tried to tell him to heal me quickly. The words didn't come though. I was already drifting towards sleep, but not of the eternal kind. Rather, of the type necessary for extensive healing.

Praise Pienne and his elixirs.

That was good, for I had a damsel in distress to save. And I never turned away from one in need, especially one I loved.

THE END

Author's Note

I hope you enjoyed reading this story. If you did, then drop a quick review at amazon. It would be much appreciated. And if you would like to receive emails to let you know when my next book is available...and there are more books about Ash's continuing adventures, as well as other fantasy books coming, please sign-up here: www.philipligon.com

More Titles from Jumpmaster Press

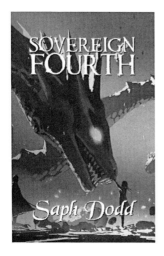

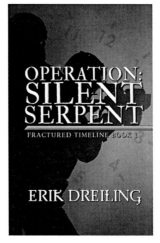

Acknowledgements

A special thank you goes to Sally and Janice for their willingness to read and critique – your comments were invaluable. A special thank you also goes to Kalisa, Kris, Haley, Leslie and Mat for their conversations, wit, and wisdoms.

About the Author

Philip Ligon's love of fantasy began in earnest when he tried to read The Sword of Shannara for a book report in high school. Though his teacher made him choose a different book for the report, he was forever hooked on epic adventures, quests, and fantastic realms. He proceeded to devour every fantasy book he could find. He threw in a healthy dose of science fiction, too.

Philip calls the hills and valleys of north Alabama home, where modern science brings what was once considered impossible dreams and far-flung ideas to reality.